SUNSHINE AND SHADOWS

Tobe Hunter held his coffee cup up as soon as he caught her eye. Roses moved behind him to fill it, then started when she felt his hand come to rest lightly against her back.

Roses was tempted to pour the coffee into his lap. Instead, she stepped back.

"I'll thank you to keep your hands to yourself, Mr. Hunter."

With a wickd smile, Tobe looked up at her. "No offense intended, Miss Jordan."

She turned away. Behind her, Tobe said something she couldn't hear to his companions, then raised his voice to say, "Just the way I like it. Dark and sweet."

She kept on walking, thankful for the dark skin tone that hid her blushes. She was going to kill that man.

ROMANCES BY AND ABOUT AFRICAN-AMERICANS!
YOU'LL FALL IN LOVE
WITH ARABESQUE BOOKS FROM PINNACLE

SERENADE   (0024, $4.99)
by Sandra Kitt

Alexandra Morrow was too young and naive when she first fell in love with musician, Parker Harrison—and vowed never to be so vulnerable again. Now Parker is back and although she tries to resist him, he strolls back into her life as smoothly as the jazz rhapsodies for which he is known. Though not the dreamy innocent she was before, Alexandra finds her defenses quickly crumbling and her mind, body and soul slowly opening up to her one and only love who shows her that dreams do come true.

FOREVER YOURS   (0025, $4.99)
by Francis Ray

Victoria Chandler must find a husband quickly or her grandparents will call in the loans that support her chain of lingerie boutiques. She arranges a mock marriage to tall, dark and handsome ranch owner Kane Taggart. The marriage will only last one year, and her business will be secure, and Kane will be able to walk away with no strings attached. The only problem is that Kane has other plans for Victoria. He will cast a spell that will make her his forever after.

A SWEET REFRAIN   (0041, $4.99)
by Margie Walker

Fifteen years before, jazz musician Nathaniel Padell walked out on Jenine to seek fame and fortune in New York City. But now the handsome widower is back with a baby girl in tow. Jenine is still irresistibly attracted to Nat and enchanted by his daughter. Yet even as love is rekindled, an unexpected danger threatens Nat's child. Now, Jenine must fight for Nat before someone stops the music forever!

Available wherever paperbacks are sold, or order direct from the Publisher. Send cover price plus 50¢ per copy for mailing and handling to Penguin USA, P.O. Box 999, c/o Dept. 17109, Bergenfield, NJ 07621. Residents of New York and Tennessee must include sales tax. DO NOT SEND CASH.

SUNSHINE AND SHADOWS

ROBERTA GAYLE

PINNACLE BOOKS
KENSINGTON PUBLISHING CORP.

PINNACLE BOOKS are published by

Kensington Publishing Corp.
850 Third Avenue
New York, NY 10022

The P logo Reg U.S. Pat. & TM Off. Pinnacle is a trade-
mark of Kensington Publishing Corp.

First Printing: May, 1995

Printed in the United States of America

Prologue

Kansas City, 1888

"Leave the lady alone."

The cowboy who'd called her a lady stood slightly behind Carolann. His voice was deep and dark and threatening enough to make the wrangler who held her drop his grip on her wrist. Quickly Carolann eased away, turning to find that her savior was the biggest, darkest-skinned black man she had seen since she'd left Georgia. She took a quick look around the room. No one seemed to have noticed. Dirty lamps cast shadows on the walls of the Painted Lady . . . a weak flickering light hung over the scantily clad whores and their customers.

"Tobe, she ain't no lady. She's just one o' the girls." The wrangler spat tobacco juice on the floor. If Madam High-and-Mighty Berenice saw him spit, the man would have a lot more to worry about than anything the darkie could do to him, Carolann thought, and giggled nervously, earning herself a look of disapproval from her protector and one of outrage from the cowhand. The wrangler reached out to grab her again. "See, Tobe, she's just nuthin'." Carolann backed out of his reach and stared at him with contempt. She might be a soiled dove, but she sure as hell wasn't nothing.

"Seems she don't want to play with you tonight, Jack. I think you may have offended her." The cowboy pushed his hat back a little on his forehead and let his hands rest easily at his sides. The seemingly casual gesture only accented the danger emanating from his taut frame. He dismissed Carolann with one brief look, then directed his gaze to the wrangler and grinned. "Come on, have a drink and we'll choose another girl for you."

"Ah, she just wants to up the price and I know it ain't more than eight bits for any woman in this place." The wrangler spat again, frustrated. This time Carolann could see Berenice had caught the action and when the madam started toward them, Carolann jumped into the discussion, hoping to end it before her boss found out she had tried to pad her take—again.

"Now, Mistah—"

"There's a whole roomful of two-dollar whores here, Jack," the cowboy said. "Why don't you choose a less troublesome one?"

Jack harrumphed. "That'll serve her right, won't it, Tobe?" He reached out for another girl who was swaying by. The white man wrapped a heavy arm around Daisy's naked shoulders.

Daisy steered the man away and Carolann breathed a sigh of relief as Berenice stopped to watch them. Carolann smiled at her rescuer.

"Tobe? Is that the name? That was right sweet of y'all to help me out. He a friend of y'all?"

The man smiled and Carolann was entranced by the flash of pearly white teeth in his dark face.

"We rode into town together," he said.

"Why, then, you just come on over here and sit down and I'll ease those aches and pains for y'all." She let her eyes linger on his thighs, then brought them back up to his face, but he didn't take the chair she held for him. Instead, he settled his hat low again, over his eyes.

"It's tempting, but I'm just here to have a drink."

"I'll keep y'all company," she offered.

He nodded toward the bar where Crystal, a pretty colored girl was waiting. "I've already found some pleasant company." Carolann could not resist making one more attempt. She moved toward him so he'd have to look down into her face and wouldn't be able to miss her ample bosom, temptingly displayed by her black satin dress. Now that she stood so close to him, she could see his face again under the brim of his Stetson. His eyes were big and round, almost black in color, and his eyelashes were longer than a man's had any right to be.

"Y'all ever had a white woman, boy?" she asked. The harshness of her own voice startled her. It had been a long time since a customer had moved her at all, let alone made her feel this rush of excitement. But he just turned away. She stopped him with a hand on his arm.

"If you change your mind, I'm in Room #4. My name is Carolann Travis." She walked away, knowing he was watching her go. She hoped he didn't drink up all his money. Though if he did, she'd give that cowboy a discounted price. He'd helped her out, and she figured she owed him one. She wouldn't mind paying up, either.

One

Tobe Hunter wished to high heaven he knew where he was. He had ridden north from Cripple Creek knowing the white men who'd trailed him wouldn't be able to travel by train. If Colonel Travis wanted to come after him, they'd have to make it the same way he did—on horseback. It had been a reckless move, riding up into the Rockies during a winter storm, when a solitary man on horseback had little chance of survival, but he'd had to do it.

This time, they wouldn't be able to beat him to the next town. He didn't even know where the next town might be.

Maybe he should have gone home to Boston, where he'd have known where to hide. He had friends there, people who would never betray him. In the East, he could have crept into one of the many hidey holes and disappeared for as long as he wanted. But out here he was free and still following the open road. The promise of excitement and adventure that had lured him away from the world he'd known still beckoned.

He was determined to keep heading west. The marshal and his men who'd been tracking him since he'd left Kansas City might have followed him north, but he didn't think they'd keep pursuing him now. No, they'd wait till the mountain passes cleared of snow—unless by some miracle the marshal convinced the colonel that it wasn't worth the risk of their own lives to continue the chase.

Even if they were still following him, they might never pick up his trail in this frontier country. Towns were spread out pretty wide in these mountains, and people were fewer still. There were not a lot of them to see him, much less describe him.

Diablo had been restless since they'd broken camp at sunrise, so Tobe gave the big black horse its head as they left the dried caked mud of the road. He settled easily into the pounding rhythm of Diablo's groundeating canter. The warm spring air cooled his face and the sunshine made the cold dark mountain road he'd been riding seem a distant memory.

They were almost on top of the girl when he spotted her sitting on the ground. She turned toward him but he only got a glimpse of wide scared eyes as he tried to veer around her. She scrambled to her feet and Diablo shied at the sudden unexpected movement.

"Damn!" Tobe cursed, digging into the horse's flanks with his calves. They flew by the spot where she'd been standing, but she wasn't there. Before Diablo could stop, Tobe jumped out of the saddle hitting the ground at a run.

The girl lay still as death next to the flowers she'd been picking. He dropped to the ground beside her, remembering Granny Gee's injunction, "Never move a man who's been knocked down till he's waked up." His grandmother, who'd raised him, would have known just what to do. He wished she were here. A moment ago—had it been one minute? two?—he'd been congratulating himself on his clever escape, but his self-confidence faded completely away as he knelt beside the small prone form.

Maybe she'd only fainted, he prayed. At closer look, she was not a girl, as he'd first thought, but a woman, her black hair gathered into a bun at the nape of her neck, the lace collar and cuffs of her dress very white against the caramel-colored skin of her delicate throat and small hands.

It was only when Diablo came and nudged his shoulder that Tobe finally moved, leaning over to put his ear to the woman's lips. She was still breathing, but the relief he felt melted away when he spotted the trickle of blood at her temple. He turned her head gently to better see the wound and saw a large rock in the grass. She must have hit it when she fell. Damn his luck! He'd have to risk moving her. He knew how dangerous a blow to the head could be, he'd seen it often enough during those years he'd fetched and carried for Granny Gee as she made her "calls."

He slid his arms under the unconscious woman's shoulders and knees and lifted her easily. Diablo trotted over at his low whistle. He climbed carefully into the saddle. Tobe gathered the reins loosely behind the girl's back and urged Diablo back toward the road. They needed to find a doctor—fast.

Her face had the innocence of a child's. What was she doing out here? Though he had travelled west in search of one of the black townships he'd read about, he had met few men of his own race, and even fewer women, and those he had were very rarely ladies, as the woman in his arms looked to be. Her light blue dress was soft under his hands, the style modest. The lace that trimmed it looked store bought, not homemade. She reminded him of a schoolteacher he'd known back East, or he guessed she might be a young matron.

She looked a lot like he'd imagined the women from one of the new colored townships might look: respectable, attractive, content. But he didn't know of any black towns in Colorado. The laws of the state forbid blacks to own businesses, just for a start. It was ironic that this black woman was the first evidence of civilization he'd seen in weeks.

She was not dressed for traveling. He figured there must be a town nearby. He would follow the road, as he'd been doing for the past week, and hope it led somewhere.

Roses Jordan awakened slowly. She was afraid that the strange sound of drums pounding in her dream was going to follow her into wakefulness. There was a bright red glare behind her closed eyelids, and that was unusual as well. She usually slept like the dead, dreamless, and awakened easily early in the morning, ready for the new day. But as she lay with eyes closed, she didn't hear the cocks crowing, but voices, quite nearby.

"Roses?" She jumped at the loudness of Dr. Forrest's deep tones and started to ask him not to shout, as it hurt her head. But she couldn't seem to raise her heavy eyelids, let alone speak. It was all very confusing and felt vaguely unreal—like a dream. But she never dreamed.

"She's trying to say something, Henry." She recognized Mrs. Forrest's voice but it was a thin reedy whine. She puzzled where she'd heard that anxious tone before. Of course! The doctor's wife was worried about one of Henry Forrest's patients. Her, Roses suddenly realized. No one had worried about her since . . . since she'd left the reservation four years previously. Roses was touched and a little surprised by Mavis's concern. The woman had always been friendly enough towards her, but Roses wouldn't have expected Mrs. Forrest to go to any trouble for her. She wondered why Henry didn't tell his wife that everything was all right. She was never ill.

Unable as she was to see the people around her, she felt strangely detached from the scene, totally disconnected from these people as well as her own body. Other than a slight stirring in the region of her heart when she'd realized that Mavis Forrest's concern was for her, she felt no fear and very little pain. She just floated, her mind puzzling over the odd set of circumstances she found herself in.

What was all the fussing about?

Roses had worked with Mavis, caring for more than a few of the doctor's patients, over the past few years, and Roses knew how much it upset the kind-hearted woman to see anyone in pain. It distressed her to hear the anxious note in Mrs. Forrest's voice, knowing that somehow she had caused it. Roses tried again to open her eyes, but they felt glued shut.

"She's coming around. Roses, can you hear me?"

"Am I sick?" she tried to say, but the words stuck in her dry throat.

"What?" The doctor's breath whisked by her cheek as he whispered in her ear.

"Ice?" a male voice suggested, and the word echoed as though caught in a well. Sheriff Alvin Carpenter, was Roses' guess. What was he doing here?

"Right," Dr. Forrest said, from further away. "Mavis, if you please?"

"Just a moment," Mavis said.

Roses tried to wave them all away, but her arm wouldn't obey her mind's commands either. That was all she heard for a while, and the red light behind her eyelids seemed to pulse and grow until something cool and dark was placed over her eyes.

"Where'd you put the man?" Dr. Forrest asked, his voice closer to its customary soft timbres.

"We got him in the jail. You sure he didn't hurt Roses none?" The sheriff's angry growl made Roses shiver, but it gave her a strange sense of comfort, too. He was angry because someone had hurt *her*. She'd been on her own since she was sixteen, she had forgotten how it felt to have someone take care of her.

"I hardly think the man would attack her and then bring her here, Sheriff. That just doesn't make sense." The doctor said.

Someone had attacked her? She didn't have any enemies, or at least, she didn't think so. Everyone in town knew her, and most seemed to like her.

"Well, he didn't know she lived here, Henry," Mavis chimed in.

Roses tried to concentrate—to remember. They were talking about what had happened to her and they were angry, or at least, the sheriff and Mrs. Forrest were. The doctor sounded calm and reasonable, as always, as he responded to his wife's shrill tones.

"Where else could she live, Mavis? There isn't another town within twenty miles of here. She's just got a little nick on her head. The stranger's explanation sounded a lot more reasonable than the stories I heard folks coming up with."

Roses couldn't follow the rest of the argument. Her mind was fixed on the words "the stranger." There had been a stranger. If only she could think, remember. She had the feeling it was important.

"Why won't she wake up, then?" Mavis demanded.

Roses felt the doctor's cool hand encircle her wrist. "I don't know," he said. "Her pulse is strong. But head injuries are tricky." Her wrist was laid gingerly on the bed, and though she tried to turn her hand to catch the doctor's, he moved too quickly. "All we can do now is keep it quiet and let her sleep."

"Sleep?" Roses tried to protest. She couldn't sleep with all these folks around. And besides, there was the mystery of the stranger still to solve. She heard the doctor moving away from the bed, and once again she willed her eyes to open. This time she managed to raise her heavy lids a little bit, but there was a piece of cloth dangling down from her forehead. She raised her head, but that only made it pound harder. The doctor was herding the others toward the door.

"Wait. What's—?" She had to lick dry lips before she could finish the simple question. "What's going on?" she managed to ask. The three in the doorway turned back toward her.

"She said something, Forrest." The sheriff whispered loudly.

"I heard. She said, 'What's wrong?' Don't you think that's a strange question for a woman to ask after nearly dying, or worse, at the hands of a stranger?"

"Not if she's been hit on the head. I've had men in my jail couldn't remember a thing about a brawl after being knocked out."

Roses couldn't figure out what they were talking about, and just as she was about to ask again, the door slammed open behind them, starting the echoes again and sending a blinding white shaft of sunlight right into her eyes.

The last thing she heard as she slipped back into the darkness was Jimmy Rawlins shouting, "Sheriff, you better get down to the jail. John Applegate and the Newton brothers are talking about beating the truth outta that nigra who done trampled Roses Jordan."

The palomino's hooves had pounded beneath her as Roses galloped away from the burial ground where she had just laid her father to rest. He had lasted less than a month after her mother had died. She had buried too many of the people she loved.

Like so many others, her parents had been growing weaker for months, underfed since they'd arrived at the reservation a year before. Food and supplies were scarce, medicine even more so.

Before they'd sickened, they'd been talking about leaving the Uncompahgre and trying to find work in the nearest town. Roses couldn't imagine life without the tribe. The Ute were as much her family as John and Mattie Jordan. Her parents were right though, there wasn't anything extra on the reservation to spare for the Jordan family, who since they weren't Ute, didn't qualify for provisions at the Indian Agency. Even so she'd been shocked when Grandfather had agreed with them that it might be best if they left the reservation.

She had tried to embrace the decision of her elders in the Ute way, but she could not. Nor could she bear her sorrow in her parents' stoic fashion—she had not spent years in slavery learning to accept the vagaries of life as they had. Roses dashed angry tears from her cheeks and bent over the horse's neck as she urged the horse on, trying to escape not sorrow but shame. She had rebelled against their wishes, even though she'd known they were right and she was wrong.

In a futile attempt to make her peace with their ghosts, Roses had obeyed her father's last request and buried him, as he had buried her mother. She'd laid his body to rest, as he had her mother's, under almost six feet of soft dirt, instead of finding a small crevice in the rocks and covering it with stones in the Ute way. Her parents' graves were the only ones dug so deep. She was afraid that their spirits would wander, unable to dig their way out and find the cave that led to the land of the spirits.

She had been one with the horse, flying over the hard desert sands, but she couldn't ride fast or far enough to leave the bitter knot in her chest behind. She would have to leave the Uncompahgre now. She had no blood ties with the tribe. Unlike her parents, she couldn't be a teacher. She shared her mother's love of books and her father's interest in mathematics, and had been helping to teach the younger children, but it was her parents' knowledge of the white man's ways that the tribe had valued. Roses knew as little of that as the Ute did. She had always lived with the People. Mixed with her grief for the loss of her mother and father was the bitter knowledge that it was their presence that had kept the Uncompahgre from adopting her totally as one of their own. The only family she had left were the Uncompahgre Ute, but she wasn't one of them.

Now she leaned over the horse's neck, urging him to go faster and faster. The burial ground had been left far behind, but she rode on, unable to escape her memories.

She was five years old when she went to her first mama-kwa-nhkap, Bear Dance. The Ute chief, Ouray, had invited her parents to come and live with the Uncompahgre Ute, and they were to meet the

tribe at the summer gathering and travel back with
them to their mountain camp.

Tribes came from all over for the annual summer
gathering, and Roses, Mama and Papa travelled west
with a small band of Arapaho. Mama and Papa had
gone to town to trade for supplies, and Roses was
supposed to wait patiently and keep out from underfoot. But she was bored. Finally, a woman recognized her boredom and gave her a water sacque and
asked her to fill it in the nearby stream.

She was alone in the reeds when the frogs and
cicadas stopped singing. But it was only when she
was halfway back that she smelled the smoke. Something was wrong. She tried dragging the waterbag
faster, but, when someone screamed, she dropped it
and ran toward camp. She stumbled and fell, skin-
ning her knee and starting to cry. But she forced
herself onto her feet again as she heard more shouts
and screams coming from the camp.

She fell out of the brush into the clearing. Many
of the tepees were on fire. Men in blue uniforms
were riding through the camp, shouting and waving
torches and guns. The steel blades of unsheathed
bayonets shone in the sun. She stood rooted to the
spot, until she saw another little girl, one whom she
had played with the day before, run and throw herself onto a woman's body. It was the sweet woman's
daughter. Roses remembered—the woman's name
had meant 'sweeter than water in the desert.'

Little Roses had almost reached the child when
she heard thundering hooves and looked behind her.
A big gray horse bore down on her. Suddenly she
was whisked off of her feet and spun into the air . . .
by a soldier, who held her close as the horseman
passed harmlessly by. She struggled to get down to
her feet again, to go to the baby girl, but when she

looked, the girl was no longer crying, or moving at all. Roses was crying so hard, she didn't at first realize that her father held her.

"Leave it be, baby, you cain't do nothing for them." Roses sobbed, as the camp went up in flames behind them.

Roses awakened late that afternoon with a dull throbbing ache behind her temples and memories of her parents. She reached up to her head and found her pillow was covered with a towel and an icepack was placed on her forehead. Mrs. Forrest bustled in and said, "Oh, fine, you're awake." Roses started to sit up, but Mavis left, saying, "I'll get the doctor," before she could ask what had happened. The words died as they formed on her lips. She remembered everything. The previous day's events unfolded in her mind with startling clarity—her first glimpse of a black man thundering toward her on a huge black horse. She had stood, then been paralyzed by a sudden memory of standing in the path of another man on a horse. In the next instant, reason took hold and she dove out of the way.

The next thing she remembered was the sensation of movement as she realized she was being carried in someone's arms. Then she'd heard frantic shouting when they'd ridden into town. That sound had faded away as she'd slipped back into the darkness. Then . . . she'd awakened for a few minutes and the Doc had been there, and the sheriff and . . . they said the man was in jail!

When the doctor came in to examine her she tried to tell him, "The man on the horse, he didn't hurt me. I fell and hit my head."

"It's all right, Roses." The doctor tried to soothe

her. "Just tell me, how many fingers am I holding up?" He held his hand out at his side.

"Three. Dr. Forrest, you can't let them keep him in jail. It was an accident."

"Mr. Hunter? Don't worry about him. He's fine. I checked him out yesterday. Seems to be a little swelling here, but otherwise, you're fine. Rest is the best thing for you. That was a pretty nasty blow you took."

"I can't just lie here." She tried again to rise, but he pushed her back down on the bed.

"Don't fret now, girl. It'll just make your head hurt."

He was right about that, but she *couldn't* stop worrying about poor Mr. Hunter as day slipped into evening. The next morning she had a steady stream of visitors. She would never have guessed so many people would drop by. Unfortunately, no one would let her out of bed, and she hadn't been able to get anyone to listen to her account of what had happened the previous day, or to free Tobias Hunter.

Mavis Forrest, who brought her breakfast, said that Tobias Hunter looked like a dangerous man; it certainly wouldn't hurt him to set a spell in the jail; and she for one would feel safer in her bed, knowing he was not wandering around the town. Roses had been relieved to see the sheriff but he wouldn't let her talk, just told her the circuit judge would be in town in a week, and he'd decide what to do with the stranger.

Mrs. Dorney, the milliner, who had been Roses' former employer and was the town's worst gossip, had been the first in line to see her when the sheriff had left.

"He's running from something, you mark my

words—" she said, "prob'ly a . . . well, something too terrible even to consider, I'm sure."

Even Annette Blackwolf, who worked with Roses in the kitchen at the Blackwolf Boardinghouse, said that it would be good for that man to see how many friends she had before he got out of jail with some idea in his head about getting even with Roses for putting him there. Roses couldn't really find fault with that line of reasoning, but she suspected a week of Mrs. Carpenter's cooking would put the man on the warpath even if he didn't already think the whole mess was her fault. Little Sparrow, Annette's mother, thought men who couldn't avoid running over little tiny girls in great big fields deserved whatever they got.

By noon Roses was chafing at the bit—eager to get out of bed. She felt like a fraud, letting Mrs. Carpenter and Mrs. Forrest care for her when she was sure that if they just let her up, she'd be fine. She felt worse when Mrs. Plimstock, as sweet and round as a berry, came by to nurse her. She couldn't get used to having these people go out of their way over her. She wouldn't have expected them to do this in a thousand years. She had always been the nurse, never the patient. It made her nervous to have them waiting on her. And everyone was so kind, as though it hadn't all been her own fault.

She tried to explain, but the rotund widow shared the prevailing view of the situation. She came into the room clucking, "My, my, my, and how is our little Roses today?" She continued on before Roses had a chance to answer the question, "Did Doc or Mavis give you some hot tea? You know the restorative power of a nice brewed cup, of course. I'll never forget how you used that Indian medicine when Todd Jennings' youngest girl got that fever. But she was

up and about before you knew it . . . playing with
the other children, no signs of a weak heart at all."
The instant Janey Plimstock paused to breathe, Roses
spoke up, hoping to divert the kindhearted woman.

"Yes, I had some chamomile tea. And I think I'm
fine now. I've been thinking about taking a little
walk, maybe down the street, to see that poor man
in the jail."

The white ruching at the collar of Mrs. Plimstock's dress shook under all three of her chins as
she stared at Roses.

"Are you addled, Roses? That man tried to kill
you."

"It was an accident, Missus. He didn't do anything to me. He just startled me, is all. I fell down.
He could have just left me there, but he didn't. And
this is the thanks he gets," Roses said, but Mrs.
Plimstock had her own opinion of Tobe Hunter.

"Roses Jordan! What in the *world* would we thank
him for? Scaring the living daylights out of all of us?"

"He didn't do anything. He shouldn't be in that
jail," Roses insisted, but her words fell on deaf ears.

By the time Janey Plimstock was ushered out of
the room by Dr. Forrest, Roses' head was pounding
again, and the doctor wouldn't hear of her getting
up to go to the jail, or even of summoning the sheriff so she could talk to him again. He closed the
shutters, put a wet cloth on her forehead, and told
her she couldn't have any more visitors until she'd
taken a nap. But she wasn't sleepy, and all of the
fussing and fretting made her more determined than
ever to get That Man out of the jail.

Tobe Hunter had never been in a town like Cedar
Valley. The only man he'd spoken with was the sher-

iff, whom he had found to be a solid, easygoing man, unless he was opposed. Toby rubbed his sore ribs, remembering his "arrest." The beefy little man could really pack a wallop. But the real danger was from the townspeople, who seemed anxious to override the sheriff's decision to wait for the circuit court judge's arrival next week and mete out a little justice of their own. Tobe had seen the aftermath of more than one lynching party. It would be best to bide his time and keep his mouth shut. It had worked up until now. He could only hope that the judge was as reasonable as the sheriff, who had told him, "You don't mess with me, I won't mess with you." Tobe believed the man would keep his gun holstered and his hands to himself until he was cleared or convicted of the attempted murder of Roses Jordan.

Meanwhile, the jail wasn't so bad. The building was new, with walls and floors of wide pine boards. The cells were spacious, even though the only furniture was a cot with a slops jar shoved beneath it. The jar itself was odd; it was an Indian water basket woven of reeds coated with resin to make it watertight.

Through the shiny new bars that divided the building into two rooms, he could see the rest of the room, which made up the sheriff's office. Two straight-backed pine chairs sat facing a table on which sat Tobe's guns and the Wanted posters the sheriff was busily rearranging. A small wood stove sat just to the right of the front door. Four or five more chairs were pushed up against the walls, next to a large rolltop desk. Tobe suspected that the judge's hearings took place in this room. The only decorations on the walls were a framed portrait of Mrs. Carpenter and an ornate gun rack.

"I'm going to get our dinner." The sheriff broke

the silence for the first time in an hour. Then he was gone. These moments, sitting alone, defenseless and vulnerable, were the ones that Tobe truly feared. He lay back on the cot, tipping his hat over his forehead, trying to think of something—anything!—other than where he was. When he heard footsteps coming up the wooden boardwalk, he prayed they'd continue on . . . that no one would stop in while the sheriff wasn't there to protect him. But apparently God was busy elsewhere. The sound of heavy steps stopped outside the jail. The door swung slowly open. Tobe lay perfectly still and held his breath.

"Sheriff? Sheriff?" Two young voices spoke almost in unison.

After a moment, a woman's voice instructed, "Go on in, boys. It's not really the sheriff we're here to see."

There was some shuffling of feet, then a strange trio entered the little jail. Roses Jordan was carried in, sitting suspended on the crossed arms of two identical teenage white boys.

"Jeremy, Jessie, you can put me down now." The twins both looked nervously toward Tobe and he could make out slight differences between the boys. One was a little weightier, the other had slightly longer hair, but two pairs of identical eyes glanced toward him and then dropped back down to look at Roses.

"I don't think Doc would like it, Miz Roses," the heavier one said.

"What Doctor Forrest doesn't know won't hurt him—or me. I promise."

Although they looked doubtful, the twins put Roses down. But as she turned away from them, one of the boys put a halting hand on her arm.

"We got to get you back right soon."

"I know Jeremy. We'll go in a minute."

"Missus Forrest will chew our ears off iffen *she* finds out."

"Me, too, Jess. I just want to talk to him. It'll be all right." Her voice was reassuring, but she came toward his cell rather slowly. The relief he'd felt upon seeing her alive and well was replaced by a stronger, less charitable emotion. A wave of anger rolled over Tobe. She *knew* he hadn't done anything to her. Why did she act so afraid of him? He'd been feeling sorry for her ever since he'd been told she was lying unconscious at death's door, but now he wondered if that had been a lie. She stopped a few feet away.

"Mr. Hunter?" she called out, sounding concerned. He almost laughed. He wanted to tell her what she could do with her little act. Bile rose slowly to the back of his throat. Who did he think she was fooling with that honey-sweet voice? She might have conned these young boys, the sheriff, maybe even the whole damn town—but he knew her for the heartless little liar she was.

She had put him through hell with this little stunt. Penned him up and left him helpless while the sheriff had thumbed through Wanted posters for his name and face. His heart had stopped every time the man had paused to take a longer look at one of the pages in the slowly dwindling stack. Tobe had been forced to sit calmly, waiting for one of the flyers the colonel had printed to come up—*"Wanted: Dead or Alive, Tobias Hunter. For the Murder of Carolann Travis in Kansas City, March 13, 1888."* By the time the lawman had put aside the parchment papers, Tobe had broken into a cold sweat. His only protection was the woefully inadequate knife that had not yet been found in his boot.

He'd had the rest of the day, and a brute of a night, to wait for the sheriff to somehow find that he'd been accused of a gruesome murder. He'd dreamt that the colonel and his hired gun had somehow tracked him here, and they'd taken turns throwing stones that turned into knives through the bars of his cell.

Roses Jordan might not know what she'd done to him, but he wanted her to pay for it nonetheless. The boys moved restlessly behind her. Tobe forced himself to keep still, because if he moved an inch, he was afraid he'd launch himself at those metal bars and wouldn't stop raving until he'd convinced everyone in this town that he was, indeed, likely to kill the woman.

"Don't get too close, Miz Roses," one of them cautioned her.

That made Tobe angrier still. What did they think he could do to her through the bars of the cell? Not that he wouldn't like to get his hands on her. "He's strong as a bull. It took three men and the wrong end of a rifle to get him in there yestiddy."

"Mr. Hunter, are you all right?"

Suddenly, it came to him. He'd find out what was going on, and he'd get himself out of this predicament at the same time. He willed his tense body to relax and let his head loll to the side. The head of the bed lay in shadow, below the window. From this angle he could see her, illuminated by the sun streaming through the door, but he didn't think she could see his face, hidden as it was by his hat brim, and the shadow. "What did they do to him?" Roses asked.

"Mebbe he's sleepin'," Jeremy whispered loudly. "Why don'tcha come back later to see him?"

Tobe felt her hesitation and willed her to keep

coming. A step or two closer and he could reach her through the bars.

"Miz Roses, what are you doing?" The alarm in Jessie's voice made Tobe's eyes slit open. Roses was walking toward the sheriff's desk, reaching for the keyring lying there. This was better than he'd hoped. He reached slowly for the knife he had moved from its hiding place in his boot to his belt. He palmed it. The boys didn't see—they were looking at her, not him.

"Jeremy, you go for the doctor. Jessie can stay here with me." The boys looked at each other but neither moved. Roses was walking back toward the cell, keys in hand. "Go on. Hurry!"

Jeremy hesitated, "I don't think—"

She didn't let him finish. "There's obviously something wrong with him. Even if he comes to, what can he do to me, with Jess here? Come on, Jeremy, I told you he doesn't belong here. This is all a big mistake. I've got to find out what's wrong with him."

"Sheriff can call the doc if he's hurt," Jessie suggested. Roses fit the key in the lock and Tobe tensed, calculating how quickly he could get to her from his bed. The boys would beat him, they were moving toward her now.

"Go on. Now!" Roses' command stopped the boys in their tracks and almost made Tobe snap to attention. She sounded just like his grandmother had when she really meant business. Apparently the twins recognized the tone of voice as well. Jeremy disappeared with a murmured, "Watch her."

Roses swung the cell door open.

"Come back out of there," Jessie said, but Roses was between him and Tobe. Tobe grabbed Roses' wrist and pulled her down to her knees beside the cot, further blocking the boy's view. He held the knife where she could see it and jerked his head toward Jessie, who was coming closer.

"Oh, my God." Roses sounded truly alarmed. "Go tell Jeremy and Doc to hurry!"' she yelled at the boy. She was a quick thinker, he had to give her that. Jessie lit out. When he was gone, Tobe sprang up, pulling the woman with him.

"Now, what do you think you're going to do?" she asked calmly. Once again, he was forcefully reminded of Granny Gee.

"Get some answers." He was already spinning her around to walk in front of him to the door. "And get out of here." He didn't figure he had a lot of time before the sheriff would be back. Roses walked calmly ahead of him, back stiff, and he had to admire her grit. Any other woman would have been screaming by now. He considered asking if she'd help him rather than forcing her, but just as quickly discarded the idea. He still didn't have a clue as to why she'd had him locked up in the first place.

"You're not going to get very far," she warned.

"We'll see about that." He looked toward the sheriff's desk, trying to remember what the man had done with his gun belt. Roses twisted her hand out of his grasp and spun around to face him.

"Looking for this?" She held up his gun. He grabbed for it, but she danced back, quicker on her feet than he'd expected.

"You don't need to do this. I was going to get you out," she said, backing away.

"Yeah? What were you waiting for, Christmas?" He gauged the distance between them. Her grip on the gun was strong and steady. She knew what she was doing with the weapon.

"They wouldn't listen to me. But they will. You've

got to believe me. If you break out of jail, it will just make things worse." She was almost to the door.

"She's right, son." The sheriff's voice came from right outside the jailhouse and Tobe froze, looking toward the half open door. Roses let her gunhand drop to her side and Tobe lunged at her, expecting bullets to erupt around him, but hoping they'd be shooting low, trying not to hit their precious Miss Jordan. But the sheriff didn't need to open fire. Roses Jordan brought up the gun she held in a metal punch to his groin, stiff armed and with all the force of her body. He came down hard on his knees, waves of shooting pain radiating outward from between his legs through his entire body.

He was still doubled over, trying to catch his breath, when the sheriff hauled him into his cell and slammed the metal door shut behind him.

"Is everything all right, dear?" The sheriff's wife called from outside.

"Yes, Dotty. You can bring him his dinner," the sheriff yelled back. "Though he may not feel like eatin' right now." He looked over at Tobe with something approaching sympathy.

Roses crossed the room toward him. "I'm sorry. But I had to do it. They would have shot you if you'd tried to escape."

"He might of preferred it, Roses, honey." The sheriff smiled. "Yessir. The man might of been better off against me and the boys," he chuckled. "Myself, I'd rather face a posse of armed men than face you, Roses Jordan."

$\mathcal{T}wo$

"Roses, Charlie Johnson wants some more eggs," Annette yelled as she scurried into the kitchen with two empty trays that not ten minutes before had been covered with baskets of fresh-baked biscuits. The Blackwolf Restaurant was so busy, they were serving breakfast in shifts.

"I got it." Roses sighed and started toward the corner of the room where Old Charlie Johnson sat with his son, Young Charlie, and three other hands from the Twisted T Ranch. How they had heard about the altercation at the jailhouse out on the ranch, Roses didn't know, but apparently Mrs. Dorney had set the town abuzz and everyone Roses met wanted to hear the story.

It seemed like the whole town had turned out at breakfast this fine Saturday morning trying to find out what the commotion in the jail had been about and why the man who attacked her had been released.

Hank Avery, the schoolteacher, was sweet on Annette, and he'd been one of the first to arrive. He said that by Friday morning when his students had come to school each had heard some version of the incident. He had asked if it was true that she and the Hunter man had engaged in a gunfight in the jailhouse. Roses explained that it was all a misunderstanding; the sheriff arrested Tobias Hunter by mistake, and he was released as soon as it was cleared up. There hadn't been a gunfight, no shots were fired at all. Roses didn't mention the attempted jailbreak, just said she didn't know anything more about the stranger. She had no idea where he had come from, or what had happened to him after he'd left the jail.

It was all true. Roses had not spoken to Tobe once the sheriff arrived on the scene. As soon as she'd explained to Sheriff Carpenter how she'd wound up with the knot on her head, he had sent her back to bed. She had spent the rest of the day Friday convincing Dr. Forrest that she was fine. But that hadn't stopped everyone from Hank Avery to Mr. Terwiliger from the bank from asking her about the man. She'd been setting the story straight since the doors of the restaurant had opened that morning.

Old Charlie, prematurely bald and weatherbeaten from years of working outdoors, but as healthy as a man half his age, was determined to get his two bits' worth of information. This was her fourth trip to his table. He had spent the morning shooting questions at Roses while shovelling eggs, bacon, biscuits, and coffee down his bottomless gullet.

"No one's seen hide nor hair of the stranger this morning, but Dan Coombs says that big black horse of his is still boarded up at his livery," Young Charlie reported, as Roses stepped up to the table.

"He must have checked into the hotel, then, I reckon." Old Charlie nodded, looking at Roses for confirmation. She shrugged her shoulders. "Nowhere else in town for a man to stay but the boardinghouse, and I don't see him here." Charlie made a show of looking around the room.

Roses hadn't considered the possibility that Tobias

Hunter might come to the Blackwolf. She offered up a quick prayer of thanks that she'd been spared that trial at least. But before she could feel truly grateful, Young Charlie blurted out the question—the one that Old Charlie must have been leading up to all morning.

"Hey, Roses, is it true you shot the guy in his, ummm, privates?"

He said it loud enough for most of the restaurant to hear. Roses stood stock still. Conversation at all of the nearby tables died down. Her stomach turned over as she realized that these people actually thought she might have shot a man. Roses had known that the people of Cedar Valley thought her an oddity, to say the least, but she was hurt to think they would believe something like this. She turned to face the chuckling farm hands, but before she could let loose with what she thought of the despicable story, Little Sparrow had appeared out of nowhere to clamp a hand around her waist and, with a well placed shove, propelled her toward the kitchen.

"Old Charlie, you better stop stuffing that boy full o' my food and your crazy ideas . . . or he'll get fat *and* stupid," Little Sparrow said over her shoulder. The men roared with laughter and conversation picked up again as Roses reached the kitchen door. Just as she headed through the exit, she heard Ansel Terwilliger say, "Well it's about time Roses Jordan found herself a beau."

She closed the door on the men's laughter, but Little Sparrow pushed it open right behind her.

"Move on in there if you don't want to hear 'em. You know this's got to stay open." Roses' friend and employer pushed her forward with all of her 250 pounds.

"I'm sorry. I don't know what I was thinking."

Roses' apology was for more than closing the door between the kitchen and the dining room.

"Forget about it, child. No harm done." Little Sparrow could hold onto her sympathetic expression for only a second. Roses was almost relieved to see the glimmer come back to the older woman's eye. "At least this time you're bringing business into the restaurant—instead of keeping it away with your strange recipes."

"Well, I think this town needs some real excitement, if they're going to blow a little incident like this into a . . . a nine-days' wonder."

"It'll be over soon enough, and meanwhile, all you have to do is avoid that stranger. Don't give 'em a cause to gossip."

"Well, I won't. I didn't. I did not tell them to arrest the poor man. All I wanted was to get him out of jail."

"Hmmmph." Little Sparrow shook her head and walked away.

It wasn't until Annette and Roses were leaving the boardinghouse that Roses found out that everyone had decided that she and Tobias Hunter were made for each other. Annette had been in the General Store when Mrs. Dorney had mentioned needing fabric if she was to make a wedding dress. At Roses' stunned look Annette told her friend she had been waiting tables at her mother's restaurant that night and had overheard a heated debate over whether or not Reverend Meeker would perform the ceremony. Roses had laughed at the time, but she sobered as she thought about what Tobias Hunter might think about all of this nonsense.

She went on to the Smiths', where she tutored the oldest daughter three days a week. When Roses arrived, Sarah and Lula were waiting.

"I'm sorry I didn't get to stop by when you were laid up yesterday," Sarah apologized. "Dr. Forest told Ben you'd be fine with a little rest. And you know Ben when I'm expecting. He worries about me doing anything at all." Sarah was seven months pregnant, and despite the fact that she'd had three children already, her husband, Ben, fussed over her like a first time father.

"I didn't expect you. I just got a little bump on my head," Roses said. "I can't believe the stories I'm hearing. Do you know Mrs. Dorney has me married off already to a man who rode into town two days ago." This was one household where she could safely tell the whole story.

"I've heard a little bit about it. Did you know this man before?" Sarah asked.

"No, I don't know him at all."

"Would you like a cup of coffee?" Sarah asked.

"Sure."

"I'll get it," Lula said.

They settled at the table. While Roses blew into her steaming coffee cup, she was aware that the other two watched her expectantly.

"Thursday morning, I was out collecting flowers for my medicines when a man came out of nowhere. He didn't see me either, I guess, not until the last minute. And he was going too fast to stop." Lula gasped.

"What was he thinking?" Sarah exclaimed.

"It was on that meadowland in the foothills, there was no reason for him to expect to run into anyone," Roses explained. "Anyway, it would have been fine, but I tried to get out of the way and I fell. I probably hit a rock, Doc Forrest said. So the fellow brought me into town."

"Where did he come from?" Lula asked.

"I don't know. I haven't had any chance to actually talk to the man. He rode into town looking for a doctor, and everyone assumed the worst," Roses grimaced. "They threw him in jail. Unfortunately, when I went to get him out, the sheriff wasn't there. Mr. Hunter didn't give me a chance to explain. He tried to make a break for it."

"You can't really blame him," Sarah said. "A strange town . . . I don't know what he must have thought. I'd have been scared to death, thrown in jail for no reason."

"Exactly." Roses agreed. "But I couldn't let him go like that. He could have been shot down in the street. So I had to stop him."

"Oh, Roses, what did you do?"

"I, um, turned his gun on him."

"Oh, child," Sarah smiled sympathetically.

"He wasn't too happy about that, either," Roses said.

"I don't suppose he was." Sarah chuckled.

Roses couldn't summon up more than a thin smile. "I was thinking of asking him to come by here later, if you don't mind, so I can apologize."

"No, no. It's fine with me. I'll have to ask Ben, of course, but I'm sure he'll understand when we explain."

"I hope so. I feel terrible about this." Sarah patted her hand. "I don't know what all the excitement is about," Roses said.

"We were worried about you. All your friends were."

Roses swallowed hard over the lump forming in her throat. Sarah's simple statement had touched a chord within her. She didn't know what to say and couldn't have spoken at that moment if she had. Roses wasn't accustomed to hearing such sentiments, even from Sarah, who was probably her closest friend.

Ben and Sarah had approached Roses a year earlier. Their eldest daughter, Lula, had graduated from the town's one room schoolhouse and wanted to continue studying to be a teacher. The Smiths had heard that Roses' parents were teachers and asked if she could help. Roses had been warmly welcomed by the entire family when she agreed. But as close as she felt to Ben and Sarah and the children, she hadn't realized how much they had become a part of her life until this moment.

While she tutored Lula, her mind was taken up with the bewildering array of unfamiliar emotions she'd felt in the past two days. She was never ill, never needed anything from anyone—at least not since she'd come to Cedar Valley some four years earlier. She didn't know how it was supposed to make her feel, to suddenly find after all this time that the people around her were so attached to her. It was, she knew in her head, natural, but in her heart it felt wrong, a mistake; she hadn't meant to care for them, just to live in peace and learn what she needed to. She didn't want to be attached, not to Sarah, or the Smiths, or anyone she would be leaving behind.

When she'd arrived in this town, she'd been on her own for a year and had been afraid she would never find a way to survive in the white man's world. She had spent the year between leaving the Uncompahgre and finding Cedar Valley moving from one town to the next trying to save enough money to go home without being a burden to the Uncompahgre.

She'd been traveling steadily back into these mountains since she'd left the reservation, instinctively heading toward the one place where she'd felt safe as a child, the Uncompahgre's winter camp, high in the Rockies. But Roses knew she couldn't really go back—not alone. She would never make it in the mountains on her own.

She'd been grateful to find work in the small town of Cedar Valley which she had stumbled on to purely by chance. She had been more than happy to find a decent job and asked nothing more than to be left alone to grieve for the life she'd left behind.

She'd had a run in with one of the local men a month after she had arrived. Larry Jenkins had cornered her behind a saloon one night, and she'd fought and bit and scratched her way free and run home to hide. She had been sure Jenkins would be after her, and hadn't had the faintest idea what to do. All that night she'd been terrified, unable to imagine what she would do next. She'd been so frightened. But in the end, nothing had happened. Jenkins never had come after her and no one had mentioned the incident to her.

A few weeks later she heard some boys talking about it. "She bit off a big chunk of his ear," one said.

"They say he carries it around in his pocket, in a handkerchief," another boy added.

They didn't seem to think anything of it, and over the years, Roses had forgotten her fear. When she had met Dr. Millhouse, her first real veterinarian, she'd known she had found the answer to her problems.

She had never met a horse doctor like this one before. Ian Millhouse had studied in Vienna and New York before coming west to get away from a family tragedy that drove him to this remote town in the Rockies. She'd met more than a few charlatans selling snake oil for people and for animals. Those men traveled to small frontier towns, looking for ranchers whose livelihood lay in their livestock, claiming to have cures for hog cholera and other diseases. Doctors, with medical degrees, were rare enough on the frontier, animal doctors were few and far between. She planned to stay until she learned enough of Dr. Millhouse's veterinary medicine to return to the Ute at the Uintah Valley reservation.

She had friends here and had made for herself a life of sorts. She had also finally understood why her parents thought the whites were as good as the Good People. She didn't totally agree. She still thought most whites were crazy, especially when they talked about "dirty Injuns," or "Injun lovers." She mourned the passing of the Utes' freedom and a way of life that was dying. But she no longer felt like a traitor to her people just because she was friendly with those who didn't understand them. She even found some white people and some colored people who didn't make her feel too dreadfully out of place. There were some folks, like Ben and Sarah, who were sympathetic to her feelings about the Uncompahgre.

People in Cedar Valley had their prejudices, but she was able to avoid the worst of them. Most everyone had been happy enough to employ her as a cook, seamstress, teacher, or nurse, and they were even beginning to respect her as a veterinarian. She knew them and they knew her. This whole episode with Tobe, from his arrest to Mrs. Dorney's wedding plans, proved they might not know her as well as she thought, but she still felt she fit in better here than she had most anyplace else she'd been since she'd left Uintah. For every person who had believed some ridiculous story about her shooting Mr. Hunter, another had let her know they cared what had happened to her. Her life in Cedar Valley was peaceful for the most part and she was content, and that was more than she had ever expected from the white man's world.

Tobe hoped it wouldn't take long to restock and get out of Cedar Valley. At the livery stable, where he'd gone to check on Diablo, the boy said that his Pa was over to the boardinghouse, having breakfast. Before Tobe could ask when "Pa" would be back, the kid disappeared back into the barn, hitching up sagging overalls over lean hips with a quick, nervous tug.

As Tobe walked down Main Street, he felt the stares of the people he passed. From the corner of his eye, he could see the curious glance at him. He was relieved to finally step through the open door of the general store.

Tobe fingered the money pouch in his pocket, and looked around at the heavily laden shelves in the dim room. Behind the counter, a heavy man was counting out change for another customer. A shelf by the door caught Tobe's eye as sunlight glinted off of bottles of golden peach and pear preserves. Tobe hadn't tasted anything that sweet in over a month, and his mouth watered just looking at them. Unfortunately, he had only enough money for essentials. He'd have to make do with dried fruit.

The shopkeeper cleared his throat, finally diverting Tobe's attention from the succulent-looking fruit.

"You staying over to the hotel?" he asked.

Tobe nodded, stepping further into the room. He scanned the walls for the supplies he needed. He'd had to leave the last town in a hurry. This time he wanted to make sure he had everything he needed.

"Sheriff put me up for the night," he volunteered.

"You don't look none the worse for wear. Roses took off part of a man's ear once."

Tobe was tempted to say what he thought of Roses Jordan, but the admiration he heard in the other man's tone made him keep his tongue. "Did she?" was all the response he offered.

"Larry Jenkins cornered her out back of the saloon one night. Guess he thought he'd have a little fun. She was just a little thing, must have been three, four years ago. Right after she came to town."

"Um-hmmm." Tobe listened as he figured in his head. If he spent all the money in his pocket, he might be able to get enough supplies to last him a couple of weeks or a month. The problem was, he didn't know where he was headed, or how long it would take to get there. He'd been planning to get work and the lay of the land in the next small town he came to before he'd run into Cedar Valley's little black wildcat.

"Yes, boy, she's a spitfire."

He was so surprised to hear the shopkeeper echo his thoughts that he looked up and caught the man's eye. He continued, "Bit off his earlobe, then spat it out in her hand and gave it back to him. You shoulda heard him holler! Nobody bothered her after that— especially after we found out she was right handy with a gun, too."

"Some women have the knack." Tobe knew more than one such woman. His own grandmother had taught him how to shoot.

"I loaned her the new Winchester rifle for the Fourth of July sharpshooting contest last year. She won a hundred dollars. I sold three rifles that week." The shopkeeper chortled in remembered satisfaction. "She was working for me then. That was before I had to fire her. She'd just go and trade my stock for any old thing. Couldn't seem to get her to understand I didn't want to trade goods, just cold, hard cash. You could understand it, her living with those Indians and all."

"She was captured by Indians?"

"Nah. At least, I don't think so. I heard her parents were teachers or something. That's where she learned to trade. Don't get me wrong, I'm not against giving time to one of the town families, but you can't just let any worthless cowpoke or Indian squaw make off with the goods. That ain't no way to run a business. And that's what I had to tell her."

Tobe nodded his understanding and pulled out his money pouch so the man would see he wasn't planning on asking for credit.

"I'm Lester Freeman." He said.

"Tobe Hunter."

"You planning to stay in town long?"

Tobe didn't see any harm in satisfying the man's curiosity. As low as he was on cash, it was definitely a good idea to do business on a friendly basis.

He shrugged. "Just passing through."

"You're from back East, huh?"

Tobe nodded. "From Massachusetts."

"You don't look like no greenhorn." Lester Freeman relaxed against the counter, obviously ready to listen.

"Well, I was when I headed west. But I hired on for a couple of months at a ranch in Pennsylvania, and then I joined on with an outfit driving cattle out this way."

"You get that horse back East?"

Tobe nodded. "He was born and bred on a farm outside Lexington."

"I wouldn't get on his back."

Tobe didn't doubt it. It didn't look like the stout shopkeeper had been on a horse's back in some years. "He wouldn't let you." His smile took the sting from his words.

A woman and her little girl came into the store and Tobe's smile vanished as the child took one look at him and hid behind her mother's skirt. The woman busied herself looking at some men's boots in the front of the store. Lester shrugged in apology and straightened away from the counter.

"Go ahead and look around. I got just about everything here. I'll be with you in a minute." He turned his attention to the couple who had just entered. "Mrs. Meeker, what can I do for you today?"

It didn't take Tobe long to reckon what he could afford and finish up his shopping. When he put his cash on the counter, Freeman added a third sack of cornmeal and a small packet of salt. "Just to show what a friendly town Cedar Valley can be," he said. The gesture sent Tobe down the boardwalk with a little more spring to his step. Cedar Valley did look to be a pretty friendly town. It was exactly the kind of place he'd hoped to come upon when he'd ridden out of the mountains, and he thought it was far enough off of the beaten track to elude the colonel's notice. He was sorry that his little accident had caused such a commotion, and sorrier still that he wouldn't be able to stay and look for work as he'd hoped. It was probably smarter to move on, anyway.

At least there was one person in this town who'd be happy to see his back. He probably couldn't leave town fast enough for Roses Jordan.

He walked back to the Cedar Valley Hotel determined to check out. But when he stopped at the desk, a small voice piped up from somewhere near his elbow.

"Are you Mr. Tobias Hunter?" Tobe looked down to see a little boy whose big brown eyes shone out of a face as dark as a roasted chestnut. He hopped back and forth from one foot to the other as he looked up at Tobe.

"Yeah, I'm Tobias Hunter," he said.

The boy held out a slightly sweaty, much folded note. "Roses said to give you this." With one last little hop, the boy turned and ran to the door.

"See ya later, Mister." The words hung in the air as the door swung closed behind the child. Tobe looked down at the scrap of paper in his hand as though he thought it might bite him.

"You sure you're checkin' out, fella?" The desk clerk chuckled. He looked from Tobe's surprised face to the note in his hand. "That'll be Ben Smith's youngest boy."

"Who?"

"The blacksmith—Ben. He and his wife are like family to that girl."

It seemed to Tobe the whole town was like family to Roses. The paternal tone in the clerk's voice was unmistakable.

"When she worked here—"

"She worked here?"

"Roses? Oh, yeah. She's worked for most every business on Main Street. I was sorry to have to let her go."

Tobe couldn't help himself. "Why did you have to do that?"

"Well, she was . . . um . . . bothering the guests." The clerk looked sheepish. "Once she told this rancher that he had the manners of a pig, because he went to bed with his spurs on . . ." The innkeeper shook his head. "But the worst was this time we had this one man, a guest staying here, rich . . ." the man rubbed his thumb and forefinger together in an unmistakable gesture, ". . . very important. He was here with a . . . friend." Tobe looked down at his hands to find himself tapping Roses' note against the countertop. He closed his hand around it and slipped it in his pocket. "Roses figured the girl knew he was married. His picture is in the paper all the time." Tobe could imagine the scene. "Turned out the lady in question couldn't read. Said she 'knew he was important, but didn't realize he was married.' Roses helped her move into another room." Tobe couldn't help but laugh with the older man.

"She seems quite . . . uhmm . . . a handful." Tobe offered. He was rewarded with a chuckle and the key to his room. "I'll bring this back to you when I get my gear."

"Take your time." Once he was in the room, Tobe took the letter out of his pocket and stood looking at it.

Roses Jordan was a puzzle. He didn't understand the affection she seemed to inspire in these people. She seemed an unusual girl, but not, to his eyes, a particularly lovable one. She had bitten off a man's ear, for goodness sakes. Although he supposed the story had grown bloodier over the years, he had never heard of a black woman who could mutilate a white man and get away with it.

Though he had to admit that the people in this town, like those in a few others he'd passed through coming west, didn't seem to treat his kind much different from their own. And apparently the only smith was colored. It was what he'd been hoping for when Tobe had decided to leave home. But he hadn't expected anyone to be treated like Roses was.

Roses had bewitched all the men he had met. He

figured he knew how she might have done that, but she didn't look like that kind of woman. Tobe was pretty good at recognizing a whore when he saw one. He'd spent enough time in the whorehouse, a privileged insider, because of his mother. Roses was an innocent, he'd have sworn it. Something about her eyes, the way she'd looked straight at him, made him believe it. But it would take more than innocence to win the town's respect.

He wondered how she'd done it. She didn't seem to possess any special talent, except perhaps her knack for acquiring jobs, he laughed to himself. And that skill didn't include keeping them, apparently. She had too soft a heart, according to the shopkeeper, and an unruly tongue, he guessed. She sounded a lot like his grandmother.

Somehow, he couldn't reconcile the pretty little spitfire with the unflappable old woman.

"Knew he was important. Didn't know he was married." He chuckled and unfolded the note.

Three

Roses finished Lula's tutoring session just as Sarah Smith finished preparing the large midday meal.

"Would you like to sit to dinner with us, Roses?" Sarah asked as always. Her tone was as inviting as the sight of the heavily laden table and the heavenly smells that wafted from the plates. Although pregnant, the older woman was as spry as ever, and all her energy went into her cooking.

"Thank you, Sarah, it smells wonderful." Roses ate her dinner with Sarah and the children most days. Since it was Saturday, Ben, Sarah's husband, would be home as well. Just as she thought it, Ben came hurrying in.

"Sarah," he scolded his wife as he saw her lifting the heavy stewpot, "Can't you ask Lula to do that for you?"

"Her hands are full," Sarah protested.

"Mine aren't," Roses said, shooing her out of the way and taking her place at the stove.

"If it were up to you and Ben, I'd be lying around the house doing nothing at all. I'm expecting, I'm not crippled." Sarah complained cheerfully as she took her place at the head of the table.

Ben barely waited until grace had been said before

he launched in with, "What have y'all been doing, Roses, to set the town in such an uproar?"

"I guess I was just in the wrong place at the wrong time." She shrugged. Quickly she told him what had happened over the last few days.

Sarah turned to her husband. "Roses wants to meet this Mr. Hunter here later on, Ben. I told her it was all right."

Ben looked surprised. "Is it true, then, that y'all are . . . interested . . . in this stranger, Roses? Ah thought that was just folks creatin' gossip."

Roses sighed. "You were right, Ben. That's what I'm going to talk to him about. I don't want him to get the idea that I'm encouraging them." Sarah raised an eyebrow at Roses. "Not that it matters what he thinks," Roses rushed on, "Just . . . well, I thought you might give him work at the smithy. I know it's a busy time for you with the spring plowing and all, so maybe you could use the help. The way everyone was talking when he got thrown in the jail, I don't know how folks will treat him."

"He might just be passing through town. I mean, he may not want the work," Ben answered. "From what I heard about him, it sounds like he's one of those saddle bums come through here on his way out to California."

"If he is," Sarah suggested, "he'll refuse the offer."

"He might not want to work in front of a hot fire all day. The work may not suit him."

"He's a big man, and he's very strong." Roses caught the look Sarah exchanged with Ben. "And of course, as Sarah said, we'd just be making him an offer. He doesn't have to accept. But I think I owe it to him to try and help. After all, this is partly my fault."

"I thought I heard tell of some pretty hot sparks flying when you two met up."

Roses felt her cheeks grow warm, but she answered calmly. "Yes, if you want to believe what some nosy old biddies imagine is true."

Ben smiled. "It wasn't just that Miz Dorney and the old ladies talking, most everyone's got some kinda idea you're interested in this fella."

"It was a misunderstanding," Roses said. "I told you."

"Since y'all feel so obliged to him, I reckon I could use a hand."

Roses grinned back at him. "Thanks, Ben. Since the Reverend Meeker came here from Atlanta, I'm afraid the town's changed. I'm not sure Mr. Hunter could get ranching work the way people have been talking about us standing in the back of the church instead of sitting down. Or not eating at the hotel dining room."

Ben nodded, suddenly sober. "You may be right, Roses. I guess I could use the help, if he wants the job. It won't pay much but he could have it for a month or so."

"Thank you, Ben."

Ben Junior, the oldest after Lula, spoke around the mouthful of cornbread. "Do you think he'd let me ride his horse, Roses?"

"I don't know, B. J. You'll have to ask him."

"If he stays a while," his mother added. "And after your father and I say it's fine. We have to get to know him."

"All right, Mama. Can I be excused?"

"May I," Roses corrected automatically. The dinner table became the center of a whirl of activity as the children excused themselves.

"Don't go off anywhere," Ben cautioned.

Roses helped Lula wash the dishes before she went out onto the porch to wait for Hunter, grateful when Sarah decided to keep her company. They sat in companionable silence as Sarah took up the little sweater she was knitting. Roses was mesmerized by the movement of Sarah's hands, as she worked with the soft wool. She was startled when Sarah spoke.

"What does he look like, this Hunter?"

Roses closed her eyes to better remember. The ease with which she summoned up the man's image was a little disturbing. "Well, he's big." When he had stood up in jail, he'd towered over her. "He's tall, I mean, and wide, but he's lean." She had felt the hard muscles in his chest and thighs when he'd pulled her against him. "He didn't look like he'd eaten much. His cheeks had that hollow look." His eyes had been the thing she'd noticed most: big, almost black, and deep set. There'd been a hunger in his searching gaze. Roses' eyes flew open.

"Yeah?" Sarah wasn't looking at her. The knitting needles went on clicking rapidly back and forth.

Roses leaned her head back against the chair. "He's young. Maybe thirty." She thought for a moment, but could only think of one other way to describe the hard edge of his voice, the banked fire of his intense glare. "He looks like a cowboy."

Tobe approached the little house slowly. From a hundred feet away he could see the two women rocking on the front porch. They didn't look up. The scene was peaceful and almost familiar. This could have been his neighbor's house back home, if the road beneath his feet had been cobblestones rather than hard packed dirt. The little single story houses on each side were faced with weathered wood, but the small plots of land were blooming with spring flowers.

The street where the smith lived crossed the main street of town right in front of the livery, where Tobe had stopped to tell the owner he'd be leaving with Diablo later on. He'd stepped on a few feet down the road, at the telltale sound of metal pounding against metal. Out in front of the smithy the little boy who'd brought him Roses' note was playing with a little girl. They were busily moving wood from the woodpile onto a precarious stack in the middle of the yard. The boy barely glanced at Tobe.

"Roses is back home, down there," he said, pointing back the way Tobe had come. The girl pulled her doll closer to her chest, the piece of wood in her hand forgotten as she stared up at Tobe.

"Howdy, ma'am." He couldn't resist teasing, and she giggled, dropping the small log she carried.

"Be careful, Ruth," her brother admonished. "You'll knock down the fort."

Tobe touched the brim of his hat and winked.

Ruth smiled as she asked, "Are you going to our house?"

"If I can find it."

"B. J. and I can show you the way," the girl offered.

B. J. sat back on his heels. "Don't be silly, Ruthie, he can find it himself. It's just a step down from the livery," he turned to Tobe, "on State Street." Tobe could hardly miss the town's newly painted street signs.

"Can you find it?" Ruth asked him.

Tobe nodded at her. "Nothing to it."

When he approached the smith's house, he found Roses sitting with a pregnant woman who had the same smile as the little girl.

"Hello." Roses stood up so quickly the chair kept right on rocking behind her. "Mr. Hunter," she said. She turned to the woman next to her. "Mrs. Sarah Smith, this is Mr. Tobias Hunter."

"Mrs. Smith," Tobe greeted her with a smile and a respectful nod. He climbed the two small steps to the porch to take her hand and she chuckled. "Call me Sarah, please." She held onto his hand a moment longer than necessary, looking up into his face with clear brown eyes as open as her young daughter's, then nodded and sat back. "Pleased to meet you. Roses, would you like to talk out here, or would you rather come into the house?"

Roses looked around the porch, as if seeing it for the first time. "We'll be fine here, I think." She answered.

Sarah nodded. "I think I'll go check on Lula," she said, heading for the door. "You call if you need anything." When she disappeared inside, Roses turned back to him. Tobe had forgotten how small she was, fully a foot shorter than he was. She had to tip back her head to look him in the eye.

"Would you like to sit down?" she offered—nervously, it seemed.

"I'm fine." Tobe shifted to lean back against the porch railing. He didn't mean to make her apology any easier for her.

"Yes, well . . ." Roses moved away and lowered her head. "I thought we should talk."

"I understood that much from your note. What was it you wanted to tell me?"

"Are you planning to stay in town long?"

She didn't believe in beating around the bush, that much was obvious. He wondered how she hoped he'd answer. "I'm not sure of my plans yet," he told her.

"If you're planning to stay, maybe I could help you."

"You? Help me?" It wasn't what he had been expecting.

"Ben said you could have a job in the smithy, if you need one. 'Course, if you're just passing through, well, I'm sorry we—I—slowed you down." She lowered her head again, so he couldn't see her eyes, but he heard sincerity in her voice.

"Do you work there?" he asked. Though it was true he'd never heard of a female blacksmith, he wouldn't put much past this woman."

"Me? At the blacksmith?" She shook her head. "No. Why?"

Tobe shrugged his answer, brushing his hat against his leg. She was looking up at him again, considering his question, and an image flashed through his mind, of Roses Jordan as he'd first seen her, sitting in a field of flowers. She had the same open curious look he'd glimpsed for a moment when she'd first looked up at him. He hadn't remembered it till now in all the hubbub that surrounded that first encounter. She came around the chair and sat down.

"If you are thinking of staying in these parts . . ." He put his hat back on and put his hands in his pockets. The desire to stay in this place had been growing all day—a ready-made job and a chance to rest for a while was too much to resist. He'd take the work. To hell with the colonel. He'd been living too long with that spectre breathing down his neck. He wasn't going to let the old man control his every action. The decision made, Tobe relaxed. Roses smoothed her palms down over her skirt.

"Well, I should probably tell you, if you hear people talking, I mean about you and . . . me . . . well, they may be saying things." She looked toward the door to the house.

"About you and me?" He could believe they were talking about him. Hell, he knew they were.

"This is a small town, and the people are . . . some of them are my friends. But you're a stranger, and you're young. So . . ." her voice trailed off.

"So they don't trust me." His face turned to stone. "I won't be here that long. It won't bother me."

She sat down again in the rocking chair, leaning forward and holding it upright with two feet planted firmly on the floor. She looked straight up at him.

"No," Roses said quickly. "That's not what I meant. They think we're, well, courting. And I'd like to change their minds."

Tobe was flabbergasted. "That's what they think we've been doing?" Tobe leaned back against the railing. "The people in this town have some odd notions. First they think I want to murder you, then they think I want to marry you?"

"They thought you attacked me. I told the sheriff you didn't—"

"I know," he interrupted. "I was there."

"You went to jail." She grimaced. "There was some kind of a blow up. And now you're out. I don't know what the sheriff told people, but they've got plenty of ideas. I don't know what made them think you were . . . interested in me. I guess it's mainly because we're both colored. And young. And single. And they don't have much else to talk about around here."

"Don't they?" He almost smiled at her look of confusion.

"They don't know what to think. There are so many stories going around. But I thought we could act like friends." Roses was clearly flustered. "I mean we should be civil to each other, and we can show them that there are no hard feelings about what happened. All right?"

He had thought after all that had already happened to him on account of Roses Jordan, he'd been prepared for anything she might say or do, but she had managed to surprise him once again. "What exactly do I have to do?" Tobe asked cautiously. After all, he did owe her a favor since she had found him work, even if she didn't know he had needed it.

"Well, I've been thinking about that. In a town this size, we're bound to meet here and there. I thought it would be best if we arranged the first time, so everyone could see right off that there's nothing special going on between us. I reckon they'll give up the notion then. Seeing us be very casual toward each other a couple of times ought to do it. We could start at church tomorrow morning, if that's fine with you."

"I won't be at the church."

Roses took his announcement in stride. "Well, then supper at the boardinghouse tomorrow night."

"And if I decide to take the job?"

"You'll have to talk to Ben, the smith. Do we have a deal?" She held out her hand and he found himself shaking it before he thought about it. The feel of her warm palm against his own both soothed and disturbed him.

Being "friends" with Roses Jordan might have some advantages he hadn't thought of, ones that even the lady herself probably didn't realize. He ignored the warning bells ringing in his head.

"So I'll see you tomorrow night?"

"Fine," she smiled.

"And then?" he asked.

"It's a small town. We're bound to have lots of

opportunities to run into each other. Accidentally, of course. Just don't run me down again."

He smiled. Things might just be starting to go his way again. He was intrigued by Roses Jordan and the town that had made her one of their own despite the color of her skin. This was why he had come west. His hometown had provided few choices and even fewer surprises. There'd been nothing to keep Tobe there once his grandmother died. The tall buildings and narrow streets had made him feel trapped. What little work he would have gotten did not suit him at all—opening doors either to restaurants or restrooms, hotels or private homes, fetching and carrying for people who wouldn't even look at him as they flipped a coin in his direction, saying, "Thanks Sam", or "Joe", or "Charlie."

He couldn't envision any kind of life for himself in Boston, despite his familiarity with that world. It had been easier to imagine riding into a frontier town and saving a damsel in distress—although the reality was quite different from what he'd imagined. Cedar Valley had become, overnight, a part of the adventure he'd only dreamed. And even though the "damsel" hadn't hung around his neck, begging him to take her away with him, he thought he'd be able to handle Roses Jordan, now that he knew her weak spot. She wouldn't be able to cause him any more trouble. She cared about these people, about Cedar Valley. She was waiting for his answer.

"It's your town," he agreed. He thought her scheme was a little strange, but if she wanted him to "act friendly," he'd be happy to oblige the lady.

Four

When Monday morning dawned clear and fair, the fourth such day in a row, Roses dressed in her favorite yellow gingham and her straw hat with the matching hatband to celebrate the coming of spring. She grabbed the flour sack that held the instruments Ian Millhouse had given her over the past couple of years. The big bag swung against her hip as she walked up Main Street to the veterinary office.

It was not just the lovely weather that quickened her step. Mondays, Wednesdays, and Fridays she worked with Doc Millhouse, the town's "horse doctor." She loved working with animals. She took pride in this work that went deeper than the satisfaction she always felt at a job well done. Learning about veterinary medicine would also give her a unique skill to bring home to the reservation. She had finally found the thing she needed, her own special *squas tenk,* medicine, to give to the Uncompahgre.

When she arrived, the waiting room was empty. It was still early, and, as she expected, the examining room was empty as well. She left her bag there and hurried to the back of the house where the doctor had his living quarters.

She found him in the kitchen, finishing off a small breakfast of cold biscuits and fried eggs. She took the coffeepot from the stove and poured two cups of the strong black brew. She added cream and sat down, placing his cup in front of him. They drank in companionable silence. When he'd drained the cup, he finally spoke.

"Morning, Roses," he said, taking his dish to the sink.

"Morning, Doc." She waited for him to rinse the dish and pan before she refilled his cup. Doc wasn't a big talker in the best of times, Roses knew better than to try to talk with him until he'd finished his second cup of morning coffee. He carried it with him and followed her into the examining room.

"I finished the paper on infections of the bones and organs," she said. Doc just nodded. "You want to look it over now?"

Doc didn't look up from the medicine jars he was sorting. "Just put it on my desk. We need more angelica and gentilia pills," Doc said. "And we'll be going over to Abernathy's later."

"Again?"

"Betsey's off her feed. Joe was by at six A.M., 'cause she didn't eat her dinner last night."

Roses winced in sympathy. She was an early riser herself, but Doc hated to be awakened for anything less than an emergency. He said it was his upbringing on the farm that made him hate to rise before the sun was up.

"Well, it *is* unusual for Betsey not to eat." She excused the errant Mister Abernathy.

There was a knock at the front door and Doc went to open up for the day, while Roses went to work replenishing their stores of medicine pills, which lasted only a short time. They had to be made fresh every week or so. Unlike the People, whites preferred their medicine modern. They seemed to feel the more mysterious the cure, the better. They thought odorless, tasteless pills and pomades were more effective than strong-smelling herbs and plasters, which were somehow "uncivilized." Roses enjoyed making the pills. Not long after she started working with Ian Millhouse, it became her regular Monday morning chore.

Roses hummed as she rolled the dough, adding salt to appeal to their more uncooperative patients. She kneaded it into a square pancake, added the powdered root of one plant, and the dried leaves from the other, then rolled the pancake into a snake. She put the roll on the pill board and grasped the wooden handle firmly, pulling it down over the corrugations carved into the board. The sharpened edges cut the snake into pellets which rolled down to the bottom of each furrow. After she had finished preparing the antispasmodic and the stomach powder, she made a small batch of soft pellets with sugar in the center, which she put in her pocket in anticipation of their visit to Betsey.

Studying Doc's books and stocking the dispensary were not exciting, but she enjoyed this job more than any other she had ever had. Doctoring animals could be dirty work, but it all washed off. While she worked in the stables and fields, Roses wore an apron she had designed herself to protect her skirts. It was made of thick leather and covered the entire front of her day dresses. It even managed to protect her from the muck to be found in Joe Abernathy's pigsty, which was where she found herself later that morning.

Most of Joe's stock was kept in his large sturdy barn. But he kept Betsey in a separate enclosure, covered with a slanted plank roof to keep the rain out. It was dry except in the area by the pig's drinking trough. Melting winter snows had created a large puddle there which Roses stepped around as she coaxed Betsey out of the corner of her shed.

Joe Abernathy had built Betsey's "house" when the pig had had her second litter of twenty piglets. No one had ever even heard of a pig that could produce that many offspring each year. Besides her private quarters, Joe had given her a special trough made from the trunk of a birch tree and carved with flowers and birds. It looked more like an oversized cradle than a pig's trough, and it had created quite a sensation when Joe hauled it home from Denver. After that, folks started calling Betsey his "baby."

Joe took the teasing with good grace. His "Baby" had reached, by the age of six years, the staggering weight of five hundred pounds. Luckily for Betsey, neither her size nor her rather nasty temper could stop Joe from coddling her.

"Is she going to be all right?" he asked, hovering at the spot on the other side of the fence where Doc always sent him to keep him from getting underfoot.

"I'm sure she'll be fine, Joe," Roses soothed, trying to look appropriately solemn. "She's a good, healthy sow." Betsey snorted and tried to stick her snout in Roses' pocket. Roses kept both pig and master happy with regular doses of sugar pills, and Betsey knew just where to find her treats. Roses thought it best to stay on Betsey's good side, since she and Doc visited regularly. And Roses had found that the only way to Baby's heart was through her stomach.

"Looks like maybe she's got a little indigestion, Joe," the veterinarian said.

"I'll get the castor oil." Roses let Betsey's head go, and the sow followed her to the gate. "I'll be right back."

Roses grabbed the castor oil from the wagon and

mixed it with beer. Like most pigs, Baby loved beer and she drank it greedily. Since they didn't want her to dirty the stall, Roses and Doc lured her out into the sunlight with a small bucket of grain and settled her by the fence in the open area of her pen.

Jessie Abernathy, Joe's wife, invited Dr. Millhouse inside for coffee while they waited for the castor oil to take effect. It was no surprise to Roses that she wasn't included in the invitation. Jessie had been one of the first of the town's "good women" to join with the new preacher from Atlanta in his campaign to ban blacks to the back of the church. She had aligned herself with him, despite the fact that most of his followers were newcomers to Cedar Valley, because Roses, to her mind, encouraged Joe's obsession with Baby.

Joe and Jessie Abernathy had come to Colorado from Minnesota twenty years before, and Jessie had never shown any unfriendliness to Roses when she had been working in town. But although most of the "older families" in the Valley which had been predominantly pro-Union during the War, ignored the preacher's proselytizing, Jessie encouraged him. Joe had never noticed the change in his wife's behavior. Perhaps, Roses thought, he just thinks I'm too worried about Baby to leave her. At any rate, Joe was too worried about Betsey to go indoors with the vet. He and Roses waited together in companionable silence in the spring sunshine.

By the time the sow was on her feet and eating again, Joe had cleared most of the muck from her pen and was sprinkling some of the last of his winter straw over the residue. He favored them with one of his rare smiles as Roses and Doc tried to make a quick exit. But he wouldn't let them go without showing his gratitude. He pumped Doc's arm enthusiastically up and down until Doc finally freed himself and headed for the gate. Joe stopped Roses, as she tried to follow, with a hand on her arm.

"I want to give you this," he insisted, pressing a silver dollar into her hand. "And perhaps you'd like some sausage to take home with you." Roses put the money in her pocket and tried to back away.

"Thanks, Joe, but I still have plenty of that smoked ham you gave me last week." Betsey snuffled and snorted as she got to her feet. Roses looked over her shoulder at the sound, then started to inch toward the gate. She was out of treats. Roses took her hand from her pocket to open the latch. She realized her mistake when she heard Betsey squeal. The sow had seen the movement and expected another sugar treat. Joe leaned down to calm the pig as she reached them, but she trotted past him. With a squeal of excitement, she slid into the back of Roses' legs. Roses tumbled backward into the icy mud of the wallow.

By the time Baby had extricated herself from under the leather apron flapping about her head, mud was running in rivulets inside Roses' collar and down her back. The apron, which had already suffered from Betsey's earlier "treatment," was heavy with the water and mud that coated it. It took the combined efforts of Joe and Doc to help her up. Both men were trying to hide wide smiles, and, as she clumped over to the buggy in her mud-filled shoes, Roses started giggling herself. Jessie Abernathy's shocked face made her laugh aloud. When Doc's shoulders started shaking, she turned to look at him, surprised at seeing the usually dour man laugh. His heavy-lidded brown eyes, usually so stern, were starting to tear.

"If you could have seen your face," Doc choked.

"That's okay." She chuckled. "I can see my feet." They both looked down at the footboard, where mud covered her from her shoes to her knees. It set them off again.

"And your hair." He was wheezing. Roses grinned, but she sobered a little when she felt the mud dripping down the back of her neck. She hoped she could save the precious lace sewn onto the dress collar. It had belonged to her mother.

Roses had promised Sarah she would help bake a pie that night, and by the time she washed up, and changed her dress, she was already late. When she got there, Lula was already rolling out the dough. "Why don't you go over to Mildred's?" she told the girl. "I'll do that."

"Go on, Lula," Sarah added. "It's such a pretty day. It'd be a shame to spend it indoors."

Lula didn't need any further urging. "I won't be long," she promised.

"Take all the time you want," Roses said. "It's a pleasure for me to work in this kitchen. I miss this in my room at the boardinghouse." When she was gone, she and Sarah exchanged satisfied smiles.

"She worries too much," Sarah said. "It's all Ben's fault."

"She likes helping you. I don't blame her. It smells wonderful in here." Sarah held up the cinnamon stick, and Roses got a whiff of the spice.

"Now, what's next?" Roses took stock.

She took up Lula's place at the rolling board. Sarah sat slicing apples into the cinnamon, nutmeg, and sugar for the pie filling. "Tobe Hunter came by after church yesterday," she announced. "I like him.

"He's working at the smithy, then."

"He started this morning. Moved in last night. Ben is letting him stay in the back room." Ben had turned the front room of the smithy into an office, but the back had remained empty until now. He must have taken a liking to Tobe right away to offer to let him stay on there. It was all working out better than Roses could have predicted. Now all she had to do was put a stop to the gossip going around town and everything would be as it had been. Tobe hadn't shown up at the boardinghouse for dinner the night before, as planned.

"I was wondering if he might come to supper at the restaurant last night. Most of the single men do." She had thought he might have decided to moved on, after all. She'd been relieved, but she had also been curious. Where had he come from? And where was he going?

"Ben brought him here to us," Sarah explained. "He's quiet, but I like him." Maybe Sarah had found out more about him.

"You said that already." Roses reminded her. "Did he say where he's from?"

"Boston."

"What did he do there?"

"He didn't say."

"Did he say where he's headed?" Roses asked.

Sarah laughed. "Nope. In fact, he didn't say much."

Roses stayed for supper at the Smiths', and although she'd worried about Ben bringing Tobe home with him again, when he didn't, she was a little disappointed. He remained a mystery.

It was dusk when she set out for home. The first thing she saw when she walked into her little room was her mud-splattered dress which she'd hung over the back of her chair. The lace collar was still damp to the touch and Roses decided to go and wash it before the mud could dry and set. Mrs. Trumbull,

her landlady, would never get her the washbasin at
this time of night, but it was just a short walk to
the creek. Though it was growing dark it was still
early. The sky was clear and the rising moon was
full as she walked past the last houses of the town
and left the road.

The night was full of sound and motion. The very
air seemed to be alive. After only a few minutes of
walking, the lights of town disappeared. It reminded
Roses of the long summer evenings of her childhood,
when she had dwelt with the People and she had
gone each night to bathe with the other youngsters
after the work of the day was done. The sound of
water rushing over stones and through the reeds
made the memory even stronger and she stopped
walking and stood listening. Nearby a larger animal
was splashing in the stream, and rather than frighten
it, Roses turned and walked upstream. There she approached the water. She could see the creek only
where starlight glinted off wet rocks protruding
above the inky surface.

The bank of the river sloped slowly downward and
she moved carefully to the edge of the water. When
she unfolded the dress, the white lace of the collar
shone clearly where it hadn't been splashed with
mud. The water, when she put her hand in it, was
icy cold. It was too dark to see properly, but she
could get the worst of the dark stuff out. At least
this way there was a chance the stains wouldn't set.
She went to work. She couldn't bear the thought of
losing the little bit of lace. It was all she had of her
mother's.

Her hands were thoroughly chilled in moments.
As a child she would have bathed in this river every
night. The Uncompahgre washed daily—out of doors
in the mountain rivers, once the snow melted. When

she'd come to live with the whites, they'd seemed
filthy and rank to her. She had found it repulsive
that they bathed so infrequently. But soon she had
discovered they thought it improper to bathe where
they might be seen. She had adopted their habits,
making do with a daily sponge bath in her room,
and bathing as regularly as Mrs. Trumbull would allow in the wooden tub in her room at the boardinghouse. Her landlady thought bathing more often than
once a week was not only unnecessary, but also un-
healthy. The closest she had come to this fresh
mountain water was wading into the creek once or
twice when she and Annette had walked by the creek
in the summer.

The discomfort of immersing her hands in this cold
water made her realize that bathing in the lakes and
streams of her childhood had been an acquired skill,
taught to her until it had become habit. She was no
longer hardened and fit from living out of doors. In
the last four years she had become as soft as the
townspeople. But despite the painful tingling in her
fingers, she wouldn't give up.

Roses' concentration was so complete that at first
she barely noticed the sound of someone approaching. It was soft whistling that finally got her attention. She looked downstream just as someone started
to sing. A man was coming upriver, singing in a
deep bass, moving toward her. The voice wasn't one
that she recognized, but she had a sudden feeling
that she knew who it belonged to.

Roses held her breath, praying that he hadn't
heard her. A cloud covered the moon. The singing
stopped.

"Miss Jordan, are you there?"

Roses sighed. He was looking for her. "I'm over
here." She heard him start toward her.

"I saw you headed out of town and I thought I'd come thank you for getting me the job." After a moment, Tobe's voice came again in the dark. "Miss Jordan?" He was headed straight for the water.

"Here," she said, more sharply than she had intended. She hoped no one had seen him follow her. She hadn't spoken to him since that day after she offered him the job at the smithy. Saturday morning at the restaurant had been a trial, true, but Sunday, at church had been even worse. Everyone had asked her about him as though she was an authority on the subject of Tobe Hunter. They thought she knew something they didn't. She didn't want to talk to him here, alone in the dark. What if someone found out? They were watching her, hoping she'd give them more fodder for the gossip mill. It wasn't fair to blame him, she knew, but everything had been going fine before the accident that had brought him into her life. She had made a home for herself, at least temporarily, and had established a fragile peace with the people here. Now, everything was changing.

On top of everything else, every time she thought of Tobias Hunter, she remembered the scene at the jail, the feel of him as he pulled her against him, and his angry eyes when he'd been locked in his cell. It was unsettling.

He stopped walking. "I'll just wait for the clouds to blow away." Roses was beginning to feel thoroughly chilled. She could barely make out his dark figure looming on the shore. After a moment, he broke the silence. "Are you all right?"

"Yes." She stood. She'd done as much as she could with the lace. "I was just washing my dress."

"*This* is where you do your laundry?"

"Not usually, but I wanted to wash some lace. It's delicate. Cold water is better for it."

"Cold? The water must be like ice. I'm not carrying you into town again, suffering from pneumonia. They'd hang me."

Roses couldn't stop herself from smiling. "I'm done now. I'll come to you," she said. She could barely make out his shadowy form, now only a few feet away. He was totally still. She couldn't even hear him breathing.

She held out her hand and touched his shoulder and he turned. He was still only a shadowy figure, but as he looked down at her, she thought she caught the flash of his white teeth as he smiled. Roses wrung out the dress. "You're shivering." He reached out and, taking the dress from her, enfolded her hand in his bigger, warmer one. She tried to pull away.

"I'll be fine. I'm warming up now. The walk back to town will get the blood moving again."

He let her go, swinging her wet dress over his shoulder. He commanded, "Give me your other hand."

His palms were warm as he gently enclosed her fingers, the backs of her hands, her wrists and forearms where her wet sleeves clung to her skin. Roses was mesmerized by the movement of his hands against her skin. His movements were brisk, impersonal, yet his touch felt intimate, sensual. It had been years since someone had touched her, soothed her, in this way. "Excuse me?" she asked, when the sound of his voice penetrated the strange fog which had wrapped itself around her befuddled mind.

"Perhaps we should start walking. Back. To town," he repeated.

"Oh. Yes." Roses turned and he followed her movement.

He kept one of her hands in his. "It's dark," he offered. She guessed it was enough of an explanation for the liberty he had taken easily. This was unfamiliar terrain for him, and not for her. It still felt odd to walk along hand in hand, but he only clasped her hand loosely in his. There was nothing threatening about it, no real reason to pull away.

He followed her lead as she started to walk downstream. She walked slightly ahead of him, very aware of the light pressure of his palm against hers. By the time they reached the road she was warm again.

She stopped walking. "Here is the road." The dried mud was light in color, almost white, visible even though the moon was still hidden by clouds.

"Thank you," he said, releasing her hand. At that moment the clouds blew by overhead, shedding light on the path, and they both looked up at the sky as the stars and the moon reappeared.

"My pleasure." She lowered her eyes and clasped her hands about her arms. He was still looking up at the sky.

His jaw was square, his cheeks lean, but already he had lost the gaunt look she'd recognized the first day in the jail. Just a few days of wholesome food and work had filled in the space below his high cheekbones. His hair was covered by his hat, which also hid his eyes. Her gaze lingered on his full lips for a moment. She forced her eyes down. He wore a wool shirt underneath his sheepskin-lined coat. Her eyes moved down to the Levis worn to the shape of his body.

Roses swallowed. He was all hard muscle. She was tempted to reach out and touch him. The feeling of his hands on hers lingered in her mind and on her skin. She shivered.

"Are you still cold?" he asked. He was looking down at her now, but she still could not see his eyes.

The hat he wore shaded them from the moonlight as effectively as from the sun.

"No. I'm fine." She answered, her voice curiously husky.

She was a healer and Roses had seen enough of men and women, birth and death, to know that what she felt was natural. It was the call of the blood to want to mate with one of her own kind. Nevertheless it made her uncomfortable.

"You're shivering," he said.

"We should get back to town. You go on and I'll wait here for a while. My landlady is used to my coming and going at odd hours. Some flowers and herbs for my medicines have to be collected after nightfall."

"My grandmother used to do the same thing," Tobe said. He sounded surprised.

"Some plants aren't effective if they're collected any other way."

"How did you learn all this?"

"A healer taught me."

"An Indian healer?"

"Ute. Yes."

"I heard you were raised by Indians." She thought she detected a note of sympathy in his voice, but hoped she was mistaken. Her years with the People were not to be pitied.

"I was raised by my parents," she answered. "When they were given their freedom, after the War, they came west. They hoped to join one of the Colonies, but they were educated house servants, not farmers or merchants, and they weren't welcomed by the Spanish townships or the settlers from the states. They tried homesteading, staking a claim on the Eastern Slope, but they would have died there if it hadn't been for the Navajo."

"Not much choice between the whites or the savages." His tone was matter of fact and her heart sank. Roses could understand his disdain for white men but she hated when anyone called the Good People savages.

"Not much choice?" she bit out. "The People are civilized, at least they have an understanding of the world." She sensed his surprise at her vehemence. But this was one area where she couldn't control her temper. She hated the ignorance that caused him to malign the Good People.

"Is that why your parents went to live with the Indians?"

"No." It calmed her to think of her parents and the way they, too, had thought the People savages, before they'd lived among them. "No, they were afraid of them when they came west. They had heard stories about Indian raids and massacres travelling across the plains. But the Navajo took them in when the whites and the Spanish wouldn't. They always counseled peaceful negotiations with the settlers from the East." She had argued with her father about his quest for peace. But she had come to agree. Even the Ute chief, Ouray, treated for peace before he died. "My parents knew, before Old Man and Old Woman, before the shaman, that there would be too many whites and they would never stop coming until they swallowed the whole earth. My parents were born with whites, bred by the white man. They knew that the People would be killed or swallowed up as well. They knew what had to be done in order to survive in the face of this invasion, and they taught me."

"They must have been interesting people, your parents?" The statement sounded more a question, and she nodded in response.

Roses had never been able to reconcile her feelings with her parents' attitude. They loved the Uncompahgre family which they had adopted but were friendly to the whites, even some of the bluecoats who'd moved the tribe onto the reservation. They thought of the soldiers as misguided, while Roses had hated the men who had taken her from her mountain home to the reservation in the desert. She had admired and loved her parents for their kindnesses but she had felt betrayed by them. It all came back to her as she stood talking in the dark with Tobe Hunter. The confusing morass of feelings and hurts she'd buried in the last few years were nearer to the surface than she had known.

Roses tried to stem her traitorous feelings, get them back under control. She was more agitated than she could remember feeling in years, and only just barely able to stand facing him. She hadn't felt this uncertain of herself since the night she had lain dry eyed and trembling, awaiting Larry Jenkins' retribution for his maimed ear. What was the power this man exercised over her? She thought he must be able to hear her heart pounding in her chest as her anger and frustration threatened to erupt and mar irreparably the calm facade that she presented to the world at large. She had met him only days ago, but the carefully constructed image she had fostered of herself as the capable, efficient, unflappable Roses Jordan threatened to fall into pieces because of him. She wanted to make him go away. But she didn't want to antagonize this man. Especially not out here, alone with him.

It wasn't that she was afraid of him. She trusted Sarah's instincts and Sarah liked him. She knew from her personal experience with him that he wasn't as dangerous as he appeared to be, because he hadn't been cruel, or overly rough with her, even in his desperation in jail. And he had been desperate, she had seen it in his eyes.

Roses finally admitted to herself that he made her feel nervous, threw her off balance, because she had felt strangely drawn to the man she'd seen that day in the jail. At first she had just felt sorry for him, and guilty for being the cause of his misfortune, but later she'd wanted to soothe the angry spirit that she'd glimpsed before he'd been able to bank it behind his hard dark eyes. She suspected there was a part of himself he hid deep inside. She didn't know why—maybe because she, too, had something trapped within her, trying to escape. She had buried part of herself when she buried her parents, and that seed of rebellion, of unreasoning anger, seemed to respond to Tobias Hunter as it never had to anyone else.

Ben thought Hunter an easygoing man, but Roses couldn't agree. Tobe was like her, keeping most of himself *to* himself. Even Sarah seemed willing to take him as he appeared, and she was usually wary about giving her friendship and trust to people she didn't know. But Roses was sure there was more to Tobe than the face he showed the world—and it called out to her.

Somehow knowing why he frightened her, why the simplest conversation with him seemed so fraught with danger, made Roses' fear and anger disappear. All that was left was sympathy. And an abiding curiosity to know more about this man. Who was he? What exactly was it, in him, that drew her to him?

She wanted to ask him what had made him so afraid—what had almost pushed him over the edge that day. But before she could think of a way to ask him, he asked her a question.

"Do you despise these people then? They seem to think the world of you."

She didn't even have to think about her answer. It came bubbling up from somewhere inside, where she'd kept her feelings locked away for so many years.

"No, I don't despise them at all. I wish . . . that they could see beyond the color of my skin and your skin. I want them to realize how ridiculous it is to think that because we're both colored we're a perfect match. They went from thinking you'd attacked me, to planning a wedding between us in one day! But many of these people care about me." It was only since Tobe had arrived that she had started to understand that she had feelings beyond simple friendship for these people whom she had come to know so well. "I cannot hate people who care for me."

It hurt to say aloud she felt. She hadn't done it in so long, she felt a physical pain in the region of her heart. And he was a part of it. She had not meant to tell him, a stranger, so much. He had told her nothing of himself, and she had revealed . . . too much.

She had to see what he thought. She reached up and took off his hat. His eyes were wide with curiosity and . . . something else. Desire. They had been dancing on the edge of a precipice ever since the night had lowered its dark curtain around them. Now, under brilliant white moonlight, they waltzed too near the edge. She swayed toward him. She might have been reaching for her dress, he for his hat, but the dance ended as their lips met.

It was a new kind of kiss, invented in that moment. He was gentler, his lips softer, than Roses could ever have imagined. Their warm lips lightly touched, and parted, only to meet again. The light caress of his mouth lured her closer, and her hand touched his chest and lingered. She was amazed at the heat she felt there, through his shirt. It echoed the heat rising beneath her skin. His hand at her back urged her closer, his tongue traced a pattern on her lips, new to her, and yet familiar. Her lips parted. She shivered again and he sighed, his breath tickled her ear. Finally his mouth fastened on hers and the kiss became greedy and insistent.

But it ended as quickly as it had begun. Perhaps a stray cloud covered the moon, or a breeze caused the grasses to rustle at their feet. Whatever it was, it brought her back to herself, and Tobe seemed to sense it. They released each other bit by bit; her hand slid down, over his waist, to her side. His fingers loosed her dress. She leaned back and away, while he stood straight.

Roses stood wide eyed, watching as he blinked, and wincing as he cleared his throat.

"Whoops," he said. Heat still shimmered through her, but that small sound cleared her mind. He had opened the door to another emotion she'd thought safely locked away, but before she'd had time to fully explore this surprising feeling, that one sound sent the door swinging shut again. She should have been glad it hadn't meant anything to him. She hadn't meant to kiss him. But for a moment here in the dark, away from prying eyes, it had felt right.

"I didn't mean to do that," he said, and the feeling was gone.

She had almost wanted to hang on to the sensation. It made her feel like a girl again, remember earlier dreams from a time before the world was turned upside down, before she had to leave her home. But she didn't want to be that girl again, suffer that pain and uncertainty again. For a moment she'd forgotten, but now that she'd regained the use of her senses, she certainly didn't want to be anything to the cowboy who called her people savages. She couldn't be anything more to him than a woman who'd set him on his way home.

She had enough to contend with . . . trying to get home, trying to bring something of value back to the people who had sheltered her in their impoverished homes, and nourished her out of their meager allowance of food. That was what she strove for, every waking minute of the day. She was going back to live with the Uncompahgre again . . . this time, forever. All she wanted now was to earn that right.

"Well, I guess you'd better go," she was pleased to find her voice was strong, even though she couldn't look at him. He turned to go. His Stetson lay on the ground at her feet. "Your hat." She stooped to get it. It had fallen from her hand at some point. He reached for it as she stood. She didn't relinquish it right away. She held it for a moment, brushed it off against her skirt, and then put it into his outstretched hand. She didn't watch him walk away.

She was halfway home when she realized he still had her dress. After all she had done to save that bit of lace, she didn't want to give it up. She could send for it through Sarah or Ben, but she would have to answer a lot of awkward questions.

She was trying to think of some way to get him a note without anyone knowing when she turned into the alley behind the boardinghouse. He stepped out of the shadows with her dress in his hand and wordlessly handed it to her. With a nod, he turned on his heel and walked away down the street, whistling between his teeth. She turned and headed up the back stairs. If she hadn't been sure before, she was now, that he would help her convince everyone that they were no more than friends.

He didn't want her. There was no need to be afraid of Tobias Hunter. There would be no more kisses. If only she could convince everyone that they had no future together—he was just another cowboy, same as all the others who passed through town, and she herself was the same old Roses, as busy as ever with her work and nothing else. No matter how eagerly the people of this town hoped for some sign of a courtship beginning between the two of them, Roses thought she had made her intentions clear— Tobe would not pursue her. It was just as well. She didn't need a man complicating her life. Certainly not this man. He wasn't at all her type. He was as backwards, about the People, as anyone she had met.

He could never understand, or go back home with her. If she did consider sparking with someone under the watchful eyes of the people of Cedar Valley, it wouldn't be an infuriating, small minded specimen like Tobe Hunter, no matter how tantalizing those brown eyes and wide shoulders. Cedar Valley could move on to some other topic of interest.

Five

Tobe really liked this town. He could almost forget that there were men out there somewhere who were, presumably, still looking for him. He felt like he had discovered a new world here in Cedar Valley. He couldn't get over how easily he'd been accepted here. By everyone except the one who had made it all possible, Roses Jordan.

He knew that the welcome he'd received, and much of the friendly feeling that was extended toward him was the result of Roses' presence in the town. She was still a puzzle to him, but she'd become one that he was determined to solve. Despite the fact that she was so well liked, she acted as though she lived alone in a desert. He had never met a woman as independent as she was.

He felt compelled to get inside the walls she seemed to have erected around herself. He thought her control had almost slipped the night before when he'd found her by the river, and they'd talked. He'd been even more sure of it when they'd kissed. But she'd managed to pull back. He wondered if anything would really get under her skin.

He looked around the saloon. Ruby had promised to give him a much needed haircut, and he'd liked the idea. He usually stayed away from whorehouses—they brought back too many memories of his mother. But Letty Dowd's saloon was a nice place, the most popular in town. Many of the regulars, like Tobe, didn't avail themselves of all the services offered, but just came for the company, or to get away from their womenfolk. Tobe couldn't bring himself to purchase the services of any of the whores, but he liked some of them. He had grown up with women like these. They helped his mama take care of him. He still had fond, if vague, memories of being coddled and pampered by big, buxom, sweet smelling ladies with knowing eyes and soft hands.

It was quiet yet, still early enough on a Monday night for men to be home having dinner with their families. He couldn't get over the fact that he knew some of those men, and was welcome in their homes. For a long time after he left home he hadn't been interested in that kind of a life. After going on the run, he had come to think of himself as different from men who lived simple, ordinary, respectable lives.

He hoped he wasn't endangering anyone else by taking advantage of this small town's hospitality. He didn't see how he could be. With the first sign of any danger, he planned to be on his way. But with each passing day, he believed a little more that he wasn't going to be found after all. He'd outwitted his hunters. Although he still woke up occasionally in a cold sweat, it was happening less and less. The pretense of cool calm he'd had to work so hard to maintain in Cedar Valley's jailhouse the first night had become real.

Sam, the bartender, wasn't working yet, so Letty was behind the bar. She poured him a drink while he waited. Ruby came downstairs, in answer to Letty's summons, just as he tipped the glass to his mouth.

She greeted him with a smile. "Tobe, chico, here you are." She sauntered over to him and offered her cheek. He kissed it, smiling back at the pretty brunette mulatta. "You want to get right to it?" she purred, her voice soft and throaty. She sounded as if he were there for something much less innocent than a haircut. The woman was made for this line of work. Everything about her, her lips, her voice, her powdered skin, was a sensual invitation. He wondered how many years it had taken her to create this enticing image.

He winked at Letty. "I'm ready as I'll ever be."

Letty warned, "Just his hair, Ruby, that's all he gets for free."

"Seguro," the prostitute agreed, pouting. "Por supuesto. Of course."

Tobe followed her up the stairs. Her long black hair flowed loose, down past her waist. It drew a man's attention (as he was sure it was supposed to) to the swaying of her hips. But when they reached the second floor, she was all business.

"This room is good." Her accent had faded a little. He hadn't realized that, too, was just another part of the act.

"Whatever you say, Ruby." He turned into the doorway she pointed out, and found himself in the biggest indoor privy he'd ever seen. The floors were tiled, the walls painted a warm pink, and soft material was draped over everything, the chairs, the tables, even the door. The centerpiece of the room was a large bath tub, the biggest that he had ever seen, by far. His wayward mind strayed, as usual, to Roses Jordan. He could easily fit with her in the claw footed monster.

"It's something isn't it? Letty ordered it, but it

was really all because of Roses." He spun around
so quickly he almost overbalanced.

"What?" He was surprised to hear that paragon's
name on Ruby's painted lips.

"She gave us some soap. Wonderful soap. Smelling of lilacs, and roses, and other flowers. We liked
it so much. And the men liked it, too. So . . ." she
gestured toward the tub.

He should have known. Of course she'd made her
mark in the whorehouse, just as she had everywhere
else in this town. But while he had almost gotten
used to hearing about her work at the school and
the bank and the store, and was pretty much accustomed to having her brought into every conversation,
this was too much. He could imagine Roses here, in
this sinful little paradise, and this time he couldn't
rein in his imagination.

She was so beautiful, and it was so easy to picture
her, rising out of that bathtub, smiling just for him.

Ruby brought him back to the present. "So, if you
will sit here? I have everything we will need, I
think."

He averted his gaze from the bath, and sat in the
seat Ruby indicated, taking off his hat and running
his hand through his unruly mass of hair. In the city,
he had worn it short, and brushed back from his
face, but on the trail it was too much trouble, so
he'd just let it grow. Now it reached to his collar,
and getting a comb through it was intimidating. He'd
combed it before he'd come tonight. He had the feeling Ruby would be gentle with him, which was why
he'd agreed to let her do this. He wouldn't go to the
barber. He was so damn tenderheaded. As he sat
waiting for Ruby to start cutting, he could almost
hear his granny scolding, *"Sit still, boy and stop*

*wiggling. The sooner you let me at it, the sooner
you can go."*

Ruby's hands were gentle as she wet a comb and
pulled it through his hair. He leaned his head back
at her command. He closed his eyes as warm water
trickled down from his hairline. The room was warm
and slightly steamy, the woman behind him hummed
softly, and sweet scent filled his nostrils. He breathed
it all in and found it calming and exciting all at
once. With his eyes closed, he could imagine the
woman behind him was Roses. He smiled as he remembered that Roses had worked in the barbershop
for a short time. She was an amazing woman.

And she was lovely. Her big brown eyes were
round and slightly tilted at the corners. Her lips were
full and pink-brown, and looked sweet as a ripe
berry. They tasted good, too. He licked his own lips,
remembering. Her arms had held him tight, she was
stronger than she looked. Her breasts against his
chest had been full. She'd been a comfortable arm-
ful. Too bad she was also such a handful. He
guessed she'd be furious if she knew he imagined
her here.

"I haven't done this in years," Ruby said, "I used
to cut my brothers' hair. We never let it get this
long." Ruby seemed to have tired of the silence.
Tobe didn't want to talk, but he felt some response
was necessary.

"Mmmm," he said.

"Feels good, no?" Her accent was back.

She came around the chair to face him and he
opened his eyes. Ruby was very pretty, her big dark
eyes dominating her face, and her creamy skin on
view everywhere, but she couldn't compare to Roses
Jordan.

"I will make you beautiful, hombre," she promised, as she moved to his side. "Then no one will be able to resist you." His half closed eyes flew open, but with the sharp scissors so close to his ear, he couldn't risk turning to face her.

"What did you say?" he asked.

"After I cut your hair, you will be irresistible to any woman you choose."

Tobe couldn't believe it. Here, too? These were the last women on earth he'd thought would be matchmakers. But why not? The women who had raised him until he was nine years old had been whores, and they had been romantics, at heart. Maybe his mother had been, too. He'd never thought to ask her. For a moment, he wondered, then he dismissed the idea. It was too ludicrous. His mother didn't have those tender feelings. Sure, when he was little, before he knew what she was, he'd thought she loved him. But if she had, she would have left all that behind and found a respectable job and lived a normal decent life with him in Granny Gee's little house.

He didn't want to think about his mother. That was all in the past. It was much more pleasant to think about the future. Tonight, for example, he was due at the Smiths' for supper. Ben had mentioned that Roses would be there as well.

Tobe found Sarah Smith's cozy little home as comfortable as any he'd ever been in. There was something about the family that was appealing, even to a man not used to minding his manners around "little pitchers." The children were good-natured, if spirited, like their mother. And Ben, as tough as the nails he crafted at his forge in public, was a pussycat at home.

His second supper at the Smith house was as pleasant as the first had been. Roses and Tobe were both treated more as members of the family than guests. Roses was clearly comfortable here, but she kept her emotions on a tight rein. He couldn't begin to guess why. Even with the Smiths, who seemed to be her closest friends, she didn't totally unbend, but only relaxed slightly—still careful never to let them see her without that smile that didn't quite jibe with the sadness in her eyes.

No one else seemed to notice the way she held herself at a distance. They all treated her with warmth and affection, but they didn't seem to see her. Not the way he did. At least with Ben and Sarah, her laughter was honest, heartfelt, the release that laughter was meant to be. It made him itch to make her laugh himself, or make her angry again. He suspected the latter would be much the simpler of the two.

Oh, she was polite, and civil, even friendly, but Roses kept him at arm's length, or even further. She didn't smile at him like she did everyone else. She didn't look at him, unless forced to. She avoided his eyes. She held back her laughter at his jokes. It galled him, though he knew it was probably better this way.

If she would have unbent, even a little, he'd have been tempted to forget himself. And she wasn't the kind of woman a man like him could mess around with. She was the kind of woman a man married. He wasn't the marrying kind. He was just passing through this town, his ultimate destination unknown. He had nothing to offer a woman like Roses.

By the time dinner was over, Tobe had decided that Roses Jordan, for all her strange ways, was as bright as she was beautiful. He sat back, listening as she argued with Ben about politics, clearly a subject they'd often locked horns over.

"But we've already had one black man in the House of Representatives," Roses said while Ben shook his head. "The vote works for everyone. That's why women need it, too."

Sarah laughingly threw in her two cents worth, "What do you want with the vote, Roses, you don't trust none of those "White Fathers" in Washington anyway? Just last week you were saying the word of a politician is as reliable as a tornado in springtime."

"But we can vote in better men. And maybe women, too, if we get the vote."

Ben was still shaking his head, but Sarah hadn't finished. "Roses, you know women are going to vote the same as their menfolks do, dontcha? At least, white women, will." She threw a laughing glance up at Ben who'd risen to put more wood on the fire. He stood up from the chore and threw his hands up, appealing to Tobe,

"Help me, Tobias, these women will not listen to reason."

Tobe chuckled. "Maybe she has a point." Roses looked over at him in shock, her mouth dropping open. "Not you," he said, nodding toward Sarah, ". . . her. Women aren't going to vote against their husbands and fathers. Won't make any difference in the long run."

"What about Nevada," Roses argued. Ben groaned. "They got the vote there, and they've voted in women sheriffs and mayors."

"They ain't elected no women to congress though," Ben pointed out.

"No, but women have to work their way up to that point. Nothing's going to happen overnight. We've got to have a voice though. What about women who don't have men to vote for them?"

Tobe hesitated, but he couldn't resist, "What kind of women are those, dried up old maids and widow women. They ain't got sense enough to get a man, I sure don't want them votin'." Ben guffawed, and even Sarah covered a smile with a dainty hand. Roses just spluttered. "No, seriously . . ." he tried to redeem himself. "Like Sarah, I don't have anything against women voting, I just don't see much point in it."

"I ain't arguin' that women couldn't do it. But why should they? They got more important things to do than worrying about votin' or gettin' lynched for tryin' like my Uncle Billy. It's dangerous enough for a black man to vote. I don' want Sarah to go through none o' that."

Sarah said, "Leave me out of this. I'm not afraid, anymore than you are, old man. I just don't see the point in arguing about something that's never gonna happen." She turned to Roses, "Honey, you know these men are gonna keep running things like they always done, and they're not gonna take kindly to us wantin' to intrude in male business. So why don't you just set yourself on something a little more likely to happen."

"If I can't even convince Ben—who is one of the best men I know—" That remark took some of the wind from the older man's sails, Tobe noticed. "How are things ever going to change."

"What do we need to worry about changing things for?" Sarah said. "We got enough to worry about with things the way they are. Men can keep their politicking, thank you."

Roses sighed, exasperated.

"Well, you changed my mind, Roses," Tobe said, "Now that I think on it, my Granny and Sarah here would be as good at choosing governors and senators as Ben or I." He had never really thought about Granny Gee as a woman who could actually have something to say about such things, but he would have trusted her judgement above most of the men he had known.

"There!" Sarah said. "See, you've done it. Now can we calm down and talk sensibly. The two of you just don't know when to stand back." She scolded Ben and Roses lightly. "It's time those children were abed." Ben and she rounded up the little ones, while Tobe watched Roses wander over to the fire. She seemed to be collecting herself, calming down, and he preferred her fired up.

"So, Miss Jordan, I guess the Temperance League and the Lady's Civil Society must seem tame to you compared to these hot debates."

"I don't know, Mr. Hunter. I've never been to a meeting of either of those organizations."

"Call me, Tobe, please." She didn't invite him to reciprocate by calling her by her first name, but he hadn't really expected she would. She'd gone all stiff on him again, and just nodded. Yet he couldn't resist baiting her. "I'm shocked, Miss Jordan. Really, I'm surprised you aren't leading the ladies in their re-forms." He didn't get any response, other than an indifferent, "Oh."

"Everyone in town seems to have some sort of story about you, you have quite a reputation. But it hasn't seemed to hurt their regard for you." As she turned away, he added, "Just thought you might want to know that."

"I can't think of a single reason why I would," she answered. "Small towns like this virtually live on gossip. I don't think anyone escapes it."

"I've never heard anyone say anything about . . .

oh . . . Sarah," he said, still trying to get a rise out of her.

"Sarah is a respectable married woman. She doesn't have people watching her every move." Her tone implied she blamed him for that turn of events.

"But you were creating talk before I came to town." She bridled at that.

"They start talking about something, and before long they've blown it into a . . . a scandal. That's why I asked for your help. And you said you would be . . ."

"Civil. And I have been."

"I wouldn't call this being civil."

"I didn't think it counted when we were here. Don't Ben and Sarah know about your plan?"

"As a matter of fact I hadn't mentioned it to them."

He bet she hadn't. He had seen the way most of the people in this town treated her. He would bet his last nickel that neither Sarah nor Ben, nor anyone else who knew her, would ever buy the idea that Roses would inspire only friendship in a man. But if she didn't know how lovable she was, he wasn't going to be the one to tell her. He could imagine the reaction that would get.

"Maybe they could help? They could spread the word that we're just friends, and that there is nothing going on between us. Shall I ask them?" He watched her sneak a look at Sarah, who was tucking little Ben into bed.

"I don't think that would be such a good idea?"

"Why not?"

"Well because . . ."

He'd stumped her. But no, he could see in her eyes the exact moment when she came up with what seemed to her a reasonable argument. "The more people who know about it, the more likely someone will mention it, and then where would we be? Everyone would just be more sure there was something going on."

"I don't think Ben or Sarah would betray us."

"There is no us," she hissed.

He smiled. She was adorable. Tobe was not going to be able to keep his hands off of her. Although he knew he should. He knew she'd rather he did. He believed that. Yet he was pretty sure she was as attracted to him as he was to her, and he could imagine that would make her uncomfortable. But she was too tempting, too seductive, too sweet to resist.

He couldn't seduce her. She was right, the townspeople would not condone that. But he could enjoy her company while he was here. An innocent kiss, or two, couldn't hurt. He'd even try to avoid being alone with her. That should make her happy. And keep tongues from wagging. Meanwhile, he wanted to figure out what made this woman tick.

Six

Even teaching church school, she couldn't stop thinking about his kiss. All week the memory had haunted her.

She had done her best to end the rumors. She had been friendly but distant when Tobe and she had shared dinner with Ben and Sarah on Tuesday night. Beyond saying that he was passing through town on his way to parts unknown, hopefully into Utah next, Tobe hadn't volunteered any information about himself. So she knew little more about him than she had a week ago. Something about the easy way he diverted personal questions kept anyone from pressing the issue. So their one meal together had been unremarkable, nothing for the gossipmongers to get their teeth into.

She had thanked Tobe for holding the door for her when they'd passed each other in the doorway of the general store on Thursday. He'd kept a polite distance between them as he greeted her with a simple, "Hello, Miss Jordan." He hadn't waited for her to answer but had sauntered on down the boardwalk without, she assumed, looking back. She'd made sure she'd acted as though she had barely noticed him. He'd been in town a week and the town still watched each encounter between them with avid eyes. She was very glad he hadn't shown up at church this morning. At least, here she knew she could relax without fear that he'd suddenly appear.

She sat with the children on the front steps of the church, showing them how to make wreaths of dried flowers to decorate the ends of the pews. Thoughts of Tobe kept intruding. She had a right to get on with her life without constantly being reminded that he was here, young, attractive, and available, by every busybody in town. She didn't need the thought of his kisses interfering with everything she tried to do. She worked hard and didn't hurt a soul. She wished things could get back to normal. Everything had been going just fine until *he* had come. She had to put an end to the gossip about Tobe Hunter and herself for once and for all.

"Repent!" the Reverend Meeker shouted, and Roses jumped. The small but loyal congregation of the First Methodist Church of Cedar Valley was once again being bombarded with a sermon full of hellfire and brimstone. Roses was very glad that she had decided to bring the church school class out of doors. It was far more pleasant to work on the dried flower wreaths for the Easter processional with the gentle spring breeze wafting the preacher's voice away.

Though he could be heard through the open windows, at least the children didn't have to watch the apoplectic minister as he lost himself in his religious fervor.

"Christ died for our sins!" he thundered, making her jump again.

Roses found it unnerving that even the most spirited of the children were subdued as the deep baritone voice washed over their bowed heads. Roses wished she could think of some respectful way to break the silence.

"Do you believe that your sins were washed away

by His blood? Do you?" the reverend boomed, and little Nettie Meeker winced, but held up the wire frame she had fashioned to hold the flowers that were to be her offering on Easter Sunday.

"Will this be all right?" she asked Roses. The preacher's daughter was a sweet child, and awfully shy, and Roses smiled as she pulled the little girl close. Holding one small hand in her own, she examined the circlet carefully.

"It will be beautiful." She declared as she handed it back to Nettie and gave the girl a quick hug. Nettie's question had broken the spell, and the other children were soon chattering away and calling Roses to come and admire their work.

While the choir sang the closing hymn and the children went to wait for their parents, Nettie sat with Roses in the sun and helped her roll the wire Ben had given them.

"Miss Roses?" Nettie asked, timidly.

Roses took a quick look at the top of Nettie's gingham bonnet, then crossed her legs under her. "Yes, Nettie?" She put her hands palms down in the soft shoots of young grass at her sides, and felt the cool earth beneath.

"Do you think it hurt Jesus to die? He must have been terribly afraid."

Roses heard the echo of older voices in the child's voice, and wondered if she was hearing the doubts of the preacher himself in his daughter's words. Death would be frightening to such a man—a man who could see nothing beyond what was here and now. Reverend Meeker now barely tolerated Roses' presence in his church. She suspected that he'd only accepted her as teacher for the church school because it kept her out of his precious church pews.

She debated briefly whether she should tell Nettie

to ask her father, but she couldn't turn away the little girl's question. If there was no answer, there was at least a story.

"My mother's mother's people told a story about why men are afraid of death. Do you want to hear it?"

Nettie smiled in her shy way and nodded and Roses went on.

"The Moon once sent an insect to men, saying, "Go to men and tell them 'As I die, and dying live; so you shall also die, and dying live.' " The insect started with the message, but while on his way was overtaken by the hare, who asked, "Where are you going?"

The insect answered, "I am sent by the moon to men, to tell them that as she dies and dying lives, so shall they also die and dying live."

The hare said, "As you are not a fast runner, let me go." With these words he ran off and when he reached men he said, "I am sent by the Moon to tell you, 'As I die and dying perish, in the same manner you also shall die, and come wholly to an end.' "

The hare then returned to the Moon and told her what he had said to men. The Moon was angry, saying "How dare you tell the people a thing which I have not said?" With these words the Moon took up a piece of wood and struck the hare on the nose. Since that day, the hare's nose has been slit, but men believe what Hare had told them." Roses opened one eye to see what Nettie thought of the story, and found the girl smiling up at her. "To know this story that I have told you is true," Roses added, as her mother had always done, "go to Hare and look at his nose."

"I don't want you telling my daughter those heathen stories," the Reverend Meeker snapped. Nettie started to step forward, but Roses stopped her with a gentle hand on her shoulder. The sight of Roses' dark hand on Nettie's pale dress seemed to inflame the rigid man. Roses removed her hand as though that scathing glance burned her.

As Nettie stood looking down at the ground, he tore his gaze away and continued, "I've told the town council that you people are nothing but a disgrace to this church, and now perhaps they will believe me." At her father's peremptory gesture, the girl walked a few feet toward her father. When she reached his side, he placed his hard hand where Roses dark one had rested a moment before. Nettie started to shy away and the minister tightened his grip. Roses winced. "Come, Nettie. You won't be attending this . . . church school again, until we find a proper teacher for it," he said.

Roses met the minister's eyes. She held his gaze for a moment, then, with an effort, she shrugged indifferently and turned away from the distress in Nettie's face. She couldn't let him see how his accusation hurt her.

Her eyes filled with tears. She didn't, at first, see Sarah, who stood not ten feet away—eyes hooded, face blank. Beside her, Ben made to move toward them. Roses stopped him with a slight motion of her hand. She walked toward Sarah and kept walking even when Sarah touched the back of her hand with such tenderness that she felt her hard-won composure start to slip. When they reached the wagon, they climbed in, and, with the minister's words echoing in her ears, Roses sat staring blindly ahead while Ruthie held her hand.

The minister was a mockery of everything her mother had believed in. She wanted to be angry with him, but she couldn't hold onto her rage. She kept seeing Nellie's questioning eyes. She didn't want those eyes to go hard, as they surely would if his daughter knew what the man really was. She could never sign the membership book in his church, but she tried to teach the children the same Christian doctrine her mother had taught her. That was her contribution to the religious life of this small community. The beliefs she held dear, humanity and compassion, were hard to find in this hard world. Roses had hoped to pass along the beautiful, hopeful stories she had learned from her parents, and to show their true meaning through her actions, as they had done. How could that man say those things to her.

He was the one who was a mockery. He had formed a club to wrest power from men in town whose beliefs he didn't agree with. He'd tried to run Lester Freedman out of business, because the man was Jewish. His attempt hadn't worked. Despite all Meeker's fearmongering, everyone knew Lester ran the best store in town. The so called Christian Men's League was nothing more than the Right Reverend Meeker's personal forum, but the men joined because they thought it was better for business, while the women encouraged them because it was a church organization. Most of its members were newer arrivals in town, but it was growing, and if Meeker had his way, he'd control every business in town, through bribery or intimidation.

Roses knew all about it. Lester and some of his friends had talked about it a lot, when she'd worked at his store. Then she didn't think it was her business to interfere. She could have told the women what was going on, but she hadn't, because she hadn't wanted the town to divide into factions. She figured

Meeker would get his when the men called a halt to his schemes. Meanwhile, as long as he couldn't hurt her friends, she wouldn't undermine the only church in town.

She didn't think anyone but Sarah had heard the minister. Even if they had, Roses was becoming accustomed to having the people of Cedar Valley talking about her. She had committed worse sins, in the eyes of the town's gossips, than being fired from teaching the Sunday School.

For example, there was her association with the women who worked at Letty Dowd's saloon. Ever since she had cured Letty's dog, Peaches, of a rash, she'd been welcome in the whorehouse. She wouldn't have gone back after that first visit, but the town council punished her by taking away her temporary job as schoolteacher and replacing her with the young, inexperienced Hank Avery.

So she continued to visit the whorehouse, though only by day and only when one of the women needed medical attention that Dr. Forrest or Mavis couldn't or wouldn't provide. It wasn't so much that the girls desperately needed her, but that she refused to condemn them because a group of straightlaced prudes required it. She hadn't flouted the town's conventions in any flagrant way since then. She'd been forgiven because some kindly souls had decided what she was doing was an act of Christian charity. Though they didn't agree with her, the good people of Cedar Valley didn't condemn her. They just treated her as an oddity.

She had become used to her unusual position in this town, but it had grown worse since the advent of Tobe Hunter. With his coming, it had been made clear, there was no reason for Roses Jordan to live singly. Not if she was like everyone else. And being like everyone else was the only unbreakable law in Cedar Valley. To break it was to risk being, at the least, ignored by every "decent" soul in town. And Roses depended on the good people of Cedar Valley to fulfill her dream of returning to the Uintah Valley with enough money saved to tide her over until she could establish a veterinary service of her own.

Most of her living was paid for in work. Her savings were adding up, slowly but surely. She was always adding a dollar here and a quarter there. She still did the odd piece of work for the millinery shop, where she'd worked when she'd first come to Cedar Valley, until Mrs. Burch had fired her for encouraging Annette Blackhawk to order a dress. Mrs. Burch didn't work for Indians. Roses was good with a needle and thread though, and Mrs. Burch still gave her some jobs. The work she did for Doc was, for the most part, unpaid. She did get the odd gift, sometimes in trade, food or fowl. Often she traded with Doc, who had a barnyard full of animals and a root cellar to store food.

The restaurant provided her meals; her clothes and hats had come from her stint at the millinery store. In addition, she had collected a lot of the supplies she needed to go back home over the past four years. Her rifle and shot had been earned when she worked at the mercantile. The girls at Letty's always kept an eye out for provisions she might need on the trail, and they had secured an odd assortment of tools and gear from their customers including spurs, awls, pincers, hammer, nails, Indian blankets, feedbags, saddlebags, even a large pair of forceps for delivering cattle.

The crowning glory of the collection was a beautifully worked Indian saddle, decorated with porcupine quills and intricate beadwork. Roses had been loath to accept it at first, afraid it had been acquired in some underhanded manner, until she'd met the young minor who had been persuaded to "contribute" it. He had been hanging around Letty's making a nuisance of himself over a sweet young girl named Bianca, and was happy enough to boast of how he'd traded for it with a Navajo he'd met down by Red Rock. Roses was able to glean from his story, that he'd been taken but good, and she accepted the saddle from Bianca who certainly couldn't use it. She'd repaid the girl, by getting her and the cowboy hitched up and sending them back home to Bianca's family in eastern Kansas.

The leather and skins she needed to make her traveling costume had been given to Roses by various farmers during the fall harvests, when she hired herself out as a cook. The townspeople for whom she did spring cleaning had provided her with books and slates, paper and pencils. She had most of the provisions she required. She lacked only a horse and pack mule, and she'd be on her way home. She'd been anticipating her return to her Ute family for so long that it was beginning to feel more like a dream than the long-range goal she'd planned so carefully. Now she felt a new urgency to make that dream a reality—all because of Tobe Hunter.

At first, as the blacksmith's wagon passed the subdued folks walking the half mile back to Main Street, she thought this might not be the best day to show everyone that she and Tobe Hunter were just friends. After the quarrel with the preacher, she didn't feel like upsetting people who were set on the idea of something more formal between them. But, by the time they reached town, she figured the incident with Mr. Meeker might have been just what she needed. The more she thought about his unjust accusations the more they irked her. She was in the perfect mood to take on anyone and anything.

She worked at the Blackwolf Dining Hall every Sunday night. Tobe would be there tonight, Ben had mentioned earlier. She kept herself busy in the kitchen with Annette while Little Sparrow opened the doors to their customers. She felt a little unsettled at the prospect of seeing him, and nervous because she didn't know what she was going to say.

The thought flashed through her mind that she was about to lose something she might not be ready to give up, like the eagle feather she had traded to Walks Softly Behind His Enemies when she was six years old for a rock which, he had said, had fallen from the Moon. But she didn't have a choice.

She had to make it clear she wasn't interested in being courted by him. If she could get him to say he wasn't the marrying kind, maybe she'd be left alone. No one could blame her for that—and everyone would understand why she didn't have time for him, then. Even if sparking was all he had in mind, she had to avoid the appearance of impropriety. She could not afford to be thought of as any more eccentric than she already was. Not understanding, or not accepting, the white man's ways had already cost her more jobs than she could count. In a town this size the supply was limited. She couldn't afford to lose any more jobs because of Tobe Hunter.

She was still trying to think of something perfect to say to Tobe or about him, to convince anyone in hearing distance that they weren't courting and weren't going to be, when Little Sparrow bustled into the kitchen, a mountain of energy, her efficient movements sweeping the air around them into unseen whirls of motion.

"We've got some hungry men out there, you two.

Where's that bread? Roses, take the meat out of the oven," she directed as she took the potatoes from the warming pan at the back of the big stove.

Roses swept into the dining room in Little Sparrow's wake. She thought she'd been totally prepared for the sight of Tobe Hunter. But when she saw him sitting with the cowboys from the Rocking T at the center table, her heart started pounding harder in her chest. Her breath was released in a rush before she managed to compose herself. She went to his table, holding tight to the thought that as soon as she'd succeeded in her task, she would be leaving these disturbing new emotions behind her.

He smiled slightly as he caught sight of her. Roses deftly placed the men's food on the table and nodded a greeting. Tobe was with some cowboys from the Rocking T Ranch. Luckily, both Young and Old Charlie were with him. If she could convince them, the news would be all over town by morning. The two men were better at spreading gossip than the Union Pacific Telegram.

Young Charlie Johnson attacked his food, but spoke through a mouthful to ask, "Hey, Roses. How are you today?"

"Fine, fine," she answered, slanting a wry glance at Tobe. "I've been seeing a little more of you boys lately. Isn't there any work out at the Rocking T for you to be doing?"

"Oh sure." Jim Ballard said. "Never a doubt. But when it's raining like this, Cookie's rheumatiz acts up. Nice to come into town to get some decent chow."

"Got to knock the mud off our boots and sit back." Old Charlie spoke with a mouthful of food. "That bunkhouse starts to close in on you after a week or so of hard rain." His long arm snaked across the table to steal the last slice of bread from under his son's napkin. "You already got two there on your plate," he told the younger man before he could protest, then continued speaking to Roses without missing a beat. "Can't open no windows. It gets a little rank. 'Sides which, a nicer group of fellas you couldn't find, but Missie, the plain truth of the matter is you can only play poker with 'em for just so long 'fore you get tired of their sorry faces."

"Tobe here has the right idea, staying in town." Young Charlie nudged his darkskinned neighbor. "It's enough to make a man think about maybe settling down on his own place. Finding a woman to bunk with." Tobe choked on his food. "Problem is, got to find the right woman."

"Guess you'll just have to keep looking." Roses' suggestion was greeted with smiles and nods from everyone but Tobe, who kept his eyes studiously lowered.

"You've got it there," Young Charlie said.

"She's right," Old Charlie commented, nodding. Roses shook her head as she moved away, but she couldn't stop the laughter that was working its way up to her throat. She chuckled as she reached the kitchen, shaking her head in disbelief. Little Sparrow looked at her suspiciously.

"What were you talking about with them from the Rocking T?"

"Finding the right woman and settling down," Roses sputtered.

Even Little Sparrow smiled at that. "Can't say they're too subtle," she commented.

"They didn't really say that?" Annette asked.

Roses got her laughter under control and nodded, but she could still feel the smile playing at the corners of her mouth. It wasn't really funny. Tobe

Hunter was moving on and she was going back to Indian Country—no settling down for them. As she served the diners, and refilled their coffee cups, she played with various scenarios. Perhaps she could just go over to his table and say, "So, I understand you're off to Utah next?" But that question might be interpreted as an interest in his future. She was so lost in her thoughts that Hank Avery had to speak twice to get her attention when she went to his table to clear his place.

"Will you be at church tomorrow?" the schoolteacher asked, clearing his throat nervously.

"I should be," Roses replied.

"I've been asked, ahem, to take over the Sunday school classes for a while."

"Oh." She had almost forgotten about her confrontation with the Reverend Meeker. She turned back to the schoolmaster, who wore his somber black suit seven days of the week. His adam's apple bobbed as he ran a finger under his shirt collar. He was a painfully nervous young man, which made him, according to the town matrons, the perfect teacher for their innocent young daughters. Usually, Roses found his awkwardness amusing, but at the moment, she was only annoyed. She had tutored some of his students, and she had helped bring him and Annette together many times. The least he could have done was refuse the preacher.

Her resentment died as quickly as it had come. She knew his position was too precarious for him to champion her cause against a man of the cloth. He could not allow even a hint of scandal to sully his reputation if he wanted to keep his position as teacher.

"I was preparing them for the Easter service. They will be bringing flowers up to the altar during the processional. The children were really looking forward to it—especially the younger ones."

He nodded. "I will continue in that same course," he said gratefully. Roses managed to smile at him and started to move away, almost bumping into Annette, who hovered behind her.

"Coffee?" the young woman offered Hank Avery, as Roses moved aside. "They want you over there," she said to Roses, nodding in the direction of Tobe's table. "More food, believe it or not."

"Cowboys." Roses managed to grin.

Tobe Hunter held his coffee cup up as soon as he caught her eye. Roses moved behind him to fill it, starting when she felt his hand come to rest lightly against her back.

Roses was tempted to pour the coffee into his lap. She stepped back.

"I'll thank you to keep your hands to yourself, Mr. Hunter."

"No offense intended, Miss Jordan."

"None taken, Mr. Hunter."

She turned away. Behind her, Tobe said something she couldn't hear to his companions, then raised his voice to say, "Just the way I like it. Dark and sweet."

She kept on walking, thankful her dark skin tone hid her blushes. She was going to kill that man. With every encounter, she felt more strongly drawn to Tobe Hunter, and it couldn't continue. He was handsome as the devil and she admitted she liked him, but from what she could see, they had nothing in common. He said he was looking forward to moving on, while she was going not forward, but back.

Her work was all she had. She needed it, and not only to get home. All these people knew of Roses Jordan was she was a very hard worker. It was all she had shown them, all she could give them. They accepted her, though they thought of her as odd, because they saw her as little more than a well oiled machine.

Tobe Hunter had reminded her that she was a normal human woman. Which might have been fine, except that he reminded everyone else as well that she was young and unattached. Her situation was uncommon and though no one had questioned it up until now, she knew that Tobe Hunter could ruin everything. It had already started. She had never, despite all the problems she had had adjusting to life in this small town, been so closely watched, nor had her normal everyday behavior caused such comment.

Maybe she should have told him she was trying to save enough money to go home, or that she was just waiting to complete her studies with Ian Millhouse before returning to the reservation. But even without knowing that, he had to know that anything that went on between them in the short time he planned to be here would cause a scandal in Cedar Valley. He might not be as vulnerable as she was, but he knew she was a respectable woman, and no one was going to condone his seducing a "good Christian girl." He couldn't want them to be badgering him to marry her. So why was he acting the fool?

She didn't know what he was thinking. He wasn't really going to pursue her—his regret at having kissed her had made that clear. So why did he keep letting people throw them together? Why touch her like that? How could he make such suggestive remarks? He was just egging the matchmakers on.

Seven

It seemed she couldn't go anywhere without running into Tobias Hunter. He had become, overnight, a fixture in Cedar Valley. It was natural that he was drawn to Ben's family, just as Roses had been. They were both truly welcome in that warm and cozy home. He and Ben Smith had become friends as quickly, working together, as she and Sarah had. She could almost relax with him in that setting. With Ben and Sarah there, she could at least respond somewhat naturally and enjoy his sly wit. But even Ben and Sarah sometimes acted as if they were a couple, so even in their presence, she kept a distance. She didn't have to come right out and say she wasn't interested in Tobe, she knew Sarah sensed her reservations and accepted them.

Elsewhere, though, the machinations of the townspeople that kept throwing them together. Despite his unfailing courtesy and the feeling she occasionally got that he was laughing with her at some joke only the two of them understood, he didn't evince any real interest in her. He didn't try to seek her out. It was unnecessary. Everyone knew Roses Jordan worked at the vet's office Mondays, Wednesdays and Fridays, did her shopping on Tuesdays and Thursdays, worked on the bank's ledgers on the weekends, and worked Saturday mornings and Sunday nights at Little Sparrow's restaurant.

Tobe Hunter was probably the only person in town that did not know how predictable she was. And so it was simple enough for people to arrange for him to be where she was.

If he did realize they were manipulating him, he didn't seem to care. She supposed he didn't have any reason to care that his new "friends" were just waiting to see her reaction when she bumped into him. But, when she saw the knowing glint in his eye when she met him on the street in front of the bank, when she returned the ledgers, she knew he had some inkling of what was going on.

He just played along though, and when she tried to ignore him and duck down the alley beside the bank to go to the back door, he let himself be herded by the "boys" into her path, forcing her to stop and say Howdy to one and all. Lanky Jim Ballard, clumsy as a young ox, almost pulled her arm out of its socket as he pumped it up and down.

"Hello, Roses," Young Charlie said, his adam's apple bobbing furiously as he tried to keep from laughing aloud. She had felt like a fool, greeting each man in turn as they tipped their hats to her. They refused to let her sidle into the muddy alleyway, insisting instead on escorting her to the bank's front door.

"Don't want to get mud on your dress." She glanced at Tobe, who raised an eyebrow at her. She knew somehow that he, too, was thinking that this was the second time mud had brought her arm in arm with him.

Roses managed not to laugh out loud. That was the devil of it all. She kept wanting to laugh with him. Demonstrating to the townspeople that they were attracted to each other at all would be courting disaster. She knew that, even if Tobe refused to believe it. Yet each time, she nearly gave in to the urge to let go of the prim facade and join in the fun with him. They could be friends, and to hell with what anyone else thought. That was the silent message in his laughter-filled eyes. She tried to put them out of her mind as she went into the bank.

"Seen Tobe Hunter lately?" Ansel Terwiliger asked. She just shrugged. He paid her quickly and she left.

The darkening sky threatened rain again as she walked home. She played with the idea that if they'd met in another time and place, they might have been friends. But she knew full well that friendship with Tobe would be dangerous, tantalizing as it might seem. She had plans that didn't, couldn't, include him. No one had discovered yet where exactly he had come from and she was sure that was because he was running from something. Whatever the reason, he made no secret of the fact that he was just passing through town, headed for Utah and points west.

Roses didn't need a friend in Utah. She had enough friends there already. The Uncompahgre Utes on the reservation in the Uintah Valley were waiting for her. Well, she amended, if not exactly waiting, she was sure they'd welcome her home. Grandmother and Grandfather might already have passed on to the Happy Hunting Grounds by now, but Running Bear and his family would always make a place for her in their tepee, until she showed the tribe her own special squas-tenk and they realized how useful her animal medicine was, and was given a home of her own.

She smiled wryly. She might be Uncompahgre in her heart, but her parents had instilled one belief that Grandfather hadn't taught. If she wanted something badly enough, she could make it happen. It was the white man's credo. But her parents had believed it, and somewhere deep inside, she believed it, too.

She was going home. She just didn't know when.

Roses lit her second oil lamp. The afternoon was dark with rain which she watched for a moment from her bedroom window before she turned back to her work. She was restless and unsettled, hemmed in by the constant patter of the rain against the walls and windows. She was still trying to settle down to her work when there was a pounding at her door. One of the maids from Letty Dowd's house stood outside, dripping wet.

"Jenny Li's baby is coming," she said, "and Doc Forrest is out of town."

It took almost no time to reach Letty's house.

"Roses Jordan! Am I glad to see you." Letty grabbed Roses' hand and led her toward the stairs. All conversation in the parlor came to a stop. "I think there's something wrong."

Roses rushed up the stairs, surprised to find Tobe mounting them beside her, taking the carpeted steps two at a time. Inside the room, Jennifer was breathing heavily, obviously in the throes of a bad contraction. Roses went forward and took her hand.

"Breathe, Jen. And try not to push till I see what's going on with that baby. Okay?"

"I'll try." Jennifer looked as relieved to see Roses as Letty had. She lay in the sheets where her water had broken. The fluid had a greenish tinge.

Quickly Roses examined the young Chinese girl.

"The baby is almost here." She assured the frightened young woman. "I want to change the sheets, Letty." She could hear Tobe's low voice mixed in with the higher ones of the women, calming them as he moved them out of the room.

"I can help." Tobe offered, and she looked up at him in surprise. "I've delivered a baby before."

Jennifer let out a little yelp of pain and Roses felt the muscles under her hand tightening. There was no time to argue with him. Jennifer was near panic.

"Everything's going to be fine." Roses told the half lie without even thinking about it. Scaring Jenny wasn't going to help her, and Roses needed to see if the baby had done himself any damage. The mercurium in the water might have gotten into his lungs, or it might not. The next contraction came suddenly, and hard.

"Okay now, you can do it, Jennifer. Your baby is almost here," she urged as Jennifer's muscles tightened again.

"Let it go, Jennifer. Push!" Tobe said, and when Roses looked up at him she realized he understood the urgency. It was the first time Roses had ever seen a man at a baby's birthing. Even the Shaman had not been knowledgeable in this area. Among the People the mystery of childbirth was given over to women. But Tobe clearly knew what he was doing.

As the labor went on and on, she wouldn't have kicked Tobe out, even if she had had the time. It didn't take long for Roses to decide he knew what he was doing.

"I can't do this. It hurts," Jenny said. "Make it stop."

"It will be over soon, but you've got to bear down, as hard as you can." Roses willed the exhausted girl to keep trying.

Her eyes met Tobe's. They were reassuring, he had no doubt in her skill. At that moment she felt closer to him than she ever had to another living soul. The delivery went fine. The mercurium in the water had not entered the baby's lungs.

"It's a girl!" Roses cried, and outside the room they heard someone take up the cry. After she cleaned the newborn, Roses watched Tobe give the child to her mother. Sighing deeply she stood, watching Jennifer Li fall in love with the daughter she'd sworn she'd hate.

Tobe Hunter would never have to pay for a woman again—at least, not so long as he stayed in the town of Cedar Valley.

As the ladies helped Roses change the sheets and repad the bed with old blankets, they made it clear she and Tobe were their heroes.

As Roses helped Jennifer into a clean nightshirt, she was offered everything from lace handkerchiefs to face powder. Letty even brusquely offered Roses the doctor's fee—for a woman as tightfisted as Letty that was the supreme compliment. Roses accepted half of the money, explaining that she'd only had to handle the last little bit of the delivery, Letty and her employees had handled the first half of the job just splendidly.

The women, who showered the new mother with smiles and hugs, and cooed over the baby, wanted to show Roses Jordan their appreciation, though they weren't sure how to go about it. They had no such problem when it came to Tobe Hunter, however. While Jennifer promised to find some way to repay Roses' kindness, Hallie and Sue hounded Tobe from the room, and he was carried downstairs in a wave of satin skirts and glittering fans and nearly drowned in the shower of whiskey and beer bought by the grateful women. Roses found him ensconced at the bar.

Letty was still trying to convince her to accept more money.

"Honey, I paid you more than that when you cured Peach's cold," she insisted. Roses had used that money to buy the women of the House some fine soaps and oils, encouraging cleanliness to stem the infection that ran rampant in the whorehouse. And it had been money well spent. Not only did the women's customers enjoy their soft-scented skin, but it turned out they enjoyed being bathed as well.

But Letty hadn't been happy, despite the results, that Roses had spent the money she'd given her on the girls. She'd suspected—a little angrily—that she'd been outmaneuvered. This time, Roses couldn't take a chance on manipulation. She wanted Letty to spend that money on Jenny and the baby, and she wanted her to be happy doing it.

"You can use that money to make sure Jennifer Li has plenty of cream and fresh fruit and vegetables for the next month or so," Roses said. Letty tended to feed her employees quantities of egg hash and meat hash. Copious amounts of onion and tomato were the only thing that kept the girls from developing scurvy.

"You've got a deal," Letty promised.

Roses turned triumphantly to the "guests" gathered in the parlor. She'd deal with finding Jennifer and Rose Li, her namesake, a proper home later. She felt too good to worry about it now.

Roses smile lit up the room and signaled to everyone there that the crisis was truly over. Tobe was amazed at how quickly the festivities rose to fever pitch. Tom Cobb was generally believed to be the baby's father because he was not only Jennifer Li's most regular customer but he had also fathered six legitimate children. He celebrated loudly with a small group of men at one table. The girls were mingling with the crowd, but no one went upstairs. He chuckled at the thought that while these men, married and single, upright citizens and hellraisers both, drank to the miracle of procreation, they were reluctant to purchase the house's wares with such a recent reminder about what a trip upstairs might just bring.

Tobe knew how they felt. The miracle that he had just witnessed had left him dazed. It made him think of his own mother. He closed his eyes against the image and took a long pull on his beer. He had so thoroughly blocked out those years when he had lived with his mother that it was like remembering another life. A life he had turned his back on at the age of fourteen. The memories usually only brought anger and resentment, but this time he felt joy as well as pain. The joy he'd felt at being his mother's hero at the tender age of five, and the pain of the loss he'd felt when he'd asked the name of the father of the unborn child in her belly and his beautiful mother had looked away without answering.

Letty's brusque offer of a bottle of whiskey brought him out of his reverie.

"To Roses and Tobe Hunter," Letty proclaimed. "The two best midwives in town." Loud laughter and the clinking of glasses dispelled the last of the tension from his shoulders. His gaze was trained on the petite brownskinned woman who stood smiling, chin up, as everyone looked from her to him and back again. Her straight back and clasped hands made her look composed, but he sensed that she was nervous, and her eyes when they met his held only chagrin. He could guess what was bothering her. He knew her well enough now. She wouldn't be happy at the toast because their names were being linked again. She had been thrust into his path at every turn and with each meeting he sensed her frustration rising.

Roses' eyes darted about the room, and he followed her gaze to Tom Cobb, whose chair toppled backward as he stood and raised his glass, crying out, "To Jennifer Li."

Tobe watched Roses' expression darken.

"And to the father," one of the men sitting with Tom added.

Letty didn't join in the toast. Neither did Delilah or any of the other women, Tobe noticed.

"Whoever that might be," someone added from the table beyond.

Tom moved so quickly that Tobe didn't have the chance to locate the speaker before Tom was hauling Young Charlie Johnson out of his seat, yelling, "You take that back."

Both Tom and Charlie were plenty the worse for drink, and each had a number of friends whose heads were not much clearer. Tobe was sure it was only a matter of time before fists started flying. He wanted to get Roses out of the house. She didn't belong here. He put down his drink and started toward her.

Tom chose that moment to lay claim to his supposed offspring. "I'll do the right thing by that baby. I'll bring her home." The statement caused low whistles and groans to echo around the room.

Letty protested, "Now, Tom, you know you're going to get me run out of town with foolish talk like that."

Old Charlie laughed as he said, "I'd like to see Edith's face if you try!"

Tom turned to Old Charlie. "Edith is a good woman, she'll do the right thing." Tobe reached Roses' side just as Letty managed to extricate Young Charlie's arm from Tom Cobb's drunken grasp. He tapped Roses on the shoulder, but she didn't pay any attention. She was intent on the argument on the other side of the room.

"Not that good. She ain't gonna want you bringing home a whore's baby. Edith Cobb is the sourest faced woman in this whole town. She'd die before she'd raise that little bastard upstairs."

"She would not," Tom argued, "Letty, you know that baby's mine, and I want to take her home." He changed his tack, struck with an inspired thought. "Edith wouldn't even need to know the baby's mine. We can just adopt her, can't we? Edith would do that. We got six already, one more ain't gonna be any trouble." Letty nodded, distractedly, trying to get Tom back in his chair. All around the room men were starting to lay bets on whether or not Edith would let Tom bring the baby into the house.

"Letty, you can't mean to let him do that." Beside him Roses spoke, startling Tobe. But no one else heard her. Everyone's attention was on Tom Cobb. Tobe took her arm, hoping to get her out of the house, before she could create any trouble. She shook him off.

"Honey, this ain't your fight." He tried to stop her.

"Jenny's got no one else to fight for her. We brought Rose Li into this world. We've got an obligation to protect her."

"Protect her from what? Her father?" Tobe asked.

"You call that a father?" Roses nodded toward Cobb's table. Letty was stroking Tom's arm, trying to calm him.

"He's willing to claim the child. And it's better than being raised in a whorehouse." Involuntarily, he shuddered. He caught Roses' puzzled expression before she moved toward the table where Letty sat with Cobb. This time she spoke more loudly.

"Letty," she said. "Let Jenny keep her baby. How would you feel if this house was taken from you?" Even Tobe knew Letty was fiercely proud of her business, despite all of her complaints. "And by some evil stroke of fate, you were forced to walk past it every day and see the new owner doing all the things you do now."

"Roses, if someone wanted this house, I'd give it to them in a minute. I don't enjoy—" Letty started to argue.

"Setting on the porch in the summer, ordering new drapes every single year." Roses finished for her. "Fighting with the town council every time they vote to shut this place down."

Tobe saw one of the girls smother a grin. Letty's shrewd eyes met Roses' determined ones, and the older women had to look away. Tobe knew, as surely as anyone else in the room, that Roses had won.

Tom Cobb wasn't going to give up that easily, though. Tobe started to move toward the little group as the tall pale eyed man turned to Roses.

"You know that's my baby up there," Tom said belligerently.

"Maybe she is. But if you take her home to your wife, you won't be able to acknowledge her. She won't know her half brothers and sisters are her own blood. Let Jenny raise her. At least her mother can tell her the truth."

"The truth is her mother's a tramp."

"What does that make you?" Roses argued. She turned away and for a moment Tobe thought Cobb was going to come after her, but after a quick look around at the men who had been listening to the exchange, the drunken man swayed and backed into a seat. Tobe watched Roses make her way toward him. The air of vulnerability he had noticed earlier was gone, replaced by determination, and, he suspected, anger. She brushed past him and continued on out of the room.

He couldn't resist the silent challenge. Foolish as he knew it was, he had to follow her.

Eight

Roses fumed as she strode down the street. Her feet carried her away from town, toward the mountains, but she was only barely aware of her surroundings. That stupid, brutal man was going to try to steal Jenny Li's baby. And Letty would probably let him.

She wanted to scream. How could Tobe help her bring a baby into the world and immediately condemn her to the miserable existence of an unwanted child? Could he not, as easily as she, visualize the life of Tom Cobb's bastard Chinese daughter in the man's white home, whether he claimed the girl as his own or not?

By the time Roses came to herself again, she was standing at the edge of town, not far from the spot where she and Tobe Hunter had embraced. She stopped walking, thinking of that night and of all the times since then she'd been distracted by the memory.

"Penny for your thoughts."

Roses jumped. She had been so immersed in her thoughts that she hadn't heard Tobe follow. She felt a rush of heat beneath her skin as she realized what she had been thinking about when he asked. She turned to face him. Deep blue sky limned his curly black hair as he stood, hat in hand, looking down at her.

"Perhaps they're worth more than that?" he teased when she didn't speak.

"No," Roses answered truthfully, "they're not important."

"No?" Tobe teased. The amusement in his voice fanned Roses' anger. Frustration washed over her in a wave, and fury lodged in her heart and throat. He taunted her with his nearness, with his white teeth and his laughing eyes. He teased her with a voice as smooth as velvet and a heart which she now knew to be as hard as rock. He tortured her with his mere presence, making her aware of desires she had never known she had, and a new knowledge, that she could slake her hunger if she wished. It was unbearable.

"Okay. If you must know, I was thinking that you are worse than Cobb. All men, the Good People, our ancestors in Africa, even the white man, know that children are our greatest gift, and our greatest responsibility. You have not only adopted the white man's ways, destroying the land, killing forests and streams working with their cattle, you've forgotten your own."

She'd wanted to make him as angry as he had made her, but when she looked up at his face, she recoiled from the fury she saw there. It didn't stop her though. "How could anyone walk away from a newborn babe? What kind of a man are you?" He turned away, back toward town. Her heart pounded in her throat in anger and frustration. He'd tormented her at every turn and now he was just walking away. "You call the Good People savages. What about you?"

Less than an hour ago, he'd joined his voice with hers to make a miracle. Had she imagined the communion she'd felt between them? Could she have been so wrong about him? The tenderness, the joy she'd felt then, had been torn away from her during that ugly scene in Letty Dowd's parlor. And it meant nothing to him. Nothing!

"Tom Cobb is a stupid drunkard. Can't you see that? Or are you really this cruel and thoughtless?"

Tobe turned back toward her and she instinctively backed away. But instead of the blazing anger she'd expected, even half hoped to inspire, his face was a cold bleak mask.

"You don't know what you're talking about. Raising a child in a whorehouse is cruel. I should know. I was raised in one."

It was like a slap in the face. After a moment she started toward him. "Don't," he said, whirling away.

"Tobe," she pleaded, but he kept walking. She picked up her skirts and ran after him. When she reached his side, he came to a halt. Slowly, he turned to face her. She raised her hand to his cheek. His skin was warm against her palm.

"I'm sorry," she said. "I didn't mean to hurt you." He gave a bitter laugh. "Or, I did, but not like that. Never like that. I didn't know. How could I?"

"If you had, would it have stopped you?" he asked, looking deep into her eyes. His own were no longer cold, but filled with warmth.

"Yes," she answered immediately.

She didn't move until he put his arms around her. Then she leaned into him. Her face turned up toward his, her eyes closed, she could only wait to see if he would respond to her mute plea. His lips covered hers, as gently as that first time. The tenderness of that kiss was unexpected.

Her own battered heart and shattered soul demanded more. They demanded release. She pulled his head down to hers and hungrily opened her mouth. He followed her lead and the gentleness was replaced with greed. His tongue dueled with hers and finally found the warm dark recesses of her mouth. Roses couldn't get enough of him. Her hands moved from his hair to his throat, the pulse she found pounding there was strong and hard and fast. It echoed her own heartbeat, the rush of blood through her veins, and the tide of warmth that flowed from her head to her toes and centered in her belly. His hands were at her hips, molding her to him.

She wound her arms around his back and held on as she sank into mindless pleasure. His lips left hers and she followed in silent protest until they danced over her eyelids, her forehead, the tender skin at her temple. She buried her face in his neck. His hands slid up her back, beneath her shawl, coming to rest right above her rib cage. His large hands nearly spanned her small frame and that made her tremble, but not in fear. She could never be afraid of this.

His thumbs painted light circles on the underside of her breasts, which seemed to strain upwards at his touch. The sensation nearly undid her. She took his chin in her hand and pulled his mouth down to hers, and as her tongue entered his mouth his thumbs covered her nipples. She could feel the heat of him through her dress, felt his hands and his thighs where they pressed against her own. She clung to him, her knees weak. His tongue escaped hers to trace her open lips. He rubbed the tips of his thumbs over her nipples and she gasped, arching toward him.

He held her, his thumbs continuing to move, over her heart, grazing her breast with each stroke, increasing the pressure each time it found the hardened nipple. His other hand cupped her, moved upwards, and he caught the pointy tip between the base of his thumb and his forefinger and squeezed gently, then, as a spasm shot through her, a little harder. She moaned against his mouth and his lips covered hers as if to swallow the sound. He squeezed and loosened his hand rhythmically, his tongue set the pace as he probed her mouth.

A shiver worked its way down her spine and her head fell back. His lips found her throat and she thought she would fall as he loosened his hold on her. His mouth moved downward, his right hand still opening and closing on her, coaxing her toward something just outside of her grasp. She felt his warm breath through her dress. She was able only to cling to him, clenching and unclenching a handful of his shirt as he suckled her, making the material of her dress as warm and soft as his wet mouth. She felt a gathering within herself, a tightening at her core, a prelude to a tremor that radiated outward. As he lifted her off the ground and into himself, she felt as though she were turning into liquid heat.

His lips were on her hair, her mouth was pressed to the base of his throat. She let her tongue glide over his collarbone and felt his answering shudder, a signal that there was more, much more, to be found in the joining of two souls. Slowly he lowered her, holding her steady, and she knew that a step toward him, only a few inches, was all that was needed to bring them to the brink of heaven again, and beyond. She could find release from the turmoil. But she could not take that step.

Instead she said, "I'm still sure that Jennifer Li, prostitute or not, will be a better parent for Rose than Tom Cobb could ever hope to be."

"Maybe you're right. I don't know these people and you do."

"Did your father claim you?" she asked. He nodded. "He was married to my mother. But he died before I was born. In the war. The one thing I am sure of is that she loved him."

"That is what is most important to you?" She took her hand away.

"Of course," Tobe answered.

"Not that she bore you, and fed you, and somehow managed to raise and educate you," Tobe looked confused. "It's more important that she loved a man you never even knew?" She let her hand fall to her side. He didn't stop her.

"Yes. Wouldn't that be important to you?"

Roses was raised by parents who believed that the Ute marriage was a civilized, if somewhat passionless process. Their own marriage had not started out as a love match, but they had grown to love each other. But for both her parents and the Ute, the most important aspect of marriage was the care of the children. The children were the whole tribe's primary concern. Yet Tobe could only feel sorrow at his mother's profession. Not all parents deserved love, or even respect, but Tobe's voice had only warmed when he mentioned his father. Roses felt as though she were being torn in half. She wanted to comfort him and soothe the pain she knew he must feel. But she couldn't find any hint of vulnerability in his voice.

Now it was Roses who turned away, not towards town, but toward the empty mountain road behind them. She crossed her arms across her chest, wishing she could comfort both him and herself. She wanted to reach out to him again, but she didn't have the strength left to argue with him, or with the voice within herself that warned her more strongly than ever that caring for Tobias Hunter might be dangerous.

"Where did you come from?" she asked. The desire in his eyes was shuttered as he stayed silent. "Is that what you're running from?"

"I'm not—"

She stepped away and he pulled her back, saying, "I don't want to put you in any danger."

"I might be able to help."

He smiled. "I doubt that."

"I'm not staying here. I'm going back home," she said desperately. As tempting as he was, she couldn't risk everything she'd worked so hard for.

"Where's home?" he asked.

"Indian country. I'm going to live on a reserve in Utah." He nuzzled her neck.

"I'm headed that way myself," he said. She didn't think it was an invitation.

"Into Indian Country?" Roses asked, to clarify.

Tobe chuckled. "Not on your life." He knew where he was going. And he was travelling light. Right at this moment it didn't matter. She hadn't expected a proposal of marriage. This was all she wanted.

"I'm headed straight into Indian Country. Back to the Ute."

"The people who raised you?" He nibbled on her ear.

"From the age of five." She kissed his chin.

"In Utah?" His hands spanned her waist.

"No, I grew up here in Colorado. The Uncompahgre had a winter camp in these mountains for hundreds of years. Maybe thousands. The Bluecoats moved us to Utah. Under their guns."

"Us?"

"My parents, me, the Uncompahgre. They promised we could stay in Colorado. Chief Ouray believed in them, signed treaties to that effect. But in the end, the government broke that promise, just like all the others. They moved us to a desert. The tribe was decimated. Not only did they take away the tribal lands, they didn't send the supplies or money they promised. When it did come, it was garbage; rotten cloth, rotten food. It killed my parents."

The sting was gone as a sensual haze enfolded her. Here in this man's arms, she felt like she was telling someone else's story. His arms held her tight, his lips were at the nape of her neck.

"Why didn't they leave?" Tobe asked. Roses felt something in her mind come awake. The voice that had gone silent, for the first time since she'd been a little girl "rescued" from the savages.

"And go where?" She drew herself slowly away from him.

"Back to civilization. Like Cedar Valley, maybe?" Tobe let her go.

"White man's civilization? The civilization that enslaved them."

"There are slaves in Africa, too, you know?"

"Of course. And even the Indians take slaves in battle. Or were you planning to mention that next?"

"I didn't know that."

"The word 'ransom'. It's ours."

"Ours?" He had withdrawn from her, not only physically, but emotionally. That was what she had wanted, she told herself.

"Indian. So, now what do you think of my plans? To go home."

"I think if you go, this town will miss you."

"Please leave me alone."

"Why are you running away?"

"I'm not running away, I'm going home."

"To starve to death like your parents. What are you afraid of? It makes no sense. The people here care about you, you said it yourself."

"They don't even know me. They don't know my

hopes. My dreams. If they did, they wouldn't approve. I'm an Injun lover. That's a crime in these parts, you know." Cedar Valley was better than some towns she'd passed through, but even here the people were convinced that it was Indians, not their own, who broke treaties, massacred innocent women and children without provocation, stole horses, and cheated the unsuspecting trader. Even those born out west had been raised on stories of cruelty and myths that no Human Being would recognize as a retelling of their own history.

"They don't care that you lived with the Indians."

"They decided it didn't hurt me any. I'm a little strange maybe, but harmless in their eyes. I can't explain it to you, there is no word for a man like "old maid," but a woman alone is unacceptable. That's why I can't afford to be seen with you. People will talk."

"Let them."

"They wouldn't give me work if they thought I wasn't respectable. It's been easy up until now. I could have had love affairs with half the men in town and no one would suspect a thing. But now you're here and they're watching us. The only respectable thing for a woman to do is marry. And in their eyes, you're perfect. You're the only unattached colored cowboy we've got in these parts."

"We're both young. And single. They don't want you to be alone. It's all perfectly natural."

"Of course it's natural, but that doesn't make it any easier."

"Make what any easier?"

"Explaining why nothing is going to happen between us."

"Something has already happened between us. And we're not finished Roses Jordan. You've only tasted the feast. Just a sample. It's in your blood now, just like it's in mine." Her body was still tingling from his touch. But she couldn't give in to his desire, or her own. It would be hard enough to walk away from him as it was. She couldn't let him divert from her purpose. They came from two different places and were going in such different directions.

"I have been working for four years to be trusted and respected here. I'm not going to risk that. Not for you, or for anyone. I have no choice but to obey the rules."

She started back toward town and he followed. She stopped when they reached the edge of town.

"We should separate," she said.

"I'll take you home," he said.

She already regretted her lapse into insanity. She'd known all along she would have to pay for the pleasure she'd gotten a taste of tonight. She hadn't known that payment would take the form of an unabashed and unrepentant Tobias Hunter. She should not have lost her temper. Her emotional outburst had cost her her strongest ally.

"Can't you just leave me be?" she asked.

"No, I guess not," was his answer.

She was exasperated, and too weary to fight with him any more. She held her head high as they walked down Main Street, trying to ignore the surprised stares of the townspeople taking a Sunday evening stroll. She didn't know why, but he wasn't going to leave her alone. She was just going to have to avoid him. It shouldn't be too long. He was sure to get tired of Cedar Valley before long.

Wednesday morning Doc left on his semiannual rounds to farms farther afield, leaving Roses in charge of the office and their patients in town for the next few days. As soon as he left, Dan Coombs' son, who must have seen Doc leave in the buggy he kept at Coombs' livery, came by to say Doc was needed at the smithy to check on a limping horse.

The horse had had a strained hock, but Ben and Tobe had already wrapped the leg when she arrived. After a quick check on the horse's bandage, Roses followed the sound of men's voices into the smith's to find the horse's owner. There she found Ben and Tobe working at the forge. Ben explained the problem, and went looking for the horse's owner, leaving her alone with Tobe.

The fire in the forge burned bright, casting a red glow on the room and everything in it.

"You're soaked through, girl. Come over by the fire," Tobe said as soon as Ben had left.

"I'd better go," Roses replied.

"Don't be silly, you might as well dry off a little and get warm. I promise I'll stay well away."

"There's no point." He looked like he would protest further, so she forestalled him by explaining, "I'll just get wet again when I go back. I'll make a run for it." Tobe was beside her in three strides.

"I think it's stopping," he said. "Besides, Ben will be back with the major any minute and you can tell him what to do about his horse's leg."

"Just tell him to change the wrapping every day," Roses said.

Tobe grinned down at her. "No crazy Indian remedies?"

"Nothing the major would do." Roses relented, moving over to the room's one window. The storm did look like it was ending. "He could chant over him." When Tobe laughed, Roses slanted a look at him from beneath her lashes. He had not said it idly, he sounded genuinely curious. She smiled. "It works for the shaman."

"Who's that?" he asked. Roses didn't see what harm could come from just talking to him for a few minutes until the rain stopped, and it could do some good. If he knew more about the Ute, maybe he wouldn't be so prejudiced against them. Maybe he'd understand why she wanted to go home.

"He's a wise man of the tribe. The elders are all respected, and their wisdom is sought, but the shaman is something more than old. He knows things about people, and about sickness and the spirits. He can guide the spirits into the body, or out of it. The Uncompahgre believe that illness is caused by evil spirits entering the mind or the body, or the soul."

"Do you believe that?"

"Yes," Roses said. She found it impossible to look only at his face. Her eyes kept slipping down, to his shoulders and arms and chest. He stood stock still before the fire. The shirt he wore fit loosely enough, but she could still see the contours of the muscles in his upper arms. The fire behind him threw much of his body into shadow, but his hands, resting lightly on the poker, were thrown into sharp relief, long fingered, warm, brown, and strong. Roses swallowed. Despite her determination to keep a safe distance between them, she wanted to touch him. Tobe cleared his throat.

From just outside Ben yelled, "Roses, you still here? I brought the major back with me." She pulled her cape, almost dry now, over her shoulders and turned to the door.

"I'll be seeing you." Tobe said.

" 'Bye, Tobe." She stepped out of the door into the gray afternoon, shivering at the impact of the cool rainy air. She couldn't help but notice how colorless everything became when she left him. She knew she'd get over it, though, when he left. He couldn't be planning to stay long. She only had to stay away from him until then.

Mrs. Dorney stopped by the veterinary office that afternoon, supposedly to drop off some piecework.

"I hear you've been keeping company with that Hunter fellow?" she fished.

"No, I hardly know him," Roses answered.

The older woman gave her an arch look. "You're not getting any younger, Miss," she said.

"None of us is." Roses shrugged. That seemed to work. Mrs. Dorner didn't ask her any more questions. She left soon after.

Roses sat in her room later that night, sewing, and trying to think of what she might have said. She couldn't concentrate on the work in her lap and finally put it down. Roses wandered over to the window and saw that it was truly dark. Nightfall had come and gone while she'd been wasting her time, thinking instead of working.

Roses had almost finished with the last of her work when there was a light scratching on the door. She lifted her head and listened. It was late. She rarely had visitors even during the day. But a few seconds later she heard a quick tapping, so light that if she hadn't been listening for it, she might not have heard it. She went, cautiously, to the door.

"Hello?" she whispered. "Is anyone there?"

"Miz Jordan?" She opened the door a crack to find Joe Watley standing in the hall, a bundle of rags in his arms. "I'm sorry to bother you, but it's Scratches." His drooping eyes gave his face, even in repose, a permanently grief stricken look. Tonight he

looked sadder than ever. She followed his gaze down
and realized that the bundle she'd mistaken for old
clothes was his cat, wrapped in a jacket, eyes glazed
over in pain.

"Oh my, what happened?" she asked.

"Jimmy and Scratches were out until dark, as
usual, but when Jimmy went to sleep tonight,
Scratches started acting strange. Usually she sleeps
with him, but tonight she wouldn't take any food or
water and wouldn't stay in Jimmy's bed."

The cat was listless and unresponsive when Roses
stroked her head, not at all the Scratches that Roses
had seen strolling at the end of the thin rope that
Joe's son used as a leash.

"Let's take him to the office, Joe," she said, quickly
grabbing the little desk lamp. She led him down the
back stairs, holding the oil lamp high.

When they reached the veterinarian's office, she
examined Scratches more closely. She found the passage she wanted in one of Doc's issues of the *American Veterinary Journal* and cursed under her breath.

"Anything I can do?" Joe asked, standing with
one beefy hand resting gently on the cat's head.

"I'm going to have to shave off some of her fur.
I don't think she's in the mood to run off, but why
don't you hold her, just to be on the safe side." She
found the spot she was looking for with the tips of
her fingers and started to uncover the wound. "See
there?" Two small but clear puncture wounds decorated the cat's hind end.

"What's that?"

"She's been bitten, probably by another cat."

"Is that bad?"

"It's not good. It's near the spine. And she's already gotten an infection. We have to keep her warm

and get plenty of fluids into her. Just like when Jimmy had the fever."

"Is that all?" Joe was relieved.

"That's all we can do for now. We just have to let this thing run its course." She laid a hand on the cat's head.

"All I can do is keep her warm and water her?"

"Keep her drinking. Anything you can get down in her. Water, tea—I'll give you a little packet of some special—anything wet."

"Whiskey?" When she looked at him she saw the hint of a rare smile. "Sometimes she takes a little from my hand." Roses raised an eyebrow.

"Mixed with water, maybe, if it'll get her to drink. But liquor tends to cause dehydration. I'm going to bandage her with a little of this willow root bark. That may help the infection. I'll show you how to do it, and you can change the wrapping tomorrow afternoon. You can use river mud, it'll draw out the poison."

"Thanks, Miz Jordan." Joe's drooping eyes shone with gratitude. "I really appreciate you coming out so late."

Jimmy Watley was waiting in the alley when she came downstairs the next morning, with a small, slightly wilted bouquet of wildflowers in his hand. Roses guessed Scratches had made it through the night. Jimmy confirmed it.

"She's better, Pa says. And he says we have you to thank for it," the boy said.

"Well, I'm glad," Roses responded, looking at the posy Jimmy was unconsciously strangling with his tight grip on the stems.

"I picked 'em for you. My pa says ladies like flowers." He thrust the flowers at her, blushing when she accepted them.

"Thank you." Roses smiled.

"It wasn't nothing." He ran off, embarrassment and pleasure shining from his bright-blue eyes.

This was her favorite thing about working as a veterinarian. As she walked to the doc's house to open up for the day, it came to her slowly. The night before had been a test of some kind, and she had triumphed. She had provided the Watleys with everything they needed. It might be time to go home.

The thought was still working its way into her brain when she reached the office and found Josiah Martin waiting for her out front. The rancher was one of the most important men in town.

"Mr. Martin." She greeted the gray-haired rancher as she reached him. She met his assessing gaze head on.

"One of my ponies is not standing right. I was hoping Ian could come out and take a look at her."

"I've been working with the doctor for a couple of years now. You may have heard." She paused and he nodded. "Doc's not here. He's calling on some of the ranches down south. I've been handling the practice for him while he's gone." Roses swallowed, but forced herself to keep her chin up as she offered, "I could come out to your place this afternoon, if you'd like."

"I guess that's all right with me. You know where my ranch is?"

"I've ridden by it."

"You have the use of Ian's horse and buggy?" Martin asked.

"I'll ride. Doc keeps a mare at the livery for me to use," she told him.

"It's an hour's ride each way," Josiah Martin pointed out.

"I'll be out to your place in a couple of hours,"

Roses assured him. She went into the house and directly to the examining room, surprised to find her knees shaking, whether with nervousness or elation she would have been hard put to decide. This was the final test. She was sure of it.

Josiah Martin came out to greet Roses as she rode up to the big ranch house. His once-black hair was now pure white, his skin dark from constant exposure to the sun. If it hadn't been for his deep blue eyes, he could have been taken for one of the People. He walked with her as she led Doc's mare around to the barn.

"She's standing funny, like maybe she has colic, but she's eating."

"Sometimes they do." Roses knew colic could be fatal to a horse. "Has she been jumping around a lot?"

"Nah." Martin led Roses to the nearest paddock. The mare was standing by the fence. Roses stroked her nose.

"Lady is twenty-two years old. Foaled out of my first string of wild ponies. My daughter's mount."

He held Lady's head while Roses examined her. "There is a blockage there, maybe colic. I think we've caught it early enough though."

Lady stamped and blew, and Martin calmed her. "Whoa, girl. Easy."

Roses cleaned the grease from her hand and arm with a length of toweling.

"I'm going to give her something for the pain, and then walk her for a bit." She prepared an injection. "The pain is what makes them jump around and hurt themselves, so after this takes effect, you shouldn't have any trouble with her, Mr. Martin."

As she was leaving, she instructed, "Keep her locked up tonight. No grazing at all. Her system needs the rest. But you can walk her all you like. The painkiller will wear off by tomorrow. If she's still "standing funny," you can give her coffee. It's a natural diuretic."

"Thanks for coming out here. I was worried when you told me Doc was away, but I can see you know what you're doing."

"Happy to be of help." He gave her a hand up on her horse, "I'll be at the office in the morning, if you need me."

He waved her off and Roses rode at a dignified walk until she was out of sight of the farm. Then she gave her horse its head and rode into the wind which had grown strong enough to blow away the gray clouds overhead. It was dark when she got home.

When she had returned the horse to the stable, she made her way to Sarah's house. She'd sent word with Annette that she wouldn't be able to tutor Lula that afternoon, but she felt too good to go back to her empty room. She had passed her final test. She had learned all she could from Ian Millhouse. She had done what she had set out to do.

The sight of Tobe sitting on the front porch with Sarah filled her with mixed emotions. She no longer had to be afraid of him. He couldn't stop her now. But there was a tugging in the area of her heart at the thought that she'd be leaving him behind. She was relieved, triumphant, because she had gotten control of her life again, but she suspected it was going to be hard to say goodbye.

At least now she knew how it was going to end.

She was ready to go home. She had to keep that thought in her mind. All she needed to do was to save money for the trip back. As she approached the house, she mentally calculated the cost of supplies, a horse and maybe a mule. A month's work, perhaps two, should take care of everything. She had saved enough money already to buy food and everything else she might need while she waited for her veterinary practice to bring in a steady income, once she was home.

She walked up the porch steps, into the welcoming light. She had to admit, it was a little bit scary to leave everything here behind. She couldn't look forward to the trip without trepidation. The first trip, here, had nearly killed her. But, she reassured herself, it would be different this time. She knew just what she was doing. She tried not to look at Tobe.

Nine

Until Roses had appeared, Tobe had been thinking about how much he would enjoy someday coming home from work to a woman like Sarah. The older woman was beautiful and serene, even with the pregnancy swelling her waist and slowing her graceful movements. But with Roses sitting on the step at her feet, Sarah's beauty became ordinary, earthbound. Roses' smiling eyes had the fire of a shooting star, streaking across the face of the night sky in a burst of fire and ice. Tobe examined Roses more closely, trying to figure out what it was about her that drew him to her. There was something different about her tonight, she was even more radiant than usual.

She sat unmoving, her head thrown back to look up into Sarah's face as though she were memorizing it. The smooth line of her brown throat disappeared into the tan collar of her workmanlike dress. Straight sleeves covered her slim arms. Only her face and hands were bared to the cool mountain air. Her unadorned dress was of the simplest style. He was barely able to make out the curve of her bosom under the loose bodice. The mahogany colored linen molded itself to her tiny waist and generous hips when she sat down, but the material of her skirt covered her legs to her ankles.

Her heart-shaped face was dominated by almond

eyes. Her nose and lips were full and round, clearly showing her African heritage, but they were so precisely rounded, so daintily drawn that they seemed unrelated to his own similar features.

There was an undaunted spirit shining through those clear brown eyes. The quick smile he'd seen her hide so many times gave her away. For all her seriousness and ambition, she had a natural joy in life that tonight glowed like a beacon from within her. He wanted, as he had at the smithy the day before, to take her in his arms again and steal another kiss. But he didn't want to take a chance on scaring her away altogether. And yesterday, at the smithy, she hadn't run away from him, for once. Throughout the past week, he had made a chink or two in her armor. She certainly responded to him physically. And what a response! She might live like a nun, and think of herself as an old maid, but she was no dried up old spinster. Her kisses gave her away. She was, underneath that prim facade, a sensuous creature. He looked at her again, buttoned up to the throat in brown linen and wondered again at the puzzle. And how long it would take him to solve it.

"Sarah, where's Ben?" Roses asked, as she leaned her head back to prop it against Sarah's knees.

"He's inside, telling bedtime stories to the little ones," Tobe answered.

Sarah laughed before adding, "He'll keep them awake for an hour. I swear he enjoys it as much as they do."

"Ben's got a way with a story," Tobe said. Both women nodded.

"He's a smooth-tongued devil," Sarah said affectionately.

"A hard man to say no to," Roses added. "Those

are the most dangerous ones." She was still looking up at the stars.

"Oh? Why is that?" Tobe tried hard to look and sound innocent. But Sarah sent a knowing glance his way as she answered for her friend.

"Women don't like to say no. It's against our nature. An unscrupulous man can use that knowledge against us."

"Women don't like to say no?" Tobe echoed, disbelieving. "You must be joking, ma'am. They're contrary creatures from the day they're born. If a man says it's day, ten to one some woman will say that it's night."

"It *is* night," Roses murmured.

"See there," Tobe said, rolling his eyes.

"She's right," Sarah chuckled. "Men are the contrary ones. And you're all as stubborn as mules, so you can't admit that you're just plain wrong."

"We're stubborn?" Tobe said. "We're not the ones who smile and tease and flirt in public and turn cold and heartless the minute we're alone."

Roses snorted, but he went on. "As for women not liking to say no, why, they're the ones who say no even when they mean yes. Men don't do that."

Roses turned to look him in the eye. "Maybe women actually mean no when they say no."

"Every once in a while, maybe," Tobe countered, "And talk about being stubborn . . . Why, just look at this whole frontier country! It's been tamed and cut back and settled and civilized, and the women did it. They wanted homes and schools and stores and churches, and by God, they got them, no matter that Indians and outlaws and all manner of mountain men and other rough types stood in their way. Men may be stubborner than is good for them, but watch out for a woman with a plan!"

Sarah's gentle smile grew wider. "You've got a point there."

Roses turned toward him, nodding as though he'd just conceded her point rather than arguing it. "But it's settlers who want walls around them. They own these buildings! And secondly, and more importantly, who are your lawyers and lawmen, shopkeepers, schoolteachers and preachers? They're men, not women. It's men who claim it and buy it and inherit it. It's men who want laws to protect their farms, their towns, their schools and their churches."

"I didn't say men aren't stubborn, I just said women are worse. And you just proved *my* point." Tobe said triumphantly.

"Amen," Ben said from the front doorway, just as Roses answered.

"Don't you get started," Sarah warned Ben. "We'll be here arguing all night. Are those children asleep?"

"Fast asleep," Ben answered, moving to help Sarah out of her chair. "Finally.

Roses stood, looking up to find the moon had traveled well across the sky.

"I hadn't realized it had gotten so late," she said. Tobe took his cue from her.

"I'd better be getting home, myself."

"I'd suggest that you see Roses safely home, Tobe, but I'm not sure she wouldn't be safer by herself. The way you two argue, I'm afraid you'd come to blows."

"I'm willing to cede the point, Mrs. Smith." He took his hat off and turned to Roses. "You've convinced me, Roses Jordan. Men are the most contrary, most stubborn creatures on earth."

Ben groaned while Sarah laughed and said, "And see that you remember it."

Goodbyes were exchanged all around, and Ben and Sarah stood arm in arm, watching them as they walked down the street. Tobe waved to them as he and Roses reached the corner and turned onto South Street. Roses was quiet beside him.

Though he knew nothing had actually been settled between them, he enjoyed walking beside her in the still darkness, the sweet-smelling air. He was more at peace than he could remember having felt in a long time. As they turned onto Main Street, a burst of laughter from Letty Dowd's broke the stillness.

"Sounds lively tonight."

"Yes." She looked toward the house as they passed.

They had reached the boardinghouse and she stopped at the front door to turn and face him.

"Well, goodnight," she said quietly.

"Ben asked me what my intentions were toward you." He had thought she would share his amusement at Ben's fatherly behavior, but she just nodded.

"You can't say I didn't warn you."

"I promised him I wouldn't hurt you."

"So don't." It was almost a whisper. He'd have sworn she swayed toward him.

"I don't plan to."

She straightened, stepping away. "We want different things. You're running from your past. I'm running back to mine."

Slowly, he closed the distance she'd created between them and reached out to touch her cheek with one fingertip. She turned her head away, looking at the darkened windows of the boardinghouse. "Everyone's asleep. No one's watching us." He bent and touched his lips to the corner of her mouth.

"Don't!" she ordered, but in a whisper.

"I thought you didn't say no when you meant yes."

She looked him straight in the eye as she answered, "I don't. I'm tempted to kiss you, but I don't *want* to. I don't need you complicating my life."

"I don't want to be a complication." He stepped closer.

"As long as you get what you want?" she asked, but she leaned into him as his arm curled around her back. "Why don't you just give up?" He chuckled in her ear and her lips brushed his chin.

"I guess you were right. I *am* more stubborn than you are."

"I'm only doing this so I can win the argument." Her gentle teasing made him smile. She was different tonight, happier, and no longer afraid.

"You win." He said against her lips. He caught her lower lip lightly between his teeth and gently pulled it down. Then he covered her open mouth with his own. The taste and scent of her was at once familiar and heady. Her hands went to his hips as he pulled her closer. He couldn't get enough of her.

Too quickly, she eased away from him.

"Goodnight, Tobe," she said again, quietly.

"Goodnight, Roses." He watched her slip into the darkened house.

He was halfway to the smithy when it hit him. He hadn't thought about the men who were pursuing him in days. Not since he'd kissed Roses, out in that meadow. He no longer dreamed of the colonel or flying knives or bullets. She'd bewitched him, just as she had everyone else in this town. Well, maybe not in exactly the same way, but she had made him forget the mortal danger he was in. When he saw her he forgot everything else. When he wasn't with her, his mind was occupied with arguments for why

they should explore the attraction between them—
some spurious, some more reasoned, but all inspired
by the vision of Roses with moonlight shining in
her eyes.

The sky was overcast and the church was filled
with gray morning light and the golden glow from
the two tall candles which stood on the altar. The
women's pastel pinks and blues, whites and greens,
were muted. The men's somber blacks and browns
suits added no color to the scene.

Roses sat at the back of the church with Tobe,
Ben, Sarah, and the Smith children. Sarah wouldn't
send Ruth to the Sunday school because of the reverend's behavior, despite all of Roses' arguments. In
fact, Roses was grateful to have Ruth sitting next to
her in the pew this morning. Ruthie's nervousness at
attending regular grown up church for the first time
couldn't hold a candle to Roses' own. She could
hold the little girl's hand in hers without embarrassment. The warm little fingers grasping hers so
tightly were all that kept her from bolting.

Roses appreciated Tobe's presence, even as he sat
on the other side of Ruthie. The Reverend Meeker
had chosen as his theme recognizing false Christians.
The sermon disgusted her now that she knew the
minister's true colors. Roses bit her tongue as she
vowed to sit calmly through the service.

"You shall take no word but the Lord's," he all
but shouted. The Reverend Meeker had never wavered from his pointed message. His righteous in-
dignation was clear.

Roses had suspected all week that the preacher
was planning something, but she'd been too busy to
find out what it might be. More than one conversa-

tion had died when she'd entered a room where Mrs. Meeker's friends happened to be gathered. Annette had even tried to warn her, but Roses had been too proud and too stubborn to heed the warnings.

She'd been tempted just that morning to delay seeing the preacher for one more week. She thought of staying home to avoid the confrontation that had been brewing since the previous Sunday. She had ignored the impulse because she hadn't wanted to explain her feelings to Ben and Sarah. And she didn't want them to know she was afraid, for herself and for them, of the southern minister's bitterness.

Ben and Sarah felt strongly, though, that the church was the center of the community. But if the hypocritical preacher from Atlanta was successful, they would be unwelcome in their own place of worship. Roses couldn't stand still for that, and it looked as if Tobe Hunter felt the same way. His jaw was tight and it made him look dangerous, like the Tobe Hunter she'd found that first day in the jail, frightening and unpredictable.

The preacher barely spared him a glance, but Tobe didn't take his eyes from the tall, black-clad southerner. Meeker was inspired. Roses couldn't help but think that if he blazed with this fever of passion when he spoke of Christian love and charity, he would have made a wonderful leader for this congregation. As it was, though, the townspeople were shifting and turning uncomfortably in their seats. More than one man had cleared his throat and adjusted his collar. Across the aisle, Mr. Terwiliger was fidgeting nervously, studiously avoiding looking over at where Roses sat.

As he finished, a collective sigh rose from the pews and the worshippers began to stand without waiting for the preacher to gesture to his wife to

lead them down the aisle. Ben was the first at the
door, which he threw open with such force that it
hit the wall with a bang that reverberated throughout
the high-ceilinged room. He herded Sarah and the
children out of the building, and Tobe stepped aside
so Roses could follow. Ben had already stalked off
with Ruth and B. J. to bring the wagon around to
the front of the church. Roses didn't follow, however,
and Sarah stayed by her side. She waited at the bottom of the short stairway that led up to the church
door directly across the walk from the spot where
the preacher always thanked his congregants for
coming. She was determined to show Meeker, and
the entire congregation, that she held none of this
against him. Tobe hovered near Sarah and Roses,
sending measuring looks at the folks who came
down the church's stairs.

The Reverend and his wife took their usual place
at the bottom of the three steps that lead up into the
white clapboard building. Mrs. Meeker was soon
surrounded by her close friends, who occasionally
darted a glance at Roses as she and Sarah greeted
their friends. As the church emptied onto the front
walk, Roses noticed three distinct groupings emerge.

The battle lines were drawn, one on the preacher's
side of the walk and one on hers. The groups nodded
stiffly at each other, and the third group, mostly
young people, stood dazed between them. Jesse and
Jeremy, the hulking blond twins, led a small group
toward Roses to pay their respects. Roses saw Tobe
relax slightly as the few churchgoing hands from the
Rocking T Ranch and some of the other outlying
farms aligned themselves with him. He'd met a lot
of men at Letty Dowd's Saloon and had become very
popular after taking part in the birthing of Jenny's
baby. His new friends didn't seem to have any ques-

tion as to which side they were on. Neither did the doctor or his wife, who flanked Roses and Sarah.

Roses hoped she was doing the right thing as she walked across the few feet separating herself and the Meekers. The reverend thanked the last couple to leave the church, the sheriff and his wife.

"Hello, Dotty," Roses said to Mrs. Carpenter, as she reached the foursome. "Sheriff."

"Good morning, Roses," the sheriff's wife answered sweetly.

"Good day, Roses," Mrs. Meeker greeted stiffly.

The sun came out from behind the clouds just as Roses said, "Good morning, Mr. Meeker."

The preacher nodded. "Morning," he said coldly.

The laughter of children burst through the air. Roses turned to see Hank Avery leading the Sunday school around the corner of the building. The children carried bright flower wreaths. It was a cheerful, colorful scene, and Roses couldn't help but feel that the worst was over. She had made it through the morning, which had been a lot worse than she'd anticipated. Nettie came running toward them, her habitual shyness forgotten as she smiled widely and grabbed her mother's hand.

"Look what I made, Mama." She held up the wreath for her mother's inspection but her smile was for Roses. "I finished it." Mrs. Meeker's smile died on her lips as she took in the direction of her child's happy smile and bright eyes.

"You'll ruin it, swinging it about like that," she said sharply, reaching for her daughter's hand.

"It's for the altar, Mama, for Easter Sunday." Nettie explained. "We all made one, everyone in the Sunday School. Won't they make the church look pretty?"

Under the full force of the little girl's smile, Mrs.

Meeker visibly melted. She was about to respond when her husband interrupted.

"There will be no heathen symbols in my church," he proclaimed as he snatched the flowers out of his daughter's hand. Families that had been standing, admiring the youngest children's handiwork, fell quiet.

"But, Daddy—" Nettie started to argue as she reached for the wreath he held over her head.

"Don't talk back to me!" he exploded, glaring at Roses and throwing the flowers away. Nettie wailed and he slapped her.

The sound of flesh meeting flesh reverberated in the church courtyard.

"How could you!" Roses cried, pulling Nettie away from him. She sank onto the step behind her and rocked Nettie in her lap while Mrs. Meeker stood speechless.

"Take her," Meeker said to his wife. Mrs. Meeker gave him a look of such fury, Roses was sure that this was the first time he'd hit the child. Roses relinquished the sobbing child to her mother and stood.

"You are the worst of your kind, and a danger to white Christians." He hissed at her.

"You're the danger to Christians of any color. You call yourself a man of God. I wouldn't be a member in your church if it was the last one on earth."

He grabbed her arm. "You don't belong in any church. You people think you can fool us into believing you've been saved. But nigras can't be Godly. Your souls are as black as your faces."

"You don't know anything about saving souls. You're trying to lead these people on your own crooked path. I've heard about your so called Christian Men's League and how you tried to get Letty Dowd to send some of her girls to the meetings. She refused you." The crowd grew silent.

The Reverend turned shades of red in his anger. "That's a lie."

"Is it a lie that you allow the men to drink and smoke there, when you tell them in public that they shouldn't?" Roses accused. "Reverend Meeker is trying to convince decent men to sin—the same way he does." She turned back to the preacher. "The sooner these people, white and black, recognize you and your lies and hatred for what they are, the less damage you can do to them. I've held my tongue for too long." She had been afraid to create a rift between the black denizens of Cedar Valley and their church. As the only minister in Cedar Valley, Reverend Meeker had too many weapons at his disposal. He could use her friends to hurt her, and she suspected he would feel totally justified in doing so. But she couldn't be silent anymore. "This is our only church. I didn't want to divide this town in half. But it's better no one goes to church than to attend this mockery of one!"

"You shall not speak to me this way. You are possessed by Satan." He lunged toward her, but Tobe was there.

He said, so softly she almost didn't catch it, "Don't touch her."

Meeker tried to push around Tobe, but he wasn't moving. Jesse and Jeremy suddenly brushed by Roses, and stepped between the two men. The sheriff pulled Reverend Meeker back.

Jeremy and Jesse flanked Tobe. Jeremy offered him his hand saying, "You're a friend o' Roses, right?" Jeremy dropped his hand when Tobe didn't even look at it. "Mebbe you should take her home." After a moment, Tobe looked down at her.

"We'll take care of him," the sheriff said. The two boys nodded.

Roses urged him away. "Come on, Tobe."

The sun was once again hidden, and there wasn't another break in the clouds in the whole of the wide Colorado sky.

They rode home in silence, punctuated by skirmishes between B. J. and Ruth in the back of the wagon whenever the younger children managed to slip out of Lula's grasp. Ben drove one handed, his free arm wrapped around his wife's shoulders, but Tobe and Roses didn't touch. She watched him as he stared unseeing toward the mountains to the East. His face was hard and smooth as a bronze statue, his skin the deep rich brown of newly tilled earth in the grey afternoon light.

They had just reached the house when Josiah Martin rode up, followed by two of his hands.

"Lady's in a bad way, Miss Jordan. She was better after you looked at her Thursday, but this morning she seems real sick."

"I'll come right away," Roses said.

Mr. Martin motioned for the men to dismount and Roses swung onto the back of the nearest one.

"Come back here when you return if it isn't too late," Sarah called from the porch.

As she rode, her mind was busy with a recitation of everything she'd ever learned about horses and colic. She couldn't let herself think about what had happened at the church.

Josiah Martin was silent and morose during the ride, so she didn't have very high hopes about the horse's condition when they arrived. Even so she was surprised at the deterioration of Lady's condition.

"I didn't let her graze," Mr. Martin said when she turned from her internal examination. Lady was beyond pain and beyond hope, and by Mr. Martin's expression, Roses could tell that he knew it.

"I had better take her out to pasture, while she can still walk."

"She can eat now?" he asked, surprised. Roses shook her head. She was going to lead the horse to a place where she could bury her.

"Oh." The old rancher sagged.

"Where do you want me to take her?"

"I'll show you." A light rain had begun to fall, and he got a slicker for each of them. As they left the barn, Roses hefted a shovel onto her shoulder. Her gun was in her bag. Nothing was said between them as they walked slowly past the outbuildings away from the house.

"Those were the last two men here, the ones who rode into town with me. The rest have Sunday off." One calloused hand stroked the shoulder of the horse beside him as he spoke.

"Don't worry. I can manage," Roses assured him.

"The only people here are my cook and I. He's old. I'm afraid I can't . . ." His voice trailed off.

"Just go on back to the farm. I can take care of it."

He gave Lady a pat and turned away. The sunset was barely a glimmer of red against the dark grey horizon. The rain had stopped for the moment, but the clouds still hung heavy, darker still in the mountain sky.

"Well," he said. Then he walked back toward the house.

Roses started working at once. This was one aspect of her chosen work that she didn't enjoy, but it was necessary. And it was better done quickly. It took her some time to dig a shallow trench next to the swaying horse. The old mare's body was shutting down from the inside.

Some animals could sense death coming. They

prepared for it, crawled away, and curled up in a ball to sleep until the end. Even men could do it. But the Horse Tribe, whom her People considered their brother, was not capable of it. They sometimes needed help to find release.

Roses offered a quick prayer in the tongue she hadn't spoken in four years, and gripped the pistol in one hand as she pulled Lady to her knees. She cocked the .45 with both thumbs, and, taking careful aim, squeezed the trigger. The shot went true, the sound reverberating across the mountain pastureland.

She had covered the carcass with a thin layer of dirt when Josiah Martin suddenly materialized at her side. He had brought another shovel from the barn. With his help she was finished refilling the hole she'd dug in just half an hour. The soft rain started to fall again.

"My daughter probably doesn't even remember Lady," Josiah said, after a few minutes.

"I'm sure she does," Roses answered, "I remember the first horse that I rode."

He smiled briefly. "So do I," he said. They finished working and started back to the house. His step quickened as they neared the north pasture fence to look at the two-year-olds who he was breaking to sell.

"That's Lady's last foal." He pointed to a three-year-old roan. "My daughter has a little girl of her own now. I've only seen her once. If they lived here, that would be my granddaughter's horse. They'd know each other already." As they watched her the mare stopped grazing and lifted her head.

"What's her name?" Roses asked.

"I haven't thought of one yet. I may sell her. If I do, I'll let the new owners name her."

Roses thought that sounded hopeful. "Is she broken to the saddle?"

"Yes. I trained her to sell last year with the other two-year-olds. I don't know why I held on to her, but I guess . . . old men get foolish notions sometimes." He shook his head, smiling wryly. "I even thought of shipping her east on the train. A present for my first grandchild."

"How old is she?" Roses asked.

"Three years," he answered.

"If you do decide to sell her . . ." Roses began.

"I should. No reason to keep her," he said.

"I'd be interested in trading for her."

"Trading?"

"Buying her."

"Oh." He thought about it. She would let it take hold. He would probably give her a good price for the horse. She would ask him during the week, when he came into town.

"I should be getting back to town. On these gray days, night comes early."

"Of course." They turned back to the house. "You can leave the horse at the livery. I told Judson to pick her up there."

She had not thought of the events of the morning for the last few hours, but as she neared town, the scene in the churchyard came forcibly back. She remembered the Reverend Meeker's fierce glare, and the sound of his hand as it made contact with Nettie's cheek. The tightness in Roses' chest grew as she left the borrowed horse at the livery stable and returned Doc's things to his office.

She approached the Smiths' house slowly. She had never before gone to the house with such trepidation. This was all the fault of the preacher from Atlanta, but she couldn't hold on to her anger. It had been replaced with sorrow and a familiar feeling of resignation. She should not have lost her temper. She had lectured him as if she had a right to tell him, and everyone else in town, how they should live, and what they should believe. She didn't have that right. She wouldn't be staying here. In fact, she wouldn't even be living here much longer anyway.

She forced a bright smile as she entered Sarah's house. She was relieved to find not only a cheery fire blazing in the fireplace, but an answering smile on every face but Tobe's as well.

"How did it go?" Ben asked.

"She was an old mare, and the colic went straight through her," Roses responded. She went to the stove to get a cup of coffee and found a napkin covered dish being kept warm atop the back burner.

"I saved your dinner," Sarah said, coming over to take some rolls from the oven.

"Thank you."

She didn't have much of an appetite, but she dug in anyway, wanting everything to appear as normal as possible.

"We had a lot of visitors after you left, asking after you," Sarah said.

Roses was amazed. "Really? Were they angry?"

"Not at all. No one wanted to say nothin' but not too many people like that preacher. Now you said it straight out, made 'em realize, they ain't too happy with what Meeker done. Don' think he's gonna feel welcome 'round here too much longer."

Roses couldn't believe it. "I thought I'd ruined everything. I didn't know how I was gonna face everyone."

Tobe said, "It should have been done long ago."

"Well, it's done now. And we're so proud of you. But we're keeping you from your dinner. Eat."

Roses was suddenly very hungry. Her mouth watered as she took in the fried chicken, cabbage and mashed potatoes and gravy piled high on her plate. Tobe was pacing before the fireplace. She was put in mind of a caged lion she'd once seen. He came over to the table with the same long strides and paused.

"You're something else, Roses Jordan," he said.

Roses sensed he was looking down at the top of her head, but she wouldn't look up at him. When he joined her, she could no longer avoid his eyes. The fire that had glowed so brightly within those black depths had been banked, but she had the feeling it would rise to the surface again with the slightest provocation. Cravenly she looked away.

Ben handed Sarah her knitting, and for a few minutes, the only sound in the room was the clicking of the long needles against each other. Roses savored the peace as much as the succulent chicken. The children were studying for the next day's classes, intent on their work, the only sign they were affected by the morning's events their slightly subdued voices. She could almost imagine that the whole incident had been a dream.

"I'd better get going," Tobe said. She hung back as he said good-bye to Sarah and Ben and the children. As he took his hat from the peg by the door, she went forward.

"Thank you for being there today, Tobe," Roses said. He smiled at her and was gone. The light from the fire seemed a little less golden without him in the room. Ben was restless after Tobe left. Roses wandered over to the window, feeling a little restless herself. The crisis was over, her decision made. She could walk away and leave this town as she'd found it, at peace.

Ten

When Roses arrived at Dr. Ian Millhouse's office the next morning, she found the veterinarian, still dressed in his traveling clothes. He had a visitor, Josiah Martin. The two men were sitting in the front room, which served as a spare but comfortable reception area for Doc's clients. Josiah stood as Roses entered the room.

"Good morning," he said. Doc looked amused as Roses stared at them in surprise.

"Good morning, Mr. Martin. Welcome home, Dr. Millhouse. When did you get here?"

"I've been on the road since daybreak. I just rode into town an hour ago. I met Josiah at the livery stable. He tells me you've been busy." The doctor's eyebrows went up in an expression of curiosity. "He's come to pay you for the work you did for him." She was relieved. For a moment, when she had seen the two men sitting together, she had the sinking feeling she might have been in trouble.

"I appreciate it, Mr. Martin. But you paid me on Saturday." Her voice trailed off. Ian Millhouse was wearing a strange smirk.

"I thought a lot about what you did, and what you said, yesterday. And I'd like you to have Lady's three-year-old," Martin said.

"What?" Roses was stunned. She'd hoped to have

a chance to buy the horse at a good price. She'd never even dreamed the rancher might give her the mare.

"The three-year-old," he continued. "My granddaughter has no need of her, and I know that you do, since you were planning to buy her. I don't feel like it would be right, somehow, to sell that foal. I hope you will accept her as a gift."

Roses stuttered. "Thank you. It's too much." She couldn't believe it. And another thought occurred to her. Now, she could leave. With this horse, she would have the money she needed for the rest of her supplies, and she could start for home with her savings almost intact.

"I think it's fitting." The rancher picked up his hat from the couch where he'd been sitting. "Doc, I'll talk with you later." To Roses he said, "The mare is at the stable. You may want to get her shoed." He left, and Roses turned to Doc.

"Close your mouth, girl, you're picking up dust," he said, as he started for the examining room. She followed him wordlessly. Once he had stored the remainder of his supplies, he sat at his desk and opened the journal to log payments and expenses.

Over his shoulder he suggested, "Why don't you go to the livery and examine that horse."

Roses couldn't resist. "If you're sure it's all right?" He turned to look at her, his usual dour expression back in place.

She decided to name the horse Bella, and to get her shoed that afternoon. After a thorough examination of the healthy young horse, she went back to work. Then she went to the smith's to tutor Lula for what might be the last time. She planned to tell Sarah and Ben that she was leaving, but Ben didn't come home to lunch, so she decided to visit again

later that evening. When she took Bella to the smithy
to be shoed, she found out why Ben had not come
home for the midday meal. It wasn't just work, as
she had thought.

Tobe was out in front of the small building when
she arrived. No shirt covered the top half of his long
underwear, and as he heard her approach he looked
up from what he was doing. His shirt was wet at
the collar and shoulders, turning the red wool of his
underwear dark. In fact, water was dripping from his
curly black hair and as she came closer, her eyes
were riveted by the sight of his chocolatey throat
glistening in the sun.

He put aside the shirt he'd been washing and came
over to her as she tied Bella to the hitching post by
the front door. He greeted her with an overly loud,
"Well, hello, Roses Jordan." He blocked the entrance
to the smithy.

"Hello, Tobias Hunter," she answered wryly, craning her neck in an effort to look over his shoulder
into the darkness beyond. The smithy door was open,
but the contrast between the bright daylight outdoors
and the dark interior made it difficult to distinguish
any of the shadowy shapes within.

"What's going on?" she asked.

"What do you mean?" Tobe answered, widening
his eyes and raising his eyebrows. He looked anything but innocent. A drop of water rolled from the
bridge of his nose to his cheek.

"Isn't this an unusual time of day for a bath?"

"Cleanliness is next to godliness, so they say." A
shadow crossed over his face, but it was gone so
quickly, Roses thought she might have imagined it.

"Church yesterday, a bath in the middle of the
work day. You're going to make it to heaven yet,"
she teased.

"Don't you mean the Happy Hunting Grounds?" His air of distraction made her wary.

"Is Ben inside?"

"Let her in, Tobe." Ben's voice was muffled, not the usual hearty bellow. She stepped past Tobe and hurried into the front room of the smithy.

"I shoed the mare for you, Roses," Ben whispered, watching Tobe walk away. "And I didn't tell Tobe, just as you asked. But I don't feel right about it."

"Roses, what do you plan to do?" Sarah had joined her husband at the smithy.

Roses took a deep breath. "I'm leaving town to-morrow."

"Leave town?" Sarah exclaimed.

"I think it's best. Doc has taught me as much as he can. I was planning to leave soon anyway. And now that I have Bella, I'm ready to begin my journey. My mind is made up." She explained to Sarah about Josiah Martin's extraordinary gift and even the practical Sarah had to admit that it seemed like a good omen.

Sarah walked with her out of the smithy when she left, still not contented with the decision, but Roses had anticipated all of her arguments and remained unfazed. Once they were out of Ben's earshot, Sarah asked, "This sudden move wouldn't have anything to do with Tobe, would it?" Roses hadn't expected the question, but realized she should have. Sarah wasn't one to let something like this pass.

"A little bit. I was planning to wait a few more months, and start over the mountains in the summer, but his being here now reminded me of something I'd forgotten."

"What's that?"

"It's hard to put into words. With Tobe here and the whole town bent on putting us together, it's a little like it was with the People when I was young. I was of their minds and hearts and they loved me, but I could never be one of them. Everyone in this town, well almost everyone, looks at Tobe Hunter and at me, and purely because of the color of our skins, they think we belong together. I guess it made me realize that no matter how long I live here, or what I do, they will never realize that I'm just the same as them."

"We're all different."

"I know. It's always been that way. The Ute and the Navajo are different. The white man and the Indians are different, but I think we're all basically the same. We want the same things: someone to love, food, shelter from the rain. But I'm homesick for a place where I can just . . . be alone, and not be lonely."

"It is Tobe, then." When Roses raised an eyebrow at Sarah, she sighed, raising her hands in surrender. "Okay, okay, I give up."

Roses smiled wryly. "I'm going to buy my supplies in the morning. I'll be by at lunchtime, to say goodbye, if that's all right with you."

"Of course it is. I just wish you didn't have to go."

Roses started home, thinking about all that she had to do the next day. There was her room at the boardinghouse, her job at the Restaurant, the bank, and of course, the veterinary office. She could leave a note for Mr. Terwiliger at the bank, but she would have to tell Doc face-to-face. She had to pack up her belongings and stop at the general store to buy her supplies from Lester Freeman.

She was glad that there was so much to do. Her leavetaking was going to be so fast, and she had so many friends that she wasn't going to be able to say goodbye to. She barely had time to think, let alone to brood over . . . anything. As she passed Letty Dowd's saloon, she decided to say a proper farewell to at least one of her friends. Jenny Li was working as Letty's housekeeper now, and she and the baby spent their evenings in their room, a converted storeroom at the back of the building. Roses slipped into the alley and went to the back entrance. She tapped gently at the door of the Li family's new residence and Jenny answered right off.

"Come in." Roses stepped into the room and stopped short. Tobe Hunter was hunkered down by the cradle playing with the baby. It seemed to Roses, looking at him peacefully entertaining the newborn infant, he was a different man. He looked up briefly to give her a welcoming smile. He looked wonderful. There was a tugging at her heartstrings as she watched him lean over the cradle. It was the first time in two days she'd seen him with a real smile. She suddenly realized she had missed it.

"Hello," she managed to say when Jenny bustled over to take her shawl.

"Hello," Jenny answered and Tobe echoed her, seemingly unembarrassed at being discovered in this unlikely place. He cooed at the baby as she caught one of his long fingers in her tiny hand.

"Would you like a glass of wine?" Jenny asked. "The girls gave it to me for Rose's one-week birthday."

"I'm not staying long," Roses responded. "I just came to . . . to check to see the baby was all right. And to make sure that the bugleweed tea worked."

"The baby's fine, and so am I. The bleeding abated after a couple of days, and I'm drinking only one cup of tea a day now, as you said."

"That's fine," Roses said. Happy, gurgling noises

from the crib seemed to confirm the young mother's opinion.

"I think she's starting to actually focus on my face sometimes when she looks at me."

"She could be." Roses approached the cradle slowly, entranced by this new vision of Tobias Hunter as he grinned down at the little doll who was guiding his finger into her mouth.

"This is the happiest baby I've ever seen," he said, gently disengaging himself as Jenny leaned over to pick up the child. "She never cries."

Jenny nodded. "Roses suggested that I cover her mouth and pinch her nose closed for a moment if she starts to cry. I've been trying it lately, and it seems to work. She's learning not to cry, and I don't think that's doing her any harm."

"It shouldn't. It's an old trick. Indian children hardly ever cry aloud."

"Do you really think that's necessary here?" Tobe asked, looking around the room. Piano music tinkled cheerily in the front of the building, and occasionally they could hear the creaking of leather boots on the old wooden staircase.

"Perhaps not. But it doesn't hurt. Letty would be very upset if the baby's crying distracted her customers or woke the girls up in the morning. So there's no need for crying."

"I guess not." Tobe looked unconvinced. Roses sighed. There was no time to debate childrearing methods, or explain Ute customs. It was good she was going home where she didn't need to explain every little thing.

"Well, I guess everything is fine here. I'd better be going," Roses said.

"Oh, stay for a minute, I'm going to feed her.

She's such a good eater. After that you could hold your namesake for a while."

"Don't go on my account," Tobe said. His easy smile was still gone, but the scowl hadn't returned. "I just stopped by to say goodnight myself." He was gone a minute after he announced his intention, and Roses relaxed as Jenny put the baby to her breast.

"She's eating well," Roses commented.

"Gaining weight each day," Jenny agreed. Roses watched the baby suckle and a feeling of contentment, of rightness, flowed over her. She knew she was letting Tobias Hunter and Edward Meeker run her out of town, but she wouldn't have to look back on her stay in Cedar Valley with regret.

She had lived well here, and done well.

"Shall I bring her to Doc's office to be weighed again?" Jenny interrupted her reverie.

"No, actually, Jenny, that's what I came to talk to you about. I didn't want to say anything while Tobe was here, but I'm not going to be working for Dr. Millhouse anymore."

"Do you think you might go to work for Dr. Forrest? You'd be a wonderful doctor for people."

"No. I mean, I am planning to work with people as well as animals, but not until I get home, to the reservation. I'm going back to Utah."

"And you don't want Tobe to know?"

"I think he'll disagree with my reasons for leaving," Roses said.

"I'm sure he wouldn't want you to leave."

Roses waved the comment away.

"Really," Jenny insisted. "It's obvious every time he looks at you. He wants you." Roses blinked at Jenny's matter of fact statement. When she looked at the smooth faced girl with long black hair hanging loose to her waist, she forgot that the Chinese

woman had been sold into prostitution at the tender
age of twelve. Yet Jenny's knowing assurance and
calm acceptance of Tobe's feeling for Roses reminded her that Jenny had many years more experience than she did at knowing men's desires.

"I know. But there's nothing to be done about
that," Roses stated firmly. Rose Li had fallen asleep,
and Jenny gave her to Roses to burp as she spoke.

"The Rocking T hands, and some of the men in
town, have been betting on whether you'll marry."

"Isn't it ridiculous?" Roses whispered.

Jenny shrugged. "Not totally, I guess. There's
something between you and Tobe Hunter. And both
of you are going to Utah." Roses gave her a wry
look.

"I'm going to the Uintah Valley. I don't know
where Tobe is headed. Certainly not into Indian
country."

"Well," Jenny watched as Roses gently lay the
still sleeping baby in the cradle. "I think you would
be a very beautiful couple."

"Not you, too," Roses complained. Jenny held up
her hands in a gesture of retreat.

"It was just a thought." But it was a thought that
Roses knew would come back to haunt her.

As she walked home a little bit later, she couldn't
get the image of Tobe and herself, as Jenny might
see them, out of her mind. The idea scared her. She
admitted, also, it was the real reason she was running, rather than walking, away from this town.

Eleven

Roses got out of town without incident, although she kept looking back over her shoulder. When half a day had gone by without the telltale echo of horse's galloping hooves pounding on the road behind her, she was finally convinced that she had made good her escape. It was silly to think that Tobe would try to stop her, when he found out she'd left. She'd been sure that when she stopped at Sarah's, her last stop before leaving town, he'd be there. She told herself she was being silly, that what felt like disappointment was just a little nervousness at finally reaching for the dream that had been so far away for so long.

She rode north and east on the white man's road, which would disappear at the edge of "civilization," bordered in this part of the world by the invincible mountains. Once in the forest proper, she'd be following the old trails. Ute Pass had been worn into the mountain by the People's moccasins since the beginning of time.

The further she rode from Cedar Valley, the more she felt her "town self" disappearing. Almost forgotten feelings from her younger days flooded through her. The landscape, barren of people, was in tune with her mood. She drank in the slightly moist sweet smelling air. Her spirit was soothed by the sight of the blue purple mountains, wreathed in gray clouds, that surrounded the valley.

She hadn't seen anyone in the fields of the farms and ranches she'd passed. Occasionally cattle wandered near fences that stretched alongside the road. She'd spotted horses in the distance at the Horace place, but the farmer and his "cowgirl" wife must have been busy elsewhere. In the middle of the week, in the middle of the day, everyone was busy working. She'd skirted Main Street as she'd ridden out of town, and she hadn't seen a soul.

Although the sky was gray, it didn't look like it was going to rain. The mule she'd bought so surreptitiously, and which she'd been afraid would be seen when she'd brought it back to the boardinghouse to transport the bulk of her belongings, plodded along behind Bella, gazing occasionally at the tall grass on the side of the road, but seemingly happy enough to plod along on the end of the lead rope Roses had tied to Bella's saddle. The hooves of the horse and the mule barely sounded on the dirt of the road. She relaxed into the motion of Bella beneath her and let her mind wander to the future.

Doc had given her a note of reference. It looked very official, and it certified that he, as a graduate of the Veterinary School of Vienna, was pleased to advise the reader that Roses had studied under him and had worked alongside him and had distinguished herself in the care and doctoring of animals. She was lucky to have known him. There weren't many men with his training in the entire country. To have found a veterinarian who had studied in Europe and New York in the small town of Cedar Valley had been a stroke of good luck that must have been arranged by the gods. She thought it would be acceptable to anyone. That should help her to start a practice with the whites who lived near the reservation.

She was pleased that she'd had the opportunity to learn from such a man. She'd read the doctor's magazines about veterinary medicine and had learned things about healing that shaman would never dream of. She'd seen with her own eyes the bacteria and microorganisms that swam unseen through the air and water of the visible world. She'd managed to teach Ian Millhouse about some of the People's cures as well. She wished she hadn't had to give up working with such a remarkably open-minded man, but, she quickly reassured herself, she'd passed the final test when she had made the trip to the Doubletree Ranch. She'd been fine without the veterinarian for the week he'd been gone, and that proved that she was ready to move on.

She was going to miss . . . everyone. She tried to be glad she hadn't had time to say goodbye to Tobe, she consoled herself with the thought that it was better this way. If she'd stayed, there would have been trouble. She suspected trouble followed Tobe. His appearance in town out of nowhere, and his refusal to tell her about his past, were enough to confirm her suspicions. Maybe he was trying to protect her, as he'd implied the one time she'd asked him straight out about his past, but that wasn't good enough. He wasn't shy about saying where he was going. Though now that she came to think about it, he'd never said exactly where in Utah he was headed, or why.

Wherever he was headed, it certainly wasn't Indian country. That much was clear in his attitude toward the human beings. Since he hadn't followed her after all, even to try and stop her as she'd been afraid he might, she reckoned she had him figured out. He would have been happy to spark with her, even to consider going further than kisses stolen in the dark—but he hadn't been interested in any more. Which was fine with Roses. She was happy alone, really alone, for the first time in years. She had grown so accustomed to living in town, she had forgotten about the blessed solitude of the open road.

It was pleasant not to have anyone but herself to please, and no one to worry about. She wasn't in any hurry. There was even a small part of her that was afraid of the reception she'd received at Uintah. A tiny voice nagged at her that she might be disappointed by the reception she'd receive from the tribe. They had turned their back on her once. But she comforted herself with recollections of her friends. Smiles Like the Moon, Running Bear, and many others had not wanted her to leave the reservation.

She was able, for the most part, to forget her fears and to concentrate on her hopes. She was a grown woman now. When she had left home, she'd been little more than a child. She was an adult now, she knew her own worth. She had proved it—over the last four years in Cedar Valley.

She had been able to make a place for herself in the white world. She could easily do the same at home.

As it grew later, she decided to keep an eye open for a place to camp for the night. She figured she'd ridden ten or fifteen miles. Roses was well contented when she came upon a stream, a tributary of the Blue River. There was a natural ford, only a foot or two deep in summer, she guessed, but slightly the worse now with the additional waters deposited by the mountain runoff and the spring rains. She urged Bella across, and the mule followed obediently.

It only took a few minutes to reach the center of

the stream. The water rushed past Bella's flanks and tugged at Roses' skirts and boots. The pull of the current was stronger than she had expected, and just as she was starting to worry, the pack mule lost its footing and let out a panicked snort. Bella fought against the pull of the rope on the saddle, while Roses tried to coax the heavily burdened mule to follow the lead rope rather than fighting it. With a few clucks and snorts of her own, Roses managed to get both animals moving in the right direction, and Bella fought her way toward shore, helping Roses to pull the valiantly struggling pack animal behind them.

When the three of them stood on dry land, Roses thanked the gods, and Bella, and went to the mule to evaluate any damage the water might have done to her belongings. Her stores were not much, but they were all that she had until she crossed the mountains and came upon another town. She was pleased to find everything had survived the dunking. Her food was dry, and nothing had been washed away. The rifle and ammunition, which were two of the few things she carried with her on Bella's back, had stayed relatively dry as well. With relief, she turned to uncovering the rest of her things.

She didn't own much. Her gifts for the tribe alone filled one large sack. She had lengths of cloth, thread, and the delicate metal pins and needles that were so much smaller than the implements she had worked with in her childhood. They would not be as easy to hide if the need to disguise one's presence became urgent as bone, quill, or stone needles had been, but she assumed that that quality was not nearly so important on the reservation as it had been in the wilderness. She pictured herself riding into camp with her booty and hummed contentedly as she hung damp clothes and yardgoods out to dry on large rocks and small bushes along the bank of the stream.

She decided not to hunt for meat for her dinner, but caught some fat frogs to cook with her flatbread over the open fire. Once she had eaten, she repacked most of her damp belongings so that she could make an early start in the morning. Roses settled into her fur bedroll to sleep alone under the stars for the first time in over four years. The night sky was glorious. The moon was covered by clouds, which also obscured many of the stars, but the sky was wide above her head, and the few stars that twinkled here and there between the clouds looked close enough to touch.

The starry sky reminded her of the first night she and Tobe had kissed. He hadn't been far from her thoughts all day, and finally she admitted to herself she missed him. She would never see him again. It took her a long time to get to sleep that night.

Roses had been on the trail for two and a half days before she picked up her first traveling companion. She heard the mewling of kittens before she saw the paw prints that led into the underbrush. Then she caught a blur of motion out of the corner of her eye. She unsheathed her rifle with one practiced motion. Just ahead a stone ledge gave access to a maple tree branch above the trail. A perfect spot for an ambush. She raised her rifle just as the bobcat sprang. She fired. The impact of the shot stopped the cat in mid-air; it landed in a crumpled ball of fur less than two feet away. Bella nickered and danced. Roses kept her seat and cleaned the rifle chamber with a flick of a wrist.

She watched the she-cat. It didn't move, except for the rapid rise and fall of its chest. Roses dismounted. Holding her gun at the ready, she approached. Unconscious, the animal looked just as harmless as a housecat. Roses knew she was more deadly than many larger predators that lived in these mountain forests.

But she couldn't resist examining the unconscious animal. And then treated the wound she'd inflicted with her own gun. The bullet had scraped along the fleshy part of the cat's shoulder. She cleaned the area with water from her canteen, and applied a poultice of mountain iris root and selfheal leaves. Then she went looking for the kittens.

There were four adorable little babies in the litter. Three were crying, their little pink mouths open wide to show off tiny teeth. The fourth, obviously the runt of the litter, was sleeping. The larger kits banged their heads into his side, vainly searching for their missing mother.

The site chosen for the nest was an indentation under the cover of an overhanging rock rather than one of the small caves usually returned to year after year to have their young. The little family was obviously alone out here, and Roses knew the mama would chew off her bandages in no time at all. If the wound got infected, the babies would die. Roses decided to make camp nearby, as it was almost dark anyway, and keep an eye on the injured animal for a day or two.

When Roses visited the nest the next day she wasn't surprised to find the poultice had been chewed off and pushed off, but she was worried by the signs of infection that the mother cat had left behind.

A few miles further along, just a stone's throw from the trail, she found a perfect place to stop for a little longer. In the midst of a clearing stood a freshwater pond surrounded by pines and aspens and thick brush.

She hadn't anticipated the problems of sharing such a small area with a hungry wildcat. Twice in the next two days, she and mama met while hunting the same game. The second time the rabbit almost got away, as Roses didn't expect the bobcat to suddenly enter her field of fire.

Though it had rained for the previous two nights, on the third the clear weather held. She kept her fire glowing throughout the night, and slept for short spells between stoking the flames but there was no sign of the wildcat. While the daylight hours had been full of hunting, cooking, and planning her triumphant return home, the long hours of the night were filled with thoughts of the people she'd just left behind, and especially Tobe Hunter.

She had thought that leaving him behind—escaping his overwhelming physical presence—would make it easier to put him out of her mind. But throughout the night thoughts of Tobe haunted her. She remembered his teasing smile at the Smiths, the restaurant, on the street, she remembered his eyes glowing at her in the red light of the forge, and gleaming in the moonlight, his hands stroking her. At dawn she felt she'd hardly slept at all. She waded into the pond. The cold water washed the tension from her neck and limbs.

She floated, enjoying the liquid coolness of the water and the rapidly warming early morning air. Bella whinnied and Roses looked quickly toward shore. The scene was as peaceful as any she'd ever seen; the flawless blue sky limned the dark-green pine trees, the sun's rays broke through the branches, dappling the roan's shining red coat, the mule grazed peacefully. A trickle of light-gray smoke rose from the fire, disappearing before it reached the top of the trees. Dust motes shone gold, dancing in the air around her, and water gnats skated over the glassy surface of the pond. Bella had gone back to grazing. Roses didn't see anything untoward, but the mule started braying.

Roses swam toward shore, barely breaking the water. She still couldn't see anything out of the ordinary. Nor did she until she went to quiet the mule, whose eyes were rolling back in her head from fear. Roses couldn't calm the panicky animal until she stood between her and the brush at the side of the clearing. When she'd gotten the pack animal as quiet as she could, she went to investigate. She found a kitten, the runt of the mama cat's litter, sleeping on the ground where she'd been unceremoniously dropped. Perhaps the campsite just seemed, to the bobcat, an apt place for burial, but Roses couldn't leave the baby there to die.

It was two days before Roses felt any degree of confidence in her ability to keep baby Jasper alive. She had not traveled one foot toward her destination since she had taken on the responsibility of raising the little hellcat. He got into everything: the food, her clothes, her medicine bag. She couldn't keep an eye on him twenty-four hours a day, but it should not have been necessary. He slept, like any other cat, ninety percent of the time. Yet he did enough damage during his waking hours to drive her to drink.

She quickly became accustomed to taking catnaps, aptly named in this particular instance. On the second night she was wide awake long after night had fallen. The kitten was finally fast asleep. The water beckoned her. She decided to take a quick swim. The sun had been shining for three days, and it was almost bathwater warm now.

She shimmied out of the Ute clothing she'd taken

to wearing the first day on the trail, down to the white man's underwear she still wore beneath the deerskin leggings Annette Blackwolf had given her. The night air was chill as she moved away from the campfire. The water, when she waded into the moonlit pond, was much warmer. The reflection of the night sky glittered on the pond surface. It rippled and broke apart as she moved through the water with long, slow strokes.

She swam halfway across the expanse of the pond and rested on a rock ledge just under the surface of the water. She undid the braids that kept her hair out of her way during the day and ducked her head back under the water, the black cap of her hair sleek for a moment as she emerged, springing into an unruly mass of shoulder-length curls seconds later. She finger-combed the thick strands, submerging again and again under the warm water as she worked her way from her forehead to her nape, until she was satisfied that all the knots were gone.

She was about to swim back to the camp, pleasantly relaxed, when an unfamiliar sound floated over the water from the eastern shore. The lethargy left her limbs, and she slipped soundlessly from her perch. Her eyes could not pierce the darkness. She had to get closer to investigate. She swam closer to the shore and tread water, listening. The water lapped gently at her chin. Pine branches swayed in the breeze, their shadows dancing over the pond's silver black surface. Suddenly a man, stark naked and pale as a ghost in the moonlight, ran out of the woods and straight to the pond, jumping in with a loud shout.

Roses couldn't believe either her ears or her eyes. She stealthily swam to the shore some twenty yards away and slipped under cover of the tall pines. She picked her way toward the spot he had come from, her eyes trained to the glitter of the pond's surface through the trees. The noise made by his mule led her to his clothes and other gear. She had just started to go through his pockets, looking for something that might identify the man as friend or foe, when behind her she heard a low growling. She turned slowly toward the sound and found herself face to face with the biggest bear she had ever seen.

She stood, and the bear reared back on its hind legs, grunting. Roses inched a foot to her left, the bear let out a tremendous roar, sunk down onto all four feet again, and stood swaying from side to side.

"Irma! What's the matter, girl?" The voice came from the shore.

Roses was astonished as the bear turned its head toward the sound and sat down. "Who's there?" The man moved toward them. "Damn!" he cursed, hopping on one foot, trying to hold the other off the ground. "Don't move, buster. I've got that bear trained . . ." His voice trailed off as he saw Roses. "Why, bless me, it's a woman!" the man exclaimed, sitting down to nurse his foot, and cursing again as his backside hit the ground. "Damn pointy rocks! Speak up. What are you doing out here?"

Roses stirred the fish stew she'd prepared and hung it over the banked fire to cook slowly in Trapper Jack's huge metal pot. Her mouth watered at the prospect of a meal that wasn't fried in her one small pan or baked in the coals of the fire. She wondered idly if she could convince the miner to travel a little ways with her, in order to combine his kitchen and her cooking skills.

"That's a sight better than what you were wearing

last night." The object of her musings emerged from the trees carrying a string of quail.

He'd been gone when she'd awakened that morning, and this was the first chance she'd had to look him over in the full light of day. He was unremarkable in his appearance except for his huge beaklike nose. He was of medium height, with mousy brown hair and eyes of the same hue. His ragged clothing had faded to a color somewhere between brown and gray.

She looked down at herself. She was wearing deerskin leggings and a soft shirt of the same material decorated with dyed porcupine quills. It had been given to her by Annette and Little Sparrow when she'd said her goodbyes.

"I'd return the compliment, but you weren't wearing anything at all last night," she joked. He didn't smile, but turned away.

She had worn these clothes since her first full day out on the trail. They were more comfortable for riding and hunting than her dresses. They were also a constant reminder of the girl she'd left behind on the reservation four years ago. At first they felt unfamiliar, but wearing these clothes made her feel freer and younger than she had in years. She didn't know if this was because they were the garb of her youth, or because wearing this attire reminded her that she'd left the white man's world, and all her old troubles, behind her.

She was very glad to have worn the outfit when, a little later that day, a Ute hunting party "dropped in" for a visit at the camp she and Jasper were sharing with the miner and his equally unusual pet.

Jack had tramped off after lunch, but Irma had stayed behind and tried to sleep while Jasper had worried one of the bear's paws. It was almost as tall as he was, but he batted at it and caught the fur in his tiny claws. Roses was keeping an eye on the duo when she became aware that there were other human beings nearby. She scanned the treeline and suddenly saw them, standing almost completely in shadow. There were four braves, two in their first manhood, two in their middle years, all dressed in only leggings and face paint.

"Hello." She greeted them automatically in the language of the Uncompahgre.

"You make a good fire, like the People." One of the older men said with a strange accent—Kiowa she guessed.

"And you speak Uncompahgre." the other said, in the same tongue.

"Would you like to eat?" she asked, her head bent and slightly turned away from the party. Out of her peripheral vision she could see them peering into the woods behind her. "I have a companion here, but he has gone to hunt."

"Wildheart?" One of the younger men stepped into the sunlight while the others stood tensely, waiting, she supposed, for a hail of bullets to erupt from the brush behind her. She recognized the man who called her by her Indian name right away. It was Hunts Too Slow, a boy she had grown up with. He hadn't changed much in his growth from boy to man. His shoulders had filled in a little, but he was still lanky. The feet he had tripped over as a boy were still enormous. His face was long and thin, like the rest of him, but his long black hair flowed over wiry muscles in his back and chest.

"I am pleased to see you, Hunts Too Slow. It has been a long time."

The other youth stepped forward.

"Hello, Wildheart." When she didn't respond he

smiled. "You don't recognize me, do you?" He peered
at her myopically. Like Hunts Too Slow and the other
two men, there was not a spare ounce of flesh on his
red-gold body, but there his resemblance to his companions ended. All three of them were whipcord thin,
but this beautiful blinking youth was perfection. His
white teeth flashed against full lips. His round black
eyes were shadowed by long thick eyelashes and
brows that were finely drawn crescent moons placed
well in his high forehead. His face would have been
womanly if it hadn't been for the patrician nose com-
plementing his other features.

Any resemblance to a woman stopped at his neck.
His body was sculpted gold. His square shoulders
and wide chest tapered down to a narrow waist and
long muscular legs. Roses blinked back at him and
he laughed, a rich sound, like the pealing of church
bells. Then she knew.

"Little Deer. You have changed." The two older
men smiled. Little Deer introduced them.

"This is my uncle, Graywolf. I don't think you
ever met him, he lived with his wife's tribe on a
reservation in the south for many years," he said of
the man who had been surprised by her ability to
speak his language. "This is his friend, Atlato." The
latter was the man who had commented on her fire-
building skills. She thought he was Kiowa. She
couldn't translate his name into Uncompahgre or English.

"Are you hungry? I was just making a fish stew,"
Roses offered. All four men nodded and started toward the fire.

Irma's bellowing stopped them in their tracks. Jasper came running to Roses' feet and she bent and
picked him up.

"Irma. Lie down," Roses ordered firmly, still

speaking the language of her People. Irma recognized the tone, at least. She subsided. Roses spoke to her in English, using the same words Jack had the night before. "These are friends! Quiet down." Irma lumbered off into the woods, and all the Ute watched in amazement, then turned back to Roses, slackjawed. Hunts Too Slow shook his head in awe.

"I thought you went to live with the whites. Have you been visiting the spirits, Wildheart?"

"No. I was learning the white man's animal medicine." Roses explained. Everyone nodded approval except Graywolf.

"White men cannot speak to animals. They just kill them and leave the carcasses to rot where they fall," he said.

"I have seen this." Little Deer nodded.

"This," Roses motioned toward the trees where the bear had last been seen, "this is not white man's medicine. This is . . . different. Their medicine is for their horses and cows and pigs, and sometimes Dog, who works with white men on their ranches and farms." This the Ute understood. However, they still watched her closely while she put Jasper down and turned back to the fire to make sure the wood she had added was blazing under the metal pot. She could hear Little Deer and Hunts Too Slow explaining to the other two men how she and her parents had come to live with the Uncompahgre. She only half listened as she wondered what Jack would do if he came back to the camp now. By the time she brought them chunks of bread and dishes of fish stew, Graywolf and Kiowa had lost interest in Roses' origins and were only interested in her "animal magic."

"Can you call wild horses to come to you tamely?"

Kiowa asked. All of the men looked so hopeful she hated to have to tell them the truth.

"No. I'm sorry. I have no more power over Horse than you do." She had to admit.

"It's a shame." Kiowa shrugged. "That would have been useful. We have no horses."

"You're traveling on foot?" Roses was surprised. "But why? Where are you going?"

"We are hunting. Meat is scarce in the desert and there is not good hunting there. The land is bad. In the high mountains are goat, good meat. White men do not chase them and could not catch them if they did. We hope to dry the meat and bring it back to Uintah. Maybe we can trap some beaver if they have not all been killed. We will trade the skins," Hunts Too Slow explained.

Little Deer added, "Perhaps we will have enough money to buy some horses."

Kiowa snorted. "We go into the mountains as hunters, but we return home as beasts of burden, carrying the meat like women," he said.

Roses nodded. "These are all the same problems we were having when I left the reservation. Has nothing changed?" she asked.

Graywolf shook his head. "It gets no better. The only change is that the People grow resigned, they accept what comes to them. We thought we could fight again if the Indian Agency did not give us what was promised. Now no one wants to fight. The young ones are hungry. They go to schools taught by white men and see that white children are not hungry. They forget who they are."

"Not all young people feel this way, Uncle," Hunts Too Slow protested. "Many more would have been willing to hunt with us, if we had wanted a bigger party."

"And we are here with you. Are we not young? Are we not risking our lives? But we are here." Little Deer added.

"To you it's all a game. You don't really remember what it was like before." Graywolf said sadly. "We lived where we wished and hunted where we wished. Even when I was a child, there were many more beaver and buffalo."

"We have to sneak out of our tents in the middle of the night and crawl to the tops of the great mountains just to hunt for goats," Kiowa said, angrily. "This is not right. But there are too many bluecoats to fight, and fewer of us all the time. We will disappear, too, like the bison."

"It is hard to believe that we had no word for evil when the whites came. There was only disharmony. Living in harmony with nature, with men and with Senawahv, the Creator were all that was truly important," Graywolf said sadly.

"But have you forgotten, Uncle, we were not always so peaceful. What of the raids and the rivalries with the Arapaho and Cheyenne? That started long before the whites came," Hunts Too Slow pointed out.

"How many times have I heard the story of how you got that silver bead in your hair?" Little Deer added.

"That is an old story," Graywolf said.

"I know an older one." Roses smiled. "Once there were no people in any part of the world. Senawahv cut sticks and placed them in a large bag day after day, until Coyote grew so curious he couldn't stand it any longer. He opened the bag, and people came out, all of them speaking different languages and scattering in every direction. When Senawahv returned there were only a few people left. He was

very angry with Coyote, because he had planned to
give the people their own lands. But since they'd
been released without direction there would be war
between the different peoples, each trying to gain
land from his neighbor. Of all the people remaining
in the bag, Senawahv said, "This tribe shall be Ute,
but they will be very brave and able to defeat all
the rest."

"That is a very old story," Kiowa said. But he
was holding back a smile, and the others were grinning, even Graywolf. They had finished their meal
and the sun was getting lower in the sky. The men
decided they should go before it became too dark,
so they could still travel a few more miles that night.

"If you meet me on your way back, my mule can
carry the meat." Roses said. Her offer was greeted
with pleased nods of acceptance. "I would offer her
to you, but she will be no use to you up in the
heights of the peaks."

"Towaoc." Graywolf said. "Perhaps we will meet
you on the path, and then we can travel home with
you." Roses watched the Utes leave. They slipped
into the trees as quietly as they had come and were
gone.

Twelve

Tobe had never seen a prettier sight in his life. The thin line of gray smoke he was heading for was the first sign of life he'd seen in two days. He had doubled back on the trail he followed, thinking he must have somehow missed Roses. He certainly should have caught up with her by now. He had followed only a day after she left. Ute Pass seemed the logical place for Roses to have traveled through. She had talked about leaving this area with the Uncompahgre. The trail was well known, if not well traveled. A southern route, at this time of year, would make sense if she planned to take the train, but with the horse and the mule, he suspected she planned to ride straight through. He and Diablo were not so heavily burdened as she was, and though she'd had a day's start on him, he was able to keep up a reasonably fast pace, despite the fact that he had to be careful not to stray off the trail. He must have overshot her. He didn't know how else he could have missed her. He could only pray that no harm had come to her.

It was late evening, almost sundown, and he thought he could just reach the origin of the plume of smoke he'd seen before nightfall. He could only hope the fire it came from was hers.

No one had ever left him before. He had left

home without once looking back. After Granny Gee
died, he hadn't thought of Boston as home, really.
But he'd known it would always be there. Even his
mother, whom he hadn't seen in over ten years, was
there if he wanted to find her. All of the places he'd
visited on his grand adventure were there for him to
go back to. This time he was the one who had been
left behind.

When he heard she had left he'd been surprised
at the burning disappointment he felt. His frustration
at having let Roses slip away had grown with every
hour since he'd learned of her departure and her destination even after he decided to follow and try to
catch up with her. He couldn't get over the feeling
that he'd been close to breaking through her defenses
and getting closer to her. And he wanted that, more
than he had known.

The trail led around to the left and he followed.
The path had been cut into the side of the mountain,
over hundreds of years, he guessed, and though it
seemed a haphazard, meandering thing, it was actually carefully arranged and very well formed. It was
also cleverly disguised. Expanses of rock in some
areas, and weed cover in others, made it almost invisible to the casual observer.

As the day's last light gleamed red in the treetops
above, he reached a place near, he was sure, where
the smoke had originated. There was still no sight
or sound of human life, but he reined Diablo in anyway and sat still, listening. Only the sound of the
horse's breathing broke the silence. But Tobe smelled
wood smoke, and a faint perfume of, of all things,
frying fish. It took him a moment to decide from
which direction that welcome aroma was wafting.
Then he turned Diablo off the path in search of the
cook.

He followed his nose through the trees to a stand of rocks, from behind which, he could swear, he heard moving water. He left the horse lightly tied to a pine branch and scrambled up the rock face to stand atop it. At his feet a good-sized pond stretched before him. A hundred feet to his left, on the southern bank, he was sure he spotted the glow of a fire. He slid down the hill of stone, impatient now.

He led Diablo through the trees, which grew close together almost up to the shore of the pool. The pine needles below muffled the sound of their approach, but as he drew close to the fire, he could see a horse and a mule. The menacing sound of a gun being cocked sounded just behind him.

"Hold it there, Mister."

It wasn't Roses.

"I mean no harm. I'm just riding the trail through to Utah," he explained. Tobe raised his hands out to his side and slowly turned to face the man who had gotten the drop on him.

"It's getting pretty crowded on these trails, these days," the old geezer said. By the look of him, he hadn't been to town in a long spell. His guns were ancient, though lethal-looking, and his clothes had seen much better days. He wore a coonskin cap, like the trappers in the dime novels Tobe had read back East. Despite his age, his eyes were clear as he sized up Tobe with a measuring glance.

"I'm looking for a woman. 'Bout five feet tall." As Tobe moved his hand to indicate Roses' height, the old man aimed the gun at his head. "A colored woman. She should have come this way, maybe a day or two ago."

"Women," the geezer spat, obviously not an admirer of the fairer sex. "Ruining this country. Whores with their crabs, and ladies with their churches. Only good woman to have out here is a Injun." The man's accent was familiar to Tobe, but he couldn't quite place it.

"This woman was raised by the Ute," he offered.

"A nigra Injun?" The old man cackled. "Eh, whaddya know." He had to be a Bostonian. Tobe hadn't heard the accent since he'd left Massachusetts, but he would have recognized it anywhere. As hostile as the old man was, Tobe felt like he had come home.

"You're from back East, aren't you?" Tobe lowered his hands, still keeping them clearly visible at his sides.

"Mebbe about a hundred years ago." The old man finally lowered the gun. "You're from there, then, eh?" As Tobe nodded, it occurred to him that the geezer didn't seem all that surprised to see him. Tobe began to suspect that perhaps he was closer to finding Roses than he had thought. Something the trapper had said about the trail being crowded came back to him. The tentative thought was knocked right out of his mind as a huge black bear lumbered out of the woods toward them.

"Oh, my God!" The bear didn't look at Tobe at all, its eyes were on the trapper. Just as Tobe was about to grab for his gun, the man held out a hand to the immense animal and he or she nuzzled it. A shiver went down Tobe's spine.

"I'm Jack Trapper." The bear rested its paw on the trapper's shoulder. Tobe managed to regain control of his tongue.

"Tobe Hunter. Friend of yours?" He indicated the bear, careful to move slowly and carefully.

"Her name's Irma." Jack Trapper turned toward camp. Tobe was relieved when the bear followed his lead. "Raised her from a cub," the old man said, over his shoulder. "She's good company on the trail.

Which is more than I can say for most people." Irma followed him, and Tobe made up the end of the train, at a respectful distance.

When he did walk into the light of the fire, he was not really surprised to see Roses there, frying fish in a large metal skillet. Here was the face that had burned in his mind each night as he'd tried to sleep, that had warmed his blood each day as he followed an indistinct pathway to heaven only knew what. This was the lady he had come for. The tension that had filled him when he'd heard Roses had left Cedar Valley slowly dissipated. He hadn't realized how stiffly he'd been holding himself until his muscles relaxed. He hadn't known that a hard knot had formed in his gut until it disappeared. "She can't cook, though." It took a moment for Tobe to register that Jack was still talking about his "pet."

"Why should she?" Roses answered Jack. Tobe noticed that Irma had made her way off to the bank of the pond and was pulling out a string of fish that had been tied to a line and left submerged in the shallow water. He marveled as Irma systematically, if not very neatly, ripped them from the string with teeth that gleamed in the moonlight, even from this distance. "She likes her meat raw."

"I'm not complainin', eh. Just pointing out a fact. Wouldn't trade 'er. Watch out that one on the edge there don't burn," Jack fussed at Roses.

"Don't worry. There's more than enough." Finally Roses looked up at him. "Tobe Hunter. What are you doing here?" she asked, as calm and collected as if she was just standing in Sarah Smith's kitchen, rather than on a mountain trail in the middle of nowhere with a trapper who looked about a hundred years old and a huge bear feasting away not ten feet from her. After her hasty, and rather secretive, de-

parture from town, Tobe had been convinced that if
she saw him coming she would run a mile in the
other direction.

"The same thing you are," he answered.

He didn't know if it was the place that he had
found her, or the short time that they had been separated, but she seemed somehow different from the
Roses he knew. Then she turned away from his scrutiny, with a nervous little duck of her head, and suddenly she was again the woman he had pictured as
he'd ridden all those wild, lonely miles in the wilderness. This was the Roses he had been looking
for—independent and indomitable on the outside,
soft and sweet and a little bit lost within.

"Hungry?" she asked. He nodded, accepting the
plate Roses gave him. He tasted the odd-looking
greens that accompanied the fish with some trepidation, and then digging in when he found they tasted
like fried onions. The three of them ate in companionable silence. Irma had wandered off somewhere,
and Tobe forgot about the bear long enough to enjoy
the hot meal. He couldn't keep his eyes off Roses
as she sat, apparently lost in thought, ignoring the
slobbering sounds coming from Jack Trapper's side
of the fire. She certainly didn't seem overjoyed to
see him, but he hadn't expected she would be. He
had hoped . . . but he'd been prepared for an argument. He was going to have a good time disabusing
her of the notion that she was going to be able to
negotiate around him. He had plans of his own for
the two of them, plans he couldn't wait to put into
motion. He could almost feel the soft sweet skin that
glowed luminous as a caramel apple in the flickering
light from the fire. The leaping flames were reflected
in the black-brown of her eyes. He watched the
spoon she carried to her lips and remembered the

caress of her tongue and the taste of her. He licked
his own dry lips and she caught the motion as she
looked up. But she didn't meet his eyes. She cocked
her head as if listening for something.

A tiny ball of fluff, no bigger than the foot of
Tobe's boot, came streaking suddenly out of the bed-
rolls nearby. Tobe recognized the markings emerging
on the little gray furball. This was no tame housecat;
it was a bobcat.

"Jasper. You had your fish already!" Roses scolded,
as the kitten climbed halfway up her pant leg, balanced itself on its rear legs, and tried to swipe at the
food remaining on Roses' dish with one little paw. He
lost his footing and tumbled over onto his back, but
within seconds the baby wildcat was back. "Jasper, I
gave you your dinner." Roses tried to sound exasperated, but she only sounded amused. "Okay, you can
have one more little piece." She gave the cat a bite
of fish, and he started to carry it away, only to come
up hard against a wall of thick black fur the moment
he left Roses' shadow. Irma was safeguarding her
ground. It was clear that she had no intention of giving
her food away to any creature this small. When the
kitten tried to go around Irma, the bear gave him a
little swat, which was enough to send Jasper somer-
saulting back almost into Roses' lap.

"Irma," Roses scolded, without heat. She put her
plate down and picked up the kitten to comfort him.
But the cat had barely noticed the blow, and still
held the fish in his mouth. Irma approached the pair,
stomach rumbling. Roses held Jasper out of harm's
way, but she couldn't really protect him from such
a large animal. The kitten did not realize that he
even needed protection. He struggled to get out of
Roses' grasp as Irma came ever closer, literally

drooling in anticipation of eating that bite of fish Jasper had begged from Roses.

The grizzly planted herself a foot from Roses and started to sway back and forth, grunting each time she hit the end of the arc. The kitten tapped the bear playfully on the nose with one quick paw. Irma responded with a roar that shook the tree branches. Just as Tobe decided that he would have to intervene, Jack's voice bellowed from the trees behind the bear, "Irma!" The bear looked reluctantly over her shoulder, and then back toward the mischievous kitten.

"Irma, come here! Now!" Jack ordered. Irma strode nonchalantly into the woods, and Roses released the kitten with an audible sigh of relief. Tobe had stood and started toward Roses when he thought he might have to distract the bear, and since he was already in motion, he decided he might as well keep going.

Roses sat looking at the kitten eating at her feet, still with that distracted air she'd worn all evening. Tobe circled the firepit between them and stopped a foot away from her, willing her to look up at him. She did. Her eyes traveled up his legs, then his body, to his face, searing him, like fire, wherever they touched on him.

Her lips were dry and pink from her days out in the sun, her skin was a shade darker than it had been, with the golden tone of absorbed sunlight. Her hair was pulled back and loosely tied with a piece of rawhide. In town she had combed it tight to her head and twisted the rest of its length into a bun at the back of her neck, out here the tight waves of hair ran riot from her temple to her shoulders, the string she had tied at her nape barely controlled the black curls close to her head, and separated them from the kinky mass that spread across her neck. He wanted to touch it. Instead his hand came out unconsciously in invitation and she stood, taking it, and let him guide her closer with a light touch of his palm to hers.

His hand came up to touch her cheek and he moved his thumb over the tiny cracks in her lips. Leaning down, he licked them, and when he would have stood away again, she followed with a tilt of her head, raising her lips for another stroke. His hand slid down to her chin and cupped the smooth skin there. The coolness of her cheek under the tip of his fingers did nothing to abate the heat growing within him. Her eyes slid closed and he sighed, and let his own heavy lids drop as he kissed her. With his mouth, he caressed the delicate half moons below her eyes, and the firm skin at her cheekbone, until he could resist no longer and he opened his mouth over hers. They stood so for a long time, drinking deeply of each other.

The sounds of the forest around him, the gentle lapping of the pond at its shore, even the crackling of the fire warming them, faded. All he could hear was her soft uneven breathing, the gasps that followed each movement of his mouth, and the thudding of his own heart in his chest. He wondered at the pleasure of feeling her in his arms again, and then marveled at how perfectly they seemed to fit together. She sighed against his mouth, and he knew just how she felt. The feel of her soft flesh under his hand was as intoxicating as strong drink.

He had never felt this way with any other woman, and he had sampled more than his share. She welcomed the thrust of his tongue into her mouth as one of her hands snaked behind his head and she curved it around the back of his neck.

"I didn't think you would be so happy to see me," he whispered in her ear.

"Neither did I," she answered, kissing him again. "I wasn't sure you'd follow me."

"No?"

"I thought you might. After all, we are going the same way."

"I'd say." He slipped his hand under her shirt at the waist and slid it up her back, over the camisole he was surprised to find she still wore.

"I mean, we're both going to Utah. Even Jenny Li knew that."

He found the bottom of the lacy cotton undergarment and worked his hand under it, sighing as he touched the smooth skin at the small of her back. He kneaded the soft flesh there.

"That's not why I came, and you know it," he whispered. She turned her face to his, and the desultory conversation came to an end for a few minutes as he explored the mouth she offered. "I missed you," he said, when he freed his mouth for a moment. Then he assaulted her chin and collarbone with his tongue and teeth.

"I did, too," she admitted breathlessly. The surprise in her voice made him chuckle. "What?" she asked.

"I didn't think you'd admit it," he told her.

"If you can, I can." She let her head fall forward against his shoulder as his lips moved lower.

"So, this is the Hunter fellow you asked me about?" Jack's voice came from only a few feet away. Tobe slowly disentangled his hand from Roses' clothing and took a deep breath before he stepped away. Roses composed herself, a hand going to her unbound hair and falling again by her side.

"This is him," she said, unnecessarily.

"Thought you said you didn't want him to catch up with you," Jack taunted her.

"I didn't think I did," Roses answered.

"Guess you were wrong, then."

"I guess I was," Roses agreed.

The old man chortled. "I knew it. I could tell. That's why you've been hanging around here for the past few days."

"No," she answered. "I wanted to dry some fish to take to Uintah with me. Who knows when I'll find another spot that isn't fenced in, or posted."

"You might not." Jack nodded. "Then again, you might find one just over the next hill. You don't know, do you?"

Tobe grinned. "It seems like the tide's turned, Roses Jordan. You can't hide anything from him. Or me."

She looked up at him, but her protest died on her lips and she shrugged. "Who says I'd want to hide anything?"

"Well, I'll be. The woman has finally stopped arguing?" Tobe wondered aloud.

"There's obviously no point to arguing with you two. You're typical men, thinking the world revolves around you."

"Doesn't it?" Tobe grinned.

Roses shook her head in exasperation. "No, it doesn't. But if it makes you feel better to think so, far be it for me to ruin your fun."

"I'll hold you to that," Tobe said.

That stopped her. She opened her mouth, but nothing came out.

Tobe relented. "So, where do I sleep?" he asked.

"Ummm, there." She pointed at the side of the fire opposite her sleeping roll, next to Jack's pile of pine boughs and crumpled blankets. Tobe walked over to the spot and dropped his blanket roll.

"Here?"

She nodded. He looked from the bare ground at his feet to her neat "bed." She'd also collected pine boughs to cushion the area where she slept, but they were carefully arranged in a pyramid shaped stack, her blankets and an animal fur rolled together at one end. Only ten feet separated the two small mounds. He could walk around the fire pit in two or three paces. "Fine," he said, rubbing his hands together. He would gap the small distance that remained between them, and soon. She shot a glance at him from beneath lowered brows. "I hope you don't snore," he said. "I'm a light sleeper."

She almost laughed, he was sure. "I don't, but Jack and Irma sure do."

"Doesn't bother us," Jack said.

"I think I'll take a quick swim," Tobe decided. "I'd like to wash. Anyone care to join me?" He didn't expect Roses would take him up on the offer, since she seemed to be standing on her dignity at the moment, but he hoped the old man would. They were going to be resting quite near each other.

"I take a bath every night," Jack said, "when I'm here at the pond."

Tobe figured the stale odor emanating from the old coot must be caught in his clothes. He hoped the trapper slept in the all and all. He wondered what Roses wore to bed.

"There's a good spot down the bank a ways. It's warmer 'cause it ain't so deep there."

"Lead the way," Tobe said, "before it gets any colder."

"Don't bank that fire, girl," Jack ordered. "We can warm up when we get back."

"All right." Roses agreed.

After gathering some tree branches to soften his own bed, Tobe followed the old man, looking back to see Roses gazing out at the water. He wondered if she, too, bathed nightly in the pond. But when they returned she was already abed.

It took a long time for Tobe to fall asleep. Roses lay so near, he was sure he would have heard her breathing if Jack's heavy snoring hadn't been so loud. He struggled to get comfortable, too close to the woman whose memory alone had warmed his blood.

He dreamed of her and himself. She came to him, the fire burning high and bright behind her, lighting her body as she slipped out of her white cotton underthings and stood by his bed, allowing him to look his fill. Her skin was the color of coffee with cream, her high, firm breasts capped with red-brown areolas, her waist slim, her hips rounded, with thick black curls at the juncture of her thighs. Her legs curved gently down to feminine ankles and small feet. She lowered herself to her knees beside him, and as he reached up to her, he awakened in the pink-tinged light of early morning.

He looked immediately over at the spot where he'd last seen Roses. Her bed was there, blankets neatly rolled again at the foot of the pine mattress, but she was gone. He stood, clad only in his long red underwear. Coffee was simmering on the fire. Trapper Jack was still snoring. Irma was nowhere to be seen. Jasper was prowling along the shore of the pond, back and forth, tail swishing from side to side as he walked. Tobe knew, then, where he would find her.

Thirteen

Roses finished washing and surfaced by "her" rock. The sun was peeking over the mountains that rimmed the horizon, the first rays just clearing the tips of the pines. The old trees surrounding the clearing confined the first tentative touch of light to the center of the lake. She hoisted herself up to sit on the stone, high enough to be warmed by the gentle rays. She looked toward shore and was surprised to see Tobe standing there, looking directly at her. She had listened to him toss and turn for hours the night before, well aware that his sleeplessness, like her own, had little if anything to do with Trapper Jack's snoring.

She had been unable to forget the blood-stirring kisses Jack had interrupted, or the feeling of breathless anticipation that overwhelmed her every time she'd looked at him the night before. She hadn't been able to sleep at all. At first light she had climbed quietly out of bed and gone to where he lay. He was asleep. She had missed him so much since she'd seen him last. She had thought her feelings for him would have lessened, but they hadn't. That became clear as soon as she saw him again.

When he'd appeared last night, it had been all she could do to stay calm until she found out what he was doing there. When he'd said he'd come for her, she'd been so happy she hadn't known what to say, so she'd kissed him, deep and long. Trapper Jack had come back then, and she hadn't had time or the nerve to try to say what was in her heart.

He was coming with her. For now, that was enough, more than enough. Tobe Hunter was here, with her. Cedar Valley had been left behind. She no longer had to worry about "what people thought". She could respond to the desire she saw in his eyes when he looked at her.

Tobe had come to find her. Now she could explore the strange and wonderful feelings he inspired in her with his hands, and lips. And she would. The next time they parted she wouldn't regret that she hadn't taken advantage of all the cowboy had to offer.

As she watched, Tobe walked into the water, long red underwear and all, purposefully striking out towards her when he had waded in to his waist. With each powerful stroke of his arms, he drew nearer. She waited for him, unmoving, the chill of her early morning dip forgotten at the thought of his lips on hers.

They met in the water. She slid off of her perch into his arms and they closed around her. Legs and arms intertwined, they kissed as the water closed over their heads. With one kick he brought them back to the surface again, and his hands found a hold on the rock behind her. They explored each other's bodies hungrily. Her hands were free and she stroked the hard muscles of his back through wool turned dark by its soaking. The thin cotton of her camisole was no barrier to his questing lips. His hot mouth replaced the water that caressed her neck and shoulders and breasts. He sputtered once and she gripped his shoulders and raised herself out of the water to her waist, holding her torso up and open to his searching lips until her bones melted and she started to sink again.

He grasped her waist and lifted her up and back until she sat on the rock behind her. His arms slipped around her hips and he buried his head in her stomach. She wrapped her legs around him as far as she could reach and ran her hands down his shoulders to his back and then to his buttocks, which clenched beneath her palms. There was an answering tightness in her belly which Tobe seemed to feel as he raised his hand to the swell of her abdomen. He raised his head to look up into her face. Catching and holding her eyes with his own, he untied the drawstring at her waist and pulled the clinging material away from her skin.

He slid one hand around to her back and palmed her buttocks, slipping one finger between the cheeks to stroke the sensitive skin there. The other hand he positioned over the dark curls at the apex of her thighs, the heel of his palm at the top of the black curls, his long fingers stretching downward, their tips just grazing the entrance to her most private place. He caught the nub of flesh between the crook of his fingers and manipulated it gently. She was open to him, her legs spread wide around his chest, but inside she felt a tightening, a pulse that echoed once, twice, and then he slid one of his fingers inside her and she nearly cried out. She bit her lip hard to stop the sound from escaping. Her fingers twined in his springy hair and she pulled his head up to hers. He gripped her tightly between his palms and she moaned, but he swallowed the sound.

She urged him upward with her hands and arms, but he didn't budge.

"Don't move," he said, through clenched teeth.

Tobe pulled her smoothly into the water with him,

guiding her hand down his chest to the slit in the front of his woolens. She pushed his hand aside as she searched for his hardened flesh and guided it through the opening. She felt his muscles spasm from his neck to his toes as she fingered the smooth cylinder of blood and sinew, and then his hands slid down from her waist to her hips to pull her body close to his. Her arms circled his neck. Her legs drifted upward around him.

"Relax," he mouthed against her lips, and she forced her hands to loosen their grip on his shoulders while Tobe stopped treading water and lay back, floating slightly beneath her. She adjusted her position so that she was above and beside him. His staff glided between her thighs and she closed her legs around it, nearly submerging them, and he smiled, pulling her close again and sinking them both. She held her breath and pushed upward against the water, he reached between them and guided his hardness into her softness. His arm went around her waist, leaving her arms free and they stroked upward as one. When they broke the surface of the lake he was inside her.

The sensation of being filled by him was incredible. She felt buoyant, but she could barely move enough to keep her head above water. Tobe was all that kept her from going under, but with his slightest kick, the smallest wave of his arm, his body moved against hers. Each time her nipples rubbed against his wool-covered chest, a soul-deep tremor went through her and she lost control.

She was drowning in pleasure and would have given herself up to it and to the lake, so long as she could continue to float in the haze of sensual pleasure Tobe had created so deftly. She didn't notice at first that Tobe had guided them into shallower waters where he, at least, could stand. Her legs were wrapped around his thighs, her arms around his shoulders, when his open mouth found hers. He moved harder, faster, and she became vaguely aware of the fact that he was no longer floating. He tried to pull away from her, to withdraw, but she just gripped him tighter. All that was important was the pool of liquid gold that glimmered deep inside her, rising behind her closed eyelids. When she opened her eyes to find Tobe, it spilled over into the lake and she rode the golden tide to its crest.

When she came to herself again, Tobe was holding her, standing chest deep in a lake that had indeed been turned to gold by the sun's rays. Reflected light danced across his solemn face as the water rippled around them, but it didn't penetrate the darkness of his eyes, turned almost black with concern. "I didn't mean to lose control that way."

His words pierced her to the heart. She pulled away abruptly. It was just like his kiss—he didn't mean it. He didn't care about her. She couldn't believe she had been so wrong. Why had she thought anything had changed? Just because he had followed her? Had he said he missed her?

"Why did you start this then?" she asked sharply.

"Because I wanted you. But I didn't mean to—" his voice trailed off.

"You didn't mean to what? Enjoy it?" She couldn't understand him. If he wanted her, why was he upset now that he'd had her? She could never regret what they had done, even now, when her heart was breaking. She was glad that she would have this memory to hold on to when he moved on. Even if he'd ruined it.

"I wanted to make love to you, but I meant to

stop earlier. I wouldn't want to . . . get you in trouble."

"What kind of trouble could you—" Suddenly, it dawned on her: he was upset because she might get pregnant. She almost laughed.

"That's all you're worried about?" He nodded. She did laugh then, but he didn't join in. "It's not the right time," she tried to reassure him, resting her head in the crook of his neck. She was so relieved. She had tried to convince herself that he didn't matter to her, that she was happy just to take what he had to give. But for that one moment when she had thought he had not meant to make love to her, she thought her heart would break.

She cared about him, despite the fact that he would not stay, did not trust her enough to tell her what he ran from, and could never fit into the life she'd planned for herself. She had given herself to him willingly, and she could never regret the outcome of the experience. It had moved her to her soul. He continued to stroke her back lightly even as he frowned.

"One of these days, you'll have to tell me what you're running from," she said. "In the meantime, it's all right, it's not the right time. I really don't think we need to worry."

He sighed, shaking his head. "That's no guarantee."

She could see that nothing she could say would enable him to forgive himself. She tried diverting him. "I'm wrinkled as a prune," Roses laughed, but he didn't join in.

Even Tobe's gloomy attitude couldn't quell her irrepressible high spirits. A tiny part of her was foolish enough to almost wish she was pregnant. When Tobe left, as he inevitably would, a baby would ward off the loneliness that had haunted her since the death of her parents. She would have a family of her own again, someone who would belong just to her.

She didn't recall when she had decided that she was never going to find the mate that was right for her, as her parents were right for each other. It had been before she had left the reservation. Since then she had met many men, but she had, when she first left the reservation, been too unsure of herself, too grief-stricken, too busy trying to eke out an existence all alone, to let her guard down and get to know them. None had been interested in her—at least not interested enough to pursue her. As she'd worked through her grief, she'd realized that most of the men she met could never live with her among the Uncompahgre Ute. Tobe had changed that. He had shown her, if she did not find love among the Ute, amazingly enough it could still happen. He had wanted her badly enough to follow her into the wilderness.

She had never thought it possible before, but maybe she could have her family and love, too.

Tobe Hunter, with his restless untamed heart, might never be hers, but he was here, now. She had to take a chance on him. She was sure it would be worth it, whatever happened.

When they had reached their campsite, they saw that Jack's kit was gone. He had disappeared back into the mountains as quietly as he had come.

"We should probably go as well," she told Tobe. "We could break camp now."

"Later," Tobe growled when her voice trailed off. "Now we can make noise." He held a hand out to her, but she danced back out of arm's reach.

"I want to get out of my wet things. Don't you?" she asked seriously.

"Yes," Tobe answered, "but not by myself."

"It would be faster," she suggested, but she had stepped back toward him already, without thinking. His wide smile was reward enough.

"But it wouldn't be nearly as much fun." His misgivings of barely half an hour past seemed to have fled. Or perhaps it was only that he was more confident of his control on land. Whatever his reason, her heart sang as he leaned over and playfully kissed the tip of her nose. "You said you wouldn't ruin my fun," he reminded her.

"So I did," she agreed.

They planned to leave the next morning. Roses didn't mention her encounter with her old friends Little Deer and Hunts Too Slow or the other braves. The men were on foot and probably laden with their precious burden of food for the tribe. There was only a slim chance that they would meet up with them on the trail. She didn't know how he would react, and she was embarrassed to admit to herself that she didn't trust his reaction. He'd never had anything positive to say about the People. Perhaps she'd changed his mind a little since he'd called them savages, but she couldn't be sure.

As they sat eating dinner, Tobe finally told her where he was headed. "There's a town, somewhere in Utah where only black folks live: the mayor, the sheriff, the postmaster, everyone."

Roses had never heard of such a thing. She was sitting next to Tobe, the dinner dishes washed and packed up. They'd decided to get an early start and had spent the evening packing up anything that was not essential for their last night in camp.

"There are a few towns like that, out here in the West," he went on. "I read about them in the newspaper back home. In California, there's a law that has permitted us to buy our own land since the fifties." His eyes were alight with excitement, thinking about the prospect of reaching his goal. His intent expression sent shivers down her spine. This was one subject Tobe didn't treat in his usual casual manner.

"I want to live where there is no 'other side of town' for my kind," Tobe said. "And where I won't have to spend the rest of my life looking over my shoulder for white men with whips, or ropes, or guns."

She couldn't argue with him. But she could try to find out why he was so frightened. "What are you running from, Tobe?" she asked quietly.

He was silent for a moment. The night was not as chill as it had been for the past week. Summer was truly on its way. They had let the fire burn down to the embers. Roses knew they would be able to keep each other warm that night.

"You don't have to tell me, if you don't want to," she said. She didn't want to force him to tell her. She didn't want anything to ruin this idyll. She leaned over to kiss him and he turned his head so his lips met hers. They lingered so for a moment, then Tobe reluctantly drew away.

"I do have to tell you, since we'll be traveling together. You may need to know. I want to . . . tell you. It's a little complicated." He sighed. "A girl was murdered. And her father thinks I did it. I guess it's not that complicated after all."

Roses could see that this was painful for him. His halting speech as he tried to find the right words told her that this was the first time he had told anyone this story. Being hunted was something that grew in a person's mind until it colored every word, action and thought; she knew that. She'd lived with the fear—the night she'd fought with Larry Jenkins, she'd waited for them to come and get her. It wasn't a feeling one ever forgot. She sat patiently, one hand on his knee.

"She was a prostitute, at a saloon in Kansas City, a southern girl. The daughter of a Colonel Travis from Georgia. I don't know why she was there, her family is very wealthy."

"Women end up in those places all of the time, for all different reasons," Roses answered. "I have seen some women, Indian, colored, and white, fall into that line of work quite quickly, while other women will starve first. It is not for us to understand. The People believe there is no dishonor in surviving, or in choosing to die."

Tobe nodded. "Carolann sure wouldn't choose to die. I only met her once, but I'm sure of that. She was a lively girl." His expression was not sad so much as reflective, as he tried to remember.

"You met her just one time? She seems to have made quite an impression on you."

Tobe's eyes focused on Roses' again and he half shrugged. "Her death made an impression on me. She was so young. I guess she was a bit of a trouble-maker, but still . . . I couldn't believe it when Jack told me she was killed." Tobe was quiet for a long time. Roses thought he wasn't going to tell her the rest, but then he started talking again. "We'd been on a cattle drive, down from Wyoming to the stock-yards in Kansas. It wasn't a long haul, but it was a tough one. The man who hired us owned a saloon in town and after he paid the men, Mr. Jones offered us one free drink there. He had the right to try and get his money back. And the place wasn't bad. To-bacca Jack, a friend of mine, he wanted to go. He didn't have much of a head for liquor, so I went, too, just to make sure he got home okay."

"Why did they think you did it?"

"Carolann had a little trouble with Jack. That's when I met her." As Roses looked at him accusingly, Tobe defended himself. "All I did was suggest he choose a different girl. She didn't mind. She thanked me."

"Oh?" Roses raised an eyebrow. "How'd she do that?"

"She said thank you." When Roses gave him a look of disbelief he admitted, "She offered more, but I told her I had already met someone else. There was this woman that I'd been talking to. Her name was Crystal." Roses kept in mind the fact that all of this happened well before she and Tobe had even met. It had nothing to do with her. But she must have looked jealous, because he added, "We just talked. It was simply nice to spend time with a woman, without having, being—intimate. Jack found a girl and I guess he passed out. Anyway, he never came back downstairs, and I finally went home. I went back the next morning but I didn't really have a chance to look for him. Crystal told me Carolann was dead, and there were some people looking for me. I cleared out. I didn't want any trouble. Later on, Jack found me at the bathhouse. He said the Madame had seen me speaking with Carolann and they were looking for me."

"Couldn't he vouch for you?"

"Maybe. But he didn't remember much about that night. When they questioned him, he hadn't even remembered talking to the girl until the woman who ran the whorehouse reminded him."

"What about Crystal?"

"Who is going to listen to a whore? I put as much distance between me and Kansas City as I could. I heard the colonel and some marshal were tracking me. They think I killed her, it's clear. They almost caught up with me in a small town west of Kansas City. I wasn't there long enough to catch its name. I rode into town, saw a flyer they had posted, heard there were two men looking for a man with my description, and lit out. But I think I lost them. Maybe when we get where we're going, I'll wire home, and see if they've heard anything back East." He lapsed into silence, his brow clear of the furrows that had marked it while he told her his story. After a moment he raised Roses' hand to his lips.

"I'm sorry," he said, looking down at their entwined fingers.

"There's no need to be." She brought his hand to her lips and gently kissed it, lingering over each knuckle. A thought struck her. "The sheriff told me there were no Wanted posters on you," she reported.

Tobe smiled. "I know. I nearly had a heart attack when he looked through them though. He just sat there at that table in front of my cell and went through, oh, must have been a hundred of them."

"He's a very methodical man," Roses smiled in sympathy.

"I thought I'd had it, then."

"You were pretty lucky," she said.

"You can say that again," he grinned wickedly. "But you still owe me one for what you put me through."

She shook her head, "I think we're square," she laughed.

"I've been waiting for that for days." He stood pulling her up with him. "For you to laugh out loud instead of holding it in."

"You are dangerous," she said against his lips.

He leaned back to look at her. "And you are beautiful." She thought he was beautiful, too. The laugh lines were still etched in his cheeks, although his eyes had grown dark and serious. His skin had the sheen of polished cherry wood in the firelight. She shivered, not because of the light breeze, but because the glow in his eyes sent a wave of desire through her.

She reached up to ruffle his shortcropped black hair with a tender hand. "You, too."

He explored every inch of her body, his hands taking the place of his eyes when the clouds hid the moon. He took his time, torturing her with searing kisses that brought newly sensitized areas to her notice in the most delicious of ways. He massaged her sore thighs, spreading them wider and wider, until nothing was hidden from his hot gaze. Her hands gripped his shoulders, but she couldn't move him. She couldn't stop saying his name, again and again, in a litany that was almost a prayer. He finished massaging the tender flesh of her inner thighs and moved his hands to the curve of her bent knees. She opened her eyes to find him looking down at the source of her desire and she unconsciously moved against his hands. He looked into her eyes and smiled, and ever so slowly lowered his head to kiss her there. Her hips bucked and she dug her nails into his back.

Only his lips and tongue moved against her, although his grip on her legs tightened in response to her frenzied movement. He held her in place easily, and his mouth stayed glued to her sex. The tender torment was so sweet it brought tears to her eyes. Her hands went to his head, whether to push him away or to pull him nearer she didn't know. Something within her pulsed, once and then again, and tremors wracked her body from head to toe.

He finally let her go, and she lay still. She wanted

to thank him, but she couldn't think of the right words. She gave him a quick smile. He kissed her forehead, her nose, and her chin and as her eyelids slid closed, he lay himself gently atop her languid body.

"I hope this doesn't mean you're too tired for more?"

"More?" Her eyes popped open. Tobe threw his head back and laughed long and loud.

Fourteen

In less than one day on the trail, Roses and Tobe
found that traveling with Jasper was going to present
some unique problems. Bella would not tolerate the
cat's presence on her back at all, no matter how
Roses tried to hide the feline. Diablo was not much
better. He wouldn't let Tobe place the kitten's basket
on his saddle horn, and he shied away from Roses
whenever she tried to hand the animal up to him.
Tobe had to climb up on his horse's back with Jasper
in his arms, a difficult maneuver that was not made
any easier by Jasper himself. All day he fussed and
fretted and tried to escape. By nightfall, Tobe was
ready to strangle him.

Roses, half amused, watched them struggle all day
long, but that evening she knew she had to do something. It would take some time to reach the Uintah
Valley, and they couldn't go on this way. She braided
strips of cloth into a leash, thinking she might be
able to let him run beside the horses. Her experiment
ended in disaster. Jasper would not obey her on a
short walk, she and Tobe were riding between twenty
and thirty miles a day.

It was Jasper himself who finally came up with the
solution. She was half in and half out of her shirt
when Jasper chose to pounce from a tree limb overhanging their makeshift "bed." He got caught up in

the folds of the shirt behind her head. After extracting the bundle of fur and claws from clothing, she realized she had overlooked the obvious solution. She rigged a sling, like one she would have used if she was carrying a human baby, and slung it around to her back like a papoose. In order to make it more acceptable to the horses, she used Bella's saddle blanket. The mare might sense that something was not right, but at least the squirming package would have her own familiar scent.

By the time Roses had finished inventing her special sling, Tobe was asleep on their bed of pine. But he awakened when she slipped under the covers next to him.

"Did I wake you?" she asked.

"No problem," Tobe said, cuddling up to her back and fitting his knees in the curve of hers. "This is the way I'd like to be awakened for the rest of my life." His hand snaked around to her front and slipped under her chemise.

"I thought you were tired." She protested without much force.

"I was, but . . ." His hand started to roam up and down her front. "Not that tired."

Her back arched, pressing her shoulders into his chest and her breast into his palm. She felt his hardness against her buttocks and reached behind her to return his caress. "My god, Tobe," she murmured. That was the last coherent thing she said all night.

They were on their way again the next morning. The trail was a blaze of spring flowers. The mountain rock was bare in places, and striations of red, white, black and grey shone through budding tree branches. Thick mountain laurel bushes and stands of white-capped candytuft blossomed in other spots. The pass wound up and through the mountains, following a path that was not always easy to follow, but its twists and turns made the steep trail much easier going. Roses explained to Tobe that the Ute, the Arapaho, the Kiowa, and other mountain tribes had been using this pass for hundreds of years, and before that the Ancient ones had traveled this same way. No one knew how old the road was. It was said it led eventually to the Great Pillar and the Great Trail to the Cave of the Winds, a mystical place given to the People by the Gods. That was the passage to another place, where their cousins lived and the white men did not go.

"Why didn't they go to this place when the white men came?" Tobe asked, sensibly enough.

"Finally they did. Many people from many different tribes went on a kind of pilgrimage to that magical place. During the wars, more than half of the people died. Those who remained were weakened by lack of food and because the barbarism of the bluecoats sapped the spirits of the Good People. But a large number made it to the Pillar." Her voice lapsed into the singsong pattern of stories she'd heard told again and again. But this was not an ancient story; those who had told it to her had lived it. She continued, "They were full of questions. What was happening and what would happen to the world? Should they pass on to the other place and never see their homes, their families, again? They stayed there for one long, hard winter, and many survived. In the spring, the People, who had come from all over the world had to make a decision. Would they go back, or would they go forward? That valley of the Great Pillar was not rich enough to sustain the lives of so many."

"Some went forward, many of the younger ones were sent by the elders. As far as I know they were never seen again. Many went back to their tribes, or what was left of them, because they wanted to see their families. They did not give up their hope for a peaceful end with the white man. Some even found the peace within themselves to try and change and live among the whites."

"Where is this place?" Tobe asked. She should have anticipated the question, but she had not. The stories that she had been telling were of a sacred place.

"I have never been there." It was all she could say. He didn't press her for a different answer, but she felt she should at least try to explain. "It is a place white men can never find. They can't see it."

"I am not a white man," Tobe chuckled.

"No, but you are not one of the People. You and your people have been too long living together with the white man. Before that, perhaps you were of the People, too. Your ancient ones are gone and you have forgotten them."

Tobe's face hardened. "We had no choice," he said. *"My* people didn't come to this country of their own free will."

"I know," she reminded him. "My parents were slaves as were their parents and their parents before them." They shared a long silence and Roses finally said, "This is a difference between us that will never be forgotten. Just as there are bonds between us that will never be severed. We are who we are, and knowing each other can only make us more, not less. We cannot lose what happened to us before we met." She reminded herself as well as him. They might not be able to live together, but she would cross that bridge when she came to it, without building more walls between them now.

"No," Tobe agreed. But Roses was thinking of Ben Smith, who, like Tobe, preferred to forget his past. Ben never spoke of his life before emancipation. Tobe never spoke of his upbringing or his mother. She didn't think he could ever be truly happy until he dealt with the demons of his past. But she couldn't let him go now. She had to take a chance on staying with him until he left her.

Maybe he would never be able to settle down. Or perhaps her home would not be the right place for Tobe to settle. But she had to take the risk. She couldn't suffer again what she had when she'd left him behind in Cedar Valley. After all that had happened between them, they were even closer than they had been then. He'd gotten under her skin. She couldn't re-erect the barriers she'd used to close him out, even if she wanted to. It wasn't worth it.

That night, as they drank Apache plume tea after their dinner, Tobe said, "This is comfortable, isn't it?"

She looked around at the campsite. They were high in the Rockies, and the trees had all but disappeared as the forest had thinned around them. During the day when they were riding, they could see views of the mountain surrounding them and the valley below. They were, she estimated, about halfway to their destination. The place they had chosen for their night's rest was covered with thin mountain grasses that clung tenaciously to the soil. Now that they had climbed so high, patches of snow and ice clung to the ground. Their bed would not be very soft. But the night sky was clear, and the fire would keep them warm.

"Yes," she nodded. "Very comfortable."

"I didn't mean this place, I meant you and me . . . together."

Roses didn't know what to say. She did feel comfortable with Tobe, in a way she never had before, with anyone. But her contentment was a fragile thing. She didn't think it was wise to talk about it. She felt superstitious. It might end tomorrow.

"I think so, too," she agreed, when he didn't say anything more.

"You gave yourself away, you know," he said, "when you said we were bound together."

"When I w-what?" she stuttered. She hadn't meant to say anything like that.

"You said there were bonds between us that would last forever." He sounded pleased. She'd have thought he would run away at the first mention of forever.

"I didn't mean to imply . . . anything." She vaguely remembered saying something along those lines, but she hadn't intended him to think she expected him to stay with her forever. She knew he'd be moving on. He had a dream to follow, too.

His grin faded and he was suddenly very serious. "You really don't know, do you?" A moment later, the solemnity was gone. "You will." His self-satisfied expression had returned.

"Okay. Whatever you say." As long as he was happy, she was content to just be with him. Whatever she had said, she knew this thing between them wouldn't last forever. Their desire for each other burned bright, now, but probably wouldn't last the summer. He was too restless, too driven to search for something she didn't understand. Like most of the men she'd known. She just wanted to be with him now. Maybe if he made it with her to the reservation, he'd like it there, and stay for a while.

The next time they parted it might hurt more, but she wouldn't again regret that she hadn't gotten as close as she could to him.

That night they fell asleep as a light snow started to fall on the mountaintop. They were snug and warm, well covered and curled together. In the early morning, before dawn, a chill breeze followed Jasper under the edge of the blankets and Roses awoke with a shiver as the wind and the cat's cold fur touched her bare skin. Tobe mumbled and, curving her arm around her waist, pulled her closer to him in his sleep. She turned her head so that her cheek brushed his and, nestled against his warmth, she drifted back to sleep.

The next day they arrived at Piñon Mesa. Tobe watched Roses grow solemn as she looked down the mountain slope. As they rode closer, Roses grew quieter and quieter. Finally, she reined Bella in at the top of a ridge.

"The bluecoats escorted the whole tribe to the reservation. Eight years ago. It feels like yesterday." She would only have been a child. "We took this same route. The border of Utah is somewhere down there." She gestured at the valley below. "We were in the rear. The trail is steep here, so we could see all the way to those at the head of the line. We thought at least the land would be ours. The treaty promised food and supplies. We had changed. Everyone wanted peace." A tear slid down her cheek. Tobe nudged Diablo with his knees and brought the horse close beside Bella, close enough to reach out and wipe the tear away with the back of his hand. Roses hunched her shoulder, catching his hand for a moment against her cheek, without taking her gaze from the valley. Her lip quivered.

He wanted to reach out and touch her again. He was afraid, though, that she was too far gone from him to take comfort from the gesture, so all he could do was sit helplessly by, waiting for her to recover herself and move on. When she turned her face toward his, her eyes shown with unshed tears, and though she tried to smile, she looked sadder than he had ever seen her.

"When the Uncompahgre crossed that border, there were no more Ute tribes in Colorado. The Uncompahgre and the White River Ute were promised land where the Great River meets another river, whites call it the Gunnison. But the farmers did not want us in Colorado at all. They place great stock in the invisible lines they draw on their maps. For them, this was their state. The Uncompahgre were moved to Uintah, south of here, and the whites kept the land. They built a town there. It is called Grand Junction."

Tobe nodded. "I've heard of it," he said.

Roses went on as though she hadn't even heard him. "The reservation land was not what was promised. The food would not have supported a population half the size. My parents were dead two years later, even though the Ute shared everything with us. We had been a part of the tribe and because we had come with them to help them, though in the end, there was nothing my parents could do to help." Roses got control of her emotions with a long, shuddering sigh. "It is done. Long ago. Though I have never forgotten this place. Perhaps now that I have seen it again, I will be able to forget it."

She sighed, shaking her head. "Let's go."

After that, Tobe was afraid to mention again Roses' admission that she, too, felt they were bound to each other. It should have been easy enough just to say it. The words hovered on the tip of his tongue, but though he wanted to, he could not bring himself to say anything. It wasn't that he was afraid she would argue with him. He knew she would argue. He was afraid she'd withdraw from him.

He didn't know when he had first realized that he loved her. Perhaps it was on the day she'd whispered his name and it floated to him across a fiery lake. Maybe it was when she'd moaned his name in the darkness of the night, as if she were praying to one of the stars shining above them. More likely it was over dinner at the Smiths' house, when her arm brushed his shoulder as she served him a second slice of the apple pie she'd baked, but, then, he hadn't known to call it love. He'd been intrigued by her, that was all he thought it was. He thought he could walk away at any time. Now that he knew the truth, he wanted to tell her, wanted desperately to hear the words on her lips, but he didn't know how to go about it. As the days passed, he was silent. In the night he tried to tell her with everything but words.

Most of the time she was so strong, so sure of herself. She didn't need him—except when he held her in his arms. Then he didn't feel separate from her; he felt they were complete together, a whole. She could not do without him, nor could he do without her, and it felt right. This love was the adventure he had been looking for his whole life, but he hadn't known it until he'd found it.

He had never been a hard man, but he had been quiet, and alone. He had even thought that he'd been happy. When he had come west, he felt like he became someone else. It was the first time he'd lived without the stigma of being a whore's son and that had changed him. Finally he'd been able to share the jokes he'd always feared to tell, afraid they would bring laughter aimed at him, rather than at the subjects he chose. When the men and women he met on his travels had responded to the new Tobe, he'd found it easy to pretend to be the man he'd always dreamed of being. A man like those his mother always seemed to be drawn to. A man something like he imagined his father must have been.

He was still a loner, still proud. But it was easier out here, in these wide open spaces, to be comfortable with strangers. They expected nothing from him, they knew nothing of him. He had no past. He was just another cowboy passing through town; a man with a horse and a gun, hard hands, and a rope that could stop two thousand pounds of beef on the hoof with a twist of the wrist.

The work he had chosen was hard, the days and nights long, and sometimes lonely, but he was accepted for exactly what he appeared to be. The disguise he had donned had become more real to him than the memory of the young man he had been when he left home to make his way in this rough frontier country. He found he attracted friends easily, and he enjoyed them. He even enjoyed the fact that they were a little bit afraid of him. It made him feel a bit like the hero of a dime store novel.

Until he met Roses. With her the facade fell away. She made him laugh, even at himself. She reminded him of the sad child he'd been, while respecting the self-sufficient man he'd become. With Roses he was able to let his guard down. He couldn't help but be honest with her. As frightening as it had been, it had given him, for the first time in his life, a sense of peace. She accepted all the different parts of him, it seemed, and so he could, too.

He knew Roses thought they would part, that she had steeled herself to go, without looking back, that she accepted it and was enjoying the time they had together. Each night they discovered new ways to pleasure each other. The connection between them seemed to him to grow stronger with the coming of each sunset, but to start to fade each morning at dawn, until by noontime, it was a thin thread which would break with the slightest pressure.

He didn't want to put any strain on her. But he had begun to think that he would be able to change her mind. Now he finally realized that if they were to stay together, he would have to go to Uintah with her, or she would have to give up her goals to go with him. And it wasn't just love and affection that she was looking for. She had a debt to pay, and she meant to repay it.

She had said long ago that she meant to go home. He just hadn't known how much it meant to her until he saw her tears. Roses was not a woman who cried easily. Her dream was as important to her as his was to him. He had dreamed for years of finding one of the all-black townships he'd read about. But in order to be together, one of them would have to give up the future they had worked toward all these years. He knew that he would be willing, but he didn't know if he would be able to do so. He was even less sure of Roses. He was sure she loved him, even if she wouldn't admit it, but he didn't know if love alone would be enough.

She said she thought it would be two more weeks before they reached her valley. Her memory of her first journey along this trail was muddled; she had been a young girl then, and on foot. She was distracted and seemed to move further away from him each day. He saw the trail more and more through her eyes. Though she rarely spoke of that first trip to Utah, she recalled it in many ways; she slipped off her shoes to hunt barefoot and silently, using snares more often than her gun. The foods she cooked were leaves and grasses gathered in the ripening forest. He saw that being torn from her home had been the same for her as leaving Africa had been for the freed slaves he had known. These were stories he had heard throughout his childhood, and while he watched her mourn the loss of her beloved mountains, he was frequently reminded of old men and women he had grown up with back home.

A week after they reached Piñon Mesa, he had begun to form his own image of the exodus she had described that day. Men, women, and children struggling to survive on the trail. He was in sympathy with the Uncompahgre and almost looked forward to meeting these people whom she loved so. He was just starting to appreciate the life she wanted to return to when four Ute braves approached one morning as they were breaking camp. They seemed to appear out of nowhere, four men, each with two long braids wrapped in furs hanging down over the fringed neckline of their shirts. They carried rifles as well as bows and arrows, and long bundles strapped to their backs. Tobe realized he hadn't heard them approach because they were shod in soft shoes that made no sound, even as they crossed the rocks. Roses did not seem at all surprised to see them, and he slowly relaxed, but Tobe didn't totally lower his guard.

Roses greeted the men in a language he didn't understand, then turned to Tobe.

"These are friends, from the Uintah Reserve. I grew up with Little Deer and Hunts Too Slow." Apparently the two younger men understood English— they nodded as he looked toward them. They didn't have as much decoration in their hair as the older men, but all four had fancy beaded bandoliers slung over their shoulders.

The older men remained impassive as she continued the introductions, "Kiowa and Graywolf came to live in the Uintah Valley after I left, but I met them last week on the trail. They were headed up into the mountains to hunt. Given the size of their parfleches, they must have been successful." She turned to watch them lay down the hide sacks she'd called parfleches. She asked them a question and nodded when they answered, before turning to Tobe to explain. "They were looking for goat, but they found mountain sheep and were able to get all the meat they needed in one day."

Tobe met the unblinking stares of the braves without flinching, and all five men sized each other up. When they began to move, the Utes moved as slowly and deliberately as Tobe did.

They treated each other carefully, despite Roses treatment of all of them as trusted friends. She was polite to the two older men, lowering her head when she spoke to them with a deference he had never seen her display to anyone in Cedar Valley. The young men she treated like family, joking with them and laughing at their teasing remarks. From the many looks and gestures that were sent his way, Tobe thought they had guessed at the carnal nature of his and Roses' relationship. Roses responded to the comments and sign language, some of it very suggestive, in an offhand manner, as though the relationship between Tobe and herself needed no explanation. The men seemed to accept that.

As they prepared to ride out of camp, the braves followed suit. Their rawhide parfleches were packed on to the mule and the party left with more than half its members on foot. Kiowa and Graywolf would not accept the use of the mare, despite Roses' repeated offers, but the Utes did not slow them down at all. They were so swift and surefooted that Tobe couldn't stop watching them. The path was steep enough to slow the horses, but nothing stopped the braves, who trotted at a ground-eating pace, without tiring, all day.

Roses and Tobe had never talked overmuch while they rode. They had concentrated on keeping to the trail. They had the evenings and nights to commune and Tobe had never felt any awkwardness at the long silences between them during the day. But with these strangers travelling with them the lack of conversation made him uncomfortable. No one else seemed to think anything was wrong so he followed Roses' lead, speaking only when he needed to stop, or to point out game.

The silence was not unwelcome, since he didn't know what, if anything, to say to the braves. He'd envied the younger two their easy discourse with Roses that morning, while the older ones looked to him quite fierce, in spite of their stoic faces. He would not have wanted to meet them alone on this trail despite their small stature, and half-starved physiques. He dwarfed all four of the men, but he would not have wanted to take on even the eldest of them by himself. They looked formidable.

The Indians kept up a fast pace without any apparent discomfort, carrying packs that he knew to be heavy because he had loaded similar bundles onto the horses and the mule. Roses told him they had risked their lives and freedom to hunt for meat for the tribe, and his admiration for the strength and determination of these men grew. If the rest of the People were anything like these men, he could see why she would be proud to be one of these Human Beings. The Ute had risked considerable danger and had sacrificed much to provide for the Uncompahgre, with no expectation of any payment or reward beyond the personal satisfaction they would feel. These men were no more savages than he was. He wondered how many of the stories he had heard of the barbarism of the race were lies.

When they decided to stop and eat at noon, none of the Indians were even breathing very heavily. He and Graywolf went to water the horses.

"You have come from the Big Water in the Land of the Rising Sun," Graywolf said.

"Yes." The statement hadn't required an answer, but Tobe was so surprised to hear the older man speak English that his response was automatic.

"I have never travelled so far. There are many dangers. I have heard that the land is very green and it is easy to grow all kinds of food there."

"Yes, there is good farming land back East," Tobe told him.

"Then why do you come here?" As Tobe met Graywolf's wary eyes, he knew the older man had a reason for asking these questions. For some reason, these men didn't completely trust him.

"I am travelling to a town I read about back home."

"Do you have people waiting for you there?"

"No. My family lives in the East, but . . . there is nothing for me to return to at home."

The Indian nodded his understanding. "There is no more land for you. Is the land good in this place that you seek?"

"It is hard, but the people are all working together to make it better."

Graywolf was astonished. "I have seen the Mexicans do this, but never the white man from the east."

"There are no white men living in the town I seek. The people are all black—like me, and Roses."

"I never heard of this." Graywolf said, shaking

his head. "I didn't know there were towns of black men. Do the black soldiers live there?"

"Some may. It is a new kind of town. I have never seen one before either."

Graywolf nodded as though he had suddenly solved the puzzle. "You will send for your family later, as the settlers who came here long ago. Are your women so weak, they cannot carry your tepees?"

"My mother is my only family."

Tobe was tempted to let Graywolf think his mother was too elderly to come west, but he couldn't bring himself to voice the lie. "My mother and I do not speak to one another."

"She is alone then."

"She is not alone," Tobe said. "She has another child, a girl." Graywolf looked at him, uncomprehending.

"I don't understand. You have a sister and a mother."

Tobe had never thought much about the sister he had never met. He had been fifteen when she was born. He always left his grandmother's house when his mother had come to visit with the little girl so he'd only seen her from a distance.

"I don't know her," Tobe said.

"No?" Graywolf was puzzled again. But, when Tobe shrugged, he didn't ask any more questions. Tobe was relieved. He could not have explained how he felt about his half sister. He had never thought to question it before.

As he rode on later that afternoon he wondered if Graywolf would ask Roses about his life back East. He sensed she was curious about his mother, but she didn't ask about her, or why he left, and he didn't want to talk about it. He didn't even want to think about Martha Hunter, though ever since he had

met Roses Jordan it had become more and more difficult to restrain his memories and the emotions they
invoked.

Roses reminded him more of his grandmother,
Virginia Grant, with her knowledge of plants and her
calm competence. But she sometimes brought to
mind the gentle loving mother he'd adored as a child.
Memories of Granny Gee were less painful. She was
the one he preferred to remember, but Tobe wasn't
sure he could explain that to Roses.

He tried to concentrate his thoughts on the vege-
tation beside the trail, which was becoming more
plentiful as they rode down into the valley. He found
that he could identify more of the trees and flowers
than he had been able to before, due to Roses' tute-
lage.

The light green plants that grew in the shade of
the taller trees made a tea that tasted a little like
ginger ale. He could distinguish between the white
birch, and the yellow now, and he saw the Mountain
Lilac, which his grandmother had called Buckbrush,
was blooming here at the lower altitude. Roses had
to let it dry and later would make cures for everything from sore throats to a swollen spleen. The
plant grew differently here, more a tree than a bush,
and the flowers were not only white, but also pink
and purple. But it was the same root his grandmother used, and he wondered if the cures she had
concocted were taught to her own grandmother by
the Indians generations before.

They decided to make camp the first night not far
from a stream. The little waterway meandered into
the thickening underbrush and he decided to wash
up before dinner in the frosty mountain stream.

When he returned to the camp, Roses was roast-
ing a rabbit he'd shot that day on a hastily con-

structed spit over the fire. She and all four of the
Indians were sitting crosslegged around the shallow
rock-rimmed pit and as Tobe approached he thought
they might be praying. But as he came closer he
heard the low murmur of a voice, he quickly discovered it was Kiowa who was speaking in the gut-
tural language he had come to recognize as the
Uncompahgre's own. He sat next to Roses in a space
that was clearly left for him.

She leaned closer and started to translate; "Kiowa
is telling the story of the last great battle in which
he fought." Her voice changed to a singsong whisper
that echoed Kiowa's rasping tones. "It was shameful,
that encounter. The Arapahoe and the Cheyenne had
returned to the reservation, after peace talks in Denver, as had been ordered by the white fathers. They
finally realized that they could not continue to stand
against the Bluecoats and all their guns. They told
stories of their battles to others, how they had won
some skirmishes, taking scalps, razing farms and
fences, killing animals and raiding along the trade
routes of the whites."

"The next day the Bluecoats retaliated with a surprise attack of their own. The tactic might have won
them some respect, as the lion respects the hawk that
swoops down to steal a tasty morsel from a fresh
kill. Except that the soldiers not only attacked without warning, but they killed and maimed women and
children.

"I was wounded in that attack. Another warrior
fell on me as he died, covering my body. I had not
the strength to push him aside. I was forced to lay
as one dead, watching the slaughter of innocents.
Since that day, I have not raised a hand against the
Bluecoats, white or black. In '88, Ouray counselled
against further fighting after the whites tried us il-

legally for killing that corrupt agent, Meeker. I stood
with him, believing Ouray's counsel to treat peacefully with the whites.

"Now our women make baskets to trade, while the
men farm. The children plead with their mothers to
sew them white men's clothes, and to tell them white
men's stories. I have not sat thus by the fire in many
moons, because I was afraid to see my words fall on
deaf ears. Chief Ouray, whom even the White Fathers
respected, is dead. Perhaps it is better that he didn't
live to see how his wife, Chipeta, is forced to live.

"I sit in silence as Old Man is pushed aside, and
Old Woman dies of starvation. I hold my tongue when
our councils talk of trading horses and furs for plows
and pipes. I know the Great Spirit, Senawahv, hears
my heart breaking. But I should have spoken sooner.
It eases my spirit." Graywolf nodded his understanding. Hunts Too Slow and Little Deer listened respect-
fully, but when he finished speaking, they turned
eagerly to Roses.

"Roses, you have been among the whites for
many moons now," said Little Deer. "What do you
think of their craziness?" Roses translated to Tobe
before she answered them in English.

"I do not think they are crazy all the time. They
need to learn."

Graywolf helped her take the rabbit from the fire
and Hunts Too Slow started to cut off strips of meat
and pass them around. Roses pulled some roasted
wild onions out of the fire at the same time. When
everyone was settled back in their places, hands and
mouth full and the Ute talking quietly among themselves, presumably discussing what Roses had told
them, Tobe asked her, "Why did you say that? You
always said they were crazy before." Roses licked
onion juice from her fingers before replying.

"I don't know. Listening to Graywolf tell that story, I suddenly remembered my father saying that the craziness must end. That we must all live together in peace. Maybe not now, but perhaps in our children's time. I thought maybe he was right. In only one generation we have seen the end of slavery, and the end of The Indian Wars."

Graywolf spoke to her in his native tongue. Roses hesitated before translating. "We are aware, whenever we are traveling and we look upon things like this mountain stream, that we as people can make it disappear if we have no regard for the growth on our land. We cannot take everything. We have to leave something for those who follow." When the warrior saw her explaining, he added something and gestured that she should translate. "Graywolf says he has nothing to offer in place of what we take tonight, since he gave his offerings in Ute Pass." The old man looked at Tobe and switched to English.

Tobe was quick to take the hint. He dug into his saddlebags and offered Graywolf his tobacco pouch. Kiowa took a pinch from the bag and threw it on the fire. Graywolf nodded approval. "We will smoke the pipe together when we return home." Tobe sensed that the small gesture had meant a lot to these men and to Roses.

Roses sighed, in satisfaction, he thought, and turned to him with a smile. They sat, all of them, in silence for a while. Finally Roses spoke. "The old ways should not be forgotten. Did you know that there was no word for "rich" in our language. When a man was rich he had many friends, when poor, he had only a few. The idea that owning things made a man rich was foreign to us, until the white man came."

"Friends are the most important," Hunts Too Slow

agreed. "But when a man wants a wife, it is not his friends who must agree, but the woman's parents. And for them, a man needs gifts."

Little Deer explained, "Hunts Too Slow is courting a woman, and her mother wants his horse. This is not a good time to talk of possessions."

"I am not rich enough for her parents," Hunts Too Slow complained. "And she will not agree until her parents agree."

"It is probably not a horse they want, but your willingness to give it for their daughter. Do you not think it may be generosity of spirit they seek?" Roses translated Graywolf's words. Hunts Too Slow shook his head.

"White men probably have this same problem." He looked at Tobe for confirmation.

Tobe smiled. "They do."

Little Deer steered the conversation back to the original topic, away from his friend's problem. "If we share this problem with the whites, then there are probably others as well. All men want the same things. Family, and friends. Everyone wants to live in peace. We must find a way."

Tobe looked around the campfire. "People can learn to live together." He turned to Roses. "Look what you have done. You have lived with the Uncompahgre. And with the whites. You're going to doctor animals for both indians and whites when you return home, aren't you?" Roses nodded. "You can teach the indians how to live and work with the whites, like your parents."

The men nodded assent. Roses didn't look convinced, but she slowly nodded as well.

He had not thought before beyond traveling to the reservation. He had not wanted to leave Roses, but he had not thought he could stay with her in Indian country. Now that he had met these men, he was actually looking forward to arriving at the Uintah Valley. The braves might seem resigned to their fate, but below their acceptance was as strong a spirit, as invincible a will, as men could have. Perhaps, when she returned home, Roses would see that whites could live in harmony with the People.

Now that he knew that he would be welcome, maybe he would stay in the Uintah Valley for a while. He had to have more time with Roses. He sensed, behind her determination to return to the Ute way of life, another purpose—something she'd never said straight out or even hinted at, but which he thought he had figured out. Roses Jordan needed to live among the Uncompahgre again, not only to repay the debt she felt she owed them, but to find out who she was, and where she belonged.

But Tobe knew she belonged with him.

Fifteen

Roses woke up in a rare state of contentment the first morning after she and Tobe were joined by the Uncompahgre. Tobe lay sleeping beside her, his arm snug around her middle. The snow that had fallen the last two nights had started to accumulate, dusting the trees above with white powder and lowering the temperature on the mountain.

She and Tobe were warm enough, the heat emanating from their bodies enough to warm their sleeping rolls, even though all they had done was lain together. She felt closer to him than she ever had before. In spite of the sorrow that had been inspired by Kiowa's stories, she was glad that Tobe had met and been accepted by this small party of Ute, it seemed to bode well for the future.

She didn't know anymore what she hoped would happen in that future. She couldn't imagine Tobias Hunter living on the reservation, even though he seemed to like their new friends well enough. Perhaps he could overcome his prejudice, but even if he did, there was still his past nipping at his heels. He was looking for a different kind of peace. She had lived with the Uncompahgre for ten years and had never become one of them. But she belonged with them, despite the differences that separated her from the tribe. Tobe was looking for some place where he could be one with the people. Roses knew there was no place like that for her. She couldn't be happy, truly happy unless she lived with the Good People. But Tobe might well be able to find it in one of these towns he searched for.

She hoped he found what he was looking for. He would leave her a different woman from the one he'd found. Knowing him had changed her. She no longer spent all of her leisure time dreaming about her life with the tribe. She couldn't see Tobe there, and it was becoming difficult for her to imagine her life without Tobe in it. He seemed to fit her, like no one else ever had. Although she tried not to hold onto him too tightly. She didn't want to scare him away. Sometimes, when she looked at him, her heart ached.

Every once in a while, she almost forgot that he was just stopping with her for a while, on his way to some place she couldn't even imagine. If he did settle in this town he was looking for in Utah, and it wasn't too far away, perhaps he would visit her. That was possible.

Tobe awakened and kissed her cheek, and she turned to face him.

"It's time to go," she said, kissing his chin. He looked around to see the Ute had already packed their gear, not that they had much to pack.

"Aw," he said disappointed, "I thought we were the first ones up."

"Not very likely," she said. "Perhaps you were indulging in some wishful thinking."

"And you weren't?" Tobe teased her. She laughed at the irony of it. He would never have guessed she'd been wishing for a lot more than a few minutes of privacy with him.

She stood and quickly pulled her outer clothing on over her camisole and knickers.

It was wonderful traveling home with Tobe and the Uncompahgre. She occasionally missed the closeness she and Tobe had shared when they were alone. But in some ways, this was the closest they had ever been. She felt herself opening up to him when he made the men laugh, just as he did with her. He still didn't understand, or couldn't see, the tragedy that she had lived through, that they were traveling back to, but he talked to her People and treated them with respect. He didn't treat the braves as savages. He didn't scorn her family, as she had been so afraid he would when she'd first known him. He was interested in their ways and curious about their thoughts, even though both were new to him.

It was on the third day that they encountered the first signs of white civilization. They had been riding steadily downward, and the trees had been thinning out. Suddenly the forest ended, and they were in an open field rimmed by grass covered foothills. Stretching across the mountain meadow was a fence that followed the contours of the land and disappeared over one of the hills. Roses looked at Tobe, and then at their companions, but the Ute did not acknowledge this symbol of the white man's presence. They just jogged along, without comment.

Roses hadn't expected to find that ranching had stretched this high into the foothills, this close to the mountains. The snow line was well behind them, but the terrain was still rocky and in some places quite steep. The land couldn't support horse ranching, it would have been covered by snow for five to six months of the year. But soon they came across an abandoned shed, and she realized the land was being used to graze sheep. Apparently this post hadn't been used in some time, probably not since the previous spring, but the track that led away from the site was wide and had been beaten down by thousands of animal hooves, including horses ridden by men.

"Sheep farming in Utah?" Tobe voiced his surprise and she nodded.

"I've heard men have been lynched over whether sheep or cattle will graze on the land." Roses said, loud enough for the People to hear. She wanted them to be prepared for what they might be walking into.

"It's happened all over," Tobe said. "I think it's always been that way. Cattle destroy the river banks, sheep the grazing land, neither side will compromise and they just keep fighting." None of the men on foot gave any acknowledgement that they had heard, and then it was too late. Over the next rise rode two men on horseback, sighting down on Roses, Tobe and the Ute braves, with their rifles.

She and her companions slowed as the armed men rode toward them. Tobe's hand went to his gun. Then he let it rest on his thigh. As the men came closer, Roses, beside him, unsheathed her rifle. She moved slowly and deliberately, keeping her hand away from the trigger. She held it up above her head, one hand on the butt, one on the barrel. The two men who were approaching lowered their own guns. Roses stopped, and the men fanned out beside her and held their ground. The white men held their guns at the ready at their sides, but they aimed them toward the ground.

"Howdy," Roses called out to them. They squinted, perhaps they were surprised to hear a woman's voice.

"Hello," one of the men said uncertainly.

"We're just passing through here on our way to the Uintah Valley," Roses explained. She thought she saw their shoulders relax. Tobe, at her side, still had his hand resting lightly on his holstered rifle.

"You going to the reservation there?" one of the men asked.

"That's right," Roses answered. "Is this your fence that we've been riding?"

"Yeah, 'tis," the other man, not much more than a boy, said. " 'Bout three miles that way." He pointed to the northeast.

"We'll get off your property then," Roses said, reining Bella to the right. "I'm sorry for any trouble we might have caused you gentlemen."

"No bother," the young one said. The other man just grunted and watched them ride off. She was sure his rifle, though lowered, was trained on them. Tobe and their Uncompahgre companions pulled along beside her, all of the men keeping the same steady pace that Roses set with Bella. Finally Tobe volunteered his opinion, "This road's gonna lead to a town."

"Eventually," Roses agreed.

"It might be smarter to go around it."

"I think you're right." She wasn't too comfortable with the idea of riding into a strange town, especially with the four men who might be in danger of arrest or worse if they were found to be off the reservation without official leave. But the fence lined both sides of the road, when they reached it.

"I don't think it's any safer to cross the fence lines," she pointed out.

"No." Tobe thought about it. "But I still think it's better to skirt any towns we see."

"I agree," Roses said.

Before they reached the first town, about forty miles down the road, the Uncompahgre had volunteered to separate from them and travel across country on their own. Roses could understand their fears. They were sitting ducks traveling down the open roadway. But she wanted to try to keep the group stay together and she talked them into agreeing to stay in one party unless it became clear it was safer to split up. She was betting on the chance that they would all fare better together, as there was sometimes greater safety in larger numbers. She'd heard of farmers and ranchers in these mountains who believed that when it came to the People it was wiser to shoot first and ask questions later.

They were able to follow a river that ran around the outskirts of the first town. Immediately on the other side were signs posted warning that all of the land was private property.

"It's gotten worse," she said to Tobe that night. "When I left the Uintah valley, unfenced range and forest had dwindled, but now there doesn't seem to be any left at all."

"The west is settled, at least this part of it is."

"All of the People are gone."

"This side of the Rockies there is some rich farmland and a lot of miners came out here during the boom."

They were camping beside the road in a stand of trees that hadn't been fenced in. The sun had just set behind the mountains when Graywolf announced, "Men coming. Five or six, on horseback." The Uncompahgre faded silently away from the fire, hiding themselves so well even Roses couldn't spot them. By the time the posse arrived, they were nowhere to be seen. Tobe and Roses each had their guns nearby but they made no move toward the firearms as the men, still on horseback, formed a semicircle between the camp and the road.

"Where are your other friends, ma'am?" A gray haired man, who seemed to be the leader asked politely.

"Who?" Roses inquired innocently.

"The Injuns." Roses recognized the voice, it was the older of the two men they met that morning.

"They went ahead," she said.

"On foot," Tobe added.

"They wanted to get home," she said, carefully keeping her voice emotionless. "We can't keep the horses on the road in the dark. We had to stop for the night."

"Why didn't you stop in town?" No one bothered to ask why they hadn't been seen coming through town.

"No money for a hotel," Tobe spoke up.

"I wasn't dressed for civilization. And we've been sleeping out under the stars so long, we've kinda gotten used to it." Roses embellished on his story.

"Those are Indian clothes, aren't they? From those Indians?" Grey Hair asked Roses.

"No. I traded for these on the Eastern slope." Roses thought the partial lie was safer than the truth. One could never tell when the epithet "Injun Lover" could presage gunfire. She wished the men would state their purpose and ride off. But it was obvious they still weren't satisfied by her explanation about the missing Indians.

"Larry says you're heading for the Ute reservation at Uintah Valley. That so?"

"We are," Tobe said. "We're visiting the agent there. We've got a message for him from back East. Then we're heading further west. Those men were our guides."

"Why'd they leave you alone, then? How you gonna find them in the morning?"

"We only needed them to guide us through the mountains. We told them we'd meet them there," Tobe improvised.

"I don't think so, boy. You're coming back to town with us."

"Why is that?" Tobe's hand moved closer to his

gun. Instantly five guns were pointed at various parts of his anatomy.

"We got a Wanted poster. Looks like you're the one they were talking about." Tobe eased his hand away from the gun, but the men were cautious. Their guns never wavered.

"Stand up, boy!"

"What's he wanted for?" Roses asked.

"Murdered a white girl in Kansas about two or three months ago." One of the men volunteered.

"What makes you think it was him?" she persisted, even as the men shifted restlessly in their saddles.

"Description fits," the man from the morning spat. "Six foot, one or two. Nigra. Cowboy. Big black horse."

"Not much of a description. That could be any one of a thousand men."

"No one asked you, girl. And, fact is, I ain't never seen no black cowboy riding alone before. Now step aside." The men were losing patience, and she didn't think they were even tempered types at the best of times. Tobe was as edgy as they were.

"He's not alone, I'm with him," Roses said.

"You're welcome to come along. In fact, we insist," Grey Hair invited.

She and Tobe stood slowly, and each of the guns rose as they did, sights never shifting from Tobe. She hesitated before stepping away from Tobe and Grey Hair glared at her. Tobe never took his eyes from the black steel muzzles bearing down on him. Roses thought she saw a hint of movement out of the corner of her eye. With an almost imperceptible shake of her head, she tried to warn him not to do anything foolish.

"We've been married over a year and neither of us has ever been to Kansas," she lied without a qualm. Tobe's brows knit in consternation, but she wasn't going to let him be taken. He kept his gaze on the men who faced him.

One moment there were six of them. Suddenly three men disappeared—pulled off of their horses' backs by unseen hands, as if blown away by the angry breath of an avenging deity. Tobe dove to the side knocking Roses to the ground beneath him as three guns went off in unison. The last three men were whisked from their saddles as silently as the first three had been. The crack of a rifle butt making contact with one man's skull echoed in the night air, and then the stillness was broken only by the chirping of crickets. The attack had been as silent as it had been swift. Tobe got to his feet first. He offered Roses a hand up and then, his gun still in his hand, he strode over to the white men's horses and examined the unconscious men lying by their hooves. The Uncompahgre held the horses' reins in their hands, but the animals were docile. The stealthy assault had not alarmed them, and they stood contentedly unaware that their riders lay motionless beside them.

Tobe and the Ute tied the men's hands behind them after Roses gave each a quick examination and pronounced, "They'll be all right. They'll have headaches when they wake up, but nothing serious. They're a hard headed lot."

They broke camp and covered their tracks behind them as they left the road and cut across the fenced in fields they had avoided all day. They took turns scouting after that, two members of their party traveling a couple of miles ahead on horseback. Roses and Tobe took turns walking with two of the men. Their stops for food, water, and rest were shorter. Roses had little opportunity to speak privately with Tobe, but she barely noticed, she was concentrating all of her energies on making it to the reservation in one piece.

It took them five more tension filled days, traveling at their new fast pace, but she was finally home.

They rode into camp in the middle of the morning. Everyone greeted them like long-lost relatives, even Tobe. The children swarmed around them and Diablo shied away. Tobe took a firmer hold on the reins, and brought the horse under control. Roses' booty was removed from the horse's saddle and the mule's pack. She unwrapped some of the meat, and candy and children's toys. The children whooped and hollered and laughed. The women smiled, welcoming her home and took treasures away for safekeeping. The men looked on enviously and finally stepped forward to swap stories about the hunt and local life with her companions.

Roses couldn't get over the faces, so different from what she'd expected. They were so very familiar and yet very much changed. Smiles Like the Moon had aged much more than seemed possible in the six years since Roses had seen her last, her big brown eyes now shaded by wrinkles, her hair graying at the temple. Little Mountain Lily was in love and inseparable from the boy she was soon to marry. Her pointy chin and long arms were elegant features now. When Roses had left she'd been a gawky child.

The provisions were unpacked as they moved toward the chief who was waiting patiently for them outside his lodge. The others stepped aside to let Grandfather greet the hunters.

"It was a good hunt," he said nodding at Graywolf and Kiowa, sparing a smile for the two younger men.

"He saw it in a vision," she translated for Tobe. Everyone smiled and Graywolf nodded, though no acknowledgement was necessary. Everyone present knew the elderly man, though frail, was as sharp as a tack. Roses watched as Tobe nodded and smiled as he, too, came under Old Man's scrutiny. Grandfather, whose stories had enthralled Roses through many a childhood evening, was now chief. His wisdom was what the Uncompahgre needed in a leader, his knowledge of battle though far behind him, would not serve them on the reservation. The Uncompahgre no longer needed a leader who was a warrior, they required a man with judgement and diplomacy.

He examined Roses carefully before he spoke to her. "You have been gone a long time, daughter," he said.

"I have been learning from the white man, his animal medicine. I think it will be of use to all of us. And perhaps I can use it to bring us closer to our white neighbors—whose animals are very important to their farms." He nodded.

"We have seen her medicine," Little Deer piped in. "She has learned much."

"What about him?" Old Man asked, pointing to the pack on Tobe's back, which held Jasper. How he had known about the cat he couldn't begin to guess, but she motioned to Tobe to turn around and she took the kitten from the strange papoose. "He was orphaned. I didn't know what else to do but bring him here." Old Man raised one eyebrow. She sensed a hint of disapproval behind his stoic expression. "I could not leave him to die."

"Death is a part of life. But he is here now, and we will decide what to do with him later," he said, turning to walk away. The People seemed to melt away, leaving only Tobe with Diablo's reins in his hand, and Roses with a frisky Jasper in hers.

"Well, where should we bring them?" Tobe asked,

one sweeping glance taking in both animals. Roses
took his hand and walked back the way they had
come. She found her friend Smiles Like the Moon
sewing outside her tepee. Her four year old daughter
took in every move as Roses and Smiles Like the
Moon embraced, and Tobe stood in the background,
waiting patiently. Roses realized suddenly that living
on the reservation, the child had probably never seen
two such dark skinned people before. Tobe soon had
charmed the little girl into smiling with winks and
nods, despite the language barrier between them.

"Old Woman has passed on," Smiles Like the
Moon told her. "It was a few years ago." When
Roses explained why she had been looking for
Grandmother, Smiles Like the Moon offered Roses
and Tobe a place in her home, which Roses accepted
for both of them.

She left Jasper with the wide eyed little girl while
she showed Tobe where all of the village's horses
were kept in common, young stallions separated
from mares only by tethers of thong tied around their
forelegs. Tobe took a quick look and started to remove Diablo's saddle. Once he had rubbed the horse
down and gotten him settled, he followed her back
to the tall canvas structure and inside.

Roses could tell by the look on Tobe's face that
he was surprised by the roomy tent. She showed him
where to stow his saddle, in the natural storage space
at the sides of the tent. To her it was cozy and comfortable. A large fire pit occupied the center of the
room, and the ceiling above it rose some twelve or
fifteen feet above it at its peak. The leather walls
were somewhat transparent and allowed light from
outside to penetrate. Roses led him outside again,
and sat beside Smiles Like the Moon, motioning for
Tobe to join her. He settled nearer to the little girl,

and played with her while Roses spoke with her old friend. Gradually, other women joined them.

At first, Roses tried to translate their words as the women spoke, but eventually Tobe suggested that she tell him later what was said. He seemed content playing with the little girl and taking in the activity of the women and men working around the village. At some point, Hunts Too Slow came and got him, and Roses watched him go, as did the other women. There had already been some questions about him, but suddenly the tone of the conversation changed.

"When will he leave?" Smiles Like the Moon asked.

"I don't know," Roses shrugged.

"Graywolf tells me he is looking for a village where everyone has skin that is dark like yours."

"Yes." Roses was surprised that Tobe had told Graywolf about his dream. "He read about it. I have never seen such a town, but among the whites they separate the people, white, black and yellow live in different places in their towns and cities, so it is not such a strange idea for them." The women were more interested in the relationship between Tobe and herself.

"He is not so ugly, but he dresses like the white man," Morning Dove commented.

"I think he is very handsome," Lily said generously, with a smile that took in the whole group. She wanted everyone to be as in love as she was.

"He is a very big man. Is all of him as large as his . . . feet?" Little Rabbit asked.

"They are like little boats," Hummingbird added.

"It is not the size that matters, but the skill," Raven Wing answered for Roses. The older woman had been married two times, and now lived with her second husband's brother. It was well known that she still hoped to have a child. She was an authority on these matters.

"Is he gentle with you?" Smiles Like the Moon asked.

"When I want him to be gentle, he is," Roses answered. Lily nodded.

"That is the most important thing in a man, he should be attentive to his lover."

Some of the women agreed, but Morning Dove said slyly, "Important in bed, but in life his ability to father children is what makes a man a real treasure." The women all agreed with that.

"My first husband and I were very disappointed when moon after moon came and still there was no sign of a child. But when he died, I mourned him for himself, for my loss of a friend, and a lover. I did not think of myself and my wish for a child," Raven Wing shocked them all by saying. "It was later, when my second husband was killed and I was still childless that I started to value that ability in a man, and to be envious of the husbands of my friends whose children were already entering adulthood. But I would not change the way of things. I miss my first love, sometimes, even today."

"Is this Tobias Hunter your first love?" Smiles Like the Moon teased Roses. Although she knew her friend was trying to divert Raven Wing from her sad memories, she was still taken aback. She hadn't been asked such a personal question in many years. She could not hide her thoughts or feelings from these women. They knew her too well. And they were very direct.

"I guess he is," she answered.

"And you will let him leave here without you, even so."

"I cannot live with him; I would miss my home

too much. I have already been away from it for too long. And I don't think he can live here. So I don't see what choice I have."

"Perhaps you are wrong. Maybe Tobe will stay with us," Lily said leaning forward eagerly. The moonstruck young girl was clearly unable to comprehend Roses' resigned attitude.

"You could make it so pleasant for him here that he would never want to leave," was Morning Dove's practical suggestion. Roses smiled and winked conspiratorially.

"That might be fun for me, too," Roses said drily.

Sixteen

Tobe had been accepted quickly by the men on the reservation, some of whom spoke English quite well. He could hardly believe that these were the same "savages" he'd been on the watch for since heading west. Roses' People had the same worries that most of the white settlers had on this frontier. They reminded him of the old men sitting around the cookstove at Lester Freedman's general store, talking about which crops would fare better in the dry soil, and how they could irrigate it. In their natural setting, living in the "old way," they had been proud warriors, but from their conversation they had always been as concerned with keeping their families safe and living according to a strict moral code of honor as they had with the glory of the hunt, or of battle.

They were forced, by being constrained to live permanently in one village, to start farming, and their conversation revolved around trying to get the hard land to yield the precious food and tools they needed to survive. Tobe did not know much about farming, especially under the conditions that they faced in this valley, but he was willing to pass along what he had heard, and the braves were eager to listen.

The farming that had been done by the People who lived in this area had been more of a harvesting of nature's fruits, and had traditionally been done by the women. The kind of planting they were learning now, as well as processes for collecting and storing wheat, corn, or any other crop were relatively new to most of the Uncompahgre Ute. Until some twenty years ago, their lives had been hunting in the mountains, trading on the plains, and traveling from winter camp to summer camp to follow their prey. Now the women's gardens were supplying the tribe with most of their food. The monies from the Indian agency could not buy enough food, and they were used to buy other supplies instead.

The hunting was sparse. Rabbit and dried fish appeared to be the main sustenance of all of the Ute living on the reservation, the White River tribe, the Uncompahgre and all the others. Their life in the mountains had been hard, but it had been the way of their fathers and grandfathers, and had been all they'd known. They didn't choose to change it, but were forced to, and Tobe thought they were remarkably resigned. It seemed to be a part of their philosophy to accept the vagaries of life with stoicism. As Roses had mentioned once, even the children cried less here.

Look as he might, Tobe could find no trace of barbarism on the reservation. The Uncompahgre had some unusual superstitions, and he'd heard some odd references to spirits, which the men seemed to feel lived in various objects, but Roses agreed, and she was as learned as anyone he'd ever met. Some of their customs and laws were quite unique, as well. Although it was customary back East for women's homes to be referred to as "theirs," Tobe had never heard of any people who actually considered the physical structures to be possessions of the women, to be passed from mother to daughter, rather than from father to son. In this village, women owned the tepees, most of the goods within them, and even more shockingly most of the horses, which were used to move the tepees from one camp to another. This tradition, while entirely new to him, was the way of their ancestors he was told. He was passed from person to person, each eager to show him the village and share their lives. They were quick to anticipate any questions and he was given a thorough tour.

Roses found him a short time before dinner and led him to a central eating area where the tribe had gathered for the evening meal. There was a celebratory dinner to honor the return of the hunters. There was music—a chanting monotone punctuated by the beat of hide drums. There was also much dancing and singing and, of course, goat meat. Every conceivable dish was cooked, soup, stew, and even a kind of pie. The various recipes were tasty, though he wasn't familiar with all of the flavoring they used, such as piñon nuts and wild onion.

The stories they told around the campfire were tales such as the one Roses had told him about the Horse Tribe, rather than accounts of battle. A favorite seemed to be about Coyote finding a baby who was a monster that bit off the hands of anyone who tried to feed him.

"And that is why babies have no teeth." The tale ended. Wide eyed children, wizened men, old before their time, and rough skinned women, relaxing after preparing and serving the bounteous meal, all smiled and nodded as the Chief concluded. The listeners' familiarity with the stories did not seem to lessen their enjoyment at all.

The hunt that had provided the evening's bounty was recounted in the Uncompahgre's own language, but Tobe understood what they were saying by their body movements. At one point the four braves who were telling the story started to gesture toward Roses, and said something that made the entire rapt audience turn toward her. Roses stood and spoke for a moment in Uncompahgre, then reseated herself beside him. Everyone was still looking from Little Deer to her and when Tobe looked curiously at her, she explained, "Little Deer was telling them about Irma." Unconsciously she relaxed against him, her body melting into his side. "I can't convince them that it was Jack that trained the bear."

Tobe got Little Deer's attention and told him, "The bear was the pet of an old man who has lived in these mountains for a very long time. He found her as a cub and trained her as he raised her."

"But you were living not only with the bear, but with a wild cat. How did you get the kitten from its mother? Beasts, like men, are fierce when it comes to their babies."

Roses' eyes glowed with suppressed laughter as she told them the story of the runt's appearance. The responsive laughter of those listening made her eyes shine all the brighter, and she turned toward Tobe as if to share her joy with him. When her eyes caught his, her voice faltered and she wet her dry lips with the tip of her tongue. His eyes followed the motion, mesmerized by the sight of her full moist lips slightly parted as she gasped. Blinking, she turned away to face her enraptured audience once again.

Tearing his gaze from her succulent lips and rose washed cheeks, Tobe took in the play of firelight over the faces of her "People," male and female, young and old, who smiled and laughed as Roses finished the story of her adoption of her rare pet. As delighted as he was to find the Indians such a welcoming lot, he couldn't wait to be alone with this woman, whose voice alone could make his blood pound in his veins. It had been too long since he had made love to her, since they had found that sweet, secret place where their souls met and merged.

The festive gathering went on for hours. News was exchanged, and plans made for the summer trip to the Bear Dance. Roses was untiring, exclaiming over the wedding of this old friend, the birth of that baby. There were good tidings and bad and she soaked everything in. Tobe imagined he could see her expanding, like a parched desert flower greedily soaking up fresh water after a long awaited rainstorm, unfurling its blossoms to the sun. Despite his eagerness to find their fur-lined bed, he couldn't drag her away.

Finally, even the hardiest young men were drooping, the fire allowed to die. Smiles Like the Moon and her rather large husband, Running Bear, had stumbled off an hour previously. Roses and Tobe strolled slowly through the quieting camp, his hand in hers as she guided him deftly past unfamiliar wooden structures.

The darkened form of tall tepees loomed up over them in the light of the half moon as they walked by. He didn't know if he could wait to kiss her. He could so easily stop and turn her into his arms. The silence was broken only by the cry of a baby and Roses' breathy whisper as she translated again for him tidbits of the evening's conversation.

"They think they may build some houses here, since the government is willing to provide most of the materials, although they would prefer adobe to wood and I think it would be safer, especially in the event of fire. The Ancient Ones lived in stone houses or sometimes in caves, huge caves that they carved into comfortable spaces. They don't need tepees if they're going to stay in one place year round. But they'll use the tepees to go to the summer gathering in Arizona."

"I thought the Indian agents were trying to stop the gathering." There had been much discussion about this subject when it had been brought up earlier.

"The Bear Dance has been held at the summer gathering for centuries, and I do not think that even the Bluecoats would stop it. I was only eleven or twelve when I last went, but I can remember what fun it was. There was singing and dancing, and foot races and horseback riding competitions. And the food! There was so much food! And storytelling, from every tribe. All the tribes gathered." She had stopped walking. Tobe thought he recognized the tent they stood in front of, it was the tepee of Smiles Like the Moon and her family. Their tent.

All things considered, making love in a tepee was the most wonderful thing Roses had ever experienced. Tobe's sighs mingled with hers as they undressed each other under their buffalo robes, then his hands found those places on her body that belonged only to him. Every nerve ending in her body came alive as his hand skimmed down her back from her shoulder to her thighs. It had been too long since he'd touched her. She wanted to take all of him in at once. She breathed in his scent as she lowered her head to his chest. She kissed the smooth warm flesh, drinking deeply the taste of him. Her fingers twined in his curly hair.

Wave after wave of spine tingling sensation ran through her. He caressed the soft skin of her thighs. She suckled his nipples as his hands kneaded her buttocks rhythmically. Her tongue played at the tips of the small buds that responded like her own by becoming rigid. He pulled away and bent down to place a tender teasing kiss on each of her swollen nipples.

She reached down between them to grasp the object of her search and urged him up, but he didn't follow. He lifted her up, with a hand under each of her arms, to lie upon him. The buffalo robe slipped down to her shoulders and he pulled it slowly back upwards, inch by inch, until they were cocooned from head to foot in the supple fur, in a warm dark cave cut off completely from the rest of the world. The only sound Roses could hear was her own heartbeat as Tobe's hands went to her waist and he held her slightly away from him. It was pitch black under their covers, but she imagined she caught the glint of his eyes as he smiled up at her. She waited, poised above him, balanced precariously on his hard body, powerless to move until he released her from the sensual spell he had cast over her.

Finally he moved, bringing his head up to hers and covering her mouth hungrily, with his lips open, tasting her. Their tongues dueled fiercely, each thrusting into sweet recesses, unmapped but familiar terrain, almost forgotten in the past few days. A shiver ran through her and he pressed his palms into the sides of her breasts, until she thought it was all that held her together, as a series of explosions started deep within. She let him mold her to him and wrapped his arms around his shoulders, hugging him close as one of his hands dipped between the juncture of her legs to the moist center of her being. He slipped just within that entrance, first a quarter inch and then a little further, and then when she would have slipped down to engulf the rest of her, he stopped her with a hand on each of her hips. Her knees came up under her as she lay suspended above

him by the strength of the two steel arms that shook
with the force of his determination.

"Don't move." He panted. "Wait."

"I can't." She breathed against his cheek, as she
brushed light kisses over his forehead, eyes and lips
in silent succor, pleading for release from the steel
grip holding her hips in place. She wanted to close
the distance between them, where their bodies were,
so loosely, joined. She wriggled and his breath
hissed out between clenched teeth.

"Don't do that," he ordered.

"Let go," she begged.

"Not yet." His voice shook. His whole body trembled.

"Please," she said. He raised his head and si-
lenced her with another soul deep kiss, and finally,
when she thought she could not bear another second
of the sweet torture, he started to lower her slowly
onto himself, down and down, until she started to
think she would not be able to fit all of him within
herself. She was full to bursting. Full of Tobe, his
flesh, his scent, his tongue, his bone and muscle and
sinew. He had insinuated himself into her deep under
her skin, and all the way to her heart.

He had bound her to him, and she could fight
him, bite, scratch and scream in silent protest against
his mouth and teeth and tongue, but she knew he
had her. As he finally released her, she grasped his
shoulders and pushed away. But she couldn't let him
go. He had won her, and gifted her with himself,
and she couldn't get enough. She strained against
him, his hands guiding her up and down, moving to
her buttocks and thighs and finally her hair, to pull
her open mouth back down to his. With each thrust
of her hips against his, she thought he came deeper
within her, claiming every inch of her body for her

own, capturing even her breath with his mouth. He brought his hand up between them and cupped her center, his palm against the sensitive button that guarded the entrance of the soft cleft. She bucked wildly atop him, wrapping her arms around his wide chest. A wave of shudders swept her from shoulders to knees as she exploded again and her heart swelled with the love she felt for this man. He, too, shook beneath her, quaking as though he would never stop as spasms wracked his body.

She lay spent, sprawled across him. She was full of wonder at the rightness of the moment, having Tobe here with all of the people she loved. He was a part of all that she loved, as he was now a part of her, and she didn't know how she was going to let him go.

One stealthy unexpected tear slipped down her cheek and Roses tried to disentangle herself from Tobe.

"Shhh." He wrapped his arm around her, stroking her back as a shiver ran through her. She tried again to roll away and he rolled with her, so the connection between their two bodies was unbroken, and he still filled her to her heart. She swallowed convulsively, but could no more disgorge the knot of unshed tears that had formed in her throat than she could force him to withdraw. Her treacherous body still wanted to wring more pleasure from him, her breasts still throbbed against his chest, the walls of her inner passage still squeezed him tight.

The release that they had fought for her had been only temporary and already her traitorous senses craved more. Her hands gripped her upper arms, her lips parted slightly as she gasped in surprise that just lying close like this could bring such delight. Her eyes closed tight against the desire that welled once again from within her. Her body ached for more, despite her exhaustion.

She wanted body, heart and mind to lie quietly in their fur-lined bed forever, but temptation lay too close at hand to resist. She turned her face into Tobe's neck and nipped his shoulder gently. He responded by starting to move slowly within her. He stroked in and out once, long and slow, then again. She felt already taut muscles stretch to accommodate him and wrapped both legs around the back of his thighs. His head went to her breast and her back arched, opening her even further to the delicious invasion. His control snapped. He molded her buttocks with big strong hands as he pounded into her faster and faster. She caught her bottom lip between her teeth to keep from crying out as she mirrored him movement for movement.

It went on forever, each sensation growing in intensity. Her fingernails dug into his shoulders. He bit her shoulder, not hard, but enough that she knew there would be a mark there in the morning. She was past caring.

"Tobe." She mouthed in his ear. As though he'd heard her, he gave her one last squeeze and ran his hands down from her hips to the backs of her knees in one long smooth caress as he moved furiously within her. He did it again. With his caress, he seemed to be trying to guide her heart out of her chest, down and out of her and into himself. He did it a third time and she would have sworn she saw sparks dancing in the air about them as he withdrew and she was left writhing beneath him as they both dissolved in pleasure.

After Tobe had fallen asleep, Roses lay awake for a long time, amazed at what he could make her feel—with his hands, his mouth, and his body. Each time they made love, she lost a bit more of herself to him. He was a cowboy, a natural enemy of the Good People. He was a drifter and a dreamer, and definitely the wrong man for her.

There was no way around it—she was in love with him. Tobias Hunter was going to break her heart when he left and there wasn't a thing she could do about it.

Seventeen

It felt strange to be back in skirts again. Roses hoped she didn't look as awkward as she felt as she and Tobe walked down the street looking for the post office. She reckoned they looked quite ordinary, Tobe walking beside her, carrying the sack containing her recent purchases from the town's general store. She had bought a small sack of cornmeal and some candies for the children.

Supplies on the reservation were as scarce as she remembered, and there wasn't much for the Ute to barter with. Their money was good only in the Indian agency store, and the inflated prices the agent charged for staples such as corn and flour made it difficult for the Ute to afford the amounts they needed. Vital foodstuffs were delivered in smaller shipments than useless goods such as tobacco or liquor. No attention was given to the needs of the people the store was supposed to serve. It was shameful. The children were barely getting enough to eat, and all she could get was candy.

Roses didn't know what she was going to do about it, though. The money she had brought with her remained largely untouched, but there just wasn't enough of it to make a difference. The Uncompahgre, like the White River Ute, needed the farm implements, seed, animals, food goods, and cloth goods necessary to sustain life. The land they had been given yielded little meat, sparse crops, and not much wood for building. But lack of water was the most critical problem. The Uncompahgre were mountain people, not like the Kiowa or the Hopi. The cloth they wore was primarily made of animal skins, not woven fibers. They had no "art" to sell to the white man; their skills were not considered by the settlers or townspeople to have any value. Their only hope was to farm, but without water, they could not even do that.

Roses hoped to get work as a trained veterinarian, but she knew it would take some time to establish herself. Not only was she Negro and female; certified animal doctors were few and far between on the frontier. Most so-called horse doctors were frauds living off the desperation of farmers, killing animals with their ridiculous potions and taking credit for cures that would have certainly occurred naturally. Roses had never planned just to hang out a shingle in town. She had thought to work her way gradually into the neighboring white community. But she hadn't known how poor the Uncompahgre were, nor how hostile the local farmers.

She and Tobe had gotten nothing but rude stares from the moment they'd ridden into town. She held her head high and turned off the wooden sidewalk into the dusty interior of the little post office, Tobe just behind her. He was acting rather strangely, very conscious of the fact that there was a Wanted poster with his name on it floating about this part of the country.

After their last encounter with white men, Roses had not wanted to bring Tobe into contact with their neighbors at all, but he had insisted that she not go alone, and the Uncompahgre were not supposed to leave the reservation. He stalked through town, returning glare for glare, and even though Roses knew he was just nervous about being recognized, she thought he was probably attracting suspicion with his surly behavior.

"Hello," she said politely to the wizened old man behind the counter. She poked Tobe in the ribs. He grunted something that could have been taken for a greeting.

"Hi," said the man, sliding from his stool to come and face them. The place was empty except for the three of them, for which Roses was grateful.

"I want to subscribe to the *Veterinary Journal*. Here is a letter to send to them." The postman examined the envelope carefully and then said,

"It'll cost you a penny." Roses pulled the coin from the pouch that hung around her neck and gave it to him, while Tobe watched the doorway, obviously jumpy at being inside the cramped little store. Apparently, he hadn't yet noticed the Wanted posters lining the walls.

"Excuse me. Can I have the magazine delivered here each month?" Roses asked. The proprietor of the establishment was stooped with age. Perhaps he had been taller as a young man, but now he was barely taller than Roses' five feet, four inches, and he was totally bald. His brown eyes were still sharp as he looked her over measuringly.

"I guess so. But you'll have to pay for it," he said. "Two bits a month." Roses gasped and Tobe spun around, his hard gaze traveling over the postman with contempt. The older man drew himself up. "That's if you want me to hold onto it. But it's a nickel if you pick it up within a day or so. I can't be cluttering up my shelves with some little—" Tobe took a step toward the counter and he gulped audibly. "Uh . . . girl's magazine."

"That's fine," Roses agreed, motioning to Tobe to back off.

"Here is five cents, on account," she said, after digging in her little purse again for coin.

"Let me take your name and address."

Tobe had finally seen the notices on the wall and he sauntered casually around the room, taking a quick look at each. Roses recognized the tension in the set of his jaw, but she relaxed as she took in his hands and arms hanging loose at his sides. To a casual observer, he would look like any other cowboy, his hat square on his head, his shoulders back, his disinterested glance at each poster just a quick scan of a face or a name. His pace was measured as he circumnavigated the room. The old man behind the counter didn't give him a second look as he found a pen and asked again, "Name and address?"

"Roses Jordan. I'm visiting friends on the reservation at Uintah. A message to the Indian agency store will reach me."

"You're staying out there? They try to keep people off the Indian land." Roses wondered what he thought the Ute were, if not people, but she replied calmly, "I was living with the Uncompahgre when they were moved to the reservation. The Agency has my name on their lists." She hoped that sounded official enough to satisfy the old man. It wasn't, strictly speaking, the truth, but she had noticed that whites put great stock in official lists and papers. Her skin color had made it easy for the bluecoats to distinguish her from the Uncompahgre when they were moved to the lands assigned them by the government, and so she hadn't been included on the rolls as a tribe member, but her parents had been listed somewhere as teachers living with the tribe. The soldiers hadn't been happy about paperwork, and they had been happy to let her parents compile the various lists and letters they were supposed to turn over to the Indian agent, and for their superiors in Washington. The lie seemed to satisfy the postal clerk. He didn't question Roses further about her address.

"What's the name of that magazine again?"

"The *Veterinary Journal*." Roses spelled it out for him.

"From back East. That's a magazine for soldiers then?"

"Not veterans. Veterinarians. It's a magazine about medical research and procedures for animal doctoring."

"Yeah?" He had clearly never heard of such a thing. "Guess they're printin' readin' material on just 'bout everything these days. They got so many o' them fashion magazines I don't know how the ladies get time to read 'em all. Why, I remember when we got everything we needed from the Sears Catalogue delivered over to the general store." Tobe came to stand behind Roses, an impatient presence at her back.

"Well, I'm a veterinarian, an animal doctor, and you know there aren't many of us out here."

"I never met one," he agreed.

"So this way I hear about things that are happening back East and even in Europe. The journal gets stories and letters about animal doctors all over the country."

"Uh-huh." She was losing his interest and she didn't want that. She wanted the little man to talk about her with the rest of the people who came in to get their mail. She knew he'd be quick to explain to the curious what she and Tobe had been doing here. She wanted to leave him with something astounding for he and his friends to chew on, something beyond two niggers living with the Indians, something that might bring in patients from the ranches and farms in the area.

"There are many people who are experimenting with cures for animal diseases."

"Did you ever hear of lung plague?" the old man asked, leaning forward. "I was raised in New Jersey, dairy country. Lung plague took our whole herd. That was, let's see, '60, 1860. That was a bad time." He shook his head.

"They've managed to almost eradicate, I mean get rid of, that disease. There is no more lung plague in New Jersey. Only in New York. It got as far west as Illinois at its worst, back in '64. But there hasn't been a case reported in two years anywhere west of Maryland. In two more years they think it will be completely wiped out. Forever," Roses was happy to report.

"You don't say?" He leaned back again, pondering her statement. "Well, I reckon it's about twenty years too late for my pa. For me, too." He chortled at his own joke. Roses gave up. It had been a lot to expect that she'd make an impression on the first man she spoke to.

"Well, I'll be back to see if the first issue arrives in a few weeks." She started to turn away.

"What did they do?" The man's question stopped her in her tracks. "To stop the plague. What did they do?" Roses smiled at Tobe and turned back to the postman.

"They had to kill the infected animals, but once they were able to figure out what caused the disease, they could tell with a simple test which animals were infected and which were not. They could weed out

the cattle that were spreading the disease and stop
them from being sent out West. And they can test
the animals that come from Europe and stop the
sales before they can spread the disease here. Children no longer die from drinking the tainted milk."

"Um-hmmm." The postman nodded. "How many
did they kill?"

"I don't know," Roses had to admit. "Thousands,"
was her guess. "But they stopped the plague, and
that's why you never see it out here."

"I guess not." The old man nodded, still not entirely convinced.

"And the Bureau of Animal Industry paid the
farmers for the cattle they had to kill."

"The hell they did!" The little man was astonished. He ran his gnarled hand over his smooth head.
"The government paid to kill them?"

"Yes," Roses told him. "It could damage the cattle industry to have the disease spread all over the
country. They knew it had to be stopped. So they
stopped it."

"I never heard of that!" All his doubts were forgotten as he marveled at the unprecedented news.

"And you learned about this from this *Vetera* . . .
what magazine?"

"I've read about the latest developments. Much of
the history I studied in books, the *American Veterinary
Review* and other publications. They're very helpful
tools in my business. They're working on Texas fever
and I believe they've got a cure for that now."

"Texas fever? That's killing ranchers out this side
of the Rockies."

"Yes, it is. But they're going to try to stop that."

"Well, whaddya know? There's some good things
about livin' in these modern times, I suppose."

Roses laughed. "I think so," she agreed. With a

wave, she turned to leave for the second time. A quick backward glance revealed the little man was rubbing his palm over his bald head as he reflected, presumably on their discussion.

Roses could have danced all the way home. She didn't kid herself that she'd broken through any real boundaries yet. After all, the man was probably not particularly influential. But he would see most of the townspeople and the farmers in the town's post office, and he would certainly speak of her.

"That's one man who thinks I might know what I'm talking about."

As it turned out, she'd convinced the right man. While she and Tobe were retrieving their horses from the hitching post outside of the general store, a round little man in a dusty black suit came rolling toward them. Tobe tensed.

"Excuse m-me." He puffed. "Miss?" He skidded to a stop a few feet away and doffed his strange-looking hat. The stranger's coat and pants were rumpled but clearly elegant, nothing that she would have expected to see in this tiny little town. A plaid vest covered his rotund stomach. "Miss, are you the veterinarian Conroy Hollis just spoke with?" He had a British accent.

"If Mr. Hollis is the man who is working in the post office, then I am," she answered.

"My name is Quentin Smythe III. And I have a job for you, miss."

Tobe raised an eyebrow at her, comically impressed by the strange gentleman.

"You do?" Roses held back a smile, looking away from Tobe's smirk.

"You see, Eugenia—that's my puppy, Eugenia—

seems to be having some difficulty giving birth. She's been trying for days and we just don't know what to do." Roses smile was quickly stifled as she looked into the man's watery eyes.

"We desperately need a veterinarian, but that is one of the many amenities that these small towns never seem to offer. I should have thought of it before, but I never expected . . . well, you know, since she's a purebred English bulldog, I didn't *plan* to breed her. I didn't know that the cook was just letting her out unattended to do her business by herself. In the *yard*. Could you come quickly? I'm afraid it may soon be too late." He jiggled nervously as he turned, looking over his shoulder to see that they followed. Roses threw Bella's reins back around the hitching post and followed. For such a heavy man, Quentin Smythe III could move quite rapidly. She nearly had to jog to keep up with him, and Tobe's stride lengthened to full stretch beside her. They exchanged amused glances as Eugenia's master continued his breathy monologue over his shoulder as he walked.

"I brought Eugenia with me when I came to America. She was all I had of home, you see, and I thought since she is a bulldog she might come in handy when I came west to the ranch I had purchased. Of course, once I saw how roughly my men handled their animals, I knew that she wouldn't fit in with the mongrels they use for cattle herding out here. So she's been a house dog, and it just never occurred to me that she would end up in this condition. When she did, I was devastated, of course, because she's a purebred and I don't even know which of the town's dogs is the sire, but even so, I thought, 'Well, my little Eugenia would have a family anyway, and why not?' . . . but I forgot about all the difficulty bulldogs have delivering babies, since it had been years since I'd witnessed it. Not since I was a boy in my father's stables, where Jose handled everything beautifully, as he was from Spain where they use these dogs quite often with their bulls. But now." He was wheezing as he turned to open the door of the last building on the town's main street. Over his shoulder Roses read "Quentin Smythe III, Barrister," but their host led them through the office without stopping and into the back, still talking. "I don't remember what Jose used to do, and no one in town ever saw a bulldog before, so they don't know what to do . . . Eugenia, darling, I'm here, and I've brought help for you." This last was said as he showed them into his bedroom, where the dog lay in a large basket at the end of his bed.

Roses went down on her knees beside the poor bloated animal. Eugenia was the strangest looking dog. Her nose was squashed back in her round face; her head, neck and body were wider around than even a large German shepherd's, her ears and tail could only be called stubby; and her legs did not look like they would support her weight. A quick examination assured Roses that most of the roundness was bone and muscle, except the belly, which was swollen to the size of a watermelon. The animal's breathing was tortured and she grunted and labored with all her remaining might, but she was clearly exhausted.

"How long has she been like this?"

"She started nesting a couple of days ago, but she went down yesterday and I haven't been able to get her on her feet since." Roses looked from his tear-filled eyes, to the wet eyes of the barrel-shaped dog, and she would have laughed at the eerie similarities if they both hadn't been in such obvious distress.

The bitch would not be able to whelp naturally. Despite the pain Roses must have caused with her probing, Eugenia didn't move convincing her that the animal was near the end of her rope.

"I'll have to do a caesarian delivery," Roses decided.

"What's that?" Quentin asked alarmed.

"I don't have a lot of time to explain," Roses said. "I'll have to surgically remove the puppies, and then we'll try to sew the mother closed again. Tobe, hand me my sack." Roses always packed a few of her medical supplies, a trick she'd learned from the medicine man when she'd been growing up among the constantly moving Uncompahgre.

"We want to keep the chance of infection down. Can you tell Tobe where to get some alcohol and some clean sheets?"

The roly-poly man sprang into action. "The alcohol's in the sideboard in the livingroom down the hall to your left." He opened a trunk by the wall. "These sheets are clean," he said handing some to her. "I'll start warming water."

Tobe returned with a bottle of whiskey and Roses sterilized her instruments and the area on the dog's belly where she would be using them. She poured ether on one of the rags Quentin had brought back into the room with him.

"It might be better if you waited outside," Roses suggested.

An hour later the operation was finished. Somehow two of the pups had managed to survive, and despite their mongrel blood they were adorable. The tiny little fluffballs squirmed and slept, waking and dropping off again every few minutes after their exhausting experience. Eugenia slept on, her breathing shallow. She was still bleeding a bit but the worst of the operation's effects was hidden by the bandages.

"Mr. Smythe?" Roses called. "Sir?" A round face appeared around the door. "You can come in now."

He tiptoed clumsily to the nest Roses had made, of an old blanket lined with a clean sheet, where the pups and their mother slept peacefully. Tobe had wrapped up the stillborn babies and taken them outside. Roses assumed he was burying them. She had taken the soiled sheets and rags and piled them as neatly as she could in the now empty kettle that had held her water. She started to rise, but Quentin Smythe stopped her with a hand on her arm.

"You've done a wonderful job here, Miss."

"Roses Jordan," she supplied her name. He shook her hand with great energy.

"I never met a female veterinarian before, but I shall be sure to tell everyone what a miracle you wrought here today."

Quentin brought them to a room on the other side of the house. A comfortable couch and a few chairs made up the furnishings, but there were books everywhere. After lighting a lamp that stood on the mantel, he directed Roses' eyes toward the painting that hung above it.

It was big; it filled most of the wall. The picture portrayed was of a dusty, lively scene. Colorfully dressed men stood in the background against the fence of a walled corral, while cattle and dogs milled around in front of them. To one side a bulldog hung from a ring through the nose of a fierce black bull many times its size. The painting had a lifelike quality that she'd never seen before. It caught the heat and dust the energy held in check of men, dogs, and cattle.

Roses was impressed and looked at Mr. Quentin Smythe III with a new respect. He had an eye for the unusual, it was clear, but he also had an appreciation for the beauty of life.

It took Roses and Tobe a good half hour to extricate themselves from his voluble company and by the time they were finally on the road out of town, Roses knew more about the breed than she knew about all the other types of dogs put together. Quentin, as their new friend insisted he be called, had even offered to lend her a book on the subject.

Roses was still marveling at her good fortune in having met Quentin Smythe III, a man who actually knew what a veterinarian was, when a cloud of dust on the road ahead got Tobe's attention. It turned out to be a bullwhacker's wagon, the five yokes of oxen a familiar sight in mountain towns like Denver, but strange to see on this straight flat road. The feet of the oxen stirred up the dust of the road so badly that Roses and Tobe rode off the road to get out of it.

"That's got to be worse than riding the drag," he commented.

"What's riding the drag?" she asked.

"Rear of the herd. I was a drag rider on the last part of the drive into Kansas City." Tobe flashed a smile at her. "Sure don't miss it. Dust in your face all day long." He shook his head.

"Did you liked cow punching?" she pressed him. Something in the tone of his voice made her suddenly curious about his trip west. He never really spoke of his past. Except for the occasional mention of his grandmother, and the one time they'd talked about his mother, it was almost as if he'd just appeared out of nowhere. Their shared experiences since meeting, in Cedar Valley and on the road, could have been the sum of his existence. Except, she corrected herself, she knew that he had taken the trouble to bring her home when she was hurt, made friends easily, knew how to deliver a baby, and had not only adjusted to life in Cedar Valley, but also managed to live with the Ute. "I did like it, learned a lot. Those men were a different breed. The way they talked, well . . ." He smiled to himself. "They cussed enough to peel the hide off a gila monster. They have a reputation for being hard men. Quiet. Loners. But not all of the men I met were like that. Some of 'em were poets, I swear." He lapsed into a soft drawl that slid off his tongue like melted honey. "And some of them could sing. Really sing. They sang to the cattle at night. There was this one boy, Billy Heart, and when he sang, we all just stopped and listened. It was so pretty."

"Do you sing?" she asked.

He shrugged, embarrassed. "I guess I can if I have to, but nothing special."

"Why do they sing to the wohan?" Roses asked, using the People's word for cattle.

"The cows get jumpy at night. Any sudden move can get them started up. If you're riding the herd, you sing or whistle so they know it's a man coming, not a coyote or a wolf."

"Would you like to go back to it? If you could?" Roses asked.

"It's a hard way to make a living, but I might at that. You don't have to answer to anyone. I liked that. But there were a lot of things I missed out on the range."

"Women?" Roses teased.

"There are always women," he shot back at her. "That's the one constant in every town, east or west. No, I meant growing up back East, in the city, there were always people. Always new things to do, and I missed that. Kansas City was exciting, and when we rode in I realized I had missed the saloons and

the people." He was quiet for a moment, but Roses
didn't think he'd finished. After he thought about it
for a second he added, "I grew up in the city, there
was always something exciting going on. Out here,
I find our people few and far between. When I left
home, I was looking for a place like the one where
I grew up, without the white bosses. Traveling out
here made me want that even more. Ben and Sarah
have a nice life, but look what happened with that
Meeker fella. One or two words and half the town
was willing to turn against you and them. I want to
live somewhere where things like that never happen.
I believe that I may find that in Utah, or maybe in
California."

He was still a loner, still just passing through on
his way to somewhere, or something, else, and she
was already close to having him take a piece of her
with him when he left. She couldn't give more, nor
could she ask it.

There was a burning behind her eyes that Roses
put down to the dusty road they travelled.

She summoned up a smile. "So, cowboy, you're
gonna own a house in town someday?" She'd meant
it as a joke, but she could tell right away she'd hit
a nerve. A muscle tensed in Tobe's jaw even as he
answered confidently.

"Maybe." He'd shut her out again. But they were
near home now, and nightfall was only a few hours
away. She'd have him again soon, when his arms
came around her in the darkness, and his soul
opened to her. She urged Bella into a canter, and
Tobe spurred Diablo to match the mare's gait.

Eighteen

The wooden stick made contact with the ball with a resounding "Thwock!" that rang across the field. Tobe punched the air triumphantly. His team yelled in appreciation of the goal he'd scored. Roses laughed at his antics as he ran back to the center of the field with his teammates. The only man playing shinny, he was a full head taller than the women who took their positions beside and opposite him, but he was not self-conscious.

He was getting the hang of the game. His early attempts to compete with the skilled female players had brought laughter and jeers from the opposing team, who'd only agreed to let him make up the other side after "testing" him by giving him a full run down the field alone with his stick and the ball. He had missed the ball as often as not. He counted on the power behind each stroke rather than concentrating on aiming carefully to propel the ball to the goal. The woman guarding the end of the field had easily managed to steal it from him in one brief foray and try as he might he couldn't begin to outmaneuver her quick feet or deft hands. But he was getting his own back, now. His team had rallied behind him, and their talent made up for his inexperience, while his speed and strength became an asset to them.

The game of shinny was a woman's game, but Tobe had watched them play all morning and when Roses was accidentally injured by a high flying stick, he'd asked to be allowed to take her place. He didn't seem to feel any embarrassment at being outplayed by women, and he refused to be manipulated, even by the catcalls of the few men who had gathered to watch the game.

"He' is light on his feet for such a big man." Hunts Too Slow came up behind Roses. "I noticed it on the trail as well."

"Not so light on his feet as they are." She gestured at the two women who were running toward Tobe, artfully passing the ball back and forth between them and forcing Tobe back. They made a move to pass by him, but his feet got in the way and he kicked the ball, almost falling over it, but catching himself at the last minute, to see one of his opponents recover control of the ball and send it flying across the field to a waiting teammate.

The final goal of the game was scored, Tobe's team had lost, but not by an embarrassing margin. The women congratulated him and he left the field at a jog to throw himself down in the grass beside Roses. Hunts Too Slow grinned at him.

"Now you see why shinny is a woman's game," the younger man said. "They will always win, and without kicking the ball." Tobe laughed.

"It's trickier than it looks, but I think I could learn," Tobe agreed without heat. Hunts Too Slow shrugged and moved away, leaving Roses and Tobe alone in the sweet-smelling grass.

The sun beat down on the two of them. There was a dull throbbing in Roses' leg where she'd been hit by an overly zealous teammate a short while earlier. But the pain faded as she soaked in the sight and smell of Tobe.

He'd once again shown her that he was a man with many faces. She'd seen more of them, she was sure, than most people, and she loved them all; the easy going cowboy as false and yet solid as a store front facade; the funloving tease, who could make her laugh even when she didn't want to; the skilled and intent lover, whose hands and mouth alone could bring her to the peak of ecstasy; even the fierce savage, whom she knew would protect her as he would himself, with his life if need be. She didn't ask any more than that. She didn't need any more.

Roses knew there was a part of Tobe that he kept from her, just as there was a place within herself that she couldn't open to him. He would leave, eventually, and she'd stay here, and they would never know what lurked in those dark places inside each other. He never spoke of his mother, and she knew that had something to do with why he was here. Maybe he would tell her before he left. If not, it didn't matter, she cared for him, dark places and all. She knew how it felt to have something so painful inside.

She had told him a little about her parents, and how she had felt about them. Now that he was here, he could see that she was different from the tribe not quite one with the Uncompahgre, no matter how much she felt herself to be at home here. Her parents had known that. *She* had known that since the day the Bluecoats saved her from the savages. When he sensed her sadness, he soothed her with his touch.

He was breathing heavily. His open shirt displayed his dark muscular chest rising and falling rapidly. The tops of his long underwear were unbuttoned to the waist, and the curly black fuzz on his chest was damp. Perspiration had made the short hair at the back of his neck, and at his temples, shinier and softer-looking than ever. Roses itched to touch. Her hands curled into fists at her sides as she restrained the urge. She lowered her eyes but was caught by the sight of his slick, wet throat and the glistening nutbrown skin in the dip below where his pulse raced from the physical exertion of the tournament he'd just played in. She could almost taste him, he looked so delicious. He lay back on the ground beside her, one hand on his stomach, the other splayed in the grass next to her knee.

The field that had been the site of the shinny game was at the western edge of the encampment, between the village and a small trickle of water that the Uncompahgre called the River, only half in jest, as it was the village's only source of fresh water. Men and women walked by on their way to and from the stream, children ran around them, following their parents or lugging water and playing games. Roses knew she should get back to work. There were a hundred chores she could have been taking care of, but she bathed instead in the warmth of the sun. Tobe's hand slid under her knee.

"Does it still hurt?" He asked.

"Not really. Then, when he started to administer a gentle massage, she reminded him, "She hit me in the shin."

"Oh?" Tobe said, his eyes still closed. Instead of sliding down to the afflicted area, his fingers moved upward. Roses bent her knee, casually propping her leg up a few inches to allow him access to her thigh. Tobe smiled slowly. To anyone who glanced at them, he would have looked like he was asleep. Roses tried to imitate his relaxed stance, leaning back on her straight arms and turning her face to the sun, but a delicious tension was growing in her, radiating outward from the spot where his soft caress was sending tides of pure sensation right down to her toes.

He scraped a fingernail lightly across the sweat soaked material of her leggings an inch below her buttocks and she shivered. Tobe was no longer smiling. His bottom lip was caught between his teeth as he moved his hand up to the crease between her backside and her slim thighs. She pictured his calloused fingertips as they roamed over her curves and then slipped between her thighs.

She was tempted to move away then, unsure of whether she could control her reaction to his touch. His hand slid over the deerskin covering her most intimate secrets and the thought flew. Her eyes slitted open. The crickets still sang in the grass; a group of children ran by, silently intent on some mysterious childhood game; one of the women who had recently played with Tobe on the shinny field strode by on her way back to the village, plaiting her wet hair. All passed by, seemingly oblivious to Tobe's probing exploration beneath her knee-length dress.

A moment later she couldn't have stopped him if she'd wanted to. She could barely control the urge to move against Tobe's hand. She would have thought the fear of discovery would dampen her enjoyment of this sensuous delight, but it only added a frisson of excitement to the pleasure she felt. Then she could not move. Her body was suffused with pleasure. She tasted the salty liquid on her upper lip and knew the sheen that covered Tobe's face and chest was mirrored on her own.

The pressure abated and she opened her eyes and looked at him. The knowing glint in his eye made her blush.

"How is your leg now?" he asked.

"I don't feel it at all," she answered truthfully.

"That's good," Tobe said. He let out a deep, slow sigh and Roses' stomach turned over, jostling her heart. She felt renewed, the heat no longer sapping her strength. Her senses were alive, drinking in every detail of the man lying by her, the rise and fall of his chest, so much deeper than her own, the breath rising from his ruddy lips, his lashes, too long and beautiful for a man, black bows against his rosy cheekbones. She looked again. His burnished chest had gained a reddish glow.

"Tobe?"

"Umm-hmm?" His somnolent voice would have fooled her into believing he was on the verge of sleep if he hadn't been so utterly still. Tobe wasn't a quiet sleeper, as Roses well knew.

"I think you'd better get out of the sun."

"Really?" He made no move to rise.

"You're beginning to blush."

"I'm what?" Raising a hand to shade his face from the sun, he opened his eyes.

"You're turning red." He propped himself up on his elbows and took a look at her.

"You don't seem to be suffering."

"I'm used to this altitude, and more. A month or so ago you were out on the plains. You should find some shade, maybe go inside. Come on." She stood and held out a hand to him. "If you want to nap, come back to my tepee."

He quirked an eyebrow at her. "Are you, by any chance, trying to get me alone?"

She wriggled her eyebrows at him suggestively, a gesture she had learned from him. "You never know." He stood up with alacrity.

"I do believe I'm going to enjoy this."

She backed away. "I didn't promise anything."

She had no intention of joining him in bed in the middle of the day. They were no longer alone on a mountaintop.

"How about a nice bath instead?" she suggested.

"That sounds like fun, too," Tobe said, closing the distance between them with two quick steps, reaching out to put an arm around her shoulders when she would have retreated. He turned her toward the water.

"I have things to do in the village."

"They can wait," he answered. He steered her upriver, toward the bathing pool that had been dammed off.

"I should get back."

He pulled her on. Though she held back, the pressure on her arm was inexorable.

"Wouldn't it feel nice to get out of these clothes, to wash in cool, clear water?"

Roses knew those honeyed tones. "Of course, but . . ."

"But what? There's no one waiting for us. Smiles Like the Moon might even appreciate a little time alone with Running Bear, on such a sweaty day." He rubbed a hand over his chest, and it came away wet. Her hands ached to follow the path blazed moments ago by his palm. But it was foolhardy to let him take her to the bathing pond. Anyone could see them there.

When they reached the spot, Tobe reached out to the drawstring at the neck of her dress.

"Wait, Tobe," she protested, trying to catch his hand.

"You already tried that. I thought I made it clear, I don't take IOUs. I'll take what's coming to me now, thank you."

"All right, but not here. Come with me." Roses

led him further upstream. There was a dip in the
terrain right above the bathing pool, which was why
the Ute had chosen this place to build a dam. He
followed her over the river and down the other side,
then across the water to a stand of waist high mead-
owsweet bushes among the violets.

She turned to him. Leaning forward, she licked
the salty moisture from the column of his throat.

He ran his hands down her arms and returned the
favor, planting a kiss just above the collar of her
dress. She held his hands, dropping her forehead
against his breast. The gleaming skin that had
taunted her was within her grasp. She breathed in
the smell of him, musky male, green grass, and
dusty sunlight, as her lips skimmed lightly over the
hollow at the top of his ribcage.

"You're all sweat and dust," she murmured. "I
could eat you up."

"I'm all yours," he answered, his voice rising
from somewhere deep inside his throat. Brief
glimpses of his brown skin had beckoned her since
the sun had first seared the enticing landscape. Her
fingers tripped lightly up his arms and across his
wide back. His hands went to her hips, as he captured her lips with his own. She kissed him, and
gently pulled away, to apply herself to the golden
brown planes and ridges of his torso.

He swayed toward her, then away, her fingertips
caressing his body while she peeled away his
longjohns and his Levis with impatient hands.

Nude, he was a bronzed statue, all rock-hard muscle covered with silky skin. He stood before her un-
flinching as she took in the sight of him. Like a
statue, he didn't move as she palmed the sides of
his waist and ran her hands up over his chest and
down over his flat stomach and lower. His breath

hissed out between his teeth as she took him in her hand and discovered the length and power of him, rigid and yet satiny in her palm. She ran her hand lightly up and down his length, and he grasped her wrists, but he didn't try to stop her. Rather he lifted her hands one at a time to his lips and kissed the heel of each in turn, then he let her go.

Roses made herself free with the body he offered her. It was, indeed, hers, as precious and as necessary to her as the earth under her feet, the sky above her head, and the air she breathed. She wanted to run her fingers over every inch of him. She circled him, kissing his shoulder blades, which gleamed darkly. She stroked from the small of his back down to his knees and back again, then left them resting lightly on the swell of his buttocks, one knuckle just slipping into the crease as she rained feather-light kisses across the broad expanse of his tawny back. Here there was no downy black fleece to wrap around her questing fingertips. A fine stream of perspiration gave his skin the patina of burnished mahogany.

She circled around to stand in front of him again, and slowly lifted the hem of her dress over her head. Then she shimmied out of her leggings. His eyes closed and he gulped, but in a moment he was watching her intently, caressing her with hungry heavy lidded eyes as she stepped from the leggings pooled at her feet and walked proudly toward him. A shout from over the rise behind her made her jump. She had forgotten they were so near the village. Tobe pulled her down with him onto her knees so they were better hidden by the scrub bush. She laid her hand against his chest and pushed him back with a steady gentle pressure until he lay stretched out before her. She lowered her head to continue the exploration she'd begun, catching a tiny fold of flesh above his ribcage in her teeth and tugging gently. His hands went to her face, but she caught them and laid them by his side as she worked her way down over his belly, hands and lips busily touching, stroking, tasting, devouring every inch of him.

He was rigidly erect. As she finally took him in her mouth, his body arched violently. She circled the base of his shaft with tender fingers and worked the flesh gently to the tip, where she laved him with tongue and lips. One large hand clamped on her shoulder as he writhed beneath her, but Roses barely felt it, so intent was she on the satiny skin she was massaging. He panted and began to move, his hips pressing forward in a rhythm as natural to her now as her own breathing.

"Wait," he gasped. She closed her lips even further over him and tiny spasms wracked his frame.

Tobe pulled her up effortlessly, sliding her over the length of his body and plunging his tongue deep in her questing mouth. She bent into him as he buried himself deep within her. They tore at each other mindlessly, savagely grinding hip to hip. He rolled them over so that he lay atop her, stroking ever more deeply into her. She moved beneath him, welcoming his urgent thrusts, wrapping her legs around him. They exploded against each other together.

When they returned to the village, they found three horses adorned with white men's saddles patiently standing in front of "their" tepee. Tobe put a restraining hand on Roses' arm as she called out, "Hallo?"

When there was no response, he ducked cautiously below the entrance flap, returning in a moment with his holster in one hand and his pistol in the other. They turned and surveyed the peaceful scene around them.

Children worked at their chores in the shadows between the conical tents. Jasper slept in a pool of sunlight near the stake where he'd been tethered. The dogs did not bark in warning as they did at the approach of danger. The only indication of anything amiss, besides the strange horses themselves, was the lack of greeting from the women who usually bustled in and out doing countless tasks of household importance at their homes at every hour of the day. There were only one or two old women in sight—but the rest could have been anywhere. After the shinny game, in which most of the women had participated, they could have gone together to the sweat lodge to unwind.

Pushing her behind him, Tobe proceeded cautiously down the path toward the center of the village, stepping gingerly on the hard packed earth, his footsteps silent. As they came close to the open area in front of the chief's house he slowed to peer around the last tent. There three white men stood, talking to two of the tribe's elders. The exchange looked perfectly normal. If it hadn't been for the fact that they had never seen a white man set foot on the land in these last weeks, they would have thought this kind of visit occurred every day. The elders spoke to the men in unexcited tones, and the whites stood calmly, hands at their sides. Occasionally, they, too, looked around, but they didn't seem nervous at all. Roses knew Tobe was thinking that they had come to arrest him, but she didn't think that was the case. If these three men were here to apprehend a murderer, they were the most stolid, unexcitable posse she had ever seen assembled.

"I'm going to see what they want," she said, trying to move around him.

"Wait!" His voice was panicky and she reached up to place a quick kiss on his cheek.

"Don't worry. The elders would have left a message at home if there was any reason for us to stay away." She walked toward the men, who turned to meet her.

"Then I'll go see what they want," he said, striding forward. She followed. When he reached the men, they turned to her.

"Roses Jordan?" When she nodded, one of the men stepped forward and removed his hat.

"Quentin told us you might be able to help us. He said you're a real veterinarian, from back East." He sounded doubtful.

"I have a letter of reference which you can read, from Dr. Ian Millhouse. He is a graduate of Cornell Veterinary School." The man nodded.

"I got a problem with one of my cows. They were quarantined before they crossed the state line, but one of the cows sounds like she has water in her lungs. I separated her from the rest but . . . I'm just hoping I won't lose the whole herd. Is there any way you can tell if they all have to be put down?"

"How long has she had difficulty breathing?" Roses questioned him.

"It just started this morning far as I can tell."

"I'll get my bag."

She went back to the tepee to get her medical supplies. "I'm going with you," he said.

"It's not necessary," she assured him. But her words fell on deaf ears.

* * *

When they reached the ranch, Quentin Smythe III was there.

"Hello, Mr. Jordan. Hello, Mrs. Jordan." He greeted them, shaking hands with Tobe. Roses darted a glance at the tall dark man at her side and found in his eyes the same dawning realization that had come to her. These men thought they were a married couple, travelling west like so many others. They probably hadn't even checked the wanted posters for Tobe Hunter. And they wouldn't associate Tobe Hunter, killer, with the nameless coffee colored cowboy and his unusual wife, even if they read the description.

"Hello, Quentin." She replied. Tobe just nodded.

"These men have a serious problem." Quentin started to say, "This is Lenny Fulsom, who owns this ranch, and these are some of his neighbors. If we've got a problem here, it could affect every ranch in the area, including mine. I told them you were the one to call." Roses jumped in as he took a breath,

"Gentlemen, this will take some time. I assume you all have other work you need to tend to." None of the men responded, so Roses tried a more direct approach. "Why don't you all go on, now, I'm sure Mr. Fulsom will pass along any pertinent information." As she put on her heavy apron, she looked around at the solemn faces of the group of men, hardened by a profession that required a tough hide and an even tougher disposition. She shooed them away like a flock of wayward chickens, waving her arms, "Go on, now. I won't know anything for certain for an hour or so." Fulsom finally joined her in her efforts.

"Go on to the cookhouse, and grab a bite of something from Tilly. She's the best cook in three counties, as you boys know." As his audience shuffled reluctantly toward the house, he called after them, "And no trying to steal her away now, you hear." Only Tobe, Quentin and Lenny Fulsom remained behind and she needed all three of them to help her draw the cow's blood and set up a makeshift laboratory in one corner of Fulsom's huge barn.

The last piece of her equipment to be unpacked was her precious microscope, which she unwrapped carefully, making a neat pile from the many layers of soft swaddling. She screwed each delicate metal section together as lovingly and as carefully as a gunslinger assembling a shooting piece with a hair trigger. When the polished apparatus sat shining on the table she released her pent breath in a sigh which was echoed by all three men, who had been spellbound by the procedure.

She prepared the slides, and leaned forward to look through the eyepiece, and felt the men lean closer as though they too could see the hidden world revealed by this unique invention. She held her breath, as they did, as she adjusted the focus and watched the fluid come alive with the movement of microorganisms invisible to the human eye. She felt as always, awed, by the revelations of the magnification. And was more than a little nervous about what she might find in these particular specimens.

It was with profound relief and only after many tests and checks of her tests that she announced to Mr. Fulsom, Tobe, and the finally silent Quentin Smythe, Esquire, that the cow did not suffer from any disease carried by germs or bacteria that she recognized. Everything appeared normal. The palpable tension of all four occupants of the room was eased.

Quentin smiled and announced, "I'll go tell the others."

Lenny Fulsom was caught offguard by a sudden yawn, at which he grinned sheepishly.

Tobe, when Roses looked around again, was sitting, apparently at ease, on an upturned barrel a few feet to her left, silhouetted by the rays of the sun shining through the open barn door behind him. She didn't move to rise from the table, and he remained in his seat, but a silent dialogue passed between them. His proud, shining eyes and her shy smile spoke volumes. She turned away to look at her equipment once again, and, with a sigh of simple satisfaction, she stood.

"I guess I'd better go see what I can do to relieve that poor animal's suffering," she said. Lenny Fulsom accompanied her.

Tobe stayed behind, planning to guard the prized microscope from anyone curious enough to approach. He thought he might burst with pride. When Quentin returned, singing Roses' praises, Tobe thought that this one time, it would be all right if the lawyer babbled on forever. A nod was all that Quentin seemed to require in the way of response, and Tobe was only half listening as he took stock of Fulsom's barn.

"Roses is not only a beautiful and feminine woman, she is also skilled. In England I have met many women crusaders, horsy women and bookish ones, but rarely have I met a woman like your wife." Tobe agreed wholeheartedly—he had become convinced, some time ago, that there were no other women like Roses, anywhere—and so he continued to admire the surprisingly well-appointed structure in which they stood.

The wide wooden planks that formed the walls were hung with shelves and hooks for the equipment the rancher needed; lengths of rope, tackle, blankets, raincoats, tarps, skins, everything a ranch required.

The wide cross beams served as support for open-
ended rooms on a second level, the hay loft on one
end of the room, a storage area on the other. There
were three or four windows, and one large one of
real plate glass.

From the size of the small town they'd discovered,
he'd assumed the local ranchers were small farmers;
if not poor, then certainly struggling—as the Indians
were—to draw a living from this harsh land. But the
size and apparent wealth of this spread had caused
him to rethink that assumption. The reservation land
might be poor, but much of the surrounding land
was lush enough to be good horse and sheep ranching country. Though he hadn't seen it yet, he guessed
there must be some good farming land in these parts
as well, since two of the committee of dour but
clearly prosperous ranchers they'd met had been introduced as farmers as well as cattlemen.

He moved to a window below which a large table
was neatly divided into two different kinds of work-
spaces. On the right writing implements, some worn
ledgers and an old fashioned inkwell clearly indicated that paperwork was done here, while on the
left a torn bit, an awl, thread and needle and various
other small tools showed that leatherwork was one
of Fulsom's talents. The window above looked out
over the farmhouse to the fields and hills beyond.

"She is a rare one. Her beauty is surpassed only
by her charm and intelligence. I'll never forget what
she did for Eugenia. And you can be sure these men
are grateful as well. You are a lucky man to have
found such an unusual woman."

"Um-hm." Tobe mumbled again, but he was diverted from his thoughts about Lenny Fulsom and
his ranch as Quentin joined him at the window, ask-

ing, "Do you mind if I ask where you and your
lovely wife met?"

"Colorado." Tobe answered, after a moment's hesitation. He contemplated telling their new friend the
truth about their "marriage." He was sure Quentin
wouldn't turn them in. He'd keep quiet if asked, if
only for Roses' sake. A lawyer's advice might even
be helpful. But Tobe was afraid the voluble man
wouldn't be able to keep his mouth shut, since he
hadn't stopped talking since they'd met. Despite all
that, Tobe felt in his gut that Quentin Smythe III
was good at his profession. He could easily imagine
Quentin pounding a jury into submission. As a lawyer, he would have to know what to say and what
to keep to himself. In the instant it took Tobe to
argue this out with himself his decision was made.
"She's not my wife," he confessed.

That shut Quentin up. Tobe almost laughed as he
watched him struggle for words to express his amazement. He couldn't believe that this man was stunned
into silence very often. He waited, for the first time
in their acquaintance, for the fat man to speak.

"She's not?" Quentin spluttered.

"It suits us fine to have these men thinking we're
the Jordans."

"Well," Quentin had recovered himself, "I won't
tell anyone else but . . ." He turned a sharp eye on
Tobe, a faint gleam of intelligent curiosity making
Tobe sure he was right about the man's talents as a
lawyer. "Why are you? . . ." Quentin swallowed the
rest of the question, once again confirming Tobe's
suspicion that this man was not the bungler he appeared. "I don't mean to pry."

"Good."

"But there must be some reason why you're telling me this."

Tobe debated with himself for a moment. "You're probably a pretty good lawyer," he said, less to have his opinion confirmed than to reassure himself.

"The best," Quentin answered without hesitation. "In these parts."

"I ran into some trouble, back in Kansas City," Tobe started.

"I thought I recognized an Eastern accent." Quentin nodded, inviting Tobe to continue.

"I drove a herd of cattle out from Pennsylvania. There was a girl in Kansas City. A working girl, in one of the saloons. A white girl, Carolann Travis." He paused, suddenly having second thoughts. Telling a virtual stranger one was wanted for murder might be like signing your own death warrant. Even though the lawyer hadn't seemed to be particularly prejudiced against Roses and Tobe, it was hard to know what side he would believe. But Tobe thought back over the way the Englishman had talked with the two of them. He had never uttered a word indicating that Tobe and Roses were beneath him. Tobe had heard that the British were like that, they'd outlawed slavery long before the war.

When the silence between them grew long, Quentin urged, "Go on." And the man's open expression tipped the balance.

"She was murdered. Her father came west and he blames me for it. He had a warrant issued for my arrest."

"Why does he think you did it?"

"I was the only black there that night and I spoke to her." Tobe said bitterly. "But I swear that's *all* I did. There were fifty, maybe a hundred, guys in the place, and I don't know how many from her past. And there was her boss. I heard . . . well let's just say I've got reason to believe there were a few people had it in for the lady. I wasn't one of them."

Quentin barely waited for him to finish, his lawyer's blood obviously stirred. "You don't know who killed her? Any witnesses?"

"No, not that I know of. I didn't stick around to find out. I hightailed it out of there as soon as I heard the first man say nigger. I knew they'd put the blame on me somehow."

"But perhaps they wouldn't . . ." Quentin's voice trailed off as he met Tobe's eyes.

"Listen Quentin, the West may be full of wide open spaces, but none wide enough to wait for a jury of my peers to happen along. At least none that I've found."

"You have an idea who did it, though."

"One or two."

"You'll need proof," Quentin said.

Tobe smiled wryly. "That I don't have."

"Can you get it? It could be your only chance. Unless you want to spend the rest of your life avoiding Kansas City."

"I wouldn't mind that," Tobe said. "But the Colonel, the girl's father, isn't gonna just sit there. He tracked me all the way to Colorado, until I finally rode up into the mountains."

"I don't know what to tell you," Quentin sighed. "You've got two choices. Go back and prove your innocence. Or just keep running." Tobe looked down at his hands. They were steady.

"That's what I figured," he said.

"Well?" Quentin prodded.

"I'd never get a chance to prove anything if I went back there," Tobe answered. "They would never listen to me. They'd just put me away. Maybe even kill me."

"You may be right." The lawyer pursed his lips, "But the alternative isn't much better."

"Nope. But it's my best shot at a long and happy life. And I'm taking it." His voice was assured. At least he'd tried, even if he had only gotten the answer he'd expected.

"With Roses?" Quentin asked. He nodded toward the door, where they could see Roses approaching, deep in conversation with the owner of the land they stood on.

"Probably not," Tobe said, gruffly. They stepped forward to meet her.

Nineteen

Roses was worried about Tobe. She'd looked everywhere and she couldn't find him. She'd asked after him among the women and among the children who had taken to following him around in the hopes of hearing one of his stories. Roses had been surprised to find Tobe had a hoard of unusual tales. They were, he explained to her, told to him by his grandmother. They were about animals, both familiar and exotic, and there were others about characters such as Br'er Rabbit, which Tobe told with an exaggerated southern drawl that made Roses laugh as hard as the children he told them to. But none of the children had seen Tobe this evening.

It was almost dinnertime and Tobe usually reported back to the tepee when his stomach started grumbling. Roses had had a sinking feeling in the bottom of her stomach ever since she'd had the fleeting thought that Tobe might have left without saying goodbye. She knew it was improbable that he had gone, since Diablo was still pastured with the other horses, but she couldn't help but surrender more and more to a feeling of hopelessness as she searched in vain. It wasn't any easier to admit that the sorrow she was feeling was in anticipation of the day when Tobe would actually leave to continue on his journey. It had been three weeks since they'd reached Indian land, and his well meant attempts to hide his impatience to move on were not lost on her. She appreciated them, but it was like watching Diablo trying to restrain himself once Tobe was up in the saddle. The man, like his horse, couldn't help but tug at the bit when the urge to cover ground was upon him. He was bored by all the talk of crops and irrigation and they both knew it.

She heard the deep rumbling of men's laughter as she approached Graywolf's tent. When the laughter died down, she recognized Tobe's voice talking about his first stampede, which had been led by a frantic cow looking desperately for her calf. He was telling the Ute about one of the older cowboys, who'd headed the cattle into a mill. All the other men whistled and shouted and forced the frightened animals to run in a circle until they tired themselves out.

As she bent to look through the raised flap of buffalo skin over the entrance to the tepee, he said, "All I was trying to do was get out of the way. I couldn't believe these crazed beasts were the same sweet trusting animals that had been so docile and . . . well, stupid, up until that moment." The men laughed. "Those big brown eyes weren't so pretty rolling all the way back in their heads." Tobe demonstrated, for the Uncompahgre who hadn't understood. Roses almost giggled. "I was scared to death. Which is probably why I rode into the middle of the herd, instead of away from it. It took two of the other men to get me out of there."

Graywolf said, bolsteringly, "A frightened animal is always dangerous."

Tobe answered, laughing at himself. "I'll never look at cows quite the same again."

After her nerve wracking search, she was relieved to see him. He was wearing deerskin leggings and

the soft moccasins he insisted on wearing at all
times. He liked to joke that he was literally a ten-
derfoot. He was seated by the fire, probably unaware
that the sun was going down, passing the pipe with
some of the older men. If it hadn't been for his
speech, he could, in the low light, have been taken
for one of the People.

Roses ducked into the tepee and waited for someone to notice her. One of the old men said in Uncompahgre, "The wohan are strange beasts, but the
buffalo . . ." He let his voice trail off, and there was
a murmur of encouragement from those around him.
Someone translated for Tobe. She quickly recognized
the story and didn't bother listening to the man who
was retelling it. Hunting stories were always popular
with men.

A fire burned brightly in the center of the room,
despite the heat of the day, and a small pile of bed-
clothes lay neatly in one corner. Tools for house-
keeping, metal and clay pots, mugs, wooden dishes
and buffalo and bone spoons and knives were hung
on the front poles or stacked neatly on stools. By
the fire were gourds and baskets holding nuts, seeds
and other provisions. Tobe looked as comfortable in
these new surroundings as he'd looked in the Smith
house.

Graywolf's sister, Lightning Horse's Wife, ducked
into the tent a few minutes later, clearing her throat
impatiently when the men ignored her.

Tobe scrambled to his feet when he saw Roses
standing by the door.

"I didn't hear you come in," he said, reaching her
side.

"I just wanted to tell you that supper is almost
ready," she told him.

Tobe looked at his host and back to her, guiltily.

"Graywolf invited me to take the evening meal here with him."

"Fine." She was relieved that she was able to sound so unconcerned. It seemed strange now that only minutes ago she had been so worried. "I'll see you later." She covered the strong hand resting on her shoulder and turned away. "Don't forget the way home," she advised.

"I won't," he promised, with a light tap to her buckskin clad behind.

But in the end he came home so late that Roses was already half asleep when he slipped into their bed. She turned into his warmth, drowsily rubbing her cheek against his arm.

"Did you have a good time?" she mumbled.

"Umm-hmm." Tobe murmured against her hair as he slipped his arm under her head.

"Good. You can trade more stories with the men tomorrow. I think I'll go into town and see if my magazine has arrived. I want to check on Eugenia and the puppies."

"I'll go with you."

"There's no need." Roses was too sleepy to argue, but she wanted to point out that he was much more comfortable, and more relaxed, on the reservation than in the white man's town.

"We'll talk about it in the morning." She nuzzled his throat and settled into the crook of his arm, but went to sleep thinking that it was one conversation she intended to avoid.

It was impossible, though. When she awakened the next morning, he refused to let her leave without him. She was too angry to listen to any of his arguments. She walked off in a huff, saying she'd rather not go than watch him jump at every shadow on the road.

He didn't follow her, but later he found her with a group of women, weaving baskets. He came up behind her as she was saying to Raven Wing, ". . . he was the stubbornest creature on earth."

"I don't think so," Tobe said, adding, "but I already lost this argument once." As she turned to him, he raised his hands as if to ward off her wrath, so she didn't bother to tell him that they had been talking about her father, whom the widow remembered well. Raven Wing winked at her, a smile tugging at the corner of her lips, but she didn't correct Tobe, either. "Is that all you women talk about?" he asked.

"We can't help it." The older woman sighed. "The foolishness of you men is a constant source of wonder to us." Tobe laughed at her good natured gibe and sat at Roses' feet. He still wore the western clothes he'd donned that morning and his cross legged position made him look like a little boy. Roses had changed back into her dress of thin hide. Her legs and feet were bare, and she had pulled her skirt up above her knees. His eyes wandered from her hands to the shadowed space between her spread knees and then back to her face. Roses was very aware of the lingering trail his eyes followed. Despite herself she found her ire dissolving. Her companion took one look at the two of them and left them alone.

"I'm sorry," he said, breaking the long silence between them. "I know that you don't need me to come into town with you. You're already won the respect of some of the most influential men in these parts. And Quentin wouldn't hurt a fly."

"I know," she said, her voice soft and husky as she looked down at the top of his bowed head. The thick black cap of kinky curls tempted her, but her hands were busy with the leaves of Beargrass. She devoted her attention to finishing the last row, tucking in the ends of the strands. She tried to concentrate on the dry yellowing fronds, rather than on the sun glinting on Tobe's swirling blue black curls. Tobe spoke, echoing her thoughts of the day before.

"I want to go with you because you're going somewhere else. I like it here but . . . it's not exactly exciting. All anyone ever talks about is irrigation and what crops to plant." He waited until she looked down at him. "You were right yesterday. I am still jumpy." He laid a hand on her knee and she looked up into his eyes. "I don't mean I'm afraid."

"I—" Roses started to protest, but he motioned her into silence.

"I'm restless. Any chance to ride away from this miniature desert is better than none."

"You and your adventure," Roses laughed. "Just living life is an adventure. Ask anyone here."

"Yes, but . . . what kind of adventure?"

Roses couldn't resist teasing. "What kind would you like?"

Tobe glanced up at her, eyes widening. "Umm, I see what you mean." He said with a smile as delighted as a child sighting his first Christmas tree. "Is it too late to go to town now?" His voice was rough.

Roses cleared her throat before she spoke. "No, it's not. But we shouldn't be too long, getting back," she relented, as she tucked in the last loose end.

"I can't wait." He offered her his arm and she stood and took it, leaving her basket with the others.

"Let me come with you. I promise I'll behave. At least until nightfall."

"All right, let me change into my dress." He walked her back to their tepee. When they had reached the tent, Spotted Chicken called him from her stool at the entrance to her home. Roses listened to her ask, in broken English, "Would you please take baby for one little time? I must go." The older woman held up one finger to indicate the short time she'd be gone. Tobe nodded his agreement and the baby was shoved unceremoniously into his arms before he could change his mind. Roses poked her head back out of the tepee to say, "That should be about as much adventure as you can handle in one day." She watched him as he tried to comfort the baby who opened her tiny mouth and let out a piercing scream as her mother toddled out of sight. Tobe smiled weakly at Roses as he hefted the solid six-month-old onto his hip and looked around for a toy to distract the infant.

"You may be right," he said under his breath, but the baby stopped screaming at that moment to turn round black eyes on him, and Roses heard him. She ducked back inside before she could start laughing at his befuddled expression.

Tobe, to his own surprise, told Roses about the conversation with Quentin on the way to town. She only interrupted him once.

"You think you know who did it?" she asked, surprised. "You didn't tell me that before."

"Crystal . . . you remember . . ."

"I remember." Roses smiled wryly.

"She told me, well, she mentioned, that Carolann was suspected of skimming—taking more than her share of the earnings."

"Would someone kill her for the money?"

"The man she was stealing from might. He beat up one girl so badly last year that the sheriff put him in jail for the night. I met the man. He'd probably think killing was too good for anyone who dared to steal from him."

"Wouldn't it make more sense to punish her than to kill her? He'd lose all the money she made for him if she wasn't working anymore."

"That's not the way those men think, you should know that."

"I guess you're right." But she thought there was something else he wasn't telling her.

"He'd want to set an example. And, if he did it, I'm sure he let the girls know."

"If he told them, though, couldn't they tell the law?" Roses asked hopefully.

"I can just see it now. No, I didn't kill that girl, Hunter did it. I don't have any witnesses or nothing, but the girls that work there can testify against him. He told them if they tried to cheat him the same thing would happen to them. So you've got all the confession you need right there." He managed to laugh, but Tobe couldn't keep a sour taste from rising in the back of his throat.

Roses barely smiled. After a moment of silence between them, she said, "Well, if you're going to be hitting the road, I know one person you can make very happy."

"Who?" Tobe asked.

"Quentin. You could take one of his pups with you for company."

"I'm not planning to go right away. Quentin will probably have homes for those mutts by the time I leave. You're not getting rid of me for a little while yet, lady."

"I don't want to get rid of you at all. But you're half gone already. Just this short trip to town has changed you." Tobe couldn't argue with her. She was right, he didn't feel restless anymore.

He was afraid to say what he was thinking, that he wished that she could move on with him. He swallowed and finally got up his nerve enough to say, "I wish we could travel on together. If you didn't like this town in Utah, we could try another."

"And another and another," she said. "Your restlessness is a part of you. I can't change that. Even if I were to promise to stay with you forever, sooner or later you'd feel hemmed in by me. The way you feel trapped, now, on the reservation, after only a couple of weeks there."

She was wrong. He could see traveling with Roses for a long time, perhaps forever. But he'd forced himself into her life and her dreams. He couldn't ask her, now, to give them up. And even if he had nerve to ask, he didn't think she'd do it. She shouldn't do it.

But she was wrong about him. With her he'd never get bored. The emptiness inside him would go away. She was strong, capable and loving. Her love didn't feel like a cage, it made him feel free.

"You could never make me feel that way," he had to say. She didn't try to argue the point with him, but came up with a stronger argument.

"I might even be able to live with that, but with the fire that burns between us, our union would eventually lead to children. And children shouldn't live like that." Tobe smiled at the thought of a pint sized version of Roses.

"They would be like you," he said.

"They would need a home," Roses answered.

"We would make them one."

"Where?" she asked. "For how long."

"I don't know. But the Uncompahgre didn't always live in one place."

"The People follow the hunt. You are not traveling

in order to hunt. You're trying to find something to fill some hole inside of you, but no place, no one can do that for you. You have to find peace for yourself. I know this because after my parents died, I felt the same way you do now. But I knew why. I faced it. That was part of why I left the reservation. I was looking for something to fill the emptiness inside, too."

"That may have been true when I came West," Tobe said, "but it's not anymore."

She shook her head. "When I could have gone back home to let my loved ones comfort me, I didn't. I had to find forgiveness for my parents. I had to stop blaming others for my unhappiness. It took a long time before I felt that I could come home. I wanted to return but only for what was really there, a hard life, but one that would make me happiest. You're still running from your past. Until you face them, those demons will always be with you."

"My past is not something I want to hold on to," Tobe protested. Roses looked at him, holding his eyes with her own.

"I can tell that's not true."

"Oh? How?" He challenged her.

"You are restless now, not because there are no new challenges to face. Nor is it because there is nothing for you to do. It is clear you are not bored on the reservation. In fact you seem to find everything there fascinating. But you have decided you're just passing through, that you want something else, just as you did in Cedar Valley. Just as you have always done."

"One thing has changed," Tobe said. "I don't want to leave you behind."

Roses didn't even look at him. "I can make my

home wherever I am. You will always be looking for
something new."

Tobe wanted to argue—to make her see that even
if what she said about him was the truth, he wasn't
the only one with a past. She was also afraid to face
her demons. That was something they had in common, and maybe it was one of the things that had
drawn them together. But it also kept them apart, no
matter how close they became. He gave up on arguing with her as they rode into town.

In tacit agreement, they rode first to Quentin's office. He opened the door and ushered them quickly
inside, checking the street before he closed the door.

"Quentin, what is it?" Roses asked, as he herded
them toward the bedroom.

"Shhh," was all he would say as he disappeared
toward the kitchen. He came back a few seconds
later, no longer skulking around corners. "My housekeeper must have gone to the store. We have a few
minutes," he said mysteriously. "This arrived a couple of days ago." Quent handed Tobe a piece of paper, folded twice. When Tobe opened it, he found it
was a Wanted poster with his name and description.
As he handed the paper to Roses, Quentin continued,
"I don't think anyone else will make the connection,
but I've heard Roses call you 'Tobe,' " he said. "I
wired a friend, a discreet friend, in Chicago and
asked him to make inquiries about Kansas City's
judges to find out who would issue this kind of warrant. Meanwhile I'd use another name, 'Tobe'."

"Let's put it this way, you don't meet many men
with your height, weight, and skin color with the
name Tobe out here in the middle of nowhere."

"You still think I should go back to Kansas and
try to prove my innocence," Tobe asked Quentin bitterly.

"You've got the deck stacked against you, my friend. But, for me, it would beat being on the run."

A quick examination assured Roses the puppies were fine and, after hearing Quentin's news, neither Tobe nor Roses was in the mood to linger in the small town. Their earlier argument preyed on Tobe's mind, especially now that he had to leave right away. But he didn't want to fight with Roses. He wanted nothing more than to be with her. Once they were safely abed, his cares fell away. He wouldn't ruin this time with her with worrying about what couldn't be changed.

"Are you afraid?" she asked.

"Not now," he answered, kissing her forehead, then her closed eyelids, and rubbing her cheek with his own.

"When will you go?" she whispered.

"Soon." He pulled her even more tightly against him and kissed her. Her lips opened under his. She was a rare one, this woman. Even in the face of his departure she gave of herself, without asking anything in return.

Their lovemaking was tender, a farewell, long drawn out and deeply satisfying, sad and yet happy at the same time. Long after Roses finally slept, Tobe lay thinking, staring up into the darkness above them. The sound of bird call alerted him to the coming dawn.

He thought of the journey that had brought him to this point. He had left home because he wanted to do something that was new and different from the life he'd known. He had wanted to forget the past and blaze a new path for himself. His only remaining family was a mother he rarely spoke to and a half sister whom he had never met. He had only glimpsed the girl, from a distance, a few times. His mother had sent her to live with friends, near the school she attended. When his mother brought her to visit his grandmother, her grandmother, he made himself scarce. Once Virginia Grant died, he had doubted that he would ever see his "family" again. So, with nothing to keep him in Massachusetts, he had left. Roses had been partially correct when she said that he was running from old demons. But she was wrong when she said he couldn't stop. With her at his side, he knew that he could.

Roses stirred sleepily against him, turning her head to look in his eyes. "I'll go with you," she said. She closed her eyes and was asleep again in seconds. He lay there, dumbfounded, watching her. He couldn't believe this miracle. And he couldn't stop the smile from forming on his lips as he joined her in peaceful slumber.

Twenty

They rode south. Roses, who had said her good-byes for the past week, didn't look back.

It was enough to be with Tobe—for now. She knew he might not want her forever. But he did want her. And he gave her something no one else could. Her Ute family and her friends in Cedar Valley had cared about her, but they didn't need her. Tobe did. She didn't know how long he would have stayed with her if his past hadn't found him here. But she did know he hadn't wanted to leave her behind. He'd told her that before he even knew the Wanted poster had turned up in town.

It was too dangerous for him to remain on the reservation. He was too easy to spot, and to track. He had to go. And she had to go with him. She needed him, too. She couldn't have watched Tobe leave.

There was nothing left, really, to keep them apart. She trusted him. It scared her, but it gave her the courage to follow her heart. He wasn't playing with her. Maybe he never had been. Perhaps the thing that had brought them together from the very beginning had been love, not just desire. She knew his feelings for her ran deep, though he didn't declare himself. She understood why he couldn't ask her to go with him. The men who followed him wanted to kill him.

They had left the mule with Smiles Like the Moon. Jasper had also been left behind. Little Deer had sworn to take him back to the mountains on his next hunting trip, and, in the meantime, to teach him the lessons he needed to survive in the wild. Roses felt a little guilty at deserting the kitten, but truly regretted not insisting more strongly that Little Deer didn't know what he was letting himself in for. But she'd had no choice. The reservation was a better place for the rapidly growing bobcat than the road, or even their final destination, which sounded like a civilized town.

The morning they left, Tobe told her all the stories he'd read about black townships in Utah and California. He also entertained her with stories about characters like George Washington, founder of Centralia in the Washington Territory, and George W. Bush, of the Oregon Territory. To hear Tobe tell it, the west was full of opportunities, some riskier than others, of course, for a colored man to make his fortune or at least his name. Nat Love and Deadwood Dick might have been outlaws, but they answered to no one.

"Where did you hear these stories?" Roses had asked him.

"I read them in the newspapers, and I talked to men and women who have kin out here."

Roses hadn't met any of the kind of men he talked about, though she knew that the tall tales were based, in part anyway, on the truth. She wasn't sure the reality of finding a place out here where she and Tobe would somehow feel they belonged would be as colorful as all that. She wasn't even sure it was possible. They still wanted different things. She still hoped to return home someday. Perhaps with him. But now that she'd been back, she felt there was more to being "home," then just coming to this place. She did hope, though, that when he found the town he had told her about, they could make some plans for the future. She told him about the people she had met, hardworking family men and women like Barney Ford, who had been a runaway slave but now owned two hotels, and his wife, Julia, and Clara Brown who had come west as a young woman and after the War had found thirty-five of her relatives living in Virginia and brought them to Denver.

"Denver isn't the place for us," Tobe said. "They don't want our kind there, except maybe to shine their boots and make their beds. In the townships, the sheriff, the town council, even the mayor is colored. You can work at any job. Not just be a servant."

"You can do that anywhere. It doesn't matter where a person lives, as long as they have a chance at a good life, a fresh start," she said, but apparently that wasn't enough for him. Roses didn't try to argue the point further.

Their first night together on the trail was full of the same magic she'd experienced with Tobe in the mountains. There was something about being the only two people in the world that made the intimacies they shared all the more exciting and overwhelming. Working together to find firewood and snare a rabbit, crawling into their bedroll and laying with her cheek on his arm, staring at the wide open sky above her was as close to being "home" as Roses had ever felt.

She could almost imagine living like this forever. She had her reservations about the kind of reception they might receive in this town Tobe was aiming for, but she kept them to herself. Since the town he was looking for had no name, and he had never had an exact location, she wasn't sure they were even going to find that specific place. Tobe's plan was to ride the length of the state's southern border. They might find it, or another town like it. Roses couldn't imagine she and Tobe could get within a hundred miles of the place, without someone telling them about a town populated completely by colored people.

The next morning she woke to find Tobe playing with her hair.

"Stop that," she said irritably. Her dreams had been full of screams and frightened horses, but she didn't remember what they'd been about.

"Why?" he teased.

"It's time to get going." She couldn't rise with his fingers twined in her curls.

"There's no hurry," he said, looking at her quizzically. "I love your hair." For some unknown reason his compliment only made her more annoyed.

"I'm glad you like it, but it's well past daybreak. We're never going to get anywhere if we spend all day abed." She hadn't meant to sound like such a scold. He released her, and she scrambled out of their bedroll and busied herself with the fire. He didn't share her sense of urgency and rolled out of bed after her more slowly, standing and stretching his long limbs.

They were shortly on their way again to wherever. Roses rode contentedly enough beside him, except that Tobe tried to jolly her up whenever she stopped grinning like an idiot for more than a minute. He kept teasing her, kept trying to make her laugh. She didn't know why she was feeling so unsettled, but his teasing didn't make her feel any better.

She finally snapped at him that night at dinner, "Don't try so hard. I'm fine, leave me be." She thought she might have hurt his feelings but he only said, "Okay, okay," while holding up his hands as if to ward off a physical attack. He was smiling like a man who had been vindicated after serving a long unjust sentence in jail.

"What are you laughing about?" she couldn't resist asking, trying to keep the frustration she felt out of her voice so he would tell her straight out what the devil he thought he was doing teasing her. As though she could somehow forget what she was leaving behind, and just be happy. It wasn't her way. He should have known that by now.

"You have been pretending not to be angry ever since we left. I'm glad to see you finally let off some steam."

She felt like one of the bacteria she examined under her own microscope. It wasn't a pleasant feeling.

"You're smiling because you think I'm angry?" He should have known by now that she wasn't one to give in to her emotions. She wasn't angry. But she was annoyed with him.

"I'm smiling because you are finally going to tell me the truth," he said, "I hope."

That annoyed her further. "The truth about what?"

He caught one of her arms in his hand and tugged at her until she turned to face him. His smile was gone.

"Why did you agree to come with me?" he asked.

"You know why."

"No, I don't. You walked away from everything you've worked for. I didn't ask you to. You offered." For some reason, that hurt, though she knew it was true. "I'd like to think it was because my charm was irresistible. But I know that's not true, so why?" She didn't know what to do to reassure him. Ever since she had decided to go with him, she had felt as though a huge weight had been lifted from her

shoulders. She was sad about leaving the Uncompahgre, but she didn't regret it. She had left her
dream behind, but it wasn't just for him.

"Because . . ." she began, then stopped. She
didn't know why she felt so tied up in knots. She
didn't know anything anymore. She'd left with Tobe
because she couldn't not leave with him. But she
didn't know where she was going, or why. This pipe-
dream of his wasn't hers, and she didn't think it ever
could be. She didn't know if they could make it together.

"Why?" His badgering tweaked her already frayed
nerves.

"Because I couldn't let a madman wander off into
the wilderness. You'll get yourself killed," she answered sharply.

"So you came along to protect me?" he asked,
the smile back.

"What do you want me to say?" she exploded,
frustrated.

"The truth. Just tell me why you came. Last night
was wonderful but you were so far away I wondered
if you ever really left at all."

Roses didn't know why he kept baiting her, but
she'd nearly reached the end of her rope.

"I wanted to stay on the reservation," she said, as
patiently as she could. "But I wanted to be with you
more."

"I love you, Roses. And I wanted to be with you,
too. But I need to know what's bothering you. What
did I do to make you angry. So . . ." he took a deep
breath. "Let me have it. Come on now, your best
shot. I know you want to."

"You have no idea what I want." She was pleased
to find the shakiness of her limbs was not echoed
in her voice.

"You're not a good liar, Roses. You don't get enough practice. Out with it. What is it you've been dying to tell me all this time?"

"Tobe." Her voice held a warning.

"Yes?" His smile was gone, his jaw taut. For all his bravado, he was as scared as she was. Realizing that, Roses' ire cooled. It was replaced by a longing so strong she didn't know if she could bear it. She wanted to take him in her arms, comfort him, and soothe away the fears that ate at him, to tell him she was his for as long as he wanted her. She could have told him she loved him, but it wouldn't have meant the same thing to Tobe that it did to her.

She remembered what he had said about his mother and father. "At least I knew she loved him." As though that made any difference to anyone. She believed loving someone meant you were willing to sacrifice everything for them, that you did what was necessary to protect them. Apparently, that was not his definition of the emotion. If he believed this was love—this haze of sensual pleasure, this desire to be together, for all she knew it was the closest he would ever come to the emotion. She could not tell this man she loved him, even if that was what he wanted to hear. And she wasn't sure that it was.

"I'm not sorry I came." She told him part of the truth, the part she hoped he *wanted* to hear.

"Good," he said, waiting. As she gazed into his anxious eyes, she almost said it. But she couldn't. If she told him she loved him, it could ruin everything. She trusted him, but not that much.

"I left the Uncompahgre because I'm happiest with you, Tobe. The man who makes me laugh when I feel like crying. The man who makes me want to cry when he tries so hard to make me happy. You." It was clear she'd stunned him. "Tobe? Isn't that what you wanted to hear? Because you were right. I was dying to say it."

She had wanted only to make him stop asking questions she couldn't answer, but in his eyes she saw not the expression of relief she'd expected, but pain. He lowered his head and she was seized by the desire to force him to look at her again so she could look longer into his soul and find the answers he sought. But he was still looking away from her when he said, "I . . . I think we should go to Kansas City." Roses, stunned, watched him walk away.

Tobe walked away from Roses, their camp, and the fire, into the night. He stayed on the road, not because of any conscious decision to do so, but because that was where his feet led him. He wasn't paying attention to where he was, or where he was going. His mind was busy, going back over what he had said to Roses and over what she had said to him. It had shaken him like a sledge hammer to the gut, hearing her confession.

She loved him. She might not know it yet, might not name it love, but that was all it could be. That was the only way she could possibly see him as she did. If he was honest with himself, he had to admit that this was what he had wanted. Her love was what he had needed. But it was more than he had dreamed. Her passion had healed him, filling the place in his soul that was empty. He was the luckiest man on earth. But he didn't deserve it.

She had given him everything he wished for, and more. In return, all he had been able to do was take away her family. Her one dream had been to return to her home. There had been an air of sadness about her since they had left the reservation. He knew now she was happy to be with him, but part of her was missing.

In order to give Roses any kind of decent life, if
indeed they were to stay together, as he'd just started
to believe, really believe, they were, he had to clear
his name. For that, he had to return to Kansas City.

Roses Jordan had understood something that he
himself had never realized. He was afraid to back-
track. He didn't know why. But for as long as he
could remember, he'd been running. As a child he'd
made up stories about his father to escape the truth,
the "war hero" was not coming home. At nine, he'd
run away from his mother, to his grandmother, fan-
tasizing that his mother would follow him, and give
up the life she lived. At fourteen, when his mother
had gotten pregnant again, he'd stopped speaking
with her at all, running from any sign of contact. At
eighteen, as soon as he finished school, he started
dreaming of coming west. He spent every free hour
researching the frontier—pretending again—this time
that he could run away from himself. When Granny
Gee died, he barely paused to grieve, so eager had
he been to get away.

He had always needed to keep moving. Even on
the reservation, as Roses had said once, when he'd
been happier than ever before, he hadn't been able
to settle down, but had felt compelled to move on.
He didn't want to be on the run all of his life. He
couldn't drag Roses down that road with him. If he
was going to hang for murder, he wanted to know
now, before he made any promises he couldn't keep.

When they reached Kansas City, they found it
even easier than they had expected to slip into town
without attracting notice. They registered in a hotel
as Mr. and Mrs. Jordan. Roses was sure the name
would bring them luck again, as it had in Utah when

Quentin had made the mistake of thinking them married. Tobe didn't plan to use the name long enough for the deception to cause any damage. He didn't have any more proof of his innocence than he had had when he'd left before, but they did, of course, have a plan.

At first he'd been against involving Roses in the dangerous game he was about to play. She had spent the entire trip, south on horseback, east by train, convincing Tobe that she was already involved. She was certain he couldn't pull this off without her. He was just as certain that he wasn't going to be able to keep her out of it. He was sure, though, that even if the whole thing blew up in his face, no one could trace him back to her, and she'd be safe. And if things worked out as planned, Roses was going to be his trump card.

He watched his ace in the hole dispose of her belongings around the room. When she was finished unpacking Roses went to the window. The shutters were painted shut but, with one well-placed whack of her palm, she forced them open. Across a narrow alleyway were the roofs of the one-story buildings that surrounded the hotel. Cheerful music floated through the balmy evening air, presumably from a nearby saloon. The voices of children playing drifted up to them. Tobe joined Roses at the window, but there was not much of a view from this vantage point. They were on the third and top floor, toward the back, and there was only an alley below them.

Tobe tried to figure out which of the rooms below belonged to Thomas "Tommy" Jones, his former employer, and Carolann's. He couldn't find it and shrugged it off. The man probably owned half the buildings in this part of town. When Tommy wanted someone dead he just raised his hand. A slight movement of his index finger would dispatch one of his hired thugs to dispatch anyone he wanted to get rid of. Tobe thought Tommy might even enjoy doing some of his killing himself. Carolann had, according to Crystal, been somewhat foolhardy in her dealings with the man. She'd tried to cut herself in on the House's earnings and, when she'd been caught, she'd tried to wriggle her way out of it with the same sultry smile that had gotten her into, and out of, so much trouble before. Tobe remembered Crystal shuddering as she recalled the scene, saying, "I'd rather give him all the money! That Tommy is one cold fish."

Being here was bringing back the whole fateful night. Walking from the train station to the hotel, he'd given Roses a quick tour of the city, skirting the most sordid areas where the saloons were already ringing with customers, despite the fact that it was still early afternoon. Walking these streets again had brought to his mind memories of his visit here the first time.

Kansas City was as big, and, in its own way, as wild, as Denver. Thousands of cattle were shipped east each week, and this was the stepping off place for hundreds of people heading west. Most business was done in an orderly fashion, but, with so much going on, the city had more than its share of confidence men and cattle barons, bankers and barkeeps, preachers and prostitutes, all intermingling within its ever growing borders.

He remembered the excitement that had gripped him then, with the wages from his cattle drive in his pocket. It had been more money than he'd ever saved in his life. He'd only gone into town to keep an eye on Tobacca Jack, but he'd gotten caught up in the infectious enthusiasm of the men he rode with, to sample all the town had to offer. All of it had culminated in the Painted Lady Saloon. Jack had promised to introduce him to a cattle shipper who needed men regularly to ride herd from Texas to Wyoming. But the other men had warned him that Jack probably wouldn't even make it back from town where he was sure to get in a brawl, or go to jail—maybe even get himself killed. So Tobe had convinced himself that Jack needed him there, in order for Tobe to get his introduction to the cattle shipper. But he had loved Kansas City.

His argument with 'Backy Jack, and Carolann's teasing response, had only served to dampen his excitement slightly. He had not thought anything at all of the comments Crystal had made about her supposed rival for his affections. He had had no idea that Crystal's prattle about the other girl would someday be of importance to him. Now, with the power of hindsight, he wanted to go back and find out what she had said about Carolann's argument with Thomas Jones.

While he washed up for dinner, Tobe tried to figure out how he was going to get the information he needed without putting Roses, who had already gone down to the diningroom, in any more danger.

Roses wanted to be sure of every detail. Tomorrow they were going into action and much of their plan depended on timing their joint efforts properly, in order to catch this Jones person, whom Tobe thought was either their killer, or their key to the killer's identity.

As Roses scanned the hotel dining room looking for an empty table, she spotted a family rising from a table in front of a window. She waited for them to leave, watching as the mother, a beautiful self-possessed woman with skin the color of coffee with cream, allowed her tall handsome escort to drape a pale scarf around her shoulders. They both had to be at least two score and ten, and an easiness between them bespoke years together, but if it hadn't been for the presence of their tall daughter, the spitting image of the elegant older woman, Roses would never have guessed their ages at anything like that much. The gentleman was well groomed with a handsome black beard slightly tinged with grey. The laughing expression in his dark eyes reminded her of Tobe. The woman was impeccably attired in a maroon walking dress that dipped low enough in the front to show off the firm smooth slope of her breast. Only the well worn laugh lines at their eyes and at the corner of their smiling mouths, which Roses glimpsed as they passed near her at the door, hinted at their years of worldly experience.

While she waited for the waiter to clear the table, Roses looked after them, watching as the girl gracefully ascended the stairs to the second floor, laughing back over her shoulder at something her father had said. As Roses made her way to the table, the tableau etched in her mind's eye, she fantasized for a moment that the trio were Tobe and her and their daughter cheerfully visiting the city on a shopping expedition and enjoying the sights. Her rueful smile was still on her lips when Tobe joined her and asked, "Is everything fine?"

"Fine," she said. "But I'm so hungry I feel like my belly button's brushing against my spine."

"I'm feeling a mite peckish myself," Tobe answered. "In fact I do believe I could eat a horse." The waiter appeared beside him. He had obviously overheard their conversation,

"The T-bone is de closes' we gots to anyting dat size," he said cheerfully.

"What is that wonderful odor?" Roses asked.

"Bar-b-que, ma'am."

"Sounds good," Tobe said.

When the food was delivered to the table, they found it to be delicious and Tobe and Roses fell to with a will. While they ate they finished making their plans. When Roses had eaten her fill she offered Tobe some of her bar-b-que, showing him that the meat was so tender it fell off the bone. He caught her hand and licked the spicy sauce from her fingertips before he let her go.

"Ummm-mmm," he agreed. "That is good." After that it was hard to concentrate on her dinner. Roses decided to skip dessert and wasn't surprised when Tobe did the same. He'd been as hungry for her as for his meal, and he didn't let her forget it. By the time they arrived in the bedroom she was feeling breathless and as lusty as she imagined he felt.

He held the door open for her and she brushed against him as she walked past, the back of her wrist grazing his upper thigh as she turned away.

"You little devil," he said, pulling the door closed behind him, and reaching for the offending wrist in one graceful movement. He swept her up off her feet and started toward the bed with her in his arms. She surrendered instantly, meeting his passion with her own when his mouth came down on hers. His tongue was plundering the recesses of her mouth when there was a knock at the door.

"Go away," Tobe growled.

"You asked for bathwater?" a high-pitched voice shrilled from just outside the door.

"Damn," Tobe swore, but he let her go and went

to the door. Roses wandered over to sit on the bed while he let the woman into the room.

"I'll be back with two more buckets of hot water in a jiffy," the sturdy looking girl promised after she'd laid the tin tub down on the floor and emptied steaming water into it from a pail she held. Roses crossed her ankle over her leg and played with the hem of her skirt, watching Tobe wander about the room from under her eyelashes. He looked over at her once or twice as he picked up first this and then that. All the while, the fingers of his left hand tapped impatiently against the spot where she'd mischievously touched his thigh.

When the girl came back, Tobe took the buckets at the door. Tobe emptied the water into the tub and turned to Roses.

"You wanted a bath?"

"That water looks like it would scald the skin off an aardvark." Roses smiled. Tobe dipped a hand in the water, barely able to restrain a wince of pain at the heat. Roses bit back a smile.

"We could let it cool off," Tobe smiled suggestively, and she laughed out loud.

"I'll never get in the tub."

He started unbuttoning his shirt slowly. Roses wet suddenly dry lips with the tip of her tongue, her gaze focused on his brown fingers undoing the buttons at his waist. When he'd finished with them he pulled the shirt out of the waistband of his Levis. His shirttails were wrinkled and slightly damp. As he shrugged out of the work shirt, Roses' hands went unconsciously to her throat. She watched with baited breath while his hands went to his belt and unfastened his pants. As he stooped down to tug off his boots, the three separate muscles in his shoulders bulged in a smooth motion that somehow made her aware of his strength and his softness at the same time. He pushed his pants down over his hips, then slipped out of them, and stood before her, nude, his hands resting lightly at his sides as her eyes feasted on the beautiful sight.

Her own breath came in ragged gasps as he leaned over to swirl a hand in the water waiting in the forgotten tub.

"Just as I thought. It feels just right now."

Like a sleepwalker she went toward him, stopping when she stood only inches away. She lowered herself beside the tub to test the water, hiding the shakiness of her legs. Her face was only inches from one chocolate colored thigh and her hands curled into fists as she restrained the urge to reach out and touch him.

"I'll . . ." she croaked. She cleared her throat. "I'll wash your back."

He was erect. He reached down to help her up, saying, "I'm in no hurry." She wasn't sure her legs would support her, but she let him tug her upwards. Her eyes flashed along the length of his body as she rose, and she trembled, swaying toward him briefly before he released her and stepped back.

"You can bathe first," he said.

Her hands went behind her to the buttons of her dress, and stayed there as she tried to take one deep breath, just one. She started to work at the hook and eye at the nape of her neck, and chanced a quick glance at Tobe, but that was a mistake. He stood regarding her, arms crossed over his chest. Her fingers fumbled at the hard-to-reach buttons in the middle of her back and he moved around behind her and made short work of them. Then he went back to where he had been standing. She worked her arms out of her sleeves and let the bodice of her dress

fall to her waist. Fleetingly, she realized it was the
same yellow dress he'd caught her washing in the
river in on the night when they had first kissed. But
a second later the thought was gone as Tobe released
a long pent-up breath in a soft hiss. She shimmied
the dress down over her hips and thighs and let it
fall in a pool at her feet while her hands went to
the waistband of her petticoat. She dropped that on
top of the dress and stepped out of the pile of clothing, moving toward the tub of water beside him.

She stepped into the warm water and extended a
hand to him. He took it and joined her, the water
swirling around their calves as he stepped in. He ran
the back of his hand down between her breasts and
sighed.

She waited for him to sit, his long legs bent at
the knee. She lowered herself into the warmth of the
water and the heat that was Tobe.

They fit together so smoothly and so perfectly that
when she started to move against him he was already
there, gliding down as she rose above him, surging
upward as she sank down and down. She felt him
deep within her, as a part of herself. They went on
and on until the city was quiet outside their window,
sating their hunger for each other only to find desire
rising again and again.

Finally Roses slept. Tobe lay, sprawled with her
above the covers. A smile tugged at the corners of
his mouth while he gazed down at the woman curled
around his waist. She slept so peacefully, that the
rise and fall of her breast against his encircling arm
was barely perceptible in the glow of the moonlight.
He slipped out of bed quietly so as not to disturb
her and gathered up his clothing, sparing a second
to salute the shadowy bathtub in the middle of the
floor with a flick of a wrist.

Twenty-one

The moon was so bright that he cast a long shadow on the boardwalk behind him as he passed through the portals of the first saloon. The harsh light and discordant shouts jangled nerves that had been quieted by hours of lovemaking. The smell of the place was even more repugnant after the smell of Roses' sweet skin. But he had work to do, and pushing his hat forward over his forehead, he strode into the thick of the crowd, looking for the ubiquitous card game at a table full of locals.

Roses found him as he exited the third taproom. It was too dark to see one's hand in front of one's face when she stumbled into him, dressed in a pair of his jeans. She lolled across the wooden sidewalk as if she had had too much drink even to stand.

"What are you doing?" she hissed, wrapping an arm around his shoulders clumsily, to make it look as if she were using him to hold her up.

"I needed information."

"You could have gotten yourself killed," she whispered.

"I only have one more stop to make." Tobe told her, pulling her into an alley and trying to loosen himself from the stranglehold she had on his throat.

"Tobe, this is Tommy's side of town," Roses insisted.

"I've got it under control. And the name of the judge we want. I've just got to talk to Crystal. I'll take you back to the hotel first." He led her back onto the street, pulling her into his body so closely that she stumbled. To any casual observer it would have appeared they were two drunks helping each other home.

"No, I'm going with you."

"It's not safe. I don't want anyone from that place to see us together."

"If they recognize you, we're done for anyway," was her argument. "Why do you have to go there at all? I thought you said Crystal wouldn't be able to help us without risking her livelihood and possibly her life."

"She can't help us publicly," Tobe said, trying to steer her back to the hotel, but he was forced to stop when she became a dead weight in his arms. "I'm going to try and sneak in," he explained. "They should be closing up for the night by now."

"I'm going with you. If you can sneak in, you can get me in. If you can't, well, you're not going into Tommy's place alone." The stubborn set of her jaw worried him. Daylight would make an interview with Crystal impossible. Tobe was running out of time.

"Come on, then," he said, roughly. "But if anything happens, I want you to—oh hell, if anything happens, we're dead."

"Nothing is going to happen," she reassured him, scurrying alongside him. "Nothing we can't handle anyway." Tobe was silent, still angry with her for putting herself in danger. As they neared the lights of The Painted Lady Saloon, she stumbled into him again. The unsteady little man with a snoutful was back.

"If we get separated, meet me at the stables," he said. Tobe's own nerves were stretched to the breaking point by the time he successfully navigated the way through the back door and up the stairs to the room he'd heard was Crystal's. He scratched at the door, once, and then again, before he heard movement inside. He cracked the door open and looked into the darkened room just as Crystal put a match to a lamp.

"Who are you?" she asked, but she kept her voice down, trying to look around him to see Roses. Luckily, she was the room's sole occupant and he breathed a sigh of relief as he put his fingers to his lips and pulled Roses into the room behind him.

"Crystal, meet Roses Jordan," he said, thrusting his companion forward with a shove to the small of her back. Roses steadied herself and walked forward, extending a hand to the scantily clad woman whose eyes narrowed as she realized the person before her was a woman.

"Well, well, well." the prostitute said, her deep voice still husky with sleep. "What have we here?"

Roses found herself looking into eyes as black as night. Crystal was a big woman, but pretty. Her skin was the color of rich loamy earth, a golden brown. Roses could see enough of it to know. Crystal was virtually nude, all her charms displayed by her sheer gown.

She didn't seem to be embarrassed to be caught in this state of dishabille. While Roses stared at her, Crystal gave Tobe and Roses a quick but thorough once-over.

"Do I know you?" she asked.

"Tobe Hunter." Crystal gasped and stepped back. "I was hoping you'd remember, but I see you do remember my name at least."

"What are you doing here?" She looked as if she'd seen a ghost. But Tobe didn't seem to think her reaction was that surprising.

"We're here to talk to you about what happened to Carolann Travis."

"Ahhh." The puzzled look disappeared. "How can I help you?"

"You knew they suspected me, I reckon?" She nodded. "Who else?"

"Honey, you were the only one. They didn't bother lookin' for anyone else. You'd better get out of town before they find you."

"But didn't you tell them—" Roses started, but Tobe interrupted.

"I guess they didn't believe I spent the whole night at the bar. Never came upstairs at all."

Crystal shrugged. "I told 'em, honey. Don't think they believed me, though. Anyways, they pretty much dropped it, till the girl's pa showed up. You know they didn't care much about her dyin'. But that man was like a dog with a bone. He was in here every night, asking me where you disappeared to so fast. Tommy tried to tell 'im, anyone coulda done it, that friend of yours for example . . . but he wanted you. Only nigra Carolann ever talked to, to hear him tell it."

"She didn't act like I was the . . . ah hem . . . first colored man she ever . . . talked to," Tobe said.

"Honey, you were far and away from her first. To hear her tell it, there wasn't a nigra in Georgia she missed out on."

Roses cleared her throat. Crystal smiled. "Sorry, honey. Forgot there was a lady present."

"It's not that. Did you say Mr. Jones tried to tell them Tobe didn't do it."

"Tommy said I didn't do it?" Tobe repeated incredulously.

"He didn't go that far. He just said there were a whole lotta guys had more reason to do that to her. He knew about Carolann's little . . . habit. Tommy couldn't get his mind around the idea of a man killin' a woman he could have for free."

"Tobe thought Tommy might have had some reason to have her killed himself."

Crystal thought about it. "It's possible, but I don't see him keepin' it to hisself.

Tobe nodded at Roses. "That's what I thought. I think I'll have a talk with Tommy about it, though."

"You're not gonna get anywhere near Tommy this week, honey. Ain't you heard? He's campaigning for sheriff." She chuckled. "Can you picture that. Thomas Jones, lawman. That man's broken every law that ever got writ, and a few they ain't made up yet."

"You don't like him then?" Roses asked.

"He's not bad. For a boss. But when was the last time you liked your boss." Roses shrugged. "What do you do, anyway?" Crystal asked.

"A little bit of everything, just about," Roses said.

"Like what?"

"You name it. If it's work, I've done it."

Crystal just said. "Ummm-hmmm," while exchanging a look with Tobe.

Tobe and Roses both spoke, at once.

"Oh, not that."

"Nothing in your line, though."

Crystal laughed, unoffended. "Well, it is hard work!" she said with a wry smile.

Roses smiled, sheepishly. "I'm sure it is," she said.

Roses hid a wide yawn behind her palm as she walked into the telegraph office. There was only one young man behind the window, and he thrust a form at her after ascertaining that she could, indeed, write. Her message was short and simple. She was only wiring Quentin to give him the name and address of the hotel where she and Tobe were staying.

She wandered out onto the street. She had plenty of time to kill before she was to meet Tobe at the hotel for a late breakfast. Her eye was caught by a swirl of sky blue skirts and she looked toward it to see the woman whose family she'd admired the night before at the hotel. A distinguished looking white haired gentleman in an old fashioned black suit was hailing her from across the street. The elegant black woman didn't respond to his greeting. She continued toward Roses, who watched curiously as the old man crossed the busy street, waving his cane to try and stop the traffic.

He came inexorably onward, to trap his quarry on the sidewalk in front of the telegraph office door.

"Good morning, Martha," he greeted her. The woman looked flustered, an expression clearly at odds with her serene features. Roses took a closer look at the white gentleman with the southern accent. His smile, she realized on closer inspection, was more malicious than friendly.

"Good morning, sir." Martha kept her eyes on the ground, and Roses again had the strong impression that last night's air of self assurance was more natural to her than the subservient posture that bowed her now.

"Have you located your son yet, Madam?" the man asked pompously. Roses didn't like him. The lady clearly wanted to avoid the gentleman, but couldn't, whether because she was frightened or simply too well mannered, Roses didn't know. It didn't matter anyway. Roses sauntered in between them and casually swept the old man's cane aside with her skirts. As he stumbled, Roses caught his arm and pulled him around toward the street.

"So sorry," she said, noting a flash of blue out of the corner of her eye. She hoped the old man would take her smile of satisfaction for one of gratitude as she thanked him profusely for his help. When she turned back onto the boardwalk, she was pleased to see that the woman whom he'd called Martha had used the diversion she'd provided to slip into the building. She couldn't miss the look of disgust that had flashed across the old windbag's face as he'd seen that his prey had escaped him, and the venomous look he shot toward the telegraph station made Roses very glad that she'd done her impulsive good deed.

She walked back to the hotel with an added spring to her step. She didn't wait for Tobe, who was late, but ordered a very large breakfast, her appetite stimulated by the strenuous exercise she'd gotten the night before. Tobe joined her at the table just as the food she'd asked for had arrived. She dug into her food, barely sparing him a glance as she asked, "Any luck? I went to the telegraph office to see if there was a message from Quentin." She looked up from her plate to see him staring at the woman she'd last seen hightailing it into the telegraph office. Roses snapped her fingers to get his attention. "Tobe?" When his eyes stayed glued on the beautiful coffee-colored woman, "Tobe?" She leaned over and tugged at his shirtsleeve.

The woman turned, hearing her, and Tobe rose from the table like a man mesmerized.

"Mother?" Tobe's shocked whisper startled her and she looked over at the woman again. Suddenly it clicked. Roses realized the missing son this self-

possessed woman was looking for was Tobe. And
the gray haired gentleman who had molested her
must have been the colonel. She remembered herself
just in time, and looked around at the dining room's
other patrons, who had noticed Tobe's odd behavior
and were craning their necks to see what he was
looking at so oddly. She grabbed his arm and pulled
him closer.

"The colonel's here, he's watching her," she said
quietly. He looked down at her, and, in response to
a gentle tug on his sleeve, he sat. Breakfast seemed
to drag on forever. Tobe ate like a man in a trance.

Roses couldn't keep her eyes off Martha Hunter.
Was this the woman of whom Tobe was so ashamed?
It was this beautiful elegant creature that he couldn't
stand to speak of or think about? She had pictured
a hardened old lady, like Letty Dowd. Why this
woman couldn't have been more than fifteen years
old when she gave birth to him.

The waiter brought them a note. After he left,
Tobe opened it. Then he handed it to Roses.

"Room 210. Colonel Travis is watching us. We'll
try to arrange a safe meeting place," she read aloud.

"What's she doing here?" Tobe asked.

Roses shrugged. "I guess we'll find out when we
meet with them."

Tobe looked around the dining room. Kansas City
was not Cedar Valley. The room was filled with people of every stamp, ranging in color from high yellow to blue black. It was an establishment that
catered to coloreds. He had felt safe here. He had
felt that he blended right in. Now that he knew the
colonel was watching, he did a quick mental survey
of the room.

There were two or three men sitting alone who fit
the description on the Wanted poster. There were a

couple more with women and children. Two men who were approximately his height were dining with other men. He imagined the colonel was having a hell of a time checking the patrons. Though he'd seen the white man, Travis hadn't seen him. He had only the general description to follow. There wouldn't be many from this side of town who would answer an outsider's questions about their own.

Roses was watching him. "Tobe, do you think we're safe here?" she asked.

"I don't know," he had to answer. "But this is probably as safe as we're going to get with Travis in town. You'd better not call me by name. As Quentin said, it's not too common."

She nodded. "What should we do now?"

"Stick with our plan," he said, definitely. "We'll take Jones tonight."

"But . . . what about what Crystal said?"

"Tommy is all I've got to go on, right now. If he didn't kill the girl, he'll have been trying to find out who did. She was his. He'll know something. That's more than we've got right now." He stood. "I think it's time for a talk with my mother."

"She's beautiful."

"I know."

"Why are you so ashamed of her?"

"It isn't her, it's what she was."

"What could she do that you couldn't forgive?"

"She was a whore. You don't understand what that means to a boy."

"But you're not a boy, you're a man."

"She sent me away. I was fighting a lot with the other boys. She sent me to live with my grandmother. I guess I thought she was angry with me for fighting. I was only nine."

It all came back to him: the hurt, the humiliation.

And then, when he was fourteen, finding out that she was going to have another baby. And keep it with her. It came to him like a bolt of thunder. It wasn't the shame of the pregnancy that made him turn his back, it had been jealousy he'd felt when she told him she was going to have another baby. All these years, he'd gone on thinking it was her fault he'd walked away. But it had been he that had turned away, in a childishly jealous rage and then refused to talk it out with her.

But she had never even given up on him, no matter what he had done to try and hurt her. Even though Tobe had lived with his grandmother, his mother had spent as much time with him as her work allowed, up until the time when he had refused to speak to her at all. How could he have forgotten?

"Let's go."

"She said to wait."

"There will never be a better time," Tobe answered.

Martha Hunter's room was on the same floor theirs was. They walked past the door to "210," looking about them for any place that might conceal a spy. There was nowhere in the narrow hall for anyone to hide.

When they reached their room, Tobe went to the window. Standing beside it, he scanned the street below.

Roses came to the other side of the window. "Anything?"

"Nothing unusual."

Tobe recrossed the room, cracked the door and looked out into the hallway. She followed him as he slipped outside. It was the longest twenty feet she ever walked.

Tobe knocked quietly. In a moment the door

opened, and mother and son stood face to face. She stood, looking at him with tears in her eyes, then quickly stepped back and waved them into the room, where Eliza stood looking at them.

"Come in."

Once in the suite, Roses looked from mother to son and back again. Martha Hunter took a tentative, uncertain step toward Tobe, and held out a hand to him.

They met in the middle of the room. They embraced, awkwardly at first. But in seconds they were holding each other as if they would never let go. The Hunters, mother and son, had found, at last, peace. Eliza was wiping a tear from her cheek when Tobe finally released his mother and turned to her. He moved across the room to take her hand, kiss her cheek. He went back to Roses' side and pulled her forward.

"Mother, Eliza, I'd like you to meet Roses Jordan." They both came forward to shake hands with her. "My sister, Eliza, and my mother, Martha Hunter."

Martha Hunter took Roses' hand in hers and smiled widely. "We met, though we weren't introduced. Roses helped me escape from one of the colonel's inquisitions this morning," Martha told Tobe.

Graciously, Martha turned to the older man Roses had seen with the two women earlier.

"My old friend, Jeffrey Lane." She turned to them. "This is my son, Tobias."

"My pleasure." He turned back to his mother. "I can't believe you're here," he said.

"I came out here after I got a visit from a Marshall McKellum. He was working for the colonel." She turned to Roses. "The gentleman you "bumped into" today."

"A visit from McKellum? Where? Is he here?" Roses asked.

"He came to Boston."

"He went all the way to Boston!" Tobe clearly couldn't believe it.

"He's no longer working for the colonel, but that hasn't stopped the old man. He hates Tobe. I think he's crazy."

"He gives me the chills. He wants Tobe dead." Eliza said quietly.

"You've grown up, little sister," Tobe said. "You're a beauty."

"You look just like a big brother ought to look. Tall and handsome," she laughed. But she quickly sobered. "As happy as I am to finally meet you, you've got to get out of here."

"Why did you come back?" Martha asked.

"We had no idea that crazyman was here. We were hoping Tobe could surprise Mr. Jones and get him to confess to the murder," Roses explained.

Jeff looked shocked. "Thomas Jones? He's been defending Tobe."

Eliza looked thoughtful. "That doesn't mean he didn't do it."

Martha shook her head.

"It's too dangerous," she said. "Tobe can't show his face in this town. The colonel will kill him. The old man has nothing left to lose."

"We might still be able to make this work," Roses said, urgently. "Tobe is going to "kidnap" Jones and threaten to kill him. He'll blindfold him and make him think they've gone out of town somewhere, but he'll just take him to a place where I'll have witnesses waiting, including the judge who issued the warrant, if possible."

"It sounds chancy. They could say a man would

confess to anything if he believed it would save his life," Lane pointed out.

Roses could see the logic in the older man's argument. "Tobe thought, from what he knew of Jones, that the man would boast about it. If he admitted that he killed her in the first place."

"The colonel will never believe it, no matter what Jones says," Martha said.

"All of this is beside the point," Eliza said gently. "My mother is right. Once Colonel Travis gets Tobe in his sights, my brother is a dead man. We've been here for over a month, sending messages to every major city out West to warn Tobe that a madman is after him. We came here to talk to the authorities, but they weren't any help. And once the colonel found out we were here in town, he started sticking to our trail."

"We know for a fact that he's sent at least one ransom note to a place called Cedar Valley that said if Tobe wanted to see his sister alive again, he'd show up here in Kansas City. Luckily, it was returned unopened to the telegraph operator. He didn't know who to address it to. He couldn't exactly send it to the sheriff," Martha said. "Now that you know the colonel can't hurt any of us, can't you just leave? Just get out of here? Change your name? If it worked here, right under his nose, it will work anywhere."

"Mama is right. You've got to leave Kansas," Eliza said.

"The colonel is sticking to us like glue. It's certainly not safe here." Jeff added his opinion.

Martha was almost crying as she said, "He's going to kill you, if he sees you, Tobe."

Roses was convinced. It was too dangerous here. "We were going to go to this town Tobe heard of . . ." Her voice trailed off. She didn't know how much to tell them. Martha Hunter caught on immediately and rounded on her son.

"Are you still looking for that Shangri-La, Tobe?" She asked accusingly. He bridled.

"It's not something out of a fairy tale, Mother. These places exist."

"I know they do. Last year a man named Samuel Fellows incorporated a town called Langston City down in Oklahoma. It was named after the black senator." Tobe's interest was immediately piqued.

"Really?"

"They've been advertising for families, businessmen, and all kinds of respectable citizens to move there." The sarcastic tone of her voice when she said the word "respectable" reminded Roses so much of Tobe that she gaped, open mouthed, at the pair. They suddenly seemed almost like an ordinary family.

Hours later, Tobe and Roses returned to their room. Nothing had been decided. Tobe still wanted to talk to Jones, even though his family confirmed what Crystal had said about his inaccessibility at the moment. Roses agreed with Martha, Eliza and Jeffrey Lane, their original plan was too dangerous.

Tobe stood at the window, lost in thought, and Roses took out paper and ink from her supplies to write a long overdue letter to Cedar Valley. She wanted to warn Ben and Sarah about the crazy military man who had traced Tobe as far as the smithy. And she told them not to contact her until she'd sent a new address, which, if she had anything to say about it, was about to become Langston City.

Tobe wandered over to the bed as Roses folded the letter and put it aside. He sat down and propped himself up against the headboard. She looked up to see what he was doing and found him staring at her.

"When are you planning to make an honest man of me?"

She laughed. But when he didn't join in, she sat, gaping at him, while her heartbeat grew rapid.

"Are you seriously asking me to *marry* you?" she asked still sure he had to be joking.

He smiled. "I think if I'm going to take your name, it's the only respectable thing to do."

"I think we have more important things to worry about right now," she said, staying away from the subject without even letting herself think about it. Marriage!

"What?" he asked patiently.

"Thomas Jones and Colonel Travis, to name a couple. And a killer, to top it off." She still couldn't get over the fact that they were even discussing this subject. He'd never touched on it before. And if she'd thought about it, she would have said she was glad he hadn't. She thought she'd better make that clear, in case he was saying this to her because he thought she wanted to hear it.

"Besides I never said I wanted to get married."

"I never said it either. And I never did. Want to. But now I do."

She supposed this had something to do with his mother. But for the life of her, she could not see what their reunion had to do with them getting married.

"Why now?" She couldn't help asking.

"Seeing my mother. I never should have run away from her. We've wasted so much time apart. People who love each other belong together. Always. I love you so much it hurts. I want to be with you forever. Marry me." She almost wanted to say yes. But how could she? He hadn't thought this out at all.

"Marriage doesn't guarantee we'll always be to-gether. It's not magic."

"But we are magic, together. And I still haven't heard you say you love me." As she started to protest, he went on. "I know you do. But I want to hear you say it in front of God and everybody. I want to hear you say it."

Roses cast around desperately for an argument that would make Tobe see reason. She had never thought to marry him, because she had never thought in terms of forever. Until now, she knew, he thought they were temporary, too. She remembered why.

"What about the colonel? The murderer?"

"We won't invite them," he said flippantly. "Seriously, I can't let them stop me from living. If I do that, they win."

She couldn't marry him. It didn't serve any useful purpose, and someone might just end up getting hurt. She had never meant to promise him forever.

She went to the bed. "Kiss me, Tobe," she demanded, sitting next to him. He kissed her so gently, she could have cried. Instead, she put her hands on his arms to pull him even closer. When they separated, they were both breathing faster. "See, I'm here. Now. Today. What if tomorrow I were not, or you couldn't be? Would that make the way we feel about each other any less than it is."

"No," he said, "I can't imagine anything would change the way I feel. But planning a life together starts with marriage. What are you afraid of?"

"I'm afraid of this conversation. You want to *plan* a life together? What about your adventure?"

"I want us to spend our lives together. That will be an adventure. I want to watch my children grow up with you as their mother. I want to tell the world I belong to you and you belong to me. I want you to be my wife, Roses." She believed that he did, for now. But if she let herself believe in forever and then something happened she wouldn't survive it.

"What if I wanted to go back to the reservation to live?"

"We'd find a way," Tobe said. "Hell, if that's all you're worried about, we can turn around right now." But she could see in his eyes that he knew it was not that. She was afraid, and he knew it. He just didn't know why. She tried to explain.

"What if you hated it there? Worse, what if we never found a place where we felt we belonged. Where you felt you belonged. I don't need that, but you do."

"I belong with you," he said quietly. "And you belong with me."

"I can live anywhere, but I can't live nowhere. I just can't do that again," she said.

"Now we're getting to it," he said. "You've never lived nowhere. With the Uncompahgre, you were a part of the tribe. In Cedar Valley, you were a part of the town. More important to them than you could see. You're the one who doesn't feel like you belonged in those places. But you did."

"But you didn't. You left. You're looking for something that might not even be out there."

He had faced his past and that had brought on this change, but he was still the same man she had fallen in love with. A cowboy, and a man on the run. She loved him, but she didn't think he'd ever find what he was looking for.

"I left because I wanted to go on to the next place, not because I wasn't happy where I was. You're right, I never belonged anywhere. Until I met you. I left home without a thought. I left Cedar Valley because I belong with you. We left the Uncompahgre because I had to."

"And if that poster hadn't shown up, you still would have left."

"Maybe, but I would have come back. Because I belong with you. I just hadn't figured that out yet. Now I know. And I think we should get married."

"Well, I don't think so. Tobe, I can't marry you, but I'm here now, with you. Isn't that enough?"

"No. It's not."

"So, what are you saying?" she asked.

"Marry me. My mother would probably love to give me away."

Roses threw her hands up in disgust. "Tobe, stop. I'm not kidding."

He held her gaze for a moment before he answered her. "I'm very serious. But I can see you don't believe me. I'll have to convince you." He leaned over to kiss her. "I will. You said it yourself: men are much more obstinate than women." She turned away so that he wouldn't see her smile. She could picture him, gray-haired and feeble, still badgering her to walk up the aisle with him. She could imagine a worse fate.

Twenty-two

Jeffrey Lane had managed to have dinner for five sent up to the Hunter suite, and after another nervous trip down the hallway, they dined with Tobe's family.

Tobe kept dropping subtle hints about marrying and exchanging pointed glances with his mother and sister. But Roses pretended not to notice. She wasn't interested in marriage. As long as she was free, in name anyway, she felt she could ride away, or watch him ride away, without dying inside.

Nobody brought up Tobe's plan. But Roses knew they didn't want him to try it any more than she did.

Tobe and Jeff excused themselves after dinner. When the men left the room, Martha turned to her. Roses was ready to offer her help in trying to change Tobe's mind, but Martha surprised her by saying, "My son tells me he asked you to marry him, and you refused."

Roses hadn't thought Tobe and Martha had had a chance to talk and she wondered what Tobe had told his mother. Whatever Tobe had said, Roses felt she owed the woman an honest answer.

"It would never work. I like to look at things the way they are. Tobe has a terrible case of wanderlust. I've moved around enough in my life."

"But you're traveling with him already," Eliza pointed out.

"For now, maybe. But I don't plan to do this forever. Eventually I think I'd like to go back to live with the Ute."

"Tobe isn't really as restless as he seems," Martha argued. "It's just this thing of his, about living in one of these townships where everyone is treated the same way and has the same opportunities. When he was little he loved living on "our side" of town. Like most kids he grew out of that. But unlike his friends, he couldn't seem to just make the best of it. Instead, he left. Looking for a better way to live. He's been talking about finding this place for years. I think he means to settle there."

Roses didn't know whether Tobe could even find what he was looking for, let alone keep any promises he might make to her along the way. She wasn't taking any chances.

"I don't think I'm the right woman for him," she said with finality, but Martha couldn't let it go.

"He thinks you are. And so do I."

"We have different backgrounds, different goals. We argue about everything."

"But you're in love, aren't you? The rest will come," Eliza said, with all the assurance of youth.

Roses looked at Martha, expecting the widow to argue the point for her, only to find Martha was nodding in agreement.

"Tobe cares for you. And I believe you care about him—"

"Well, of course I do, but . . ."

"But nothing. It's the only way to get him out of this town." The bald statement was a surprise. But the logic of it was irrefutable. The idea took hold immediately.

"You mean get him to agree to leave? Use the marriage as a bribe?" Roses asked.

"I think it's the only way. If you care about my son at all, I beg you to consider it."

That night, in bed, Roses told Tobe, "Your mother agrees with you. She thinks we should get married." She had already decided to do it.

He smiled. "I'd love to have my mother at my wedding." He turned his head to kiss her forehead.

"I'm afraid she can't be here," Roses said. "I'll marry you, but only in Langston City."

"Langston City?"

"Now."

"Wait, Roses." He leaned up onto his elbow to look into her eyes as he asked, "You're going to marry me?"

"That's what you said you wanted."

He laughed. "I do. God, you know I do." His arm tightened about her shoulders.

"And I want to get you out of this town." He loosened his hold on her to look into her eyes once again. His smile never wavered, but he drew back a little.

"I see. We're back to negotiating again." She couldn't quite look him in the eye. She focused instead on his lips. He lay back down.

After a few minutes, she whispered, "Tobe, I wouldn't do this if I didn't care about you."

"I know," he said.

She wished it could be different, but she had no choice. This was the only way she could think of to get Tobe away from the man who wanted him dead.

Neither of them were asleep when the door to their room swung slowly inward. Tobe pushed Roses from the bed and rolled off after her, just as their unexpected visitor opened fire. The hall light had been extinguished but in the moonlight coming through the window Roses could make out nothing distinctive about the face of the shadowy figure in the doorway, but the dark skin of his hands and face. The killer was black.

Tobe's guns hung from the bedpost on the other side of the bed. Roses knew the exact moment he decided to go for his holster, and reached for the arm that had been holding her down as Tobe withdrew it. But she missed.

In the second it took him to roll across the bed, unholster one of his guns and shoot, one word flashed through her mind, "Yes!" She would marry him, not as a bribe, but because she couldn't live without him.

Tobe squeezed off a second shot, and the assassin recoiled off the door jamb and out into the hall. Tobe rose to follow. The wounded man fired wildly. A bullet hit the bed right by Roses' head. She ducked. Tobe flattened himself against the wall by the doorway, then poked his head out into the hall, his gun at the ready. Roses raised her head again, unable to stand the suspense. There were no more wild shots.

"I think I hit 'em," Tobe said, bending to examine the floor. There indeed was the telltale sign—blood. The splatters took an uneven path down the hallway. Tobe followed it, Roses right behind him. The blood spots thinned into a trickle and Roses was afraid they would end, but it led them on. The killer had even slipped on some of his own blood at one point.

A couple of doors opened as their fellow guests came out to investigate. "Go back to sleep," Tobe urged the first. When one of the men started into the hall, almost stepping in one of the bloody puddles, Tobe just barely stopped him in time with a sharp, "Watch where you're stepping." The man looked down and stepped back.

"What happened?"

"That's what we're going to find out." The man looked at them, his eyes resting on Roses' bare ankles for a moment or two. Roses was suddenly aware they wore only their underclothes. Tobe waved him back into the room with his gun hand. "You'd better get back inside, we don't know if this guy was alone." The gentleman quickly retired.

The gruesome trail continued down the stairs.

"He's lost a lot of blood, he can't get far," Roses whispered. But just in case he had made it out of the hotel, she ran back to the room and quickly pulled on her dress. She grabbed Tobe's pants and his gunbelt and ran back down the hall, but Tobe had already descended the stairs and disappeared. Halfway down, a young man came rushing up to her.

"What happened?" he asked. "There's blood all over the place."

"Where?"

"The back door, by the kitchen."

"Someone took a shot at us. My husband has gone after him. His family is here. They're in Room 210. Please tell them what's happened."

"I've got to inform the owner of the hotel first, I'm just the night clerk," the young man said. "And I think I should call the sheriff."

"You can do all of that after you talk to our friends. Please, my husband may need help."

Precious seconds were lost while she waited for him to agree, but he finally nodded. He ran on up the stairs while Roses continued down. She ran through the back door, noting the blood on the door-jamb where the killer must have slammed into the wooden frame. She picked up the trail right away.

The space between the blood spots widened, the man must have started running when he got outside. Confident that Tobe had to be just ahead, she ran down the alley toward the street.

Suddenly, a shot rang out. A hand snaked out to grab her by the waist. Tobe pulled her into an alcove and pushed her behind him. She followed his gaze to a pile of wooden vegetable crates, stacked high, across the alley.

"He's hiding back there."

"If we can keep him pinned down, I'd guess he'd pass out from loss of blood," Roses volunteered.

"When the sun comes up, he'll be able to see us. There's no cover here."

"He doesn't have that kind of time. Someone from the hotel is going to get the sheriff," Roses told Tobe.

As if on cue, another shot rang out. It hit the wall, harmlessly, two feet away from them.

"Then we don't have much time, either," Tobe said. Raising his voice, he shouted, "Give it up. The sheriff's on the way."

There was no response.

"Tobe?" Someone whispered loudly, from the backdoor of the hotel. Roses recognized Jeffrey Lane's voice. Another poorly aimed shot rang out from behind the tottering barricade.

"Jeff? You got him?" Tobe didn't bother to lower his voice. Anything they could hear, the man lurking in the shadow across the alley could hear as well.

"Yeah. I saw it."

"Go around to the front."

They were going to squeeze him out. Roses gave Tobe his gun belt and held his gun while he buckled it on. When she tried to hand it back to him, he said, "Keep it. I'll use my other gun. You can cover me."

"You take it. I don't shoot at people."

"Then just make a lot of noise with it. And stay down."

He doubled over and ran toward the killer's hiding place. Roses heart rose to her throat but she aimed the gun at the wall three feet above where she'd last seen the killer's gun flash, then opened fire. The report of his own gun answered her and she ducked back behind the protective wall.

Tobe had reached the end of the flimsy pile of wooden boxes furthest from where the assassin hid. Jeff opened fire from further down the alley, then slipped back around the front of the building as the hidden gunman opened fire. Tobe slipped behind the wall of slatted wooden crates and was lost to her view.

She heard him say, "Drop it!" And then nothing.

Heart pounding, she waited for another flash of the gun. She lowered her gun, to the spot where she thought the killer stood. Then sagged in relief as Tobe yelled, "It's okay. I've got her gun."

"Her?" Roses made her way around the vegetable crates, Jeff just behind her. It was the prostitute, Crystal, dressed in a man's clothes, who lay bleeding and unconscious at Tobe's feet. She didn't move as he bent to lift her up.

"Bring her up to our room. My supplies are there," Roses directed.

Roses was checking the tourniquet she'd wrapped around Crystal's leg when the sheriff walked into the room, Thomas Jones in his wake. Martha and Jeff had been closeted with the sheriff in their suite for a good quarter hour, filling him in on the night's events. When he'd arrived, he'd taken one look at

Crystal and sent the night clerk back out for a doctor, then demanded an explanation.

"I don't think she'll lose the leg." Roses told him, watching Jones stare unhappily at the woman unconscious on the bed. He didn't have the look of a man whose assassination attempt had just failed. He looked sadly, even sympathetically at the unconscious woman on Roses' bed.

"Where's Hunter?" the sheriff asked, unconcerned about Crystal's condition.

"Not far," Roses answered. "Why?"

"I think I should talk to him." His hard voice sent chills down her spine.

"Didn't Jeffrey Lane tell you—"

He cut her off. "Yeah, I know all about it. Seems Crystal here killed Carolann Travis and tried to kill you two to shut you up. I got it. But I want to see the man that caused all this ruckus. He seems to be the key to all this."

"Here I am, Sheriff. But I don't know any more than you do." Roses thought she should have known he wouldn't stay hidden in Martha Hunter's bedroom. He had wanted to be with her when Crystal woke up. To ask why she had done this to him.

"You don't, huh? How's that go? One girl's dead cause she talked to you. Another one's probably going to the gallows."

Jones spoke up. "Mr. Hunter was just in the wrong place at the wrong time, in more ways than one. Crystal and Carolann were at each other's throats from the moment they met. Mr. Hunter here just happened to speak to both of them on the night it finally came to a head, that's all. Crystal told you she spent the night with him, and that's what put you on his trail, but some of the other women said they saw him leaving, alone, that night."

"Well hang it, Tommy, why didn't you tell me this before?"

"I tried, Sheriff, but that old man, Travis, he had you hot on the trail of Hunter here after Crystal told him her story. To tell the truth, I wasn't even sure which story was true."

"I think Crystal told the truth, and her lying in that bed now proves it." The colonel stood in the doorway, behind Tobe, his gun trained on Tobe's back, his face twisted in a grimace of disbelief. Crystal moaned, and the colonel turned to look at her, a fleeting glance, but one which gave him away. He knew her well.

The sheriff inched to the side, angling around Tobe. He couldn't see Travis from where he had stood. At his movement, the Colonel's attention snapped back to the men in front of him.

"I'll kill him, Sheriff."

"Crystal lied to you." Tobe's voice was convincingly steady but the Colonel didn't move. His gun remained aimed at the middle of Tobe's back. "She killed Carolann, I don't know why. But she tried to kill us, that's proof enough for me. If I'd killed your daughter, do you think I'd have left Crystal alive to tell the story. Just one more bullet and she'd be quiet forever."

Roses tried to gauge the reactions of the others. The sheriff was nodding. She thought Tobe had persuaded him.

"You shut your mouth, boy!" the colonel barked.

"Colonel, you don't want to shoot that man in front of all of us. You'll hang. I was just trying to get to the bottom of this myself. We'll get the whole story now. You killing him wouldn't help anything," the sheriff said.

"It would be worth it," the ex-military man stood

his ground. "Keep your hands at your sides. You, too, Mr. Jones."

Jones held his hands up. "I don't even have a gun, Colonel. I just want to tell you you're making a mistake, Hunter didn't kill Carolann, Crystal did. Think about it. Why else would she come here and attempt to kill these two?"

"I don't think she did. I think they brought her here and shot her. They were gonna kill her. She told me the whole story yesterday." Roses looked at the woman in the bed. She'd seemed to be on their side. Roses still couldn't believe she'd been the killer after all. But the colonel wasn't finished. "Hunter and his woman paid her a little visit two nights ago and told her if she didn't change her story, they'd kill her." Crystal suddenly came alive under Roses hands. Her head rolled to the side, and her mouth worked, though no sound came out.

"Why didn't I hear about any of this?" Tommy asked.

"Or me?" the sheriff joined in.

"She said you wouldn't believe her. She appealed to me for help. She knew I wouldn't let Hunter get away with this."

As the woman in the bed moved again, Roses suddenly believed it had been Crystal who had been behind everything. It was Crystal who had killed Carolann, and framed Tobe. But why? Martha Hunter spoke from behind the old man.

"Why, colonel? What was Crystal to you? Why did she hate Carolann so much?" The Colonel's gunhand wavered for a moment as Roses stepped aside, so he could see the woman on the bed. But at a slight movement from the sheriff, it came back up. Martha kept after him. "Who is she, Colonel? Why did Carolann die?"

A tear rolled down the old man's cheek. Tobe dove to the side, and the sheriff pulled his gun, but the old man let his gun fall to his side without firing. Martha nudged him forward with the rifle she held to his back, but he didn't need much urging. He walked to the bed where Crystal lay.

"She was Carolann's mammy. My wife died when Carolann was born, and Crystal took her place as a mother to my child. She was only a baby herself. Twelve, thirteen, maybe. But, she was so good with the baby. And she was so beautiful. I—I couldn't resist her. She lived with me, like a wife, until Carolann grew old enough to understand what was going on. Even then . . . even then I couldn't let her go. I needed her. Carolann did everything she could think of to get rid of her. It started out with little things, but it became an obsession with Carolann, to make me choose Crystal over her. But I couldn't do it. I couldn't choose between them. I loved them both. Until Carolann let me catch her one night with a black buck she'd brought in from the stables. She told me, 'How did I like it?' How did it make me feel, to see her rutting with some darkie like he was our equal. I tried to get her to stop, but she, she kept talking, saying how she could see why I liked it, because she'd been sleeping with nigras, too. All of 'em. Anyone she could get to go with her. I threw her out of the house. Told her I couldn't stand to look at her. And then I threw Crystal out, too. I didn't know they'd find each other. I didn't know." He was suddenly an old man, bent with age and grief.

By the time they'd gotten Crystal and the colonel squared away, the sun was high in the sky. They sat drinking much needed coffee in Martha Hunter's suite.

Eliza shook her head sadly, "She was friendly, right off. The only person we talked to here who said she didn't think Tobe had done it. It was that that made her so believable. She sounded like she was defending Tobe, not pointing a finger at him. She sounded like she was on Tobe's side."

Martha took up the story. "When she told us how Tobe had stepped into an argument between Carol-ann and another man, it didn't occur to me to wonder why she was volunteering all that information. I never noticed that it was her alibi for him that gave him the means and the opportunity for murder. I never thought to ask you if you spent the night with her, son. I'm sorry."

"It's understandable," Roses told her.

"I should have known something was wrong with her story. When she said he'd spent the night with her, fallen asleep in her bed, I should have known he hadn't. He wouldn't have changed that much. But I believed her when she said he'd . . . purchased her services."

"She was beautiful, intelligent, and she seemed to believe in Tobe's innocence," Jeffrey said. "How could you have guessed?"

"If only I'd asked him that one question, we could have figured out what had happened."

"Maybe not," Tobe said. "We all trusted her. If you had told me about her story, I probably would have thought she'd been trying to protect me. We just didn't know enough to figure out what was go-ing on. You saved my life, mother. You knew. When it counted, you knew."

Jeff, the voice of reason, said calmly, "We weren't about to ask Tobe something like that in front of Roses anyway."

Tobe smiled, "Thanks for your support. I may need it. She probably won't marry me now."

"Of course she will," Martha said. "You two were made for each other. And now that all this has been cleared up, you can have a proper wedding. I'll arrange it."

"I wouldn't care if she wanted to jump backwards over a broomstick," Tobe said, "but Roses doesn't want to marry me. She only agreed to it to get me to leave Kansas City."

"That's not true. She loves you. Don't you, Roses." Eliza looked from Roses to her newfound brother with amusement in her eyes. "That saving your life thing was just an excuse to get that ring on your finger, brother dear."

"I don't think so." He turned to Roses, "What do you say, Roses? Are you still willing to make an honest man of me?"

"We'll talk about it later," she said.

"See." Tobe turned to his family.

"What kind of proposal was that," Eliza said, sounding disgusted, but Roses noticed that twinkle was still in her eyes.

"She didn't say no, Tobe," Jeff pointed out.

"Why shouldn't she marry you?" Martha said, all wounded maternal dignity.

"Why indeed?" Tobe turned to her again. His lips curved upwards in that familiar smile, and she found herself responding to it as always, wanting to smile with him. He was shameless, putting her in this position.

"I told you we'd discuss it later," she stated, looking away from Tobe at the others, and finding herself the focus of all eyes as they regarded her quizzically.

"You're going to have to tell them sometime," Tobe said. "My mother's already planning the wedding. See that look in her eyes. I remember that look. That means she's planning something."

"Oh, you!" Martha laughed. But she didn't contradict him.

"She's going to be very disappointed when you don't show up at the church."

"I would hate to disappoint her," Roses said, smiling.

"That's good enough for me." He grinned wickedly at her and Roses' hand flew to her mouth but not quickly enough to hold back a little bark of laughter. "I think I can work with that," he said to his family.

He was sure he could persuade her, now that he'd remembered her weak spot—Roses' soft heart.

SENSUAL AND HEARTWARMING
ARABESQUE ROMANCES FEATURE
AFRICAN-AMERICAN CHARACTERS!

BEGUILED   (0046, $4.99)
by Eboni Snoe
After Raquel agrees to impersonate a missing heiress for
just one night, a daring abduction makes her the captive of
seductive Nate Bowman. Across the exotic Caribbean seas
to the perilous wilds of Central America . . . and into the
savage heart of desire, Nate and Raquel play a dangerous
game. But soon the masquerade will be over. And will they
then lose the one thing that matters most . . . their love?

WHISPERS OF LOVE   (0055, $4.99)
by Shirley Hailstock
Robyn Richards had to fake her own death, change her
identity, and forever forsake her husband Grant, after testi-
fying against a crime syndicate. But, five years later, the
daughter born after her disappearance is in need of help
only Grant can give. Can Robyn maintain her disguise
from the ever present threat of the syndicate—and can she
keep herself from falling in love all over again?

HAPPILY EVER AFTER   (0064, $4.99)
In a week's time, Lauren Taylor fell madly in love with
famed author Cal Samuels and impulsively agreed to be his
wife. But when she abruptly left him, it was for reasons she
dared not express. Five years later, Cal is back, and the
flames of desire are as hot as ever, but, can they start over
again and make it work this time?

*Available wherever paperbacks are sold, or order direct from the
Publisher. Send cover price plus 50¢ per copy for mailing and
handling to Penguin USA, P.O. Box 999, c/o Dept. 17109,
Bergenfield, NJ 07621. Residents of New York and Tennessee
must include sales tax. DO NOT SEND CASH.*